09/24/08
3

Praise for *Bright of the Sky*
Book One of The Entire and the Rose

"At the start of this riveting launch of a new far-future SF series from Kenyon (*Tropic of Creation*), a disastrous mishap during interstellar space travel catapults pilot Titus Quinn with his wife, Johanna Arlis, and nine-year-old daughter, Sydney, into a parallel universe called the Entire. Titus makes it back to this dimension, his hair turned white, his memory gone, his family presumed dead, and his reputation ruined with the corporation that employed him. The corporation (in search of radical space travel methods) sends Titus (in search of Johanna and Sydney) back through the space-time warp. There, he gradually, painfully regains knowledge of its rulers, the cruel, alien Tarig; its subordinate, Chinese-inspired humanoid population, the Chalin; and his daughter's enslavement. Titus's transformative odyssey to reclaim Sydney reveals a Tarig plan whose ramifications will be felt far beyond his immediate family. Kenyon's deft prose, high-stakes suspense, and skilled, thorough world building will have readers anxious for the next installment."

Publishers Weekly Starred Review

". . . a splendid fantasy quest as compelling as anything by Stephen R. Donaldson, Philip José Farmer, or yes, J. R. R. Tolkien."

Washington Post

". . . a bravura concept bolstered by fine writing; lots of plausible, thrilling action; old-fashioned heroism; and strong emotional hooks . . . the mark of a fine writer. Grade: A."

Sci Fi Weekly

"Kay Kenyon's *Bright of the Sky* is her richest and most ambitious novel yet—fascinating, and best of all, there promises to be more to come."

Greg Bear

Hugo and Nebula Award–winning author of *Quantico* and *Darwin's Radio*

"Kenyon writes beautifully, her characters are multilayered and complex, and her extrasolar worlds are real and nuanced while at the same time truly alien."

Robert J. Sawyer

Hugo and Nebula Award–winning author of *Rollback* and *Mindscan*

"Kay Kenyon takes the nuts and bolts of SF and weaves pure magic around them. The brilliance of her imagination is matched only by the beauty of her prose. You should buy *Bright of the Sky* immediately. It's astounding!"

Sean Williams, author of *The Crooked Letter* and *Saturn Returns*

Also by Kay Kenyon

BRIGHT OF THE SKY

Book One of The Entire and the Rose

A WORLD TOO NEAR

A WORLD TOO NEAR

KAY KENYON

BOOK TWO *of* THE ENTIRE AND THE ROSE

an imprint of **Prometheus Books**
Amherst, NY

Published 2008 by Pyr®, an imprint of Prometheus Books

Inquiries should be addressed to
Pyr
59 John Glenn Drive
Amherst, New York 14228–2119
VOICE: 716–691–0133, ext. 210
FAX: 716–691–0137
WWW.PYRSF.COM

12 11 10 09 08   5 4 3 2 1

Library of Congress Cataloging-in-Publication Data

Kenyon, Kay.
    A world too near / Kay Kenyon.
        p. cm. — (The entire and the rose ; bk. 2)
    ISBN 978–1–59102–642–6 (alk. paper)
    I. Title.

PS3561.E5544W67 2008
813'.54—dc22

2007051802

Printed in the United States on acid-free paper

In memory of our mothers,
Catherine Kenyon and Kathleen Overcast

ACKNOWLEDGMENTS

IN WRITING THIS BOOK, I benefited greatly from the counsel and insight of my agent, Donald Maass, and from readers and fellow writers Karen Fishler and Barry Lyga. My thanks to them for their continuing dedication to this saga as it unfolds. I owe a special debt to Robert Metzger for advice related to physics and fiction, an interface of talents that I deeply envy. I take full responsibility for my willful liberties with science. On the local front, I am indebted to Pat Rutledge, owner of A Book for all Seasons in Leavenworth, Washington. Love and thanks to my husband, Tom Overcast, my steady supporter and foremost reader through many drafts and by now innumerable pages. For astute copyediting, I could hope for no better than Deanna Hoak. I especially thank my editor Lou Anders, Pyr editorial director, for his enthusiasm and inspired shepherding of this series into print, including the remarkable contribution of artist Stephan Martiniere.

PART I

A
BURNING
ROSE

CHAPTER ONE

Storm wall, hold up the bright,
Storm wall, dark as Rose night,
Storm wall, where none can pass,
Storm wall, always to last.

—a child's verse

ABOVE THE FORTRESS THE SKY DIMMED TO LAVENDER, a time that passed for night in this world. Here every creature knew by their internal clock what time of night or day it was, all but Johanna Quinn, a woman of Earth. Between this universe and the next only a thin wall intervened, a permanent storm that forbade contact between Earth and the Entire. Or so most believed.

Johanna hurried down deserted corridors following the heavy drumbeat of the engine just ahead, a bass thrumming that pounded in her ears and the hollow of her chest. Coming to a divide in the hall she took the left branch, remembering her partial and wholly inadequate map. This hall too was deserted, and she rushed on. She prayed not to be discovered, although she had her alibi, thin as it might be.

Johanna wondered how he would kill her when the time came. There were good ways and bad, and she allowed herself—amid all her sacrifices—to have a strong preference in the matter. Her captors could do what they wished, of course. They were Tarig.

Tonight only one Tarig inhabited the Repel of Ahnenhoon, and Johanna profoundly hoped their paths would not cross. Her presence in this hall was not strictly forbidden, though. In her ten years of captivity she had earned a

15

degree of freedom. Like a butterfly with a pin through its body, she could move up, down, and in a circle. Enough freedom to have learned by now how large, how vastly large, was her prison with its thousand miles of corridors and mazes. Even so, few sentients lived here—a measure of Tarig confidence regarding assault and their preference for solitary lives. However, they had not reckoned what havoc a lone woman could wreak.

Something yanked her from behind. She stifled a gasp, staggering. But it was only her long hair, caught for a moment in a knot of cables snaking along the wall. She tucked her hair into her tunic collar and hurried on, following the thunder of the engine, louder now as she approached its seat.

Up ahead was the opening she sought: the deck that circled the containment chamber. She passed through the arch and onto the catwalk where in time of siege defenders of the Repel might take aim against intruders. That Johanna was such an intruder her lord would be surprised to discover.

She gazed out on a broad valley of giant and baffling technology. Lights winked across acres of metal machines—many presumably computational devices—separated by paths as narrow as the Tarig who had made them. Alongside these machines tall struts held up silos of churning material, and these in turn sheltered docks of instrumentation, arcane in design and disorienting in their scale. An occasional gleam announced the work of molecular fabbers cleaning and repairing. Standing on the high deck Johanna could easily see the great engine nesting at the center of the cavern. It shuddered and boomed, knocking all other sounds out of the air. The engine of Ahnenhoon.

From this distance it looked no larger than her fist. It crouched in two lobes like a metal heart. Within sight but not within reach. At floor level the engine nested in the center of an unbreachable maze. This was why she had come here tonight: to look for patterns. Somewhere in this cavern lay a path—a continuous course from the perimeter of the walls to the engine. Someday she would walk that path, to the heart of it. She gripped the rail and peered, searching for any route she could spy from this vantage point. Her eyes grew weary with the paths and their twists. She prayed for keen sight, being one who believed in prayer. But each lane that she traced through the valley of machines came to an end or fed back to the beginning. The maze held.

Nearby, perhaps three miles distant, the wall of the universe formed a barrier between this cosmos and Earth's. The wall, crafted by vast and fault-less technologies, resisted penetration. Yet this lobed engine could reach through, bringing about the collapse of all that she loved: the Earth and everything else beyond imagination to the ends of the folded, curving universe. It would not, Lord Inweer said, happen today or next year, but soon. In response to the siren call of the engine the Rose universe would fall in on itself in an instant. Thus collapsed it would burn so very brightly. A fine source of fuel and virtually an eternal one.

For all her intent gaze the maze kept its secret. No paths pierced the heart of the chamber; at least not one she could see. This excursion was a failure. God, of course, didn't owe her a revelation.

She felt more than heard a presence behind her. Turning, she saw her servant. The vile creature had followed her.

"SuMing," Johanna said, keeping her voice even.

SuMing bowed. As she did so her braid fell forward, a great rope of hair that hung to her waist.

"Did you bring my shawl? One is cold."

"Your shawl is in your apartments of course."

"Then you have a long walk back, SuMing."

With a hint of a smile, SuMing bowed to her mistress. She had no choice but to fetch the shawl. As she turned away she stopped suddenly, then bowed again, deeply this time, as another figure appeared from a side corridor.

It was the Tarig lord. SuMing must have alerted him. Johanna bowed to Lord Inweer. "Bright Lord."

In the early days his form had disquieted her, but no longer. Her lord's face was fine, even beautiful. One could become accustomed to anything, living with it long enough, Johanna had learned. The Tarig even seemed normal with their muscular, attenuated bodies and seven-foot height.

Standing before Johanna now, Lord Inweer's skin gleamed with a copper tinge as though he were cast from metal. SuMing hurried past him, causing his slit skirt to billow. "Stay," Lord Inweer said. The servant stopped and turned back, waiting on her lord's pleasure.

However, Inweer took no further notice of SuMing, his eyes fixed on her mistress.

"Johanna," he said, his voice smooth and deep. "We find you abroad. Not sleeping, hnn?"

She had planned what to say if caught. With all the poise she could muster she turned from him, looking down into the chamber. "It called me. I had to see it."

In four strides he stood next to her, his gaze sweeping the great hall one hundred feet below.

To Johanna's dismay she found herself shaking. She breathed deeply to control this, but Inweer had already noticed.

"Afraid of heights, Johanna? Or afraid of us?"

"Both," she answered, though only one was true.

On her back she felt the pressure of his hand, heavy and warm, without claws. Perhaps he believed her. She had served him well, and received his indulgence in return. Until lately, since the news had come that Titus Quinn had been seen again in the great Tarig city far away. And that he had fled, taking all the Tarig brightships with him. Now Inweer had cause to worry where her loyalties lay. He suspected that she still loved her husband, and she let him believe that. It conveniently explained her agitation these days. But she hoped that Titus had forgotten her. He should concentrate on more urgent matters. Such as this engine. If he knew it existed. Pray God that he did know it existed: She had risked everything to ensure that he did.

Inweer guessed that her thoughts were of her husband. "Titus did not rescue you when he came to the bright city. Did you think it possible?"

"No. Still . . ." She put on a wry smile. "My husband was always unpredictable."

"We recall." Once, long ago, Inweer had known Titus in the Ascendancy where the Tarig had kept him. All the ruling lords had known him. One had died of the experience.

Inweer watched her with an unblinking, black gaze. "You must shut your ears against the engine."

"I can't."

"Other things which we required of you were eventually possible. You recall?"

Now he toyed with her. She dared to leave his question unanswered. Instead she murmured, "Why did you ever tell me, my lord?"

In his chambers one ebb-time when he had held her as she wept, he had murmured the thing that he thought might release her from longing. He had told her the purpose of the engine.

"We should not have done it if it deprives you of rest. An error?"

She put her hands on the railing, feeling the engine's drumming even there. "Perhaps." You made a mistake, she thought, a most profound mistake.

"Yes, an error," he conceded. "We wished for you to give up your hope of home. It had sickened you. We favor that you remain well." He added unnecessarily, "You will never go home."

"If not, I wish always to be with you, Bright Lord."

"Yes," he murmured.

If it appeared that he had forgotten SuMing he now made clear that he had not. "SuMing," he said, "come to us."

SuMing appeared by his side, bowing low. "Bright Lord?"

Without looking at her but still gazing outward, he said, "Climb onto the railing."

Her mouth quivered, then released the words, "Yes, Lord." Wearing practical tunic pants, she climbed up, sliding her legs over the railing, locking her hands in position. She teetered ever so slightly.

Lord Inweer said, "Johanna, are you cold? You shake."

"Yes, very cold."

"SuMing," he said, "remove your jacket."

To do so SuMing had to remove one hand from the rail to undo the clasps. After a long fumbling at knots she undid the five buttons, dipping one shoulder to let the jacket fall away, leaving her with a small shift for a top.

"Hand it to your mistress."

She did so and Johanna took the garment, locking glances with the terrified girl. The silks of the girl's tunic rustled in the air currents from below.

"Now jump," Lord Inweer said.

Without hesitation, SuMing let go, pushed off, and plummeted. In an instant Inweer had grabbed her braid, stopping her fall and ripping a terrible shriek from her. Then she hung quietly, her braid clutched in Lord Inweer's hand.

Inweer's outstretched arm did not tire. He turned to Johanna. "Shall I open my hand?"

Below, SuMing hung perfectly still, keeping a terrible silence. Johanna wished she were strong enough to rid herself of this enemy. But not this way. "No, my lord," she whispered, "I will teach her to better please us."

He cocked his head. "If so."

She nodded.

Then Inweer raised his arm, lifting SuMing's limp body in an effortless maneuver that hauled her onto the railing. With his other hand he pulled her knees clear and deposited her on the floor, where the girl collapsed, twitching. A trickle of blood fell down her neck.

Ignoring SuMing, Inweer resumed his conversation with Johanna. "It all has a price," he said, gazing at the engine. "Even the gracious lords must pay a price for all we do."

Johanna watched SuMing shivering on the floor, her scalp pulled halfway from her head. She could not go to her yet.

Inweer went on. "You understand the price?"

"Insofar as I can."

"You can understand."

In saying this he required her to leave him blameless in the matter of the engine. The Tarig universe was failing, its power source rapidly depleting. Only one decent substitute existed: Johanna's universe. So the burning of the Rose was the price for the billion sentient lives gathered here in their far-flung sways and in their common hopes for life and love. The same things that people on Earth desired, which only one place could have.

SuMing inched away from the precipice and pulled herself into a ball, hugging her knees.

"SuMing," Johanna said, "can you walk?"

"Yes, mistress," she whispered.

"Then go to bed." Even traumatized and bleeding, SuMing should get out of Inweer's sight quickly.

SuMing looked up. Her expression might as easily have been hatred as gratitude. She crawled backward for a small distance, eyes on Lord Inweer. Then she managed to stand up and stagger away.

Johanna felt a cold river move through her, the currents of things to come. The person sitting on the rail might easily have been herself. It helped to watch how others faced a terrible death. SuMing had been brave.

Inweer held out an arm for her. "Now you will rest?"

She laid her hand on that hard skin, that tapering arm.

It would all be so simple if she despised this Tarig lord. But that was far from the case.

She looked into his dark eyes. "Yes," she said, answering whatever he had asked her. She must always say yes. Loving him, it was easy to do. In most things she gladly obeyed, serving him in all ways but one.

CHAPTER TWO

Titus Quinn watched with only a few misgivings as his niece and nephew played with the world's most comprehensive standard-gauge model train collection outside of a museum. It was worth upward of a half-million dollars, and used to be off-limits to touching, except by himself. Today he allowed six-year-old Emily to hold the train set controls, and eleven-year-old Mateo to polish a locomotive. They were his only family in this universe, and he meant to cherish them until he returned to the other one.

"All aboard," Emily declared, presiding over the Ives New York Central model train, just pulling out of the station by the bookcase. She slammed the start button with her fist, causing Quinn to wince. The S-class locomotive strained to life, hauling four illuminated passenger cars plus flatcars, boxcars, tenders, and a caboose.

Next to him at the dining room table, Mateo polished up the Coral Aisle, using the special cloth that Quinn reserved for the locomotives. "When will Mom and Dad be back?"

"Tomorrow, Ace. You get to see them tomorrow."

Mateo's face fell. "Maybe they'll stay longer."

"Hold on," he heard Emily say.

The Ives New York Central barreled toward the sofa, zooming too fast into the turn. He saw the trajectory, and knew it would be grabbing air. He jumped up, gesturing uselessly. "Emily . . ."

Too late for interventions, the locomotive jumped the tracks coming out of the turn, flying a couple of feet before folding back on the tender unit and first three passenger cars. It fell to the floor with a sickening clatter.

Reaching Emily's side, Quinn saw the tears welling, her face starting to come apart with shock. "Hey, don't worry," he told her. "They make these trains real strong."

Emily's mouth crumpled, but she held on to her dignity.

At Quinn's feet, the locomotive lay, still humming with power. He shut down the system with a signal of his data rings, the ones he'd forgotten he wore, that could have avoided this accident if he'd been paying attention.

Mateo ran over to survey the damage. "Boy, did you screw up," he told his sister. "You broke it."

Quinn snorted. "Hey, a simple crash like this? Hell no. We'll just pick it up, okay?"

She nodded, sniffing back tears. "We'll fix it?"

He paused, thinking of a small alien girl who had recently been sure he was a man who could fix things. The day, already rainy, seemed darker for a moment. There were things he'd done on his mission for Minerva Company that haunted him.

"Sure, we'll fix it. But later." He stood up, needing some fresh air, even if it was sodden with cold spring fog. "Get your coats, guys."

"It's raining," Mateo said.

"You bet. That's why the coats." Quinn led the way, stopping Emily on the porch to redo the mismatched buttoning of her yellow jacket.

Outside, the rain had upgraded into a wet fog, with the sky brightening to a lighter shade of gray.

Not like *the bright*. The bright sky of the Entire. The place that, after only a few weeks' absence, had begun to pull on him like a force of gravity. When he went back, he would be not a sojourner, but a strike force. *Fire, oh fire*, the navitar had said on that impossible river of the Entire. And, *Johanna is at the center of it.* In two utterances predicting that the Tarig would burn this universe, and that Johanna would warn him of it. Before she died.

"Uncle Titus?" Emily gazed at him. He was still holding on to her yellow jacket.

How could they burn a universe—collapse it in an instant? There was a way, the physics team said, and it elegantly bypassed speed-of-light issues and all the other objections. A quantum transition. If the universe, our universe, was not at the lowest-energy state possible, it could make an instantaneous quantum leap, turning matter—all matter, everywhere—into hot plasma. This was just one theory of a dozen or so that attempted to explain what Johanna said the Tarig knew how to do. And were starting to do, at Ahnenhoon.

"Uncle Titus?" Emily repeated, trying to pull away.

He released her. "Stay close so I can see you, okay?"

She ran off down the strand toward her waiting brother.

When he was around Emily and Mateo, the Tarig seemed remote, hardly credible. Even after years in their presence, he still knew little of them. Where did the Tarig come from, really, beyond the legends they fostered? Were there limits to their powers? How did they manipulate matter and energy as they did? They hoarded much, and even those sentients who knew them well were not privy to essential Tarig secrets.

He watched Emily in the hillocky sand, her small legs pounding, hands held out for balance. His daughter had loved the ocean. Did Sydney miss it where she was? She would be grown up now, and beyond sand pails and shell collections. Perhaps beyond him as well, although that did not bear long thought. He lengthened his stride to keep the kids in view. As they raced down the beach, Quinn ran too, into the stinging air, icy with moisture.

Out of a curl of fog a figure appeared, near the dunes. It startled him. The whole beach hereabouts was his. Others were not welcome.

The figure stood on the beach, dressed in a parka and what looked like suit pants and city shoes.

"Who the hell are you?" Quinn said. The stranger remained silent.

"Kids! Over here now. I want you over here." Quinn walked up to the intruder. "So who the hell are you?"

The man sported a day's growth of beard and piercing blue eyes—but watery, as though unused to salt air. The breeze rustled graying hair. He made no move to respond.

"Pissing me off," Quinn growled at him. "This is my property."

A reaction finally, a sour face. "Property. Like that other place? You know. That belongs to everybody. Not just you, Quinn."

This stranger knew his name. Quinn was suddenly conscious that he hadn't come armed on this excursion. Usually, outdoors, he carried a knife, an artifact of another place. But not today.

"That's fine," Quinn shot back. "But you're on my property, fellow. You'll leave now. Might try calling for an appointment." Quinn looked down the beach. The kids were walking back toward him.

"Property," the man said. He looked beyond Quinn, to the surf, the horizon. "Who do you think owns the water out there? The damn ocean." He came closer, and his breath smelled of whiskey. "Everybody owns it. Same as the other place."

"Other place?"

An unpleasant smile. "Yes. The Entire, isn't it?"

Quinn hoped he'd heard wrong.

"The Entire," the man repeated. "What you call it, right? Doesn't belong to you or your damn company. Belongs to damn everyone. Think you're the only one wants to have that nice big life?" Spoken with righteous contempt.

"Get out of here. I'm calling my security. You better be gone."

"Okay, sure. We'll talk later, when you're in a better frame of mind." He emphasized *frame of mind* viciously. "Just want you to remember me, Quinn. And that I know. There's lots of people who know. Keep it in mind." He started to back off.

Mateo appeared out of the fog, coming to Quinn's side. Quinn put his arm around Mateo's shoulders.

"Where's your sister?" Quinn murmured to him.

The figure in the parka moved off toward the dunes. He climbed the first dune and stood for a moment, a shadow against the glowering sky.

"A little warning," the man shouted at Quinn, his voice tinny. He disappeared down the other side of the dune, leaving Quinn unsettled and nervous.

The fog blew in wisps, and the waves crashed again in normal cadence. "Where's your sister?" Quinn asked.

"I don't know."

That jerked Quinn to attention. "She's not with you?"

"I thought she was here with you."

Then, Mateo in hand, Quinn ran down the beach. She was up ahead. Surely just up ahead. Quinn ran until Mateo cried out, and then Quinn stopped, knowing he had run farther than Emily could have gone in a couple of minutes.

Shouting her name, he raced for the dunes. He didn't look at the surf. She hadn't gone near the water; she was smarter than that. In the dunes, his instinct told him. He raced to the edge of the dunes, and crested the first one, looking wildly at the grasses and gullies. Seeing no one, he charged over the next ridge, and the next, calling. But she was gone. Gone with the man in the parka. Kidnapped.

The enormity of this thought tightened his innards. *Emily*, he said, barely breathing. Grabbing Mateo by the hand, he raced down the beach toward the cottage. There was only one road in and out of here. Sometime in the past few minutes he'd heard a car engine. Whoever it was had come by car.

Quinn stormed into the cottage to grab his keys, yelling for Mateo to go to the car. They met there and piled in. Quinn gunned the sports car out of the garage, yanking it around to climb up the driveway, and careened out onto the road. Choosing the direction toward the highway, he voiced a security alert and saw by the light on his dashCom that it had gone out. He drove fast, straining to see ahead in the fog.

"Did that guy take Emily?" Mateo asked, looking miserable.

"I don't know." He tried to wrap his mind around the situation. The word was out; people knew about things Minerva had hoped to keep to themselves—things too big to keep to themselves, too big to patent. And now people were using Emily to be sure they got a piece of paradise. They might be surprised to learn what paradise had in store for them. . . .

An incoming voice message from his security backup brought his attention back to the moment. He answered. *Come by air. Come now.*

He jammed around a curve, all the while drenched in a sense of the unreal. How could this be happening? How could he have let her out of his sight?

"Uncle Titus, slow down." Hunkered down, Mateo held on to the edge of the bucket seat.

Yes, going too fast. Too fast in the fog, with bad traction, and reinforcements coming anyway. It would all be over soon. It would—

Something in the road. Steering to avoid collision, Quinn slammed on the brakes, jolting the two of them forward, into the dashboard. A few picoseconds before impact of head to steering wheel, the vehicle's interior phased into a yielding matrix, softening the crash impact. The rear end skidded to the side, sending the car nose first into a ditch and knocking Quinn's breath out of him.

Quiet settled around him. "Mateo?"

A shaky voice. "I'm okay."

Quinn hauled himself from the car and ran down the road to the place where he'd seen a streak of bright yellow. He cried out, "Emily? Emily?"

A high-pitched voice threaded to him; perhaps Mateo—Mateo, whom he'd left in the car, maybe hurt. God, the world was a jumble. He whirled around. Standing at the side of the road a short distance away was Emily.

Her jacket was still buttoned all the way to the top, and she stood just as she had on the porch. Racing to her, he scooped her up, hugging her fiercely. Her arms went around his neck, bringing the smell of wet wool to his nostrils.

At last he released her. "Where've you been, honey?" His voice, shaky.

"Went for a ride." She looked worried.

"A ride?"

Then Mateo joined them, looking tussled but not bruised.

"Those people," Emily said, looking down the road. "I didn't want to go, but . . ." She took one look at her uncle's face and started to fall apart.

"No, honey," he said quickly, relief washing over him in progressive waves. "I'm not mad at you. It's fine. You're fine, sweetheart. I just love you, that's all."

Mateo looked at his sister and shook his head slowly. "Screwed up again, Em."

Clutching Emily to his chest, Quinn looked down the dirt road, where the would-be kidnappers had fled. If they'd meant to keep her, they could have. This was just a little shot over the bow from the man in the parka.

He took Emily and Mateo to the side of road and sat down, an arm around each of them. He'd known, he'd always known, that the larger world mingled with the personal. Great events corkscrewed into small ones, leaving holes, sometimes eternal ones. His life had been like that lately.

Fortune hunters could break into his own backyard and demand that he change his *frame of mind*. They could demand answers to a few questions,

questions new in the history of the world. Questions such as, Who does the universe next door belong to?

And who gets to decide?

Stefan Polich kept well back from the edge of the sixty-story drop, high railing or not. The item he held in his hand was too precious to risk a slip. On the outside, it was merely a gray velvet case the size of a dollar bill, but it held a costly payload.

Stefan turned the box over in his hand, hearing the soft clunk inside, a reassuringly heavy clunk, and an expensive one. The contents represented thousands of person-hours, crammed into the short period of time that Titus Quinn had been back.

A security guard came to the edge of the patio, nodding to signify that Helice Maki was here.

"A moment," Stefan muttered. Let her wait. The woman plagued him— newest, youngest, and oddly, most dangerous member of the board. It rubbed the wound raw to remember that he was the one who'd put her name forward in the first place.

His glance came back to the gray velvet case. Calibrated to maim, not to kill. All the scientific resources and capability of the fifth-largest ultratech company in the world assured him that this thing was calibrated precisely. Local effects, devastating ones, with an internalized mortality sequence to ensure containment. He believed his people when they told him this. He prayed they were right. Prayer sat uneasily on him, but to lead you needed a little faith. That was something Stefan had recently decided, now that he was dealing with the most startling turn of events: contact with a stage-four civ- ilization, one that had created, or at least enlivened, a separate but proximate universe. These beings might normally have little reason to regard the Earth, Minerva, and its CEO except for one inescapable fact: Their universe was porous. One could enter. Cause trouble. The two universes were linked, like conjoined twins. Unfortunately these twins shared only one heart.

Slipping the gray box into his jacket pocket, he nodded at the guard, dreading the confrontation with Helice. Small of stature, large of ambition. Had he erred terribly when he refused to let her go to the other place? Denied her ambition, she had undermined him at every turn.

Helice came in, surrounded by three of the tallest security staff Stefan had ever seen. He thought that she looked like a human among Tarig—beings Quinn described as unnervingly tall and steely. But as to predators, in this case it was the short one.

He waved her in. "Helice, good. Have a seat."

She pulled up a chair by the door, leaving her bodyguards at their posts. Stefan glanced at them. "Privacy, Helice."

"These are dreds," she said, using the pejorative term. "Harmless." She meant they were stupid. A dred had an average IQ—by definition around one hundred. But stupid or not, they understood they'd just been insulted.

Seeing Stefan's discomfort, she waved the guards away. The brutes went through to Stefan's drawing room, lurking just beyond hearing range. Since the world had cracked open, Minerva board members went under guard, a caution against competitor firms sniffing around the edges of the secret of the Entire. They'd come to the brink in a damn hurry, since that innocent day when a postdoc student discovered right-turning neutrinos and the other place had announced itself with particles of impossible angular momentum.

"Nice view," she said. "You can see forever." The city sparkled in the night glow of lit skyscrapers, gilded by rain.

"Wish I could. Wish I could damn well see tomorrow." When the board would vote on whether to send Quinn now, rather than later. Perhaps, if Helice had any clout, they'd also vote on whether to send the man at all. Someone had to go, and soon—now that the secret was out, proven by the man who had trespassed on Quinn's property yesterday.

Stefan poured two glasses of wine, noting how young Helice looked. She *was* young. Twenty years old, the youngest quantum sapient engineering graduate in Stanford's history. Helice had surrounded herself with prodigies like herself so long she had little tolerance for people of average—or even above-average—intelligence. Stefan, on the other hand, had attended enough diversity training to understand that simple folk had their place, and it wasn't a bad one.

Helice broke into his thoughts. "When we first found it, we thought it would save us." She referred, of course, to the realm next door. Its inhabitants called it the Entire, without regard for the fact that it was not all there was.

"Yes. We thought so."

"Now it's going to kill us." Helice looked wistful, rather than afraid. Perhaps one so young could not imagine her own death, much less the death of everything.

Stefan still had trouble grasping the news that Titus Quinn had brought home. That to preserve their unnatural environment, the lords of the Entire would burn a natural one. It would be no act of malice or even ill will; they needed this universe to sustain themselves. Once Tarig engines were up to speed, the combustion would be instantaneous, forming a concentrated heart of fire that would last the Entire billions of years. It was a loathsome act, like dining on a child.

It was shock enough to discover an alien civilization. That it far surpassed human achievements staggered him. The Tarig had, Quinn said, found a barren universe and shaped it to their own desires. With powers like this, what chance did the Rose, as they called our cosmos, have?

Stefan put his hand on the gray box, taking comfort from it.

"Sending Quinn is a mistake," Helice said.

"Maybe. But there's no time to train someone new." Ever since Emily Quinn's brief abduction, they'd been racing to advance the schedule. Competing factions had now come into view. "We have to move quickly."

Helice shrugged. "We'll let the board decide if that's so."

"Perhaps the board will be persuaded by this." He pulled out the velvet case, setting it on the table between them.

Her eyes flicked to it, then narrowed. "Oh. You *are* ready, aren't you." Her forehead wrinkled to indicate she was thinking—thinking faster and better than most.

Opening the box, Stefan exposed the bracelet. Noting her expression, he said, "Don't worry; it's empty. The nan won't be ready for a few days. But this chain is what Quinn will carry with him when he goes. It'll create a limited but effective local collapse. Everything in a mile-wide circle will fall into nanoscale chaos. Hard, built structures will fall to sludge."

"And people."

"Yes, if in the vicinity."

Helice picked up the six-inch length of it. Heavy, it draped against her hand.

"We call it a cirque," he said. "He'll wear it on his ankle." He took it from her. "It's hollow, although to the naked eye it doesn't have much thickness. When live, it'll be molecularly dense, loaded with nan." He indicated three indentations in the length of it. "Quinn will press these links in a certain sequence, and that will bring the nan together in a stream, to share information. From there it'll build a surge momentum capable of mutating the environs where it's released."

"Surge momentum. You mean a nanoscale changeover."

"We don't like to use that term." Ever since nan technology became practical, alarmists had warned that the molecular process could get out of hand. Go uncontrolled, in a chain reaction. "We'll be under control," he said. "There's a phage system that shuts the whole sequence down after an hour."

He indicated that she should hold out her hand. When she did, Stefan slipped it around her wrist and inserted the two ends together to make a circlet. "That's the first step. Form a circlet. After pressing the codes into the indentations, the timing is fifty minutes. Time for Quinn to get some distance."

She dipped her hand, and the metal strip fell off her wrist onto the table. "Oops. Good thing it's not loaded."

He stared at her. She had actually dropped a billion-dollar bracelet. Stefan picked it up and replaced the chain in its case. He strove for patience. "We'll give this to him as soon as the board decides the schedule. It can't be soon enough. Quinn might not be ideal, but he's all we've got, I'm afraid."

"We're all afraid. The board's afraid."

"No, not all of them. Only *your* people on the board." Of course it only took 51 percent to quash the whole deal. They could agree with Helice that Titus Quinn was too shaky, too odd, too driven. They could argue that they needed someone under better control. Someone like Helice. Sitting across from him she looked damn cocky, as though she'd counted the votes and liked her tally.

She gazed out over the city. "All you need to do is compromise a little."

"Send you instead?" How could she still be harping on this? She was young and inexperienced. Without the language, without decent cultural cover. She knew nothing about the place except what Quinn had told them in debriefings. And by her own admission, he'd withheld plenty: the name of the Tarig lord who could be subverted, for instance. All to make himself indispensable.

"Yes, send me." She pinned him with a gaze unfettered by wine and goodwill. "I'd stay on task. The man can ruin our only chance. Over there they don't know that we know what they're up to. They won't be on guard yet. We have one chance to take Ahnenhoon out of action. If Quinn blows this—goes looking for the daughter, whatever—we won't get a second chance. Kiss the Earth good-bye, and wave a last time at the stars. It's all for burning." She smiled prettily. "That's my pitch for the board tomorrow. Like it?"

"No." He rose, and went to the railing. His hands made sweat marks on the railing. Looking down, he got that little jolt from the profoundly dropping view. If he just knew which way the board would vote. Christ almighty, the Tarig wanted to burn the Rose like an enduring source of coal. Might take a few decades, but they'd already started the process. Stars sucked out of existence . . .

He turned to her in frustration. "What do you want, Helice?"

"To win." She joined him at the railing.

"What would you settle for?"

"I'm not sure I have to settle."

He stared out into a wall of rain borne in on a bank of fog from the river and deflected by the veranda's climate control. "The thing that bothers me? I just don't believe you. You don't think Quinn will fail. You just want to go there yourself, and would sacrifice everything to do it. Sorry. It paints an ugly picture of you, I realize."

"I don't deny it. I want to go."

"Clouds your judgment, you know."

Her voice went low and throaty. "I was there when he came back—you remember? I listened to him for weeks. Every day, we debriefed him—six, seven hours at a stretch—and yes, I was intrigued. It would take a heart of stone not to . . . not to want to go. The creatures. Those sentient species. The storm walls. I want to see these things for myself. I want that." She stared into the rain as though she saw them now. "There are other sentient races out there, Stefan. We may never find them otherwise. But they're in this one place. So yes, I want to go."

After a pause she said, "But that's not the reason I'm volunteering. I don't expect you to believe me."

"Just tell me what it'll take to not hear your pitch tomorrow."

She said simply, "Send me with him. He goes. Okay. But I go with him."

Stefan looked at her with new appreciation. The woman *could* compromise. She wanted it that much. She wanted the Entire in a strange, unreasoning way. Her fascination might arise from how the place had affected Quinn. A man obsessed. And Quinn had brought her down that path slowly—without, at first, her even noticing it.

She wouldn't give up; Stefan knew that. He fingered the velvet case in his pocket. So much depended on the little circlet and its delivery to the right place: the core of the enemy.

"All right," he said. "You go."

A smile hit her lips and stayed.

"If you're set on this, make sure your papers are in order." Tellingly, his mind had jumped to the notion that she would die in the Entire.

She whispered, "Thank you, Stefan."

It wasn't a good compromise. Helice could slow Quinn down. She could blow his cover by doing the wrong thing, saying the wrong thing. On the other hand—a critical other hand—she might keep the man on track.

Now that he had overcome the last barrier to Quinn's departure, he let his mind settle uneasily into the image of Titus Quinn taking possession of the cirque. The man who'd been, until recently, a hermit, and halfway mad. "You think he'll do the job? You think he can focus on what we need?"

"Frank opinion? He's not your man. He's got too much personal history tied up in this. The wife, the daughter. Their home is, or was, the Entire."

"But this"—he spread his hands in front of him—"is his world. We'll be utterly dependent on him. I don't like the man, but he's no coward."

She conceded, "Maybe not, but the question is, would he rather save us, or go after his daughter?"

Stefan muttered, "Damn the daughter, anyway. Why couldn't she have died like her mother?"

Helice turned a sweet expression on him. "You could always give *me* the cirque."

Relentless, she was. "Let's just say you'll be backup. If he fails, then you deliver it." Every person on the board had misgivings about endangering the Entire with this nano weapon. The place was a rich region to develop, and in some respects the company's future depended on it. Its byways might offer safe paths to the stars of this universe. But before Minerva could develop the Entire, they had to overcome it. Some might find that distasteful. But he trusted Helice Maki had none of those scruples. She would cleave to her mission like a pit bull.

She nodded, her eyes exultant. "You can count on me, Stefan."

He imagined the furor when he broke this news to Quinn. "He won't like you going along, you know."

"He'll be okay," she said. "Because we're not going to tell him."

CHAPTER THREE

T HE YOUNG WOMAN'S FACE held an unsettling combination of ecstasy and innocence. Titus Quinn watched her fluid movements through the window of the Deep Room, that light-filled tank where, as an mSap engineer, she programmed the machine sapient. Her lips moved as she voiced code, but with audio off, the impression was one of a woman dancing in light.

Quinn spoke to Caitlin standing next to him. "She looks too young to train an mSap."

"You have to be young, remember? Who else could keep up?"

The empty warehouse was a new acquisition. It worried Quinn that Caitlin was here with only two bodyguards—presumably lurking on the grounds, though Quinn hadn't actually seen them. Lamar Gelde was waiting outside, along with two cars full of security staff, all of them uneasy to be making an unauthorized stop for Quinn's personal business.

"She's a renormalization expert," Caitlin went on. "This sapient's not brand new. It used to work for the Coastal Desalinization. She's retraining it, bringing it around to seeing things our way."

Quinn didn't like the anthropomorphic references. The mSaps were just machines, not really sapients or some kind of AI. Quantum processors did not a consciousness make.

In the Deep Room, the engineer turned around. Her arms fell to her sides, and some of the light of the mind-field subsided. She looked in their direction, placidly, with that flat, hostile look of the wholly self-absorbed.

"Can she see us?" Quinn asked.

"If she's paying attention to us. She's still thinking, though."

Oh, *thinking*. When you said that about a savvy, one who tested in the upper limits of human intelligence, you said it respectfully. Normal snobbery metastasized into something truly ugly these days, establishing a chasm between *middies* like Caitlin and the technical smart-asses like this young engineer. It gave Quinn a creepy feeling, this intelligence divide, in a world where the rigors of advanced quantum physics and biomolecular engineering evaded the understanding of all but a few. He was one of those, but he'd bypassed the advanced degrees for a fast-track career as a starship pilot. So much for smart.

He and Caitlin left the observation chamber, entering the warehouse proper, soon to house Rob and Caitlin's new software company. She stopped in front of a double-paneled wood door, stranding her code into the smart surface, releasing the locks.

They entered the office, cozy with rose-colored carpet, an expensive desk, and a view out to a parkland—a far cry from Rob's former life tending savants like a groomer in a stable. Now Rob was an entrepreneur, thanks to his brother's millions—Quinn's travel fees for duties performed in the Entire. Quinn was glad that his brother had finally relented and taken the loan.

Caitlin settled herself into a leather sofa and he sat next to her, glad to have a moment alone with her, wishing he could tell her what he was facing. She'd always been his confidante. But for her safety, he could tell her nothing. And what would he say, anyway? The world will end in fire, Caitlin. You think the world is eternal, but it's not. It's fragile. A dry forest waiting to catch a spark. That's what matter is. Latent fire. He pictured a hot wind sweeping over Portland, a storm of heat and smoke . . . and shook off the vision.

"How's Emily?"

"Fine, thank God. She's doing fine. It could have gone badly, and didn't. You're not still thinking you're responsible?" She shook her head dismissively. "I'll get us a drink." Rummaging in boxes on the floor, Caitlin tucked her dark blonde hair behind her ears as it fell forward, casually feminine. She found two cups and a bottle of scotch.

"I don't have much time, Caitlin."

She smirked. "You've got time, Titus. They've got to wait for you. They control so much, but not everything."

She was right. He wasn't a slave to their agendas. He was the only person who'd been to that other place and had any idea of how to survive there. The thing that he wanted to tell Caitlin, and couldn't, was that he might not make it back. He would be entering a Tarig fortress. He hadn't thought much about escape. He couldn't think past Ahnenhoon.

She poured him a drink and they toasted each other.

"I'm going back, Caitlin," he said finally. "Leaving tomorrow."

Watching Titus, Caitlin took a swallow to cushion her dismay. So soon. Just when she had adjusted to having him back, and with that altered face—more narrow, the eyes too dark, covered as they were with lenses that were supposed to make his eyes look blue. She thought she detected a ring of amber around his irises. But every time he spoke, she found the old Titus. No one was quite like him, with his mannerisms, his way of moving and of thinking. When she'd married Rob she foolishly thought he might be something like his brother. But Rob was only Rob, and the recent vacation hadn't helped.

Titus said, "I'm worried about you and the kids. It feels like hell to be leaving like this."

She gestured around her. "You regret that we've got our dream company, that we work for ourselves and don't even need to work?"

"I regret the bastards are crawling all over you like flies on a picnic."

The biggest fly was Stefan Polich, the man who'd personally threatened to destroy her son's upcoming testing results if Caitlin didn't spy on Titus, report on him. She'd expected retaliation when she'd told him to go to hell. Now that Titus was leaving, she braced herself for something along those lines.

"We'll survive," she said. "I don't walk around being scared. Besides, what can you do? You're going. You have to go."

Titus hadn't told her why. And she wasn't going to ask. He looked like he had things on his mind. That surely would be the adjoining universe, the place where Sydney might still be alive. Caitlin had last seen Sydney and her mother at Minerva's private airport—Johanna holding Sydney's hand, Sydney hoisting her own duffel, just like her father's. That was the last Caitlin ever saw of her niece and sister-in-law.

She wished she'd never been party to the information that Johanna was dead. It removed a barrier between her and Titus. He had to love somebody.

A man like that would love somebody, love them ferociously. Here she sat, the good little wife and mother, the good sister-in-law, never breaking the rules, never letting herself go.

Her hand shook as she poured another splash of the scotch.

Misinterpreting, Titus said, "Let me get you more security. My people this time."

"Titus, no. I'm not going to live like that. Shut up about it. Besides, you think because you're leaving we're less secure? After what happened on the beach? Christ. Get you gone, and we'll be better off." If he was gone, there'd be no danger of her letting go. Everyone was definitely better off with her *not letting go*.

"If they tinker with Mateo's Standard Test, I'll keelhaul their asses using the biggest ship I can hijack."

She smiled at the bravado. "But we won't ever know if they tinkered. He either tests savvy or he doesn't." She figured Mateo could well be one of the superintelligent. He had his uncle's genetic heritage, his grandfather's.

Titus was looking out the window but not seeing the view, she guessed. It seemed to her that he was already in the other place.

"There are some dark things over there," he murmured. Perhaps he saw that world right now, instead of the patch of woodland outside the window. "They can hurt us."

"Titus." The unpleasant thought struck. "You're in danger. This trip isn't just for Sydney, is it?"

A silence stretched on. Then he said, "If I don't come back I want you to have it all. You and Rob. Everything I have. You'll need it."

She put down her scotch. She didn't want to talk about money. About life with Titus gone. "We need you, Titus," she said, wanting to say instead, *I need you.* But she was the good sister-in-law. It was such pure shit.

She looked at him calmly, dropping her guard. "It isn't working. Rob and me, it isn't working." Noting his frown, she said, "You want us to be happy with each other, I know. You want us to be a good family." The bitterness in her voice surprised her. When Titus didn't respond, she continued. "You want us to be what you used to be. Well we aren't. We're just Rob and Caitlin, and it isn't good. It can't ever be good."

He shook his head. "I knew there were issues. Rob isn't always—"

"Isn't always what?" She let that hang in the air for a moment. "Isn't you, Titus. He isn't you." The words were such a relief, she felt a mountain of tension leaving her body. No, Rob wasn't a desiring creature, a striving creature, with quick, unholy passions and the drive for adventure. Just once in her life she'd like a man to make love to her as though he'd sell his soul to do it. She closed her eyes. God, it was all such a mess. When she opened her eyes, heavy tears stuck in the corners.

She wasn't sure who moved first. They'd been sitting side by side, and now she was in his arms, with tears their excuse. To hell with the excuse. She wanted him to undress her right here on the couch.

"Please, Titus," she whispered.

"Caitlin, Caitlin," came his throaty reply.

She pulled her head away from his shoulder and kissed him. She couldn't stop herself, and was glad she couldn't. His hands raked through her hair, and he kissed her back. Titus was in charge, no question, and she would have done anything, wanted him to take her to the limit. His hands were on her, and she almost cried out at the pleasure of it.

Then he pulled back. He put his hands on the side of her face, looking at her with an intensity that froze her.

He stood up, turning away. "Jesus," he whispered.

It was all clear to her in an instant. He was saying no. Of course he was. He couldn't be a son-of-a-bitch who'd bed his brother's wife.

"Caitlin," he said. "I can't. We can't do this."

"Speak for yourself," she said, catching her breath.

He looked at her, emotions warring on his face. "I am."

She calmed herself, pulling her hair behind her ears. "Is it because of Johanna?"

"Because of Rob."

She nodded. She wanted him to spell it out, wanted it to be clear now that he was leaving and might not come back. "Was I ever someone you could have loved?"

He looked at her, his face tight with emotion. "Christ, Caitlin, how can I answer that? How can you ask me?"

She knew it wasn't fair. Either answer would make her miserable. She stood up, smoothing her outfit. "Well, just so long as I was someone you could have fucked."

He grabbed her arm. "Jesus, that's ugly."

She knew it was. She smiled, and gently took his arms away. "I'm sorry, Titus. I'm a little out of my mind right now. We both are."

He stepped back, composing himself as well, but not willing to let it go just yet. "Are we? Out of our minds? I could still throw caution away. Could you?"

"No," she said, creating the hardest smile she'd ever faked.

He stood looking at her.

"You go now, Titus." The sooner he walked out of there the better. She felt like tinder near a fire. She wanted to burn. But she was able to hope, too, that he'd just go.

"You and Rob . . . ," he began. "I'm sorry."

"Not your fault." Not his fault for being the charismatic older brother. "We'll get by. We always do."

He was still hesitating to leave. Finally he spoke the words that ended it all right there. "I'm not saying that you should stay with Rob. That's none of my business, I know that. But if you don't stay, I'm not in line, Caitlin. I can't be and still live with myself."

"I know," she whispered. The awful thing was, she *did* know. She understood how it had to be. "Go bring that youngster home," she told him. "Bring yourself home." She still meant that with all her heart.

And then he was gone.

"She took it badly?" Lamar Gelde looked worried as Quinn climbed into the backseat of the company car, middle vehicle in a caravan of security.

"Yes."

They pulled away, accelerating after reaching the smart surface of the arterial.

Lamar nodded. In his seventy-six years, he had never married, had never studied women's behavior. But he said with elaborate weariness, "Women hate to say good-bye."

"Yes."

The city passed in a blur as the custom security vehicle eased into the automated flow of the freeway, where at need the chauffeur could override, pulling out of the linked formations of cars. Riding in the front passenger seat, a thin man with a ponytail kept nearby vehicles under surveillance, assessing armament with enhanced glasses made to look like sunglasses. The man on the beach hadn't been armed, but the next interested party might be.

Quinn sank into the backseat, thinking about Caitlin. He kicked himself for not having known how she felt. For not knowing how vulnerable he was when a woman he found attractive offered herself to him. It had been three years since he'd been intimate with a woman, so he was a sitting duck for acts of kindness. A few acts of kindness spooled through his mind.

"Want to stop off at Rob's?" Lamar asked.

"No." Not even. He'd call Rob to say good-bye.

The cars sped onward toward the airport, the dashCom winking with traffic flow predictions. From there it was a short jaunt by hyperjet to the mid-Pacific space elevator. Time to go. High time.

Quinn murmured to Lamar, "You're sure we're ready for this?" Minerva had had only a few weeks to plan the mission. This time he would go armed into the Entire, something he hated, even if there was no choice.

Lamar nodded. "It wasn't hard once they put their savvy minds to it. A bit of nan and the damage is done." Lamar smiled, revealing good white teeth, the best money could buy. Quinn didn't begrudge him his vanity. In his youth Lamar had been a handsome man. Lamar was now something better: a *good* man. The only man in the company who'd stood up for Quinn when he first came back from the Entire messed up, memory erased, family lost. *Gone over the edge*, said Stefan Polich. Lamar had been his only ally and got booted off the board as a result. These days he was Quinn's handler because Quinn wouldn't allow handling by anyone else.

Half of Quinn's mind was still back with Caitlin. Pray God she didn't hate him. Things he should have said crossed his mind, and then what he *had* said: *I'm not in line.* Ugly. Blunt. Maybe it needed to be.

"I'm sorry about where you're headed," Lamar was saying. "It's damn dangerous. I owe your father more than to send his boy into this madness."

"Is that what it is? Madness? They're burning stars, Lamar. Beta Pictoris. The Trapezium Cluster. Hoping to do worse."

Lamar sighed. "Sons of bitches. Like being eyeballed by a tiger for a snack."

"My father would want me to go." And then, mind back on Caitlin, moving to a safe topic regarding her: "But if I don't come back, you take care of Caitlin Quinn. My assets go to her and her family, and you keep Stefan and Helice at bay, their hands off her, off her assets. Even if she and my brother aren't together, Caitlin's still family. Understood?"

Lamar raised an eyebrow. "Is that how it is?"

"Just in case, that's all. They've already threatened her. Stefan will go after the boy. So will Helice. If they get paranoid and think I've betrayed them, they'll squash her."

"Stefan would, maybe. I'll watch him." He left unsaid, *Helice.*

A heavy silence descended. The longer it stretched, the more uneasy Quinn felt. Was there something here he should know? Did Lamar not get Helice's character? Or had she bought him out? He hated to be suspicious of Lamar, of all people. But Lamar still let it sit. Quinn was leaving his family in the man's care, and now suddenly he didn't feel perfectly at ease.

"Helice is young," Lamar said. "She's making the mistakes of the young. She doesn't like you; I recognize that. But you could win her over if you weren't so goddamn stubborn."

"I don't want to win her over. She's a vicious brat."

"You never forgive, Titus."

Quinn let it go that he'd called him Titus. He went by Quinn now, as Lamar damn well knew.

The car peeled off the freeway, went to the driver's command, and under local control, sped toward downtown.

At Quinn's inquiring look, Lamar said, "We've got one more stop. Hope you don't mind. It's the morgue."

When they came to a stop, Quinn saw a figure standing, hands in coat pockets, hunkered against the wind now blowing sharp off the Willamette River.

Lamar let the window down as Stefan Polich approached, peering in.

He fixed Quinn with a gaze. "Think you'd recognize the man from the beach?"

He did. Even lying still, the sneer gone and the eyes closed. Yes, it was the man in the parka who'd known Quinn's name, known the name of the Entire.

"That's him," Quinn confirmed. He pulled the sheet over the man's face, covering the damage from a gunshot in the mouth.

"Killed himself before we could question him," Stefan said. "He was armed, after all."

"What about the others?"

"Police are looking. But we're looking too. I don't think they're as eager as we are."

Yes, eager. And not for Emily's sake, but because the man had said that the Entire didn't belong to Minerva. That might be true in the larger sense, but not in the Minerva sense.

"So who was he?"

"His name's Leonard Garvey. A sapient engineer, down on his luck. A drinker. We don't see a connection with the major companies. Pray God he was on his own."

"That'd make a pretty good prayer. 'Please, Lord, secure my bottom line.'" He brightened, getting into the baiting of Stefan Polich. "But then, that *is* your religion, isn't it?"

Lights gleamed off metal trays, waiting to receive the dead. They were alone in the basement lab, except for Leonard Garvey, failed sapient engineer, failed kidnapper. *Think you're the only one wants to have that nice, big life?* By that did he mean long life? If so—and Quinn fervently hoped it wasn't so—then quite a lot was known out there about the Entire. Some knew the very thing that inhabitants of the Entire most feared would be known. That nice, big life.

"What's this about, anyway?" Quinn asked. "You didn't need to come to the morgue."

"No one knew I was coming here. I needed some privacy." Then, with disarming honesty: "I don't trust everyone at Minerva."

"Really."

Quinn's sarcasm killed the conversation for a minute as the two men sized each other up. They despised each other, and being on the same side hadn't changed that. Quinn had once had a thriving career as a captain of an interstellar ship. It was a risky job and paid accordingly. But Quinn would have done it for nothing. When his ship broke up in the Kardashev tunnel, Stefan couldn't get past the fact that Titus Quinn was apparently the only one who survived. Quinn couldn't get past it either, but that didn't mean he forgave Stefan for firing him or for putting him in a badly maintained ship in the first place.

"The truth is," Stefan continued, "someone talked. Someone in my group. That's why Garvey came after your niece; that's why there's movement afoot to figure out what the Entire is. Where it is. Everything we've worked for and which will only be solely ours for a little while longer. We'd hoped for a few months. Anyway, it's why you're going early."

"You can't keep the place secret for forever."

"No. But they'd stop you, Quinn. They wouldn't trust a renegade pilot running loose with military nan in the other place. Why would they? They don't have the background or the trust. They might accuse us of making up a threat. We have to act before the feds or the companies make an issue of it. Before fighting over the Entire obscures what needs doing. You see where it could go?"

Quinn did. He thought the secret worth keeping to prevent public mayhem. There were no useful precautions, no shelter from the holocaust. The only refuge, the Entire itself. With humans decidedly unwelcome, an exodus in that direction was suicide.

This wasn't a decision Quinn would leave up to a summit of corporations. So once again, and against his instincts, he found himself aligning with Stefan Polich.

Stefan looked around, scanning the scrubbed-down room, smelling of antiseptic and toxic fluids. But Quinn no longer had heightened capabilities of smell. Originally implanted so that he could avoid ingesting toxins in the new land, Quinn had found that some enhancements were impossible to live with. Millions of years of evolution hadn't prepared humans to detect smells like a predator. He'd had the Jacobson's organ removed from his mouth. Sometimes plain human was enough.

Looking up, Quinn noticed that Stefan had taken something from his coat pocket and now held a small box covered in gray velvet.

Quinn knew what it was. The weapon. The nano device.

Stefan opened the case, revealing a silver chain. "A cirque. The designers call it a cirque. It goes on your ankle." Pushing the box back into his pocket, Stefan held the cirque with exaggerated care. "It's live. Loaded, you understand?"

Quinn did. It was lethal now—its contents sequestered in three chambers, each one with only partial instructions of how to digest an industrial complex the size of New Hampshire. He gazed at the burnished metal chain. It was attractive, like an antique Rolex.

"The code is four, five, one," Stefan said. "A total of ten. You press the first indent four times, the second one five times, the last one, once. Each indentation is a different width, beginning large and ending small. Once the code goes in, the cirque opens, comes off your ankle. Then you press the links again, in reverse sequence: one, five, four. Active, good to go." He eyed Quinn. "When you make the placement, hide it. The nan needs time to share information. Give it an hour. Once fully enlivened, it will spread as fast as a forest fire under a stiff wind."

Stefan dragged a chair away from the wall. "Put your foot up here. Either one. See how it fits." He handed the cirque over.

The carbon nitride casing was reassuringly heavy. Quinn put his left foot on the chair seat and linked the two ends, fitting them with a click. Active nan, military grade, riding his body. *Give me something I can't lose*, he'd told them. *Something I don't have to carry.* And here it was.

"Test it," Stefan said. "That it comes off."

Quinn examined the chain, noting again the three indentations on the loop. He pressed down the sequence: four, five, and one. Nothing happened. For a moment he thought, They mean for me to go down with Ahnenhoon.

"Pull it open."

Quinn did, and the chain detached, coming away in his hands.

Lowering his voice, Stefan said, "From now on we don't talk about the cirque, and we don't look at it. There'll be no physical exams. No baths, either, by the way."

"It's okay in water, though?"

"Yes, but let's not chance it."

"Not very reassuring."

"Okay, take a bath."

Looking at the cirque, Quinn thought he could do without.

"You don't have to do this, you know," Stefan said. "We could send someone else. You could brief somebody, train them. I'm not saying you have to go."

"How sure are you about this thing?"

Stefan looked him straight in the eyes. "We're not one hundred percent. But it's the best we've got."

Quinn liked that bit of honesty. "Do I really have an hour to get away?"

Stefan smiled. "So we're still trying to kill you?"

"Do I have an hour?"

"Don't wait an hour."

Stefan glanced at the cirque in Quinn's hand. "You know the value of that thing? Ounce for ounce, the most expensive artifact in the world. We're giving it to you to do what needs to be done. If you're not up to it, tell me now."

"Who else is there?"

"That's no answer."

"I thought it was." He looked at Stefan Polich, reminding himself that he wasn't doing this for Stefan or for Minerva. It was for the Rose. For the people he loved, for Mateo and Emily, and for everyone else, as well. He would have done it even if Johanna, in her message to him, hadn't begged him to act. She had reached out to him in a recorded warning, one she'd sent to him when he had first been imprisoned in the Entire. He hadn't found it then, and never knew what she took to her grave knowing: that the Tarig meant to destroy us. Last time back, he'd finally heard her warning. But even without her urging, he would have tried to stop the gracious lords, as they termed themselves. At close quarters with them for so long, he'd had time to grow familiar with their ways. No one else had a ghost of a chance of stopping them.

Stefan was waiting for Quinn to answer.

Quinn took the cirque in both hands and, leaning over the chair, clicked it into place around his ankle.

They left the morgue, entering the corridor where their respective security staffs waited. The chain traced a cold circle around his ankle. He'd have to practice taking it off, so he could do it in a hurry.

He didn't for a moment believe he'd have an hour to get away.

CHAPTER FOUR

I N ZERO-G, Lamar Gelde felt like his stomach was floating free. The shuttle between ship and space platform had no rotation, so for these interminable minutes of approach to the dock, he was getting a good dose of weightlessness. He was strapped in and all loose objects were secure—the intercom kept reminding them not to take out anything that might escape and become a projectile—but he couldn't do anything about his stomach.

"I'm too old for this nonsense," he grumbled.

Next to him, Quinn smiled indulgently. Fine for him, thirty-four years old and accustomed to the topsy-turvy from his starship days. He resented Quinn at the moment, and it flooded him with relief to discover hard feelings against a man he'd wronged.

The forward screen showed their slow crawl approach to the Ceres platform, toward the dock mast. Rivets, handholds, grappling arms, and solar arrays bristled from the platform's pockmarked hide. It had grown massively since Lamar had last been here, when he'd first watched Quinn enter the adjoining region. Since then the whole complex had become dedicated to dimensional interface, growing all the time. Crawling with workers and bots, its irregular design hid modules and compartments that most of crew never saw, and weren't meant to.

A solid clunk announced they had docked. Several technicians debarked first, leaving Quinn at the last to help Lamar. Releasing the seat restraints they lost contact with the deck. Lamar went sideways in orientation to the former floor and flailed for a moment as he tried to right himself. At his side Quinn said, "Don't struggle. I'll steer us through."

Lamar felt Quinn's steady hand on his elbow. With a practiced assurance,

Quinn used the handholds to guide Lamar toward the open hatch, through which a cold current of air now rushed. The dock mast had no rotation either; so still adrift, Lamar followed Quinn's example in gripping the safety line and pulling himself to the lift. Arriving, they found the doors closed, the lift in use by the first contingent of passengers heading to the upper decks. Lamar and Quinn waited with their three guards, men in bulky jackets trying in vain to form a security perimeter here where all orientations were temporary and likely to float out of control.

Out of control. That was about the size of it. Damn Leonard Garvey anyway, trying to abduct the child, scaring the bejesus out of all of them. The man was a lunatic, a drunk, a security leak. It made Lamar sick to think how full of holes all precautions had become. The platform itself might be alive with spies, probably was, with all these newcomers. Helice said they were screening for federals too. Well, they could handle government types: shoddy, underpaid, bantam-weight goons. These were the types responsible for cobbling together the dole, the entitlements that somehow people thought they had coming. So 75 percent of company earnings went to prop up the unfit and envious. And while the feds might be easy to fend off, the industry competition was more worrisome: EoSap and TidalSphere among them. Lamar glanced at the three security men. Who could you trust anymore? The question brought his own duplicity to mind.

"Are you okay?"

Quinn thought his distress was the zero-g. Lamar clutched the handhold. "I don't know, to tell you the truth." He wanted to say, Helice is going with you. Just let her, Titus. Things have grown beyond you now, and it's no ill will I bear you, far from it. I loved your family, your father, and you. But it's all bigger than you know, Titus. And it's bigger than Helice going along for the ride—much bigger.

Quinn gently nudged Lamar toward the now-open door of the lift. "We'll get you some solid ground."

Solid ground. Would there ever be such again? "I'm sorry," Lamar said. Indeed he was sorry—for the Helice deal, and for so much else.

"We'll be there in a moment. You'll be fine."

"No, but I *am* sorry." It felt awful to say it and know that Quinn didn't understand. Lamar wasn't cut out for intrigue. God help him that it had ever come to this. He gripped Quinn's forearm. "Just remember that I'm an old man; can you do that?"

Quinn looked amused. "Lamar. Don't worry. Someday I'll tell you about the time my chief navigator threw up in zero-g."

"Please don't," Lamar said, now genuinely sick.

"Take hold," the intercom voice said. "All lift passengers take hold. In five, four . . ." The voice counted down, and they pulled themselves down the handholds toward one of the walls designated in large letters as FLOOR.

Gravity came on, jarring them against the hard deck. Lamar bent over, bile running up his esophagus. He waved help away as the four others held the door open.

One of the security had fetched a rolling chair. Good grief, a wheelchair. He sank into it, and off they went down the corridor. Someone put a lap blanket over his knees, and his humiliation was complete.

Helice Maki looked around the antiseptic cubicle. Just a short walk now to the transition module. She was ready for it. Despite how little she knew about her destination, she was ready. Quinn would lead the way, teaching her as they traveled—he'd have to teach her or risk exposure to his enemies. Language came first. She had rudimentary Lucent, even though Quinn had refused to give lessons. Such a power-grab. Who did he think *paid* for his little visit to the Entire? In any case, the first time he returned from the Entire he had raved for days in a semiconscious state. All recorded. It had taken her people two years to crack Lucent from the fragments, but you can't keep a good mSap confused for long.

She did a few deep knee bends to keep her circulation going and to fend off a mild nervousness. For a few minutes more she had to rely on Lamar and the others. Had to trust Stefan to remain befuddled. Stefan Polich believed in her passion to deliver the cirque and the nan. Quinn and Helice to the rescue. It *would* be a rescue, just not the one Stefan had in mind. Poor Stefan. A man who had faith in technology and human enterprise. Well, that *did* have a certain ring, yes it did. But how totally unimaginative. More typical of dred or middie thinking than his intellectual class.

In moments she would be in the Entire. It thrilled her, and beyond that, it was fun. Deadly serious, too, of course. She didn't relish killing anyone, but deaths would inevitably occur. For example, she was going to be rid of Quinn at the first opportunity. After he had made all the introductions.

Walking amid his security phalanx, Quinn followed Lamar in his wheelchair, feeling a little light-headed. Sudden gravity demanded adjustments. As did suddenly leaving the universe. They were heading directly to the transition module with no sleep period, no delays. All for the purpose of staying ahead of the competition. Even if the competition had no idea what the stakes really were.

He had no reason to hope that, this trip, he would see anyone whom he'd known in the Entire. Like Anzi, the woman who had guided him. Her uncle and master of the sway, Yulin. His fighting master Ci Dehai. The timid Cho, who had ferreted out Johanna's message in the library. The scholar Bei or the navitar Ghoris. The alive brightship that had deposited him at his home at the end. He wanted to find some or all of them again, especially Anzi. But the Entire was not just a world, it was a universe; smaller than the Rose, but not so very much smaller. And he'd be in a hurry.

Pressing against his ankle was the cirque—a weight he still was not used to. Just his imagination, probably, that it threw him off his stride. Just his imagination that the nan in their separate links were scratching at the doors between. Once the tiny chambers opened and their contents shared information, the nan went into changeover mode. Changing things. *Changing.* A nice word for a nasty business. He didn't like bringing military nan into the land where his daughter lived. There was just the slightest unease in his mind that the weapon could not be controlled.

His goal was clear if hopelessly general: After Ahnenhoon he would go to the sway that held Sydney. Despite weeks of feverish thought, he'd formed no sensible plan to do so. He only knew, had to believe, he would find her.

Construction and tech uniforms everywhere, crowded corridors. From belowdecks came the high whine of robotic assemblers. Minerva was getting ready to ship out needed equipment, if all went well. If peace could come of Quinn's act of sabotage. If the inevitability of contact with humanity could persuade the Entire to make concessions for travel.

"Sir." A stocky fellow with sandy hair had introduced himself to security and managed to fall in step beside him.

"Mikal," Quinn said. Mikal James, program chief for the transition.

Mikal nodded at him and Lamar. "I hoped to meet you at the dock. Running behind, as usual."

That didn't bode well since Quinn was about to be lifted out of the universe in a controlled quantum implosion of which this man was nominally in charge. "Glad to see you. Set to go, then?"

Mikal hesitated a split second. "Yes." A terrible smile, meant to be reassuring.

The issue was interface, crossing, correlations. Mikal headed the team of physicists who'd worked out what they'd do today: how and where Quinn would enter the Entire. Getting home was even more complicated, but *getting to* was devilishly hard. The universe next door shifted. Connections came and went, and Minerva had damn little by way of maps or orientation to place. In Entire terms, they lacked the *correlates*, the formula predicting time and space connections between here and there. This was the most closely guarded Tarig secret, akin to the navigational charts of medieval times, those secret maps hoarded by the Portuguese in a desperate and losing gamble to keep Cathay and the new world to themselves.

So when Mikal had responded, *Yes, set to go,* he meant, *Yes, I have a way in.* A way in that would put him in safety relative to the main things that could kill him, such as the storm walls and the River Nigh. Marking these entities were emissions of exotic matter, forming a signature—a loud one, but nothing compared to the bright, which shone like a beacon now that they knew what to search for.

In front of Quinn, security staff wheeled Lamar onward toward the wing housing the transition module. Here, the press of workers and crew grew thick.

By way of explanation, Mikal said, "Station's at capacity for personnel. We're perfecting the crossover. For objects of scale."

Of scale. Material of the sort it would take to sustain a delegation: supplies, equipment, terrain vehicles, replacement parts. They believed in the possibility of making peace with the Tarig. They wanted to believe that eventually, they would be welcome.

"So you can send objects of scale now?"

"We're a long way from perfection." Mikal glanced over at Quinn. "You'll be fine. It's larger-mass objects that give us problems. Ships, for instance. We're far from that goal."

Ships. Damn right they couldn't send ships. Although, if Minerva—if all the corporations—were content with the Entire as a route to Rose destinations, then he was much more at ease. It was staying and settling that he'd promised to guard against. Promised Su Bei, just one of those who lived in the new land who didn't trust human actions, but who *did* trust Quinn to temper those actions.

What he could do to preserve the Entire, he would. Perhaps the enmity of the Tarig would be enough to restrain human immigration. But both the Rose and the Entire would have to come to terms with each other, and sooner rather than later. Because the correlates existed. Because he thought he knew where.

Because, this trip, he intended to bring them home.

Dressed in a paper lab coat, Quinn stood in the control room with Mikal and Lamar. Just as he had asked, no one else was present, much less Minerva bureaucrats.

The interface module stood out from the main platform some two hundred yards, connected to this sector of the platform by an access tube. Here in the control room Quinn couldn't see outside, but he remembered the cold chamber with the harness that hung suspended from the ceiling. They'd lift him up, so that he'd be out of contact with the deck. He didn't ask why that was necessary, didn't ask for details of the quantum implosion and inflation process of which the nearest analogue was the Big Bang. As alarming as that summary was, Quinn didn't dwell on it. What bothered him was the entry point. Last time he had landed in a wilderness where he nearly died of his injuries. He accepted that danger. He just didn't want to fall between. From lessons learned in the Entire, he knew there *was* a between.

Glancing at the control room monitors, Quinn saw the transition chamber with the harness at its center. Embedded in the walls were 4310 titanium nozzles, giving the chamber the look of an inverted sea urchin.

He turned to Lamar, getting a reassuring smile

Lamar quipped, "No pictures in your hip pocket?" Pictures of Sydney. Quinn tapped his head. "Got hers up here."

"I know you do." Lamar reached out a hand. Quinn shook it.

Looking at Mikal, he asked, "How long do I have to wait in that rat hole?"

"We never know. I'll try to make it short."

Time to go. The hatch to the sterilization booth lay before him. There, he would be sonically cleansed of microbes that they might not wish to unleash on the Entire. Just as he made ready to go through the door, Quinn noticed Lamar's pinched expression, the sheen of sweat on his high forehead. What the hell did he mean, *Remember that I'm an old man?*

They were waiting for him to pass through the door.

Quinn pulled off the paper gown, handing it to Lamar. Then he opened the hatch and walked through, closing the seal behind him.

Watching Quinn pass through to the sterilization chamber, Lamar realized he was holding his breath. He dragged air into his lungs. Waited.

After a few minutes, Mikal said under his breath, "Leaving sterilization booth."

That meant Quinn was in the tube, and dressing in his travel clothes—garments assembled according to his strict instructions, including the Chalin knife he'd brought home last time.

"In." Mikal nodded at the screen. Quinn had entered the transition module.

"Module two on screen," Lamar said, finding a chair next to Mikal.

Then, side-by-side monitors showed Quinn and Helice adjusting straps, getting hooked in. She in her module, he in his.

Lamar and Mikal waited, in company with no less than three mSaps. When the three agreed, Mikal would enable the transition, not before. This time, one machine sapient alone would not decide when and if they were good to go. Coordinating between mSaps was Mikal's job. The computers didn't talk to each other, but would decide independently.

Lamar wiped his perspiring hands on his slacks. This was taking longer than before. He looked up, hoping to catch Mikal's attention, but the man was focused on panel displays.

On the second screen, Helice was bearing up well, looking oddly elated. In his own module, Quinn's expression was controlled—what many people mistake for coldness but which is actually intense concentration. He was a pilot. Maybe not one in a cockpit this time, but nevertheless going somewhere fast, and needing all his reactions intact when he got there.

Lamar looked at his watch. It had been ten minutes, but felt like an hour.

Even in this remote section of the platform, distant clangs of tools announced the continuing construction. For a moment, Lamar fancied it was fists beating on the bulkheads, trying to get in, trying to sabotage them. Why didn't the Tarig come to the Rose, after all, put a stop to this. . . .

"We've got something," Mikal said. "Aligning. Aligning now."

Lamar pushed himself out of the chair, heart racing.

"Okay," Mikal said, "locked on. Have one. Have two." He was noting the judgment call of the mSaps.

"Have three."

Agreement. Mikal's hand went to the toggle. "We're good. Transition."

He threw the switch, but immediately they were in trouble. The screen flashed a sickening warning, pulsing with error warnings. Two more strobing screens joined in, now accompanied by a shrill machine scream. The display for one of the mSaps went black, burst back to life in a scramble, an awful haze of decoherence. Mikal was swearing, hunched over the keyboard, as screens flipped and savant backups yelped frantic messages.

Mikal shook his head. "Should have waited, God. . . ."

"What's going on?" Lamar staggered closer, staring at the screen. Helice hanging suspended.

But Quinn had gone. The harness hung by a wisp of material that stretched to a long, melted filament.

"God . . . ," Mikal said. "We lost it, lost it. I should have waited."

Helice was still in the module. Left behind. She had to go.

"Send her," Lamar barked.

"Can't," Mikal barked. "Lost it."

"No you didn't. Look." Lamar pointed to Quinn's harness. It was moving on its own, moving backward, sliding sideways, disappearing inch by inch into nothingness. They still had connection. Two mSaps said they had connection; one said no. "Send her."

"I can't. We've only got two—"

Lamar fumbled in his coat pocket and drew out a small pistol, bristling with wires. Hand shaking, he pressed the gun against Mikal's right temple. "Send her. Do it now." As Mikal hesitated, Lamar made a dent in his skin with the barrel.

Mikal threw the switch. Then he lurched away from the computer banks, backing away from this apparent madman who shared his control room.

But Lamar's attention was all on the second module. Helice was folding together like a book closing. She became a thick line, then a thin one.

Gone. But her harness hung in the air, burning.

"Shut off the goddamn racket," Lamar growled.

The emergency noise subsided as Mikal whispered, "We just killed them. You killed them." He looked at Lamar with loathing.

"Don't be an idiot. We had two agreeing." Almost dropping the pistol from the sweat streaming off his hands, Lamar jammed it into his jacket pocket. Until now he hadn't known he had it in him, to use a weapon.

"I'll report you." Mikal was still trembling.

"Go ahead."

Lamar felt his own legs shaking. He tottered out of the control room. "Goddamn mSaps," he muttered.

How many mSaps does it take to screw in a lightbulb?

Answer: What's a lightbulb?

It took a human to make the tough decisions. Helice had to cross over. Everything depended on it. Lamar might be an old man, but he knew that much.

PART II
THE
ENGINE
OF
WORLDS

CHAPTER FIVE

The Radiant Path is the sum of perfections. All that the virtuous sentient could desire is found in the five primacies and the million minorals. Since the gracious lords have gathered the supreme pleasures of all that is into the Bright Realm, let the discreet sentient be content. Scholars, in their agitation, must peer into inferior places. This the vows permit, to document the dark of the Rose, the kingdom of the evanescent. Peer, scholar, into the veil-of-worlds, much may the scattered glories of the Rose satisfy you. Behind each scholar's life lies a pile of redstones, the sum of squandered days.

—from *The Book of the Thousand Gifts*

ENHU HAD BEEN WAITING SO LONG AT HIS POST that when something finally happened, he dropped his pipe and staggered to his feet, agape with surprise.

The floor was strewn with bedding, the remains of meals, and candles, some of them flaming. He grabbed a guttering candle and peered into the cleft at the end of the chamber. A V-shaped wedge pierced the wall, broad end facing out, the crevice clogged with a standing wedge of thick fluid.

Inside it, streaks of light skittered, dimmed, bloomed again. The floor pounded in heavy, slow beats. Something was happening behind the veil-of-worlds; and then, slow-witted, he realized it was a crossing—the one he'd been sent to assist. Already a sac had formed, and he could make out a wavering shape inside it. Benhu sprang into action. The computational devices lay stacked on either side of the cleft, with tendrils inserted into the veil. Benhu removed the cord from around his neck and fumbled at the knot, finally pulling off one redstone and inserting it into the master well. Benhu had no true understanding of any scholarly thing, but he followed Lord Oventroe's instructions with precision. Still, events were not unfolding as expected. Light boiled inside the crevice, rumbling horribly. Furthermore, it appeared that two sacs were budding inside instead of one. The foremost sac twisted, shrank, and nearly collapsed. Then it bloomed vigorously, showing a lumpish being encapsulated there.

Startled into action, Benhu dropped the second stone into the master well, and then pressed his body sideways into the matrix that filled the wedge. A vacuole of air formed around him, and he waded with great difficulty toward the new sac, where he could just make out a body, curled up and twitching. Moving closer, Benhu realized with dismay that the person was in distress. He lost no time in pushing his own sac against the other one until they merged. Immediately, he regretted it.

Smoke filled his nostrils. He fell to his knees, gagging. Then, in desperation, he began dragging the body toward the outer chamber, coughing and struggling the few yards to the edge, where he burst through, releasing his burden along with a miasma of acrid smoke.

On hands and knees, Benhu coughed and gasped, eyes watering and beard slicked wet with ooze. Then, wiping his face with his sleeve, he looked down at the person he'd rescued, who moaned, showing signs of life.

To his horror, it was a woman.

He shouted in dismay. Grabbing a candle, he looked closer and saw that she was bleeding. Her chin and neck were burned raw, and she was shaking. He rushed for his blanket, covering her and trying to summon his wits. A woman? By the vows, this was not Titus Quinn.

Titus Quinn! He'd forgotten the second sac. Rushing back to the veil between worlds, he saw the remaining sac hovering in the center of the gelatinous mass. It contained a larger body than before. Benhu wondered if he could enter a second time and not lose himself for eternity. The computational boxes stacked nearby were still firmly attached to the veil with filaments, just as the lord instructed. But the lord had said nothing about *two* crossings. He had described, however, Benhu's fate should he fail. Benhu muttered, "God not looking at me," and shouldered himself in, half striding, half swimming toward the pouch of air.

He struggled toward the sac, peering into the obscuring gel. Finding the air pouch, he thrust himself inside, seized the man by the arms, and dragged him toward the outer chamber. The man's larger bulk made it slow going, but eventually Benhu managed to push out of the veil. Turning to finish his task, he pulled on the man with all his strength, freeing first an arm and then head and shoulders. Bracing his feet on the floor, Benhu yanked hard. The man shot out of the matrix, colliding with Benhu, who collapsed backward onto the floor.

The room stank abominably of burned skin, guttering candles, and the horrifying viscous lake wherein the veil-of-worlds bridged over to the places that shall not be named.

Head on knees, Benhu sat stunned for a few moments. When he'd collected himself, he turned to face a long knife blade.

A wild man with plastered-back hair bent over him, grabbing his collar. "Name, on your life," he snarled.

"Benhu, Your Excellency. But here is a more important name: Jesid. You have heard it?" Lord Oventroe had bid him use this name as a code.

The man narrowed his eyes. "Jesid?"

"Yes! Listen to me. Jesid the navitar. Does that get through to you?" He saw the man relax a bit, and to preserve his dignity, Benhu yanked away from his grip. Jesid was a name Quinn would know, Oventroe had said. By the man's reaction, he did. So this *was* Titus Quinn. The knife was still pointed at his throat, but softer now.

Titus Quinn spat and wiped his face with his slimy arm. Benhu removed his jacket and offered it for a towel.

Accepting it, Quinn said, "Who sent you?"

Benhu now began to feel more in control, but wanted the knife put away before he divulged intelligences. He glanced at the blade. Quinn lowered it, but kept it ready.

"The lord you once met sent me. By the bright, do not say his name, not even here." Benhu watched as the man wiped himself down, using his jacket as though the expensive garment were a rag.

"I met more than one lord, Benhu."

Benhu felt like a veldt mouse frozen in the gaze of an Adda.

"Say his name," Quinn said.

Poor as a beggar, and yet Titus Quinn was presuming to give orders. Benhu decided to overlook his tone for the sake of what the man had just been through.

"Say his name," Quinn repeated.

"The gracious Lord Oventroe." By a beku's balls, Benhu thought. This pathetic man of the Rose, dripping with goo, daring to give orders, acting like a mighty legate when he was only a suppliant. Benhu stood up tall. "Fifty days I've waited in this stinking place, at my lord's will and to your great advantage. Fifty days of dried food with vermin for company, and candles for daylight.

"The result being," he went on, "you are here unscathed instead of burned or blown to pulp." He couldn't help but smirk. "You think you can cross without dying in the dark? Quite wrong. The only thing that saved you was that I drew you in." He jerked his head at the crevice. "She almost died, too. Still might."

Quinn looked at Benhu with an unnerving sideways glance.

"Yes, she lives, don't worry. Burned, though." He pointed at the figure lying in the shadows on the floor.

Lurching to his feet, Quinn strode to the woman's side. He could surely see that Benhu had taken care of her: a blanket, and laid out comfortably. It was all he'd had time for, but the man seemed enraged.

Quinn stalked back to him and grabbed him by the front of his shirt. "A bad mistake, Benhu. Send her back."

Benhu was aghast. "Back? Send back? The lord said nothing about—"

Quinn yanked Benhu around to face the veil-of-worlds. "Put her in there and do what you do. Now." Shoving Benhu away, Quinn rushed to the unconscious woman and began dragging her to the veil.

"No," Benhu said, running to prevent him. "You can't do that. Put her down." He pulled on the woman's arm, slapping at Quinn. A nasty blow sent Benhu sprawling as Quinn continued to haul the woman toward the veil.

Benhu crouched against the wall, rubbing his sore shoulder. "Go ahead and kill her then. I have no part in this."

During the dragging, the blanket had come off the still-unconscious woman, and now Quinn saw her wounds. He paused, breathing heavily from his exertions and the stress of the crossing.

He whispered, "Why can't you send her back?"

Benhu thought his dignity better served by standing up. He did so, rising to his full height, considerably less than Titus Quinn's. "First, because in her condition, she wouldn't survive a crossing. And second, because the gracious lord gave me no instructions as to the particulars of reverse passage. In other words, I don't know how."

Quinn fixed him with an awful stare. "Any more than a beku can pilot the Nigh?"

Benhu straightened his clothes. That was a foul thing to say. "I should have let you suffocate in that stinking jelly. Ever watch a man suffocate?"

"Yes."

Indeed, Quinn looked like a man who didn't care when or how he died. Those kind were the most dangerous. And though he would sooner have kissed a Gond, Benhu was now stuck with him. He put on his most superior demeanor. "I will await your apology outside."

Quinn growled, "What am I supposed to do with *her?*"

"I don't know or care. She's yours now."

Benhu walked out of the chamber, eager to exit the chamber in case Quinn dispatched the unfortunate woman with his knife. Whoever she was, she appeared to be about as welcome as a horde of gnats on a beku's arse.

CHAPTER SIX

O divine art of subtlety and secrecy! Through you we learn to be invisible, through you inaudible, and hence we can hold the enemy's fate in our hands.

— from Tun Mu's *Annals of War*

BEHIND JOHANNA LOOMED THE STORM WALL. She made it her practice never to look at it, with its towering blue-black folds, like an aurora borealis gone dark and mad.

"He's not coming," Johanna murmured. She looked out toward the mustering grounds six stories below. At her side, Pai held a square sunshade. A rivulet of sweat traced a path under Johanna's jacket. So much depended on the creature making an appearance.

"We can wait a bit longer," Pai said. She had steady nerves, this Chalin woman who had become her friend and chief spy, although Johanna and Pai carefully hid their friendship behind a façade of arrogant mistress and timid servant. Pai's golden eyes swept the yard, searching for the appearance of Morhab the engineer. Today the grounds were empty, the phase of day too hot for long exertion and the troops having no maneuvers planned.

In an arched doorway nearby, SuMing stood in the cool shade, watching them, ready to serve if called. She wouldn't approach the edge of the walkway, having developed an aversion to heights. So still and quiet, this young retainer. So . . . chastened. SuMing's neck didn't bend naturally any longer, having healed poorly. She might well blame Johanna for this, but she was still her servant and now better knew her place.

Pai wasn't Johanna's only agent. There was also Gao, who was at this moment searching through the chamber of Morhab the Gond and desperately needed Johanna to delay Morhab from prematurely returning.

"Pai, where is he?"

"Still in the watch, mistress. I'm sure."

As Heart of Day beat down on the yard, a dust devil skipped along, leaving a powdery tail in its wake. On these grounds officers would drill the garrison, although no one could remember if the Paion had ever infiltrated this far.

They called this fortress the Repel, after its function to repulse Paion incursions. Laid out in a half-moon shape against the storm wall, it possessed five domains. The innermost, and so-called fifth domain, was the centrum, her home and the home of Lord Inweer. Four lines of defense enclosed the centrum and thwarted an enemy that, when it came, would likely come in hordes. The fourth domain was the gathering yard, where the stark grounds would afford an enemy no cover. The third domain, the watch, served as a barracks, and was a stone fortress in its own right. Before the outer wall of the watch lay the second domain, the sere, a sector of blackened soil exposing trespassers to incineration. Some days Johanna could see a thermal column rise above the watch, bearing the charred dust of some hapless creature. Facing the plains of Ahnenhoon in first defensive position was the legendary terminus, a maze that swallowed any life that ventured inside. Open doorways riddled this outer wall, perhaps more unnerving than a solid buttress would have been. Johanna's understanding of the domains was collected from legend and hearsay. There were no maps or layouts, except in the minds of its Tarig builders and in the locked chests of Morhab, Lord Inweer's master engineer, the highest position of any non-Tarig in the Ahnenhoon Repel, save only the generals of the army.

Gao had access to Morhab's chests. In past forays he had found pieces of maps, fragments showing the centuries-long building and rebuilding of the five domains—most particularly, fragments pertaining to the engine's containment chamber. He committed these to memory, assembling a piecemeal understanding of the immensity of the Repel.

To distract Johanna, Pai pointed into the distance. "See, mistress, there is a sky bulb floating."

Johanna made out an airship, a mere speck hovering over the plains. It might be filled with Paion, but if it signified a fight, the sounds of battle didn't travel this far. The Long War, as it was called, hardly registered on Johanna's life, though she lived only a few miles from its eternal clashes. The daily presence of war-at-a-distance made her complacent.

The Paion, whatever they were, attacked only at Ahnenhoon. The lords could certainly prevail over the Paion technologies—but they were afraid to use weapons of devastation in a universe so susceptible to collapse. So Johanna believed. Thus the fragile Entire was protected from ruinous weaponry, and those who loved fighting could have a nice little war. The war had a side benefit: it gave cover to the great engine that throbbed beneath her feet. The denizens of the Entire—at least those who lived in the Repel— believed the engine created a protective field around Ahnenhoon, hindering if not preventing Paion intrusion. A nice fiction, and a useful one.

Pai whispered, "He comes."

A sled had emerged from a low door in the watch. The engineer, at last Johanna could identify his huge form even from here. If Morhab found Gao snooping, it could all be laid bare. Laid bare to her lord—and she hadn't the stomach to imagine it.

She turned from the overlook. "Let us greet my friend Morhab," she said, striding past SuMing with Pai rushing to keep up, holding the sunshade and pretending to protest at Johanna's hasty departure.

Down the winding stairs Johanna went, sweating with exertion at descending the Tarig-sized stairs and steeling herself for the encounter with Morhab. Here in the depths of the centrum, surrounded by acres of such stone as the Tarig devised, Johanna heard the drumming of the engine. It pulsed in the stone, in the air, in her feet. Pai said she couldn't often hear the engine, leading Johanna to suspect that she carried the hateful noise inside her head— the thrum, thrum, thrumming, like a dark god moaning in his sleep.

Her lord was the keeper of the engine. He wanted her to forgive him that, and perhaps she did. It wouldn't stop her from bringing the engine down. Then she would face Lord Inweer, a thing she dreaded far more than facing this odious Gond. That gave her more courage, and she continued her rush down the stairs to the gathering yard.

Morhab required a powered sled or litter for his mobility. Legless, he had the body of a bloated snake, like all Gond. His massive head was crowned by two short horns, and ended in a pointed chin trailing a wisp of a beard. Vestigial wings lay slick upon his back, rustling now and then as though stirred by a memory of flight. Had the creature been smaller—Morhab was the size of a steer—she might have borne the sight of him more easily.

There was, however, the fact that he looked like a demon.

His drooping red gums, along with the horns and long chin, made the Gond look unnervingly like Satan in his guise of a cloven-footed, horned beast. Well, the Gond didn't have legs or hooves, so there was that discrepancy, yet the impression was so vivid that she had taken to crossing herself when meeting Morhab.

There might be a factual basis for this coincidence. Johanna knew that the Gond, like all Entire sentients except the Tarig, were copied from different races in the Rose. Pai and SuMing, as Chalin, were of human form. The Gond must have an analogue race in the Rose. Perhaps the Gond had come as an alien species to visit Earth long ago. People of the Middle Ages might well have given them a bad reception, and the violent encounters could have spawned a legend of evil. Still, all logic aside, Johanna shuddered to meet him.

"Open the door, SuMing." Obeying, SuMing pushed on the massive metal barrier that swung easily on its hinges, allowing the three of them to enter the gathering yard. Pai unfurled the sunshade again.

"By the bright, pick up your feet, Pai," Johanna snapped. She hastened onto the parade grounds, where she spied Morhab's sled, still on the other side.

From her spies, Johanna knew that Morhab would be in the watch today, inspecting improvements made to house a fresh contingent of soldiers—Hirrin by species, with their own billeting needs. Now the engineer's course took him on a diagonal across the yard toward one of the centrum's several doors. Morhab must have seen Johanna, because the sled's course swerved to meet them. The creature was easily lured. Bloated in form and self-regard, he couldn't imagine that she found him loathsome.

Propelled by silent means, the floating conveyance lumbered under its weight of Gond, attendants, and equipage. It stopped in front of her, swaying slightly as Ysli and Chalin attendants jumped down, bowing to Johanna.

"Master Morhab," she said, bowing low. When she rose again, her smile was fixed and convincing, she trusted.

Morhab's profound bass voice came to her, clotted, as though he needed to cough. "Now then, Mistress Johanna. Too hot for strolling," he said, "unless you came to see me." He tucked his wings closer to his body, as though aware they were not his best feature.

She was already feeling nauseous, but took a cleansing breath, determined to be at least as courageous as Gao.

"Master Morhab, I saw you from the ramparts, and hoped for diversion from a day already long." She added, "Although I'm sure you have great matters in hand. No time for idle women."

The Gond's mouth was too large to be fully expressive, so Johanna could never judge whether a Gond smiled. But she thought he was pleased. His nostrils expanded, drinking in her scent. Morhab glanced at his stonewell computers built into the half-walls of his sled, monitoring his numbers and perhaps judging whether he did have time for her. But his curiosity won out.

"You will join me here." He waved his thin arms at his attendants, one of whom bent down to form a step with his laced hands.

Johanna looked to the stone embrasures of the centrum, wondering if anyone watched her. Lord Inweer might well look down and wonder why she would seek out a creature that he knew she disliked. Her ready answer: *For the sake of Gao, my lord. That the engineer treat him well.* She pretended to take a kindly interest in Gao and his family, but it was more than that. It was the first layer of lies that had by now grown deep.

Johanna allowed herself to be helped into the sled, where she sat opposite Morhab on a seat littered with scrolls. He leaned forward to push them aside, coming so near that her gorge rose from his breath. His carnivore diet mulched in his huge stomach and vented abominably.

He turned his prodigious head toward SuMing and Pai. "Yes, board, sharing with my retainers." They climbed next to Morhab's servants, sitting with feet hanging over the edge of the sled.

Johanna smiled at Morhab. "I would take it as an extreme indulgence if you would continue your inspections of the gathering yard, Master Morhab. We will ride for a time and observe your important work." She knew very well he wasn't inspecting the yard or its surrounding walls today, but hoped he would change his plans.

A Ysli servant came around the perimeter of the sled. "Mistress," the Ysli said, extending a hirsute hand and handing up her sunshade. Taking it, she popped it open, it being her custom to block her view of the relentless bright.

Observing the parasol, Morhab remarked, "Delicate." The word sounded strange coming from such a mouth. In close approximation to him, Johanna was acutely aware of his massive and useless body, its lower half hidden by a moist blanket that served to condition his skin. Morhab turned to adjust his pillows, using his short arms and exposing his glistening wings, like a beetle's.

The sled moved out again, loaded with its riders and stonewell computers. The engineer drove the sled faster than she'd hoped, and worse, instead of following the wall of the watch, he was still heading to the centrum.

Johanna tossed her hair back from her face, capturing Morhab's eye. In what she hoped was an even tone, she said, "Too busy then, to indulge bored ladies?" The engineer's nostrils flared. Gonds could smell strong emotions; this one had mistaken her scent for a strong attraction to his person.

"Today, too busy." He waved at his stone wells, their screens springing to life at his gesture, scrolling with mathematical characters. "Not too busy at other times, mistress." His eyes scanned the glyphs. "You must visit again when leisure permits conversation. I have meetings with personages, and reports to make."

Why had she not known of *meetings with personages?* But her spy network consisted of only two people, both of them lowly. *Oh Gao, hurry, hurry*, she prayed. If captured, Gao might expose her, and then so much would be lost. Such as the blue sky of Earth . . .

Morhab went on, "Not even for you can high matters wait, matters pertaining to the welfare of the Repel."

The welfare of the Repel. Also her concern, but in the opposite direction from Morhab. When Titus came to destroy the fortress, she must know how to destroy its heart. Day by day, her fate hung on the wits it took to run her spies and keep them safe. She used those wits now to let a tear escape from her eyes. It moved down her face, drawing Morhab's sudden and discomforting stare.

His reaction was sour. "Must have her way, I expect."

She dabbed at her eyes. "The master engineer is perceptive. One cannot hide one's sadness."

"Sad," Morhab repeated. "Despite all advantages." His style was to alternately flatter and instruct her, a strange little sandwich of habits used to manipulate those around him.

"Yes, despite all advantages," Johanna said with some bitterness. Then she smiled, to soften her lapse.

They came to the wall of the centrum, where the sled triggered a door to open, and they slid inside, into the cooling dark of the fifth domain. Lights bloomed around them in response to their entrance, but Morhab suppressed them with a flick of his hand toward his sled panels. They sat in darkness, the servants on the back and sides of the sled completely still and the only sound the groaning of the engine, buried deeper in the centrum.

Morhab's deep voice came to her from nearby. "Comfort is needed." His voice went soft. "One can hardly presume to comfort a lady where a bright lord fails. . . ."

"Oh, the gracious lord doesn't fail," Johanna was quick to say. "But he is busy, of course, and one . . ." She was steeling herself to be comforted by the Gond. It might only be a touch, a small, intimate conversation. Surely not so bad. She went on, "One is lonely."

"Cross over," the deep voice came to her.

She was frozen to her seat. Did he mean that she should come across to his seat?

"Such a little space to traverse," he murmured, his voice still loud in the stone hall. The hall wasn't completely dark, but the shadows fell deep, and Morhab's face was thankfully drowned in shadow.

How much time did Gao need?

She rose, and finding the parasol still open, closed it as a way of gaining time.

"Yes," Morhab said. The way he said it, with that long exhalation of breath, teasing out the word, caused her to panic. She hadn't moved.

Morhab's hand came forward to her waist. Perhaps he couldn't see in the dark that he had touched her person. But the hand stayed. Then it traced the line of her waist, venturing neither up nor down, but slowly traversing her body. Suddenly Johanna found herself clutching that Gond hand with both of her hands, as though locked into a friendly handshake.

"The engineer is more than kind," she blurted. "Such kindness reminds me that one is never completely alone." She straightened. "How much better one feels. Indeed." She released his hand and almost fell back onto her former seat.

Silence from across the sled, as Morhab adjusted to the rebuke. Then the lights came up, showing Morhab's face in a horrible grimace. His mouth drooped, the lower gums red and wet.

"I have mistaken you," his bass voice rumbled. His eyes, so large and wet. The little hands twitching in his lap. She felt faint.

He went on, "And you have mistaken *me*."

The sled lunged forward. She gripped the seat as they sped down the corridor, the wind of their passing rippling Johanna's silks. She shivered, chilled by the sled's speed and her inexcusable cowardice. Perhaps she would only have had to endure his closeness, perhaps his arm in comfort around her. Her thigh pressed against his body, no more.

She couldn't.

The sled came to a jolting halt by the stairway by which she could return to her apartments. "Let this sad lady leave to find other diversions," he said with irony and poise. His cold tone signaled an appalling turn of fortune for Johanna's relationship with the beast.

She stumbled off the sled as servants hurried to assist. Pai scrambled up on the platform to snatch the sunshade, drawing a mighty scowl from Morhab.

Then, standing with Pai and SuMing, Johanna bowed low. "One will always be grateful for small kindnesses."

But Morhab was not deceived. He looked down on her like a king on his throne, or perhaps the lord of hell, whose subjects had failed in fealty.

Unconsciously, she crossed herself.

Then the sled rushed off, hurtling in the direction of Morhab's apartments.

As they prepared to ascend the stairs, Johanna saw someone far down the hall. A man stood, dressed in green silks, a long queue down his back.

It was Gao, finished with his assignment. She couldn't show her relief.

Turning to Pai and SuMing, she said with some peevishness, "Gonds can be so difficult to please." She nodded at her servants. "Let us find other diversions, then."

"A cup of wine?" Pai suggested.

"Or two," Johanna breathed.

Without looking at Gao, she led the way up the stairwell. In the narrow confines of the enclosed stairs, the engine boomed, muffled and deep.

CHAPTER SEVEN

*Heaven is the moral realm, where the vows, bonds, and clarities
are observed with piety. There is no heaven after death, but a sentient who is a citizen of the Entire is already a citizen of heaven.*
—from *The Radiant Way*

CIXI STOOD ON THE RIM OF THE FLOATING CITY high above the sea. Inevitably here, one thought of the fall. The four-minute ride, as it was called. A grand way to die, if one had to die violently. Standing on an outer ledge of the Magisterium, in the golden hub of the radial universe, she bowed to the lords' domain, a gesture of reverence. *May they fry in the bright.*

Beneath her, five pillars plunged down from the bowl of the city, their feet melting into the Sea of Arising. Legend said that the pillars were the eternal connection between the Tarig and their subjects. In reality, the pillars held up an aristocracy cowering in fear. Cixi had spent one hundred thousand days seeking to know the reasons for their fear. Fear implied a weakness. To raise the new kingdom—the Chalin kingdom, with Sydney at its head —she must discover this weakness. Until then, she remained a most ancient and loyal servant of the Tarig.

Rising from her bow, Cixi tapped her fingernail twice to quell the incessant clamor from her minions, scrolling their miniature and often mindless messages. Let them be silent. She had more important matters just now.

Preconsul Depta was late. She was the closest confidante of Lady Chiron, and although only a miserable Hirrin and lowly preconsul, she held the high lady's authority and took liberties because of that, such as suffering her betters to wait for her.

The field barriers wavered in a gust of wind. Wearing her high-platformed shoes, Cixi placed each step with deliberation. One couldn't easily fall through the invisible railing, but one could push through and jump. Once, long ago, a small human girl had threatened to jump, keeping her jailors at bay. They had summoned Cixi, who had coaxed her back. Since that hour Cixi had loved the child, and in return, Sydney loved her. Then the fiends had blinded her dear girl, giving her to the barbarians. Even before that awful day, Cixi had hated the Tarig, but they managed, in their inimitable way, to constantly replenish hatred.

Even if they could not replenish the power source of the world.

It was on this matter that current matters stuck, drawing in all manner of trouble—trouble that was about to become rather larger than ever before.

Because Titus Quinn had stumbled upon intelligence best left hidden.

Three hundred days ago, Quinn had been in the Ascendancy—in full view of them all, she remembered with mortification. Hiding in the bright city for many days, he abandoned his disguise and left in spectacular fashion, killing a lord and leaving behind his daughter whom he had come so close to finding. He escaped the Entire by a means so bold it took her breath away: He freed the brightships, enabling them to slip away into their nether worlds between the atoms of the Entire. . . . Oh, that was so like Titus Quinn, to make the grand gesture of emancipation.

Well, now the lords had new ships, and better ones. Not sentient this time. You can't trust a machine that can think. Cixi snorted. Even *she* knew that much.

The question that occupied the best minds in the Entire these days was *why* Quinn fled.

Four days ago Cixi had discovered why. He had learned the purpose of the engine at Ahnenhoon. Not even the denizens of the Entire knew *that*. For the Rose to know was unsettling. Titus Quinn had discovered the Tarig intended solution to their power needs and by now had surely informed his masters in the Rose. This was the matter on which all matters most profoundly *stuck*.

Cixi had immediately reported her discovery to the Lady Chiron, but oddly, the lords did not seem to be on alert.

"High Prefect," a voice came from behind. Depta, at last.

Cixi turned up the corners of her mouth. "Pleasant to see you, Preconsul." Cixi inclined her head somewhat, but Depta gave only a slight nod in turn. *Damn the four-footed fool.* Cixi reigned over the Magisterium and its thousands of legates, stewards, factors, and clerks, as well as preconsuls, consuls, and subprefects. Add to this her recent stunning, even brilliant, intelligence to Lady Chiron, and a considerable amount of deference was in order.

Depta walked down the ramp way from an upper viewing post, her long neck craning for a moment to take in the sights. Like many denizens of the Ascendancy, Depta did not often come to the lip of the city, it being considered vulgar to stare at the view.

"Let us walk, High Prefect."

Cixi understood. Their conversation must remain private, and moving was better than staying put. The narrow walkway afforded just enough room for them to walk side by side. And because Depta was a Hirrin, Cixi for once could have a standing conversation without looking up.

They walked as Depta murmured, "Lady Chiron is deeply stirred by your investigations and cunning, Cixi."

Depta had omitted her title. Such overfamiliarity needed a rebuke, but Cixi forbore. "A trifling thing."

"Perhaps. We would have deduced the same, eventually. But the lady approves that you informed her before others."

Cixi allowed irritation to creep into her voice. "Naturally I informed her first. It was the lady's request, as surely you remember, Depta, since you conveyed the request to me."

The preconsul sighed, stopping before a landing and gazing down. "It is said that some sentients fear heights. They say that when standing near a precipitous drop, they are convulsed with fear. Do you credit this tale, Cixi?"

Cixi saw the barrier's shimmering field bend for a moment under a gust. "I have little time for children's tales."

"But some tales are true," Depta insisted.

For a cold moment Cixi wondered if Depta was threatening her. Was it possible, even thinkable? If so, she had horribly misjudged. Where were her advisors, minions, and spies who hadn't heard the whispers, or read the signs?

She said, carefully, "Those who have reason to fear heights, should fear them. Those who might slip, for example." She was not one of those, if this long-necked minion didn't know.

Depta turned back, smiling. Her unfailing sweetness didn't fool Cixi. "Lady Chiron is happy to keep your counsel to herself for a time. You understand?"

The bright shone down on Depta's too-small head, her broad back bearing the icon of the flame bird. Cixi noted all this while her mind furiously parsed the preconsul's words: *Keep this to herself. The other lords will not be told.*

She bought time: "Mmm. Indeed, Depta."

"The lady wishes no others informed until she approves. It is her judgment."

Heaven give me mercy, Cixi thought. Chiron required treason, then. The Repel of Ahnenhoon was in jeopardy, now that the Rose was alerted. This, one must keep to oneself?

Why would Chiron not tell the three lords who shared her power? They were already guarding the Inyx sway where, if Quinn wished to take Sydney, he would have to go. But they didn't expect an assault on Ahnenhoon. Now only Chiron was to know.

Depta stepped closer. "Swear by the bright, Cixi."

The Hirrin was still impudently saying *Cixi*. As she stood perilously close to the edge, a strange sensation forced its way through the pores of Cixi's body, leaving her dizzy and dry-throated. It was stark fear, a sensation she had almost forgotten.

"Swear," Depta repeated.

Cixi had paused a long time. She turned to look the Hirrin in the eyes, acknowledging the weight of what she was about to say. She whispered, "What the bright lady bids me to do, I do not presume to question. I will keep my counsel, Depta."

The Hirrin resumed their walk. "No sentient being is beyond hope," she intoned.

Meaning, even you can do things right. The outrage of the insult could keep. Cixi would remember it, and revenge would come in due time. For now, her mind raced at the implications of Chiron's order to *inform no others* of Quinn's likely return. Perhaps the lady wished for the glory of Titus Quinn's capture. Or perhaps to prevent his capture. Was it love, then?

With Cixi's thoughts churning, they came at last to a door on the fifth level, deep in the underbelly of the Magisterium. Here was a chamber that could only be entered from the outside. A door retracted into the floor.

They proceeded down a corridor, Cixi leading the way, coming at last to a dimly lit chamber. In the center a cage held the hostage, the despicable steward Cho, who stood up, gripping the bars. As they approached, he bowed gracefully low, the picture of appropriate behavior, despite being stiff from questioning.

That this menial steward could be a traitor had surprised and intrigued Cixi. It wasn't often her minions broke the rules, and never in as spectacular a manner as he had done. He had given into Quinn's hands the very thing that now imperiled the kingdom: a redstone from Quinn's wife, with intelligence from Ahnenhoon about the engine.

That redstone might never have been found. Though Cixi had her minions scouring the Magisterium, it took hundreds of days before they found the pulverized redstone that, reconstituted, revealed how Quinn had come into his forbidden knowledge.

Easy enough to track from there who could have helped Quinn find such an obscure redstone in the deep vaults of the library.

At the rear of the chamber, someone stirred.

A Tarig had been seated against the wall, and now stood, moving into the light. The Lady Chiron. She wore a long silver skirt slit to her thighs, and a beaded white vest that sparkled like shards of ice. Chiron approached them, carrying something in her long fingers.

Depta and Cixi bowed low, with Cho bowing repeatedly once again.

When Cixi rose, she saw that the Lady held a garrote. Did she plan to execute Cho after all?

"Bright Lady," Cixi said, "my life in your service."

"Yes," Chiron said. Her black hair was enclosed in a net studded with diamonds. Chiron turned to Depta. "How is our kingdom, that you have viewed from the balconies?" Her voice was as deep as Lord Nehoov's, or as Lord Hadenth's had been. It lent her authority—not that she needed more.

Depta answered, "Glorious, my lady. One worried about sure footing at such heights. But there was no slipping."

Chiron turned to gaze down on Cixi. "Ah. A fine walk, and good conversation. You are content, High Prefect?"

Cixi stepped back a pace to look Chiron in the eyes. Damn them, for being so tall. And what was being asked? Did Chiron wish to know if she was content with what she had sworn? No, by the bright, if it meant that Quinn would not be pursued with all the resources of the realm; no, if Chiron meant to forgive and protect him.

She forced a pleasant expression to the fore. "Yes, Bright Lady. Naturally, I obey."

"Hnn," Chiron mused. "Is it natural for you to obey, Cixi?"

Chiron stood against the backdrop of the bars of the cage, mistress of the world. For now, one must agree to all she said. Someday the fiends would be driven out, and Cixi's own Chalin people would reign. Someday she would raise the true kingdom, with her dear girl replacing this strutting creature-queen. But for now, one said yes.

"Yes."

Chiron tapped the garrote against her thigh, rustling her soft metal skirt.

Cixi glanced at the device. God has noticed me, she thought. Chiron had intended the device for her. The lady fingered it absently. Cixi stood stunned. She could have died here, a grubby, miserable death. No glorious dive from the rim, to be sung and woven into legend.

Chiron gazed at Cixi with unblinking dark eyes.

After one hundred thousand days of service, they had sent Depta to her with a question, which, if she had answered wrong, would have been followed by death at Chiron's feet. She had come so close to the wrong answer, never guessing the price.

Chiron murmured, "We will bring Titus Quinn home. His apartments have been vacant a while, and he should occupy them again. This would please us. We will watch for him at Ahnenhoon, ah?"

Chiron meant *she* would watch. The other lords would be focused elsewhere.

Cixi found her voice. "Good hunting, Bright Lady. Do bring him home. Many here wish to see him again."

Chiron laughed, a deep, throaty sound that even in Cixi's long association with the Tarig she had seldom heard. "We will hunt, yes." She turned, waving the garrote at the cage. "This one has revealed nothing additional today. Still, he will be preserved." The steward's life was forfeit, but Lady Chiron kept him as a hostage in case there were ties of the heart between the two men—Quinn being notoriously susceptible to friendship.

Chiron tucked the garrote in her belt and walked away, disappearing into the corridor. Depta followed her without properly taking her leave of Cixi— another slight, but one that barely registered in Cixi's present state of stunned relief.

Cho stared at Chiron's departing form. As a steward, he wouldn't have seen high dealing among the exalted of the Magisterium. He shouldn't have seen this much. When the lady Chiron was done with the creature, Cixi would personally stand on his neck until his hours were over.

Cixi murmured, "It seems you will not suffer the garrote today, Steward."

Nor would she.

CHAPTER EIGHT

More bitter than a sip of the Nigh, an underling grown proud.
—a saying of the Magisterium

FIRST- AND SECOND-DEGREE BURNS extended from Helice's neck up one side of her jaw.

"Don't leave me," she whispered.

Quinn knew that it must hurt her to speak. The crossing could have killed her. Killed him. Either Minerva had botched the insertion, or Benhu's efforts to pull him into a veil-of-worlds had gone awry. Benhu admitted nothing, of course—instead boasting of a job well done; but Quinn suspected that Lord Oventroe's programming had faltered when two came through instead of one.

Benhu crouched over Helice, smoothing ointment on her wound. She winced at his ministrations. Well equipped with medicinals, he must have been told to expect injuries.

Quinn watched closely as Benhu finished swabbing Helice's wound. Threads of black shot through his hair, and his face bore a few creases, making him perhaps a hundred years old. Although thin, Benhu had a pot belly, and his face was long, accentuated by a wispy mustache stretching to his chin. To Quinn, he looked like a criminal gone to seed. He wore the white tunic and jacket of a godman, but only, Benhu claimed, as a disguise. The fellow, bumbling and officious, did not inspire confidence.

Helice turned toward Quinn, her eyes sparkling in the candlelight. "Don't . . . leave me . . . here. Promise me."

That was exactly what he planned to do. "I promise you're going back where you came from; that's what I promise."

She shook her head, frowning from the pain. ". . . know you're upset. Had to come, had to. You'll see."

Benhu snaked a look at Quinn. "If she doesn't shut up, she'll break open her wounds. Tell her."

"You tell her—you're the one that brought her over."

"I can't. She doesn't understand decent speech. Use your own gibberish, and tell her to stay still."

It could have been worse for Helice, though her burns were serious and her eyebrows singed off. She'd already shaved off her hair, of course; brown hair wouldn't do among the Chalin. As for the yellow eye lenses, Quinn had removed those so that she didn't dare go out of the chamber. This place was, Benhu had said, an abandoned scholar's center, but not completely isolated. They could well meet others in the vicinity of this reach once they emerged from the cavern. Benhu should stay here and nurse Helice while Quinn went on, but the godman already refused to do so, saying, *I am to help you, not her.*

A shudder rippled over her. Quinn said, "Give her something for the pain."

Benhu pointed to the ointment. "This *is* for the pain."

"Why should I trust you, anyway?"

Benhu looked mightily offended. "If I wanted to kill you, I could have done it when you were powerless and lying like a puking, helpless baby."

"If you want to help me, tell the lord to ship her home. You know how to contact him. Tell him I won't tolerate her, and she goes back."

Helice watched them argue, looking worried, probably guessing it was about her. She tried to grip Quinn's arm, but he moved out of reach, having no patience to listen to her. He was sure she had come here seeking glory, or to manage him, or for some other devious purpose that could get them both killed. He left her lying there, and rested against the smooth adobe of the chamber wall.

Helice was badly hurt. Minerva's *improved* crossing was no better than using a raft to cross the Atlantic. They needed perfection, not improvement. They needed the correlates. *An open door*, Oventroe had called it. If, as Benhu claimed, he worked for the lord, then Quinn had a fighting chance to secure them. If he won Oventroe's trust. In his brief meeting with the Tarig lord, Oventroe had said, *It is too much to give for no advantage.* He would see about that. Time was when finding the correlates had been important for the sake of commerce. Now hopes of trade gave way to the needs of war. He didn't want to think of his mission as war. *Sabotage* was a better word, and the one he clung to.

Benhu capped the ointment and wiped his hands on a silk rag. He sidled against the wall, resting. It had been a long day, and Benhu was not young.

Quinn stared at the veil-of-worlds where he'd come through. On the surface, a dark starscape shimmered. He was a world away from home. Last time here, Anzi had been at his side, his teacher and finally close friend. Now he had the likes of Helice and Benhu.

"How much time has passed since I left?"

Benhu nodded. "You'll be wanting to know that, of course. Well, to do the sums . . ." His eyes cut sideways as he calculated. "Thirty arcs, give or take a handful of days."

Three hundred days or so, then. Sydney was still young. He hadn't allowed himself to worry about the chaotic relation of time between here and home. Or so he thought. A long breath shuddered out of him.

Benhu was prattling on. "You can be sure I haven't had the time to be waiting thirty arcs. No, we figured out you'd be here about now, and I came as my duties allowed."

"*We?* You and the lord figured it out?" The godman's boasts were ludicrous.

"Oh, time correlations are all very complicated, and the lord and I couldn't define it more than we did."

Quinn leaned forward, putting an edge in his voice. "How did you know even that much? How did you know when I'd *want* to come, be *able* to come?"

Benhu looked affronted. "Well. The lord discerns when your side begins its probes—the tests that herald your crossing. Then he alerts me, and setting aside my many obligations—"

"I don't like you, Benhu. You stretch the truth. Why should I trust you?"

"My lord wants what you want," Benhu muttered.

"And what do I want?"

"Oh, to stop the engine, of course." He grinned. "Don't be surprised. The lord knows why you're here. Did you think it a secret? Well, it *is* a secret, between the three of us, I assure you."

It *should* have been a secret. Sharing it with this tattered godman, much less a Tarig lord, stung Quinn with dismay.

Benhu drew a pipe out of his pocket and loaded it with a gray weed. A candle gave his punk a flame and he puffed out a noxious stream of smoke. "You'll stop the engine, the lord says. For the sake of converse. He says that your world and mine should work together, not crosswise. It makes sense, but against the vows, of course. The lord will persuade the other lords; don't worry about that. Inevitable, the lord says, because as for going to and from, once it starts, you can't stop it."

"Get to the point, Benhu." Quinn wondered how the godman knew his mission. How *Oventroe* knew it.

"So, the lord says peace is better than war, and converse better than everyone pretending no one else exists." Benhu gestured with his pipe as he talked, punctuating his main points. "This Ahnenhoon thing, this engine, the lord's against all that. Just like you are. You're here to tear it down, of course." He squinted through a haze of orange smoke. "How do you plan to do that, by the way?"

"If the lord's against this Ahnenhoon thing, why doesn't he take it down himself?"

Recognizing the word *Ahnenhoon*, Helice tried to sit up, pushing herself up on one elbow. Gently but firmly, Benhu pushed her down again.

Noting that Helice was paying attention, Quinn took stock of the fact that she might be not only an inconvenience, but an enemy. He put nothing past her. He murmured, "We will not speak the lord's name around her. She is not to know."

Benhu nodded, eyes wide at the thought that his lord's name might have been overheard by one whom not even Titus Quinn trusted.

Quinn continued, "So why doesn't your master get rid of the engine himself?"

The godman resumed sucking on his pipe. "Maybe he's testing you. And think of this: How could a Tarig walk in there and not have a retinue, and not attract notice?"

"You're guessing."

Helice was growing more agitated and tried to sit up, slapping Benhu's hands away. She managed to drag herself to the chamber wall, where she propped herself up. She looked like a monstrous gnome: small, hairless, her skin livid and bleeding. "Can't you talk in English?"

Quinn turned on her with incredulity. "He doesn't speak it. That's your main problem here, Helice. You don't know Lucent. Did you think about that before you planned this maneuver? Did Lamar think of it, or Stefan?" No wonder Lamar was acting so guilty. The son-of-a-bitch had caved in, never warning him.

"I'm smart; I can learn," she whispered.

"No Helice, you're dumb. This stunt proves it. You could have died, and still may. If the burn doesn't get infected, then you'll give yourself away the first time you open your mouth. Dumb, very dumb."

He turned back to Benhu. "Why is it *my* bloody job to stop the engine?"

Benhu spat back, "The lord doesn't tell me everything, and he won't tell you either, even if you are the princeling, Titus Quinn."

Quinn snatched the pipe from the old man's hands. "I don't like that term, Benhu." He drowned the pipe bowl in the nearest cup of water.

Benhu scrambled to retrieve it, pulling up a stinking bowl of wet embers. He stared at Quinn blamefully.

Quinn didn't trust the man any more than he liked him. And why trust Lord Oventroe, either? The lord claimed to want *converse*, but what of the Entire's predicament—the storm walls that couldn't be sustained without the Rose? He wasn't sure that Benhu knew about that, and held silent on the topic.

"Water," Helice croaked, and Benhu seemed to understand her accompanying gesture. He poured her a small drink in a bowl, helping her to sip.

Quinn said, "Did your boss think I'd trust you so easily, Benhu? Did he think I would come all this way only to have an old godman dogging my steps?"

Benhu was working on drying out the pipe, probing it with a stick and wad of cloth.

Quinn persisted. "Well, did he?"

Benhu snaked a look at him. "He said I should win you over."

Helice was struggling to her feet. Benhu scrambled over to help her, chattering for her to lie down.

She swayed, but remained standing. "Where does a person take a pee around here?"

Quinn translated the request to Benhu, who pointed down the corridor toward the wastery and offered to take her there.

"Can find it myself," Helice said. She walked away, wobbling, her blanket over her shoulders.

Benhu fussed with his wet pipe a moment. "I should have brought an extra."

Quinn took Benhu by the front of his jacket and twisted the cloth close to the man's neck. "I don't want to hear about the pipe again. Start winning me over." They glared at each other until Quinn won the staring contest and released Benhu, shoving him back against the wall.

Benhu cringed in the shadow of the taller man. He didn't like this strutting Titus Quinn, but the man's temper could get out of hand, and it was not his intention to take a beating. He inhaled deeply, trying to focus. *First, win him over. Tell him about his daughter.* But no instructions about what to do with the injured woman. That was a prickly problem—one the lord would expect him to solve. But how? Perhaps take a clue from Quinn himself. He wanted her gone. So, then. Leave her here? No, when discovered, she would raise alarms all over the sway. Benhu brightened with a new thought. Kill the woman? Release Quinn from this burden he obviously detested, proceed with the task the lord had set him. He drew himself up straight. There. Perhaps he could be creative, after all.

The elegance of this idea improved Benhu's mood, and he settled into his story. "Your daughter," he began. Quinn made eye contact. Oh yes, now the princeling would pay decent attention. "What would you say if I told you that your daughter is under the lord's observation? Would you be happy to have news of her?"

"Yes."

Benhu looked at the pipe longingly, but it was in no shape to light. If he was going to kill the woman, he'd certainly need a smoke to settle his nerves. Before and after. Yes, better and better, to rid the journey of a problem—a problem Titus Quinn was clearly unwilling to handle by himself. Maybe the man of the Rose had no stomach for killing.

As Quinn's look became more menacing, Benhu hastened to say, "We know where she is, of course."

"Even I know that much, Benhu. Tell me something I don't know."

Benhu held up a finger. "Mind, not all of what I can tell is pleasant." The man was bound to be touchy on the subject, and Benhu wanted no outbursts. "The Inyx," he went on. "You've heard she's with them?" At a nod from Quinn, he continued, "That's both good and bad. Good, that she's a long way from the Ascendancy where the lords would have toyed with her. Bad, that you can't get there unobserved. She's fallen in with a band of Inyx that has a new leader. The leader is your daughter's bonded mount. She rides the beast, though they are sentient, if you count herd beings who can't talk. They live like animals. But she's healthy, and riding the chief, and has managed to cajole him into getting her sight back."

"She can see again?"

"So the lord says. She has some privileges as the chief's rider. So the Tarig sent her a lord to fix her eyes, beyond what the Inyx can do, of course, they being without deep knowledge." Benhu shrugged. "She's bold, to make demands on Inyx and Tarig alike. And get by with it."

"She's well? Healthy?"

Benhu shrugged. "Yes, the lord bid me tell you. Happy, even."

"That I doubt."

Benhu glanced at the doorway, but the woman hadn't returned. Benhu didn't have a weapon. Perhaps a large stone could be used to cave in her skull. Or, better yet, borrow Quinn's knife. Maybe the man wasn't so scrupulous if someone else did the blood work.

Benhu looked into Quinn's face, feeling contempt return toward this man of the Rose. He found himself needling: "Ever think your child would end up among criminals and barbarians?"

"Stick to the point, Benhu, or that pipe's going where you won't use it again."

Benhu paused for dignity's sake, then said, "She has a guard. A big Chalin who fights for her when she needs it. And she needs it, because she's got a scheme going where every rider should be equal to their mount, saying how they communicate better mind-to-mind if everyone has rights. Not everyone approves, and her mount is full of the scars to prove it. So your girl is a troublemaker, Quinn. But the lord says she's got a measure of safety, with a few followers who'll protect her. It's a good situation considering she has to live among the stinking beasts."

"Can you get her out?"

"Out? Out of that sway? No, that would draw attention. Besides, the bright lords are watching her sway. They expect you to go there, of course. Try to be patient about the girl. When your side and ours come to agreements, you can ask for her. But for now, why should the Tarig grant you concessions? They'd rather sink you in the Nigh than look at you."

"The Inyx creature that my daughter rides . . . he can sense what she's thinking?"

"Of course."

"Can the beast know I'm here, then? Can he read my thoughts?"

Benhu shook his head. "Not how it works. They can talk to each other across primacies, but not to the rest of us. Takes two of the beasts to get a strong connection. To read other sentients, they need to be close. You aren't close."

Quinn closed his eyes, trying to think straight. His heart had lifted to hear that Sydney was well—that she could see once more. But he was no closer to freeing her. This Benhu was worthless, no one to bargain with.

He murmured, "I want you to contact your master, Benhu. Now." The first issue was Helice. Let Oventroe deal with her.

The stonewell computers weren't used for communications, not that Quinn had ever seen, so that wasn't an option. There must be some way for Benhu to report to the lord. Near the crevasse where the veil-of-worlds flickered, several boxy computational machines lay stacked on each other. The machines were shape processors, based on molecular computing, where biologically based molecules recognized patterns through shape-fitting, lining up like jigsaw puzzles and crystallizing out the answers. Quinn looked at the string of redstones around Benhu's neck and wondered if one of those stones could be used to send Helice back.

A noise drew his attention. Helice stood at the entrance to the chamber, steadying herself. She stared at the veil-of-worlds, gleaming at the moment with an incandescent sheet of stars. "I'm not going in there again," she announced.

She pushed away from the door and walked unsteadily toward them as they sat near the wall. "I know you're planning to get rid of me. I know you think I can't hold my own. But I've been thinking. Why not use my injuries as an excuse for me not to speak? A fire, the larynx damaged. It's perfect. And I'd keep up; you wouldn't have to carry me or fuss over me. If I fall behind, leave me."

She stepped closer. "Please, Quinn." She turned to Benhu. "Please, Benhu."

So, she'd figured out the godman's name. She turned to Quinn. "How do you say *please* in Lucent?"

"I'm not your language teacher, and I'm not your travel buddy, Helice. I'm leaving here in the morning, and you're not coming along. I'm leaving you with Benhu, and you can live in this cave or cross over as you like. But I'm leaving. Alone."

She stood watching him, trying to stand steadily, trying to control her emotions.

"Sit down for God's sake," Quinn said.

But she stayed put. After a moment she said, her voice soft, "I know you have great responsibilities. You have big endeavors on your mind. Believe me, I know. But I can help you in ways you can't even imagine yet."

He stared at her wondering what she might mean. "Like?"

She waved the question away. "We have time to talk. It'll take us a long time to reach the Nigh. I'm not even sure Benhu *doesn't* speak English. Are you?"

Quinn glanced at the phony godman, wondering this for the first time.

Helice went on. "It's even possible something will happen to you, and then who'll carry on? I can be your backup. Meanwhile I'll be learning the language, picking up the manners. I can help you, Quinn. This is too important for just one person."

"No," he said, keeping eye contact.

She turned away, almost falling down. Then, standing in the center of the chamber, she turned back to him. "You arrogant son-of-a-bitch. You think you're so irreplaceable."

"This time maybe I am."

Her voice ratcheted up. "I just want you to know something, Quinn. I'd rather set my clothes on fire than go back into that nightmare crack. I risked my life to come here. It's not going to be for nothing."

"Super achieving again?"

"No, it's not just that." She reacted to the disdain he couldn't conceal. "You are such a bastard, Titus. Do you think you're the only one who can make sacrifices? Sacrifices for something worthwhile?" She staggered close to him, trembling, blood cutting a track down her chin. "You think you're the only one who's looking for something fine?"

"Look somewhere else, Helice."

She shook her head, smiling a burned-out smile. "You aren't the god-damned king of the world. Sometimes other people's lives matter. Even I matter, Quinn. I *matter*." She stopped, swaying on her feet.

He moved fast to catch her as she fell. Lowering her to the floor, he came close to her face, smelling putrefaction and ointment. He eased her down, putting her head in his lap. Benhu covered Helice with a blanket where she lay.

"Goddamn it," she said, trying to control the pain. The tears festered in her burns.

"Salve," Quinn told Benhu.

Benhu brought the jar, saying, "She's a troublemaker, isn't she? Makes lots of trouble, crying and ranting. Not good."

Ignoring him, Quinn dipped his fingers in the balm and dabbed it in the lesions.

As she tried and failed to sit up, he muttered, "Take it easy, Helice."

"Not easy," she whispered. "Not easy. Don't want easy."

"No," he said. "I can see that."

As Benhu crouched nearby, frowning with worry, Quinn considered Helice's proposal. He wondered if there was more to Helice Maki than the pampered, brainy snot he'd seen at Minerva. Maybe she wasn't much better than that, but she had some courage.

She began to relax as the salve took effect. They huddled there on the floor with her head in his lap, Helice helpless and forced to depend on his goodwill. He had little to spare when it came to her. It was a damn miserable situation and no good could come of it, even though Helice seemed to hunger after *something fine*. Damn the woman, damn her anyway.

She closed her eyes, allowing herself to rest. Now and then she trembled with exhaustion and pain, but gritted her teeth against crying.

The woman was tough. But tough enough to make the trek to Ahnenhoon? Was she tough enough to stand before a Tarig and not quail, or to wear the cirque, if it came to that, and release the devouring nan? And if it came to Helice as a backup, would she sacrifice herself if necessary? He watched her as she slept. Wouldn't anyone give their life for the Earth? He warred with himself over the answer.

The candles guttered into hot pools of wax, then cooled. When he rose, shifting her head and shoulders to a folded blanket for a pillow, Quinn had made up his mind. In the end he couldn't decide what Helice would do on this journey, but she was coming along. He had no choice.

"She's coming with us, Benhu," he said.

Benhu pulled on his beard, frowning. "Is that wise, Excellency?"

"We'll find out, won't we? Your job is to make sure she passes as Chalin. Any mistakes, you're to blame."

"Yes Excellency, but . . ." The godman cut a glance at Helice. "But she's badly burned. You can't blame me if she dies of it. That wouldn't be fair."

Quinn was in no mood for his whining. "Is that what they told you about me? That I'm fair?"

Benhu could hardly answer such a question, and didn't. But he nursed Helice through a long night, and by morning she was at least no worse.

Quinn waited three days for Helice to recuperate. Under Benhu's ministrations her burns knitted swiftly, responding to biomolecular rejuvenation and her sheer determination.

When they finally emerged from the chamber, gusting winds buffeted them, bearing the sweet, lucid smell of ozone. Helice stared around her at the minoral, one of the most bizarre regions the realm presented to a newcomer.

Here, the land narrowed, with the storm walls converging on a darkened tip:

the reach. In this extruded finger of the Entire, the towering storm walls churned. Skitters of lightning laced the terrible high walls like cracks showing through to magma. In explaining Entire geography to his Minerva handlers, Quinn had used the analogy of the Entire having five main treelike trunks radiating from a center. These were the primacies. On one side of each primacy, twigs called minorals grew out, ending in tips called reaches. From the minoral protruded nascences like root hairs. It all seemed so logical to him, but others, like Helice, couldn't imagine it. Now she could test her conceptions against the real thing.

Helice craned her neck to look at the storm walls, and Quinn remembered his own first reaction to them—that they were tidal waves. Eventually he had conquered the impression that they were moving toward him.

They had a short hike to the dirigible that Benhu had moored near the grave of the godman scholar Zu Cheng—the reason that Benhu would give, if asked, for his presence in this minoral. Glancing at the storm walls, Quinn thought of the child's verse: *Storm wall, where none can pass; Storm wall, always to last*. Some nursery rhymes were lies. One could pass, if imperfectly, and the walls could not last. The Entire itself couldn't last—and the thought disturbed Quinn almost as much as the threat that hung over the Rose.

When they got to the simple grave, Quinn saw that the airship, secured by ropes to a few stunted trees, was not large, perhaps only thirty feet long. How such a small volume of buoyant gas could carry a payload of three passengers and fuel, Quinn wasn't sure. Even solar-powered, the rigid framework and passenger car would add substantial weight to the craft. Apparently the Tarig perfect technologies trickled down to godmen. What else could the lords do, claiming to be gracious masters?

They found the grave site deserted, with the only sound the flap of Zu Cheng's flag in the wind. *One Who Served Knowledge and Misery.* No higher compliment for one who tended a scholar's veil and the Miserable God.

With Benhu at the controls in the passenger car below the main cavity, the dirigible took them in silence down the minoral. They had a long journey to reach the Nigh, where the exotic river would allow travel over the immeasurable distance to Ahnenhoon. But to reach the Nigh, they couldn't travel by a costly dirigible, lest it draw attention to them. Benhu's plan was to travel to the great river by more humble means, in the company of godmen.

Seen through the airship's lone viewing port, the valley soon widened, and the storm walls did not crowd so close. In the distance, the walls appeared like mammoth escarpments. It was more comforting to think of them as solid rather than shifting, but it was no wonder that the population clusters of the sways were built far from boundaries like this.

Out the viewing port a crackle of light revealed a nascence spitting its fires. This was the third tier of the geography of the Entire, the smallest and most ephemeral. The sight of one seemed more ominous to Quinn than it once had.

Quinn glanced at Benhu lounging at the crew station controls, steering the ship with no more piloting skills than a Sunday driver. It made him uneasy to rely on the blustering godman. Once he thought the man spotted the cirque around his ankle—that innocent chain, that might merely be an ornament. For a moment he caught Helice staring, too. He pulled his pant leg down, careful not to touch the cirque.

Though it lay next to his warm skin, it was always cold.

Helice looked out the viewport, nearly giddy with what she was seeing. The storm walls, the bright. In the back of her mind she was parsing a few equations on transference of energy across branes. Because the Tarig *were* transferring energy. Just a guess, but she figured they weren't creating the bright—not exactly. They were stealing it. She got lost for a while in the math. It took her mind off the nasty burns.

This venture wasn't quite as easy as she had expected. In the luck of the draw, Quinn had come across unscathed, while she had gotten fried. Her little team back home better appreciate all that she was sacrificing for the cause. Yes, Quinn still looked like the big hero, and she looked like shit. That had darkened her mood for a while until she had figured out how to use it to her advantage. Look brave and plucky. Yes, men love that.

The little speech about *something fine* hadn't been just for show, however. Partly for show, but not all. Everyone wanted a worthwhile life. Was that too much to ask for? Some people—Titus Quinn, for one—seemed to get the good things of life on a golden platter, things like his regular family and his luck in finding the Entire, things that she could have appreciated more than he did. Things that she deserved, instead of having to claw her way to the top of the heap of the company that pretended to be in charge of things they had no right to control. Leonard Garvey, who'd had the good sense to kill himself, had been right to say that the universe next door did not belong to Quinn or Minerva. There were larger concerns here than Quinn or Minerva.

That was where she came in.

She glanced at the cirque around Quinn's ankle. Four, five, one, and then the reverse. A simple little code. The trick was getting Quinn to sit still while she took the chain. On that score, there were a number of possibilities. Then, off to find Sydney Quinn. The girl—or was she a woman now? That was unclear, but in any case, Quinn's daughter would teach Helice the language. She needed a bolt hole until she had Lucent and the cultural stuff down pat. The girl would befriend her as no one else was likely to, particularly since Helice had a number of inducements to offer. Inyx welcomed all riders, so all she needed to do was find a contingent of them and pledge her loyalty.

She'd have the cirque, and soon she'd know the ropes—all good preparation, but she was far from ready to confront the Tarig. They would merely use her, and that was a bit reversed from what she had in mind.

CHAPTER NINE

Calendar. Practice of the Rose. An iterative system of reckoning days with reference to planetary orbit *around a* star. *Allows correspondences between sequential phases of 365 days. Often subdivided into* months, *being divisions of the* solar year *roughly based on relation of* orbital moon *to a* planet.

—from *Arcane Nomenclature of the Dark Cosmologies*

JOHANNA COULD REMEMBER EVERY DETAIL of her journey to Ahnenhoon four thousand days ago. Eleven years, it had been, but of course the Entire had no years, no seasons, no star.

She remembered the scorched light that had fallen on her from the sky as her jailor led her across the hangar of the brightships. The impossible light pressed down, drowning out shadows, stealing her breath. Though she hadn't known at the time, this was what the light of day looked like in her new home. Across the huge expanse of the hangar she saw the lip of the bay jut into empty space. Close by in their docks, the brightships glistened like iridescent, sleeping beetles.

A Tarig ushered her to the nearest ship. His four-fingered hand firmly gripped her upper arm, guiding her along, but not requiring that she match his own huge stride. She would not be hurried, and the creature tolerated her slowness. From the moment she was taken prisoner she had resolved not to act like one. Even knowing nothing, disoriented and terrified, Johanna's instinct was to act unafraid. In interrogations she had insisted on water to drink. They believed that she required a glass of water by her side to talk. It was a small victory, but it gave her a tiny bit of power. Then, with the cup of water constantly replenished, she told them all the lies she could dream up.

They left her for days at a time in a small, windowless room with awful glowing walls that faded and revived on a regular cycle. When she lay on her pallet she felt a tingling sensation over her whole body. In the mornings, she and her clothes were somehow clean, even her long hair. She would rather have been dirty than to be cleansed like a piece of equipment, but after several days she got used to it. That would be her advice to any newcomer: In time you get used to it.

You will call me lord *or* bright lord *or* gracious lord, her Tarig captor had said, in her language.

The Tarig who accompanied her that day of her journey to Ahnenhoon had been Lord Inweer, although at the time he was just a ghastly creature—human-looking, but too angular, and many details wrong, in the face, the hands, the skin. The iris of his eye was large and midnight black. The skin, bronze and flawless. The fingers, capable of extruding long claws. She had never seen Lord Inweer display a claw, but could feel them embedded in his hands.

During her detention in the place that she later realized had been the great city of the Tarig, she had waited for the day when she would be in the same cell with her husband and daughter. If she'd known that the time would never come, that she would never see either of them again, she would have gone mad. If, boarding the ship that day, she'd known it signaled her permanent banishment from Titus and Sydney, she would have fought against that rigid grip on her arm. She might have rushed to the lip of the bay. But Johanna hesitated to take her own life. It was the hardest stricture her faith imposed on her. Even harder than forgiving them.

Then Lord Inweer—one of the ruling five, she would later learn—had taken her in a brightship to Ahnenhoon. At the time she could have had no conception of that journey. How far. How vastly far. Even now, she had difficulty grasping that the Entire couldn't be measured. In the Empty Lands, the firmament knotted and folded so that the Entire couldn't even be defined by light-years. Similarly, time here wasn't divided into years. This world traced no path around a sun. They had no anchor in the universe.

These things no longer seemed strange.

Nevertheless, she had the habit of counting the days, dabs of paint on a strip of silk in groups of 365. By this means she registered the arrival of months, seasons, and special days like birthdays, which she knew might be wildly unrelated to the true days of the Rose, but to which she stubbornly clung.

Johanna became aware of birdsong. She stood in her forest cell, listening, although there were no birds in the Entire, not ones that flew. The song was an excellent reproduction. She let her eyes rest on the green hills and her trees filled with dappled light.

Down the slope of the hill, she could just make out the pitched roofs of her silking shed, where she kept her prize spinners. Under her direction her overseer bred the insectoid spinners to produce the finest blue filaments. Today she wore the resulting indigo silks, the blue that had become her signature color. It should serve to set her apart from others who would attend the upcoming reception, since blue wasn't a common color among the Chalin. Her collar was high, the skirt of her gown slit on both sides to the knee. Against custom, she let her hair fall free.

Waiting for Pai to summon her to the event, she sat in a gazebo, its canopy offering shade from the omnipresent bright. It was her habit to always shield herself one way or another from the bright. If it bestowed long life as people claimed, she wanted no part of it. Although her lord had put resources at her disposal to create this park, he couldn't manage her most important criteria: a discreet source of light. Some days she thought he hadn't tried very hard. Still, it was a far cry from former days when her quarters had been a stone cell.

In those first days in the lord's presence, Johanna had proven herself capable of conversation that he found interesting for at least short periods of time. She didn't cower or fawn, but expressed forthright opinions; this demeanor horrified her guards. Once, in Deep Ebb, two of them had dragged her from her bed and beaten her, so that she would learn to show respect, they said.

When she limped into the Inweer's audience chamber the next day, and the lord wasn't pleased, these same guards had fallen in front of her begging for mercy. But Johanna guessed they hated her, and turned away from them.

Inweer gave his first evidence that day that he favored this human woman. He approached the nearest guard and, bending the unfortunate man backward over his knee and using his steely arms as a vise, broke the man's spine. The second guard wept in terror, but the lord spared him.

The next day Johanna became the mistress of a suite of rooms.

Soon her confinement relaxed to a wing of the centrum, the innermost circle of the Repel. Then, in time, she went where she pleased, even to the lord's apartments when the Lady Enwepe wasn't in residence, and sometimes, even if she was. So long as Johanna showed deference to Enwepe, the lady appeared unconcerned about favorites or the scandal that a Rose woman might have favors, might have what some would call freedom.

The sweetest privilege was her forest. Johanna had designed every acre, every feature to match a temperate Earth forest. On her canvases, she drew scenes with the glorious Tarig paints that could be retracted and altered in color. Using this guide, her overseer of grounds would create the living flora, modifying it under her direction, until they had grasses, beech trees, ponderosa pine, rock outcroppings, streams, and bracken. Sometimes the overseer was able to find records of scholars who had catalogued Earth plants, and by these means he devised more botanically correct specimens.

She painted a portrait of Sydney. When the overseer saw the painting, he lamented, *This I cannot create.* She hadn't realized it was her subconscious desire that he do so. But only God could fashion a child, and He had decided to take this child from her.

The lord heard about the painting of her daughter. As they shared an evening meal, he asked if it was a custom of the Rose to make a painted likeness of a sentient.

"Yes, my lord. A treasured Earth tradition."

He gazed at her with his black eyes. For her sake he blinked occasionally, having learned it put her more at ease. It was a small kindness, or perhaps a gesture of vanity. This time, though, his gaze held steady. "For the sake of this girl, do you wish for justice against us?"

A dangerous question, but she dared to say, "Some days I do. But other days I pretend my lord would return her to me if circumstances permitted such a favor."

He had stopped eating, and now paused before saying, "There is no difference among us, Johanna." Meaning *among Tarig.*

He had said so before, in that show of unity Tarig affected. She dared to say, "And there is no difference between me and any other mother of the

Rose." She looked at her hands, folded in her lap. She had practically said she did blame him, if he followed the nuances, and the lord always did.

"Here, you are not a mother."

She had gone too far, but still, the rebuke galled. "What am I, then?"

"Lady of blue silks. Mistress of the forest. This lord's companion."

He had failed to say, *Lord Inweer's enemy.* Then, too, perhaps he had forgotten that she was Titus Quinn's wife. If she was. Perhaps, when Titus came back, she would find out.

Of the three prisoners of the Rose, only Titus had escaped. Then, some three hundred days ago he had returned, infiltrated the Ascendancy, and fled after a destructive rampage that deprived the lords of one of the ruling five and all their brightships. She could only hope that he had fled in that manner because of an urgent need to go home; she let herself believe it was because her message had been received. This warm coal of hope, faint as it was, she fanned to brightness. Perhaps the Rose could never overcome the lords, but the only chance they had was to be conscious of the Tarig threat.

She didn't begrudge that Titus would have gone to his daughter last time, and not to his wife. No doubt he thought Johanna was dead. That was the story given out, so that Titus Quinn would never have reason to come snooping here, at the end of the longest primacy in the lobed universe.

But once Lord Inweer had unwisely told Johanna of the purpose of the engine, Johanna resolved to change all that. Such a stunning error on Inweer's part. She remembered how they had lain together for hours, the lord being inexhaustible. At last he lay back.

"You withhold from me, Johanna."

She was astonished that he thought this. "Do I?" She was prepared to prove otherwise, but he rose, donning a long, sleeveless robe.

"You are not completely present when we lie thus. Ah?" He turned to look at her with a quiet, startling intensity.

"My lord, not true . . ."

"Yes, true." He strode away to the veranda facing the storm wall. When he turned back to her, he stood in the door frame, backlit by the quilted, dark walls of the Entire.

"There can be no going home, Johanna. There can be no Rose."

Thus he had begun telling her the reason that she would never return to Earth. Because it would not long exist. When he had finished, he left her lying in his bed, feeling like a mote in the eye of a storm.

She never knew if, afterward, he was more satisfied with their intimacy. She hardly cared. Her thoughts were now on leading Titus to Ahnenhoon.

First, she had prevailed upon a friend to bring a redstone message to the Magisterium and hide it in the library there. The scholar Kang had been her original interrogator, first at the Ascendancy, and then at Ahnenhoon. Finally relieved of duties, Kang had been allowed to leave; she did so with Johanna's redstone. She never knew if Kang succeeded. But, trusting one day Titus would find her warning, Johanna began looking for a vulnerable spot to direct the Rose strike when it came. To this end, she needed an agent who could uncover and comprehend the layout of the containment chamber of the Repel. If Johanna could have found a good excuse to befriend Morhab, or had the mechanical knowledge to profit from that association, she would have pursued the plans herself. But, needing to be removed from suspicion, Johanna waited for an opportunity to bind a suitable spy to her service.

This opportunity came with the arrival in Ahnenhoon of the engineering steward Gao. He was a minor worker, but one with a problem. Assigned to Ahnenhoon, a lifetime posting, Gao had been chosen for his lack of family ties, among other criteria. However, once relocated to the Repel, word reached him that his lover in his home sway had been pregnant when he left, and now he had a son whom he'd never seen, and many regrets for not having married the mother.

Pretending to be touched by a situation so similar to her own, Johanna persuaded Lord Inweer to bring the woman and child to Ahnenhoon, incurring the fierce gratitude of Gao, who now had love in his life, and a son.

Even then, Gao might not have been suitable for her purposes. But their friendship developed, following those pathways that no one can predict. He listened to her story, stricken that she had given him family joys that she would never again have. Reasonable or not, he considered her a queen in bondage. His duty, as he saw it, was to ease her heart, at whatever risk to himself. That she had to send him into such peril made her sick with worry.

Even so, it was worth it. After hundreds of days of Gao's patient investigation, she had learned a great deal about Ahnenhoon, its byways and its heart.

So that when Titus came, she could guide the knife.

From a balcony, Johanna, Pai, and SuMing looked down on the throng below, gathered to welcome a dignitary and—since he was related to a traitor—to observe him. Assembled in such finery as the austere Ahnenhoon had to offer were some two hundred fortress functionaries, visiting military officers, servants, legates, and retainers. It wasn't a large enough crowd to take command of the assembly hall, suited more for parade muster than a party, with its burnished metallic floor smooth and vast as a glacier. But it was an event no one who could be spared from duties would miss.

Far across the hall, Lord Inweer was just arriving with Lady Enwepe. As the only Tarig in the hall, indeed in Ahnenhoon, they commanded attention, although they wore no formal costume. It would have been gilding the lily to put a gown on Enwepe, certainly. More delicate than Inweer, her bronze features were flawless. Her long skirt, a metal mesh, fell nearly to the floor, straight and without ornament. A simple vest left her well-muscled arms exposed. It was the same garment that Inweer wore. Exquisite and stark, there was nothing about the Tarig of the fleshy, dissolute, or fading. Johanna had learned to find them beautiful.

"Here is the chief engineer," Pai said. Pai had been leaning on the railing, surveying the crowd below, while SuMing stood back from the edge of the balcony.

There, cutting through the eddies of guests, was Morhab, bedecked and booming, reclining in a sling borne by four solid Jout attendants, their petaled skin forming a natural armor. When he looked up to see her, Johanna bowed, but he hadn't forgotten her recent slight, and turned away. It was worrisome to have Morhab against her, but better to have him focus his irritation on her than on one of his engineers. Johanna continued to take stock of the hall. Somewhere among that crowd was Gao, watching for his chance to come near her, to report whether that day in Morhab's quarters he had at last learned enough to crack the maze.

Preconsul Zai Gan, the guest of this reception, had arrived in the hall, and approached the lord and lady. Even at this distance, Johanna saw how large he was, as squat as Inweer was lean. It intrigued her that this man represented merely two degrees of separation from her husband. Zai Gan was the half brother of Yulin, who was the master who had helped her husband adopt his Chalin disguise. For a moment she felt that relation to Titus, and it shook her.

Yulin had fled, gone somewhere in the realm to evade Tarig justice. In his place, Zai Gan was installed as the new master of the Chalin sway. This call at Ahnenhoon was one of several visits of state that he undertook to express his loyalty, distancing himself from his brother. To most sentients, it was unimaginable why Yulin had betrayed the gracious lords. But Johanna could well imagine. By sheer force of personality Titus could persuade you to enter hell, create a stir, and depart again. So Yulin committed treason, setting himself against the lords, and against his half brother. Changes were coming to the Entire. The first vow, to withhold the knowledge of the Entire from the Rose, was irrevocably broken. Titus had broken it, as had everyone who helped him.

Johanna turned to her ladies, both dressed for the occasion. SuMing wore common red, her hair cut to chin level, just covering the scar in back, where her scalp had separated from her skull. Pai wore soft yellow billowing pants and a quilted jacket. "Now then," Johanna said, "to the hall."

She had considered leaving SuMing behind in the apartments this ebb as a penalty for stealing her tally of days. Over time this tally had become a calendar, of the sort unknown in the Entire. By now SuMing had no doubt arranged for Lord Inweer to see it. SuMing hardly dared give it to him directly, but ways could be devised. The calendar only marked the passage of days, but it suggested that Johanna wished not to be with her lord. Of course he knew where she wished to be. But it was no doubt displeasing to see the prisoner's scratch marks on the wall.

She walked that impossible line. *If I cannot be home, then let me be with you.* Such emotional demarcations hardly mattered now, if Titus came. But the tally of days might put her lord on guard, might suggest that Johanna expected to go home. Then Inweer would watch for Titus. He must not watch.

From behind came a deep voice. Turning, Johanna saw the guest of honor approaching with his aides. Zai Gan was on course for a table laid out with food, but he had detoured to stand before her. In his elaborate padded jacket, he looked like a bear in circus clothes. His amber eyes were shrewd as he studied her.

She bowed, just enough.

"A pleasure, Mistress Johanna," Zai Gan said. "One heard that you would be on display." This brought a rustle of amusement from his retainers.

"I fear we are both on display, Master Zai Gan." She looked around her to emphasize that he, too, was a center of attention, and not in a good way "The stares of underlings are so vexing, don't you think?"

A shadow crossed Zai Gan's face as he realized she was sparring with him. "One must be careful to give no cause for staring, Mistress Johanna."

She sighed. "Well, one cannot help one's relatives, of course. And that is vexing, too."

Zai Gan hissed, "A brother is more easily set aside than a husband of the Rose."

She must let him win; he was a guest. "Wisely said, Master Zai Gan. I must rely on Lord Inweer's favor, as always."

Pai was tugging at her arm. She let herself be led to a refreshment table as Zai Gan—surrounded by his aides, who were not now so jolly as before—watched her retreat.

"Mistress," Pai scolded. Pai had perfected this scandalized carping, and it had become a game between them.

"Hush, Pai," Johanna snapped back. "He is a pompous fool."

"A powerful fool," SuMing murmured with a hint of reproach.

Johanna set out into the crowd again, vowing to use better judgment. The façade of normalcy was her great asset right now.

She spied Gao at last, sipping from a cup of spirits and looking lost. "Here is Gao," she said to SuMing. "Shall I ask after his young boy?"

"He is only a servant, mistress." SuMing was following Johanna, but Pai expertly diverted her, engaging her in gossip while Johanna moved in on Gao. He bowed low.

"Engineer Gao," Johanna said. "How is your good wife? Does she still spin her tapestries?"

Gao was a poor dissembler, but he recognized their code word for the map of the Repel, and mumbled, "She progresses. The design emerges."

Johanna laughed. "I fear she will never finish such a painstaking work."

"Soon, mistress. Perhaps it is good enough even now."

As SuMing approached, Johanna backed away. "You are a good husband, Gao, to care about women's hobbies."

Her spirits lifted. *The design emerges*, he had said. *Perhaps good enough, even now.* Johanna didn't wait for him to respond, but swept off through the crowd as though in search of higher conversation.

The guests eyed the woman in blue, always a curiosity. A darkling. A favorite of Lord Inweer.

No one watched more carefully than Morhab. Surreptitiously, he tracked Johanna as she flitted from one courtier to the next, bowing to every petty lordling, smiling at the traitor Zai Gan, even bestowing her charms on the inconsequential Gao. His gut churned, seeing her debase herself for others, but not for him. Until that day in the gathering yard, he had smelled her awe—secretions that flowed from her body, that maddened him. If she had touched him, just once—not that foolish clench of his hands . . . if she had touched his person just once in admiration, he could have cherished it for a thousand days.

At times Morhab had imagined more from the lady in blue: some ecstatic commingling that the gracious lord might even condone, if it brought the lady happiness.

But that day in the darkened hallway of the centrum, he smelled the same churnings as before, and this time he knew them to signify disgust. For his person. As though he were some unwashed clerk or godman. He was fastidious about his grooming, his paints, and his ointments, yet she found him objectionable. It cut him deeply, more each time he laid eyes on her and imagined what she must think of him. Why then, had she come to him that day? He would give very much to know.

For now he was content to have purloined her record of days. Let the gracious lord see her for what she was: a vicious, lying, and stinking wand of flesh, unworthy of the lord's care. If Inweer cast her out, Morhab would be waiting.

The party formed its knots and whorls of conversation, changing randomly, joined now and then by the major players: Inweer, Enwepe, Zai Gan, and several military officers.

Johanna mixed too, feeling like a foreign bee in the hive, aware that she had set in motion events that would change everything. *The design emerges.* If so, then things would utterly change. Strangely, it wasn't her own death she most dreaded. It was facing Lord Inweer just before he carried out his justice.

And there her lord stood, a short distance away, in conversation with a Chalin man whom Johanna didn't know.

As she approached, Inweer said, "Ah Johanna, you have attended after all." A high-ranking soldier nodded to her. "Meet our general, among those who serve us."

"Ci Dehai, mistress," the general said. His fine brocaded jacket fought with a profoundly mutilated face.

She rose from a deep bow. "My high pleasure, Excellency." She cut a glance at Inweer. "And why wouldn't I attend this splendid gathering?"

Inweer looked at her with such a penetrating gaze that she had to force herself to breathe.

"There is," he said, "a Rose custom of counting days to a certain number, and then starting over again, hnn?"

She fixed her smile in place. "Yes, a minor thing. It's called a calendar."

Ci Dehai nodded. "A practice of the dark universe." Whether he was one who tolerated or disapproved such things, his half face made it impossible to read.

Inweer continued, "So today is a day you might have spent alone. Without duties. A day you count as recognizing your birth."

And so it was. And designated as such on the pilfered calendar.

"A foolish custom, my lord."

With a dangerous calm, Inweer said, "We never knew you to be foolish."

She must remember that he despised courtiers' manners.

Ci Dehai mused, "The same days rotate, coming again and again. A strange concept; but one does not begrudge a sway its particulars."

Inweer turned to him. "But you are not so tolerant of the Paion, ah?"

The general offered a half grin in response. "Bright Lord, their days come not again if they meet my army." He cut a glance at Johanna, a gaze that pierced her social façade for a moment. She wondered if it was her fate to draw the interest of ugly men. Morhab, she noticed, hovered nearby, keeping her in view.

Johanna tried to slip away, but Lord Inweer wouldn't permit it, instead dismissing Ci Dehai and keeping a firm grasp of Johanna's arm.

"With me," he said, and walked her through the crowd as sentients bowed along their path. By now Pai and SuMing were left behind, surmising that the lord wanted no audience for what he would say.

For privacy, the lord might have stood anywhere and commanded a wide circle of space, but he led her toward the edge of the room. To her surprise, he took her through a doorway and then down the corridor to a way door, an access portal used only by the lords.

"Your guests, my lord . . . ," she protested.

"Will wait for us," he finished.

They entered the small compartment, and Inweer spoke his destination. "The forest." Standing there for a brief moment, the thrum of the distant lobed engine rumbled faintly in the stone around her. Then the door brightened and dissolved, allowing them to step through to her preserve.

A subdued light fell over them. A wrong light. The grounds and their greenery took on blotches of shade, deepening the colors, cooling them. What blight had come to her preserve? Johanna was filled with dread.

But then she looked up.

A swath of blue sky spilled across the heavens. It was like a cooling hand on her forehead, as though she had wakened from a feverish dream. Gone was the curdling, silver light of that terrible river of the sky. In its place was translucent blue air. With a star burning overhead.

She fell to her knees, falling into her new shadow. "My lord," she rasped, words sticking in her throat. She looked up, and the sun was too intense to look at, but it was the perfect golden white of Sol—she could tell by the quality of light on her hands. She closed her eyes, and let the light fall on her lifted face.

Inweer folded his long body and sat in the grass by her side. "If the colors are in error, we will change them."

She dared a glance at him. "Change nothing."

He almost smiled. "So you command?"

"No. Please. Change nothing, my lord."

They sat beside each other, viewing this display of perfect verisimilitude.

"Does the sun move across the sky?" Johanna asked. "And set?"

"It does," Inweer said. He watched her closely. "You will have your night, ah?"

She closed her eyes, thinking of the glory of sleeping under her trees in the true dark. She resolved to sleep thus, tomorrow night. Tonight, she would come to the lord's chamber, to give her thanks truly.

At last she asked, "Why, my lord?"

He stood, and took her hands to raise her up with him. "A gift to acknowledge the return of the day of your birth."

Her birthday. That was the lesson he took from her calendar, not her faithlessness, her truculence. "Thank you," she whispered. "It pleases me very much." And it did. Underneath, a bit of rot: the knowledge that she had betrayed him. Today, and every day for so long.

He watched her thoughtfully. "We would see Johanna happy."

"I am happy." There was a part of her that was, that he would honor her so. And another part that couldn't bear it.

Lady Enwepe appeared from a notch in the forest, and stood looking at the odd sky. She joined them on the small green sward where they stood. She noted Johanna's wet face, but ignored the tears. Enwepe knew what they were, having no doubt seen them in her Chalin subjects. Perhaps she was embarrassed for Johanna, or more likely, indifferent.

"A pretty toy," the lady said gazing upward. "Let fat Zai Gan behold this, Lord, and know our power."

Inweer said, sweetening his gift even more, "Only if Johanna wishes. This is her forest."

CHAPTER TEN

What are the Paion?
No one knows.
Where do they live?
No one goes.
How do they look?
No one sees.
Why do they fight?
Themselves to please!
　　　　　　—a child's rhyme

RACING ALONG THE SPINE OF THE HILL, the Inyx mount sent shards of rock scattering beneath his great hooves. Sydney leaned into Riod's neck, gripping his rear horns, thinking—and trusting he would step into her mind to hear—*faster, faster, my heart.* As he put on a burst of speed, she turned around, waving in wild joy to Mo Ti. Her Chalin lieutenant hailed her in turn, riding Distanir with grace despite his size.

To one side the storm wall loomed high like a canyon palisade. The wall was far enough away not to perturb the atmosphere in this region of hills nor show more than the largest spikes of lightning, but Sydney thought it the fairest sight she had ever seen. For days she had judged each new sight as the best, changing her mind as new wonders presented themselves: the golden steppe stretching to the ends of the universe; her beloved mount's face, framed by the double row of curving horns; the bright overhead, with its endless rounds of waxing and ebbing; Mo Ti's hands that she sometimes held in her own, wondering how someone so large and gnarled could be so gentle.

115

Blind for four thousand days, she had won her vision back from the hands of a Tarig surgeon. Now, sighted and newly risen in stature, she toured the roamlands absorbing its wonders. Although most of the steppe was uniformly flat, here the land was deeply folded by storm wall shock waves. Buckled rock, chasms, and pinnacles clustered in a tangled distortion of land. A thousand shades of yellow and gold gilded the formations. Some miles behind clustered the massive encampment of the Inyx herds, drawn together now in one conclave. Akay-Wat had come ten days ago with the last of the far-flung herds, bringing the final contingent under the banner of Sydney and Riod.

While great events awaited her in the encampment, Sydney took this day for herself, riding out to the region of the Scar, a thing she had heard of but never seen. Improbable as it seemed, there was a formation on the storm wall, ancient and massive. They learned the location from Akay-Wat, that Hirrin lieutenant of Sydney's who, traveling widely in recruitment of the herds, had come upon the Scar.

Astride Distanir, Mo Ti rode at Sydney's side. His rumpled face looked like a misshapen potato sitting on the body of a troll. But she loved this Chalin man, more so because his face and body were like no other. Scarred by the Long War, bulked up by some accident of birth, twisted by his late gelding, Mo Ti's was the best face she knew, besides Cixi's.

Sydney asked Riod to set out along the hill crest, and he did so, content as always to bear Sydney and be on the land.

Best rider, Riod sent, sharing Sydney's appetite for farther landscapes. She placed her hand on his neck, feeling the warmth of his coat, taking comfort from his solid presence.

Riod glanced now and then at the storm wall, and as he did so, his strong feelings came to her—flickers of memory from his youth when he watched his mother face her death in a last ride. He had been a young foal when his ailing mother took a pledge to end her days in the ceremonial way. He had followed her into the steppe. She must have known that he pursued her, but her mind was almost gone by then, and in any case her thoughts were all on eternal things. The wildness of the storm wall that day stopped the young Inyx farther away than he'd wished. The ground trembled, the air boomed, and the smells frightened him.

He watched his mother run her last race, speeding for the dark wall. As she grew close to the curdling dark, spears of lightning ignited around her, then appeared to sprout from her forehorns, although young Riod couldn't think why. She plunged into the embrace of those black arms and disappeared, leaving behind not even a dimple. He watched the path left by her hooves until her hoofprints blew away.

Today Riod looked for those hoofprints, although this wasn't the place.

Yes, my heart, Sydney sent. *You loved her so.* Not that she knew anything about mothers, or cared for her own. Johanna, Sydney thought, have you walked into the wall by now? If she had any decency, she would have, not live for the fiend, nor pleasure him as the rumor had it.

The day burned away its last hours as they picked their way along the ridge through uplifted rock formations and across tumbled scree slopes. Riod had never seen the Scar, having confined his life to his traditional roamlands; but lately even he had begun to think of wider lands. In the past, the herd was enough, bound together in a keen weaving of minds. The mounts spoke heart to heart. Riders too, in their way: the Inyx read strong rider emotions and shared these thoughts among themselves and the riders. Formerly Sydney had fought this. Now she treasured it, provided that Riod metered out her thoughts only to Mo Ti and Distanir, shielding her from idle probes. Mo Ti had brought her into high schemes; because of this she must hide her intentions for a little while longer.

She looked up to see Mo Ti and his mount where they had climbed to a rock prominence and stood silhouetted against the bright. Mo Ti had dismounted and stood gazing outward.

Sydney joined him. Before them was the Scar.

Here at ebb-time, shadows curled into the boiling porridge of the sky. In turn the walls fell sere, and in this dimmed state, a vast formation hung on the wall. Large enough to swallow the Entire's largest city, the Scar was a pale rosette burned into the storm wall from the ground to the bright.

The four watchers stared. How could the shifting field of the walls hold a scar? The edges of the scar flickered as though the wall would reclaim its territory, but the oval held. Like a magic cheval glass, Sydney thought, where you might walk through to another place.

This was not far from the truth, according to legend. Here, the Paion had once broken into the Entire. Battering at Ahnenhoon for five thousand years, they infiltrated in small surges, but here, long ago, they had swarmed through in a massive incursion. The assault brought the lords themselves to do battle, where many Tarig died, but far more of the Paion, until the hordes were beaten back and the entry point choked off with Tarig skill.

Sydney, Riod, Mo Ti, and Distanir looked at the Scar and shared the same thought. *The fiends can die like anyone.*

"Why did the Paion enter here," Sydney asked, "so far from great centers?"

Mo Ti answered, "They struck where the Tarig least expected, taking them unprepared. It is a precept of war, my lady."

"Why don't the fiends plug Ahnenhoon as they did this place?"

Riod sent: *Ahnenhoon is a thin place; it cannot bear strong defense.*

Even the Tarig had limits. So she had come to believe under Mo Ti's urging. Within a few hours, they would have their first sense, she fervently hoped, of Tarig limits. It would begin this ebb with the great gathering of the Inyx herds.

The Ascendancy was not yet within her grasp; but already she reached toward it. She thought of that city as a spider's lair, the place where she had lost her family and suffered blinding under the claws of Lord Hadenth; where she had hung in the sky ready to fall to her death. Soon she would sweep the spiders from the castle. The Scar brought her thoughts to the Paion and how they might be allies to bolster her cause; but no one had ever spoken to a Paion, nor even seen one beneath their carapaces of battle.

Mo Ti's attention swerved up primacy. He turned on Distanir's back and squinted. A brown curtain hung faintly in the distance, nothing more than a blemish on the horizon.

Distanir caught Mo Ti's concern, and his nostrils flared, trying to catch the scent on the stiffening breeze.

"Windstorm," Mo Ti said.

Sydney took stock of the cloud. "Far away."

"Traveling fast." He checked their position relative to the ridge and its paths. He had seen dust storms before—great disturbances spawned by the restless storm walls interacting with hot thermals rising off the steppe.

"To the camp now, mistress," Mo Ti said, and Riod urged compliance, turning to retrace their path.

Riod and Distanir kept a brisk pace along the ridgeline of the hills, where now and again advance curls of wind announced a high wind coming. In the distance, a curtain of dust climbed the sky, throwing a carnelian shadow over the steppe. Even a windstorm could be beautiful to the formerly blind.

Coming at last to the edge of the hills, they descended quickly along a narrow cut in the escarpment, with switchbacks bringing the steppe into view now and then.

On the flats below was the encampment, a herd of ten thousand mounts and their riders. Sydney could just make out the center pavilion where a red tassel blew in the wind, marking it as hers. Surrounding this tent, many smaller ones housed the riders, while the mounts preferred no confinement at all. At Sydney's instruction, the mounts intermingled without respect to herd and shared their thoughts, mind to mind, in the Inyx way. Some riders were still abroad, but came galloping in before the approaching storm. A team of Laroo raced into camp from the Nigh-ward side, tails tucked in, their fur whipping in the wind. Once, many of these Laroo had opposed her, but now her old Laroo enemy, Takko, was a trusted lieutenant. Mo Ti had coached her well on qualities of leadership and the subversion of enemies, shaping her with a patient hand. The riders, that motley assemblage of castoffs and ruf fians, expected more of their leader than of themselves, so Sydney must know how to bind a crowd's allegiance, and wash her face once in a while.

Soon she would adopt a new name, a Chalin name: Sen Ni, leaving behind her old self for the new. "When?" she had asked Mo Ti. "When shall I have the new name?" He had answered, "When we are stronger, when the day comes that we are ready to act."

For hundreds of days the encampment grew ever larger, as the far-flung herds came in to her summons. They found her sighted, and promising sight for all. They found her Riod's equal—no longer a slave. Conforming to her new catechism, they accepted free bond with their riders, or they left. Few left. The vast encampment of a united Inyx was the proof. Now their combined powers would penetrate the minds of the Tarig leaders—the only beings whose heart-thoughts the Inyx had never glimpsed.

She turned to Mo Ti as he descended behind her. "The windstorm is fierce, Mo Ti. Shall we wait on this ebb's purpose until it passes?"

Riod heard and sent his assurance that the storm would make little difference.

"Let them gather," Mo Ti said. "The storm will give an excuse for a close crowd of mounts."

They weren't ready to share their purpose with the riders. Too many newcomers had come into camp for trust to be universal. The Inyx would cloak their thoughts this ebb.

As they reached the flats, the approaching curtain of dust rose into the sky, staining the light a bruised orange.

Deep in the ebb, the winds still scoured the plains, sending the riders to ground, keeping them huddled in tents and dozing instead of gaming or carousing.

Sydney hugged her mount fiercely. "Go softly, my Riod." He'd have to move quietly through the thoughts of the Tarig, leaving no signature of Inyx intrusion behind. He and the ten thousand mounts. Riod left her then, moving between the tents, making for the nearby crowded pastures.

Hair whipping around her face, Sydney watched him go. Mo Ti and Akay-Wat waited by her side. She rested a hand on Akay-Wat's strong Hirrin back. The three remained wordless, as though their silence might lend force to the herd's effort. This was the culmination of their long work to unify the sway, the thing Mo Ti had come to her to champion: to use the one power that Tarig lacked—speaking of heart to heart—to penetrate the shrouded world of the Tarig. Who were these beings who dominated the All so completely, and shared so little? What did they fear, that they built their city impossibly far from ordinary reach? *Find the weakness*, Mo Ti had said. *Then strike.* Sydney had asked, *Strike how? As we are able*, he answered. *As opportunity presents. Discredit them. Undermine them. Crush them.*

Sydney wasn't trained to battle. She hadn't thought of strategy. But Mo Ti had. That his cunning and insight had come from Cixi was something he hadn't revealed to his mistress. This was Cixi's command, for the protection of the most shocking traitor in the Magisterium, the high prefect herself.

As the ebb deepened, Sydney and her two captains went to separate tents so as not to draw attention to their vigil. They sat alone, listening to the wind punch against pavilion walls, drive down the rows of tents.

Sometime later, able to hear the separation no longer, Sydney wrapped herself in her heaviest jacket and wound a cloth around her head, one that could be pulled over her eyes against the dust. Pressing against the wind, she made her way toward the Inyx gathering.

In the shifting light she saw the thousands of mounts. Curtains of sand fell down and parted, giving glimpses of their motionless forms, standing as though asleep, heads down against the storm, nostrils clamped narrow. Not only motionless, but silent in a way that Inyx were seldom silent, they stood without tendrils of thought or emotion. They were closed to her, folded in on themselves. She walked among them, a girl among ghosts. Somewhere Riod stood his post as leader. She thought she could feel him spread thin, a mist of atoms. But his thoughts were invisible to her. Was he already flying far overhead? Or even now moving like a slow wind through the Ascendancy? The herd was to follow his lead, retreating quickly should he raise an alarm, should the fiends recognize that they had visitors.

She took a moment's refuge from the blowing dust in the lee side of a dun-colored mount. He didn't notice her pressed against his side. A trickle of anxiety came from the Inyx, piercing her mind like spilled ink on paper. Startled, she moved away. Touching them was a mistake, but she wanted that touch. This was the first time in thousands of days that she had not felt a warm frame of Inyx cognition. She looked around her, feeling separate, abandoned, and exalted. They were flying to the heart of the bright beast. She let her mind go blank, scoured by the grit-studded wind.

Blank was best. But leaving her thoughts behind, she found that she had become larger, vastly larger. If she trusted her sensations, she would say she hovered above the backs of the gathered mounts, looking down. Flying.

A gust of a thought came to her. *Burning hot. Sweet burning fire.*

An image of fire swept out of reach, traveling through the Inyx throng. But now there were more gusts: singing thoughts, shouting thoughts. She covered her ears against the volume, though it only pinned the shouts inside her head. On her knees now, not flying, hands over her ears, she bore the load of the sky, the column of air above her filled with a terrible weight of mind. She curled into a ball, her head in her thighs. Inyx thoughts marched over her, relentless.

Oh, there were Tarig here. Or shadows of Tarig. Or shadow thoughts of Tarig. Riod was here. He was in the lair, fearless and stealthy.

She was no match for the herd mind and its combined bravery. Lest her fear dilute their strivings, she staggered to her feet. Dragging herself to the edge of the herd, under fathoms of voices, she forced her steps toward her pavilion. The weight of the herd's purpose clung to her, though she was out of its footprint. By the time she plunged through her tent door, she had not one step left in her. Sleep was the safest place for her, the best place to remain out of Riod's way. She dropped onto the pallet. Sank down to oblivion, chased by a last chorus of singing mount voices: *They do not sleep.*

Waking, Sydney found the waxing bright streaming in. Her head felt swollen, her muscles lethargic. Somehow she wrenched herself into a sitting position, feet planted on the floor. It was then that she saw Riod in the open drape of one side of the tent. Covered with dust, only his eyes were clear and recognizable. Sydney went to him.

Mo Ti came too, as though he had been watching for Riod's return.

"Beloved," Sydney said, pressing her hand against Riod's massive face.

Two fell, Riod sent. *It sickened them.*

He spoke of the mounts. But Riod's sending was strong and healthy. He shook his hide, sending dust cascading from his horns and coat. "Did you see them, beloved?"

They are there.

Sydney caught Mo Ti's eye. He stood like a great stump of a tree, waiting.

Riod continued his sending. *White and thin. No colors among them. You each are a color, in heart-sight. But they are not. All of them are hot and clear, without distinction.*

He held Sydney's gaze a long while. *You understand? We found them in the ebb, pursued them through the primacies. None slept, but none knew us. They do not sleep. You understand?*

"What shall I understand, Riod?" She glanced at Mo Ti, trying to decipher what Riod was telling them, but Mo Ti had no help.

They are not as we are.

Mo Ti spoke for the first time. "How are they, then?"

They are all the same.

Sydney's thought came unbidden: Hadenth, who clawed my eyes, was the worst of them. He wasn't the same as the others. She remembered him well, that fallen lord.

Hadenth is not dead, came Riod's startling thought. *Not all the way.*

Nothing more coherent came from Riod, nothing of Hadenth or how one could be dead but not all the way. Still, it was an hour of sweet victory, and Sydney hugged her mount fiercely, then hugged Mo Ti. They had touched the minds of the fiends and melted away again without detection. In the coming days, they would do so again—and again.

And they did, fine-tuning their approach, pursuing the lords. Formerly, of all sentient creatures, the Tarig had been impenetrable to the Inyx. When a mount probed a Tarig's thoughts, that mount found a wall. Nor could the Inyx send either thought or feeling to a lord; they seemed insensible to speaking heart to heart—or defended from it. But a united assault had penetrated where individual attempts failed. One more thing Riod and Sydney learned: a united sending from the massed Inyx could range instantly across the Entire—not just to the Ascendancy, not just in a focused direction. Spying wasn't the only Inyx advantage now; communication came into their arsenal. The gracious lords controlled communications by allowing it only at light speeds, and only under certain conditions. The lords themselves had the bright to send messages. Bright speed was fast indeed. But the Inyx had heart speed, faster yet. Sydney and Mo Ti celebrated.

It was a short-lived celebration.

Riod reported each day after probing in the ebb. He was learning how to keep the mounts from sickening under the pressure; learning better how to distinguish one Tarig from the next, despite lack of color signatures. It wasn't all they needed to know. But Riod was patient—as relentless as Sydney in his loathing of the lords.

It was during a morning's debriefing on the heart-to-heart probes that

Sydney and Mo Ti first fell away from each other, when distrust seeped into their friendship—on the back of grim news. The news was bad enough that Mo Ti waited a few hours to tell Sydney, and that delay did not help him.

Riod had been recounting the ebb's progress, which this time had yielded no strictly new apprehensions of the lords. Mo Ti hardly listened, keeping apart in Sydney's tent, distracted and quiet.

Riod turned his massive head toward the man, and for a moment the two looked into each other's faces. *Tell her*, Riod sent.

"Yes," Mo Ti said. But he remained silent.

"What?" Sydney whispered.

As Sydney watched him with growing unease, Mo Ti began, "I have had a report, mistress. Hard news." Again he hesitated, while impatience streamed from Riod.

Finally: "The Tarig have deceived us."

Sydney's chest constricted. "In our ebb-time work?"

"No, my lady. That work is safe. But as to your person . . ." She nodded for him to continue. "There is a corruption in your sight. They placed it there, when they sent their surgeon to heal you."

Sydney stood very still.

"They watch through your eyes, mistress."

Her voice was barely audible. "Watch? How can they watch?"

"I do not know. They do. So my sources say."

"Sources?" Sydney put a hand to her eyes, pressing her palms into them. Riod nudged her quietly, offering his comfort, but she pushed him away, beseeching Mo Ti. "The fiends see through my eyes?"

Mo Ti watched her with dismay. "Perhaps not perfectly."

"Why would they want my eyes? Can they have guessed our plans, and mean to keep our progress in view?"

"If they thought us traitors, we would be dead. Here is the reason, so I believe: The Tarig think Titus Quinn might come here, to this sway. Because of you."

"He is back?"

"He may come back, it is thought. They think he tried and failed to come here last time."

Her voice was small. "And did he?"

"Mo Ti does not know. It is possible."

"He didn't come for me in the brightship. Why should he come now when he doesn't have a brightship?"

"I do not know. But the Tarig are desperate to find him."

"Why so much effort for . . . such a man?" She put her hands over her eyes once more. "Why ruin me for him? Why, Mo Ti?"

He had no answer. He would rather have taken out his own eyes than have Sydney suffer this violation. She knew that, but still, wasn't it Mo Ti himself who had persuaded her to accept the Tarig surgeon? *Take this gift*, he had said. *You need your sight to win the herds, to show them a new way. . . .* Sydney murmured, "I knew I shouldn't trust the surgeon. Now we know the price for Tarig gifts."

The sounds of the camp came to them distantly—the sounds of riders milling at their tents and speeding off on their mounts to test their skills and ride for the joy of it.

Inside the tent the three of them stood quietly, absorbing the news. "What sources, Mo Ti?" Sydney asked at last. "How would you know what the Tarig have or have not done?"

A long pause stretched out, until it became clear that Mo Ti wouldn't answer.

Riod sent, *The high lady of the floating city. The high lady speaks to him.*

Sydney cried out, "A Tarig speaks to him?"

"No," Mo Ti said. His voice went low. "Cixi. It was Cixi that told me."

Now Sydney had to sit down. She huddled on the side of her pallet, staring at Mo Ti. "Cixi? How do you know Cixi?"

"I will tell you, though it means my life." He turned to Riod, and opened his heart to all that he had so carefully concealed.

Riod picked up the flood of images and shared them with Sydney: Mo Ti kneeling before Cixi, receiving her instruction; Mo Ti traveling at Cixi's request to the Long War battlefields, and there finding an excuse to displease his superiors, securing his banishment to the Inyx sway. All as planned by the high prefect, all carried out by her obedient servant, Mo Ti.

Sydney murmured, "Cixi might have told me this. You might have told me this, Mo Ti. She sends word to me sometimes. She might have told me, if this were true."

Mo Ti said, "It is true, I swear it. She and I convey messages on the bright. I send a message by one of the riders who goes to a navitar loyal to Cixi, and through the navitar, our words find each other." Mo Ti looked to Riod. "These thoughts must be shielded from the herd, Riod."

Riod concurred. He was already doing so.

Mo Ti continued, "I was to prepare you to raise the kingdom. No one must know; her position is too unsafe. She is surrounded by spies. Thus she bid me keep this secret. I was content with this plan at first, but as I grew to love you, it has weighed heavily." He went to his knees in front of her. "Forgive me, my lady."

She gestured at him. "Stand, Mo Ti. They see all that you do." She paused. "You must greet Cixi for me, next time you send to her."

He winced at the sarcasm. "She loves you above all, mistress. As do I."

The day's happiness, beginning with Riod's successes with the ebb's work, had now utterly vanished. Sydney's gaze was strangely lit. From shock. From hatred.

"The mantis lords are inside my head, looking out, Mo Ti. How can I bear this?"

He reached into his pocket and drew out a strip of black silk. "A blind-fold, lady, if you wish it."

She reached for it. "If I wear this, the fiends will know their ruse failed."

Mo Ti said. "Let them know. Will they dare punish us, when they troubled to be sure all this was done in concealment?" She nodded then, and he tied the strip behind her head. She felt calmer once the blindfold was in place.

Mo Ti said, "When you ride, ride free of the blindfold. The herds came to see our success, not our setbacks."

Her voice was flat. "Yes. Our successes."

Mo Ti left at Riod's bidding, and then Riod and Sydney were alone— alone, as they had been in the beginning. The two of them, mount and rider, kept silent company for the rest of that long day. Over and over, she touched the blindfold, making sure it was secure, that the fiends could see nothing. Riod would now transmit glimpses of the world to her. That was how it had been before, and how it was again.

CHAPTER ELEVEN

Whom God would destroy, he first marks well.
—Hoptat the Seer, *Ways of the Miserable God*

IN THE CAMP OF THE GODMEN, Benhu bowed low, so low it brought his nose close to his protruding belly. Quinn and Helice bowed also, acting their roles as followers of the Miserable God.

A wealthy godman, his clean robes evidence he could afford someone to launder them, accepted their obeisance and the gift of their dirigible, which he had commandeered. He also evinced an unwelcome interest in why a poor godman like Benhu and his associates would travel in such luxury, while the thousand servants of the Miserable God traveled by humble means. Around them, the crowd of godmen milled, preparing for their cross-primacy pilgrimage to the Nigh.

"I made pilgrimage to Zu Chang's grave," Benhu said. "I needed transport for the sake of my bad leg." He gestured to clarify which leg prevented him walking up a minoral. "It is your conveyance now, quite rightly, and fitting for your person. No beku for such as you, naturally."

The wealthy godman, bald but sporting a full beard that was black with age, put his hand on the guy ropes that held the dirigible grounded. He plucked at one of them absently and narrowed his eyes at Quinn. "You'll minister at Ahnenhoon?"

"It is our plan, Venerable," Quinn answered. This was the first test of their cover story, that of providing spiritual comfort to the armies.

"Two cripples and yourself?"

Both Benhu and Helice looked decrepit. Benhu had fashioned Helice a

127

walking stick, upon which she leaned, looking every inch a godwoman, deformed, shabby, and long-suffering. A soiled white godwoman's coat covered the nicer silks she had brought from the Rose, which despite Benhu's urging she wouldn't give up.

"No one is without merit," Quinn responded with a mindless smile. "I come new to service of the Miserable God. A late vocation, for which one might use a tutor." He glanced at Benhu.

The venerable murmured. "Ascendancy accent."

"Yes, Excellency. I make no pretenses, though. My mother was a mere steward, though her grave flag is in the bright city."

The godman sized up the airship. "I will pay the contract on this sky bulb. It will free you from an onerous payment." As the three bowed in agreement, the godman glanced at Helice.

"Not garroting, was it?"

Quinn hurried to say "No, the vows forbid. My friend, Li the clumsy, tipped over a candle that caught her bedding ablaze." He shook his head at Helice. "Her throat. A terrible thing."

He caught Helice's eye, and she took her cue, bowing deeply. With her yellow eye lenses and bandaged neck, she could well pass for Chalin, but her injuries also drew attention.

Quinn added, "Many days to you, Excellency. Ask the God of Misery to take no notice of one so low, that she may regain her speech."

The godman nodded, and then turned his attention to his acquisition, sending an attendant up the hanging ladder to the passenger cabin with instruction to prepare the deck for the comfort of the venerable.

As they walked away, Helice's eyes were alight. "I passed."

Quinn put his hand on her shoulder in companionable solicitude, but his fingers dug into her shoulder. "Shut up, I told you." She was giddy from stimulation, gawking at the mass of godmen and their gaudy wagons. Quinn led Helice away, worried more than ever about their disguise. Her wounds looked like an aborted garroting. Only the lords killed that way, and then did it so slowly, restricting the windpipe so suffocation took hours. Why hadn't he thought of how her wound looked? Now, all the way to Ahnenhoon, she would attract attention.

Hundreds of white-robed servants of the Miserable God clustered on the plain, looking like a swarm of moths drying their wings. Among them, beku crowded, either saddled or hitched to wagons, though a few godders planned to walk for the sake of misery. The wagons sported lurid images of death and mayhem, in the hopes of drawing the notice of the deity and to keep Him from casting His eye on more worthy sentients.

Over the expanse of the veldt flowed the bright, the source of heat and light, varied in its intensity between day and ebb. Helice was seeing this marvel for the first time, and she seemed to be thinking hard about how it could be. However the photons had been generated in the past, it was on the verge of failure now. Helice and the Minerva team had rustled up some theories on how energy could transfer across branes. Her theories were only a shadow of Tarig knowledge, though. She realized that, and it must have grated on her. Quinn was sure that when Helice looked on the sights of the Entire, she saw more than its bizarre beauty. She saw power.

Benhu left to find them a conveyance of some kind. It wouldn't be an Adda. The place was still far distant where Adda roosted, ready to ply the trans-primacy winds. As Benhu wound into the crowd, Helice's brow furled. "*Dov jhiqat*," she said in Lucent. *One feels ill*—their signal that she needed privacy to talk to him.

Quinn shook his head. Not a good time. They were surrounded by Chalin, Jout, Ysli, and other beings, any of whom might be curious and listen too closely.

"Now, God damn it," she muttered, not in Lucent. She glared at him, and to prevent a scene, he made a show of helping her to a rock outcropping, passing on the way a cook fire where an industrious godman offered them a skewer of meat at a bad price. At the outcropping, Quinn helped Helice to sit in what passed for shade in the Entire.

"Ren Kai," Helice said, using the name Quinn had assumed.

He put his arm around her shoulder as an excuse to come closer to her, so that she could whisper. "Be quick, then."

"This isn't quick."

"Give me the short version."

"There's been a mistake."

He looked at her, thinking *she* was the mistake.

"Mistake," she repeated. "Dreadful one." She glanced at his ankle with its small cold chain.

He waited, an uneasy wariness coiling in his gut.

She went on. "I have my own people. At Minerva. You knew?"

"Of course. Your heart's set on Stefan's job, right?"

"Yes. But that's not the mistake." She glanced up, checking for Benhu. "You have to take off the cirque."

"I intend to."

"No, take it off and bury it. Right here, as soon as you can." Her eyes pleaded with him. "It's not what you think." Her next words came out in a tumble: "Quinn . . ."

"Ren Kai," he muttered.

"Ren Kai. My people looked at the nan program. It's not localized in its effects. It will spread, spread everywhere. There's no stopping it. Those phage agents—they can't overpower the nan. This land won't survive, or what will survive won't be worth having. Stefan never knew. Only my people. And now you."

"No stopping it? The mortality sequence . . ."

She shook her head. "Ineffective. Stefan admitted they weren't one hundred percent sure. Turns out, they were one hundred percent wrong."

He remained silent, staring at her.

"My team studied the Entire. I thought I'd have to go over on my own, and I was going to build my own transfer capabilities. I wasn't limited by Minerva's thinking. We spent all our time focused on penetrating the Entire with our probes. We came at it from a fresh angle, and when we did, we were able to calculate the mass and energy of the Entire. Then we set a simulation of the nan program into a modeled Entire. And it just kept going; the nan just blew past the phage constraints, feeding on the bright. It never stopped."

The words ignited a vision in his mind that he didn't want to see, didn't want to believe. "It doesn't hold up, Helice. You could have told Stefan. They could have stopped this until they recalibrated things. He'd never endanger the Entire. This place is too valuable, even if he has to share it."

"I couldn't tell Stefan." She snaked a worried look at him. "If he knew I was siphoning off resources to my own effort, I'd be out of there. With nothing.

But I wanted to tell him." She held her fingers a millimeter apart. "I came *this close* to shit canning the whole mission. Instead, I persuaded him to send me along to be your helper in delivering the cirque. But what I really wanted was to tell you privately, without revealing to Stefan that I've been working against him. Don't curl your lip—it's just business. And for the sake of business, you better hear me. No one wants to ruin the Entire, and you're going to."

His hand rested on the chain around his ankle. Cold. Humming. Unless his imagination conjured the feeling. Four, five, one. The sequence. Press it down. All hell breaks loose. Stefan admitted they weren't sure of the effects. But *this* . . . He ran his hand through his hair, gathered in a short queue.

"Think about it this way," her voice wheedled at him. "Why on Earth would I lie?"

"Don't ever say that word," he snapped. "Never here, never name our home."

She snapped back, "Don't use that tone of voice with me. I'm the only reason you're not going to fuck up, big-time."

He didn't want to believe her claim. But what if she was right? He looked at her, trying to see past her surface to the real Helice. If there *was* a real Helice. On her brow little hairs peeked out: start of eyebrows. Her neck, shriveled and scabbed, looked angry and sore.

"Why did you wait this long to tell me?"

"I didn't want to tell you in front of Benhu, and we haven't been alone until now. Maybe he does understand English. I don't trust him."

Quinn sat in silence for a moment, trying to gather his thoughts.

"Bury it. Get rid of it," Helice persisted. "Then go get your daughter, Quinn."

"You don't care about her."

"Frankly? No, I don't. But you need to get that done, and then maybe we can trust you to help us solve our problems a different way." As he waited, she said, "A weapon isn't how we deal with the Tarig. We've got to persuade them."

"This from the woman who likes to torture children?" He couldn't forget her threats during his first sojourn here—that if he didn't come back, she'd ruin Mateo's future.

She rolled her eyes. "From the woman who wants to exploit this universe sensibly. Without destroying the golden goose."

He hacked away at her arguments. "Minerva should have been running simulations. Where the hell was their modeling work?"

"They *did* model the nan sequence. They just didn't do it as well as we did. I was personally involved. And I did it right."

His heart was sinking like a stone into a tar pit. Damn her, anyway. Damn her for keeping this secret, for choosing her own corporate skin before his mission, before their lives. The bright fell on his head, driving out his thoughts, his hopes. Bury the cirque in the ground, she said. Abandon the only weapon they had. How could he do that?

He spotted Benhu approaching, sitting on a beku-hauled wagon that was scarcely bigger than the hauling beast. Benhu had found a wagon, but now what good was it? The image came of sharing a cross-primacy journey with Helice, cooped up in a box the size of a double coffin. He didn't relish sharing the ride. Even if she wasn't outright lying about the cirque, she meant to destroy his mission, preferably with his cooperation.

He started to rise, but she gripped his arm. "Where are you going?"

Quinn shook her off. "Damn you to hell."

She held his gaze, and he saw not the slightest trace of remorse. "I'm not lying. I've got no reason to lie."

He stalked away, disgusted, sickened.

She scrambled after him, saying "Ren Kai, Ren Kai." She almost bumped into an old Chalin godwoman, who cursed her and pointed to her murmuring, "The garrote." Helice caught up to Quinn, pulling on his jacket.

He grabbed her shoulders. "You know what you've done, don't you? Have you got any idea? You've put yourself ahead of the damn whole world. You remember what we came for? Do you?" He shook her.

"Yes," she whispered.

He doubted that she did. She hadn't seen the navitar on the River Nigh. Hadn't seen the needles poking up and down from the clouds, like the future trying to slash its way in. The navitar had said, *I see the world collapsing, the fire descending. I see a burning rose.* To save the Rose, he held the cirque. The chain containing just a little too much force . . .

He remembered the navitar saying *One world excludes the other; both cannot be true. The rose burns, and the All flies apart.*

And could the Entire come apart? The Entire was fragile. Those who lived in the embrace of the storm walls knew that their world depended on the walls standing, on the bright flowing. They expected it would always be so. That there would always be peace—or at any rate, no wars that used virulent technology. No wars with the Rose universe.

In his peripheral vision he saw someone approaching. He turned to find the old godwoman, still harrying them, saying, "Tarig lords could finish the job, a rude girl who can't excuse herself for thrashing an old woman. . . ."

Quinn tossed the godwoman a small coin from the money Benhu had doled out. "Born in a minoral. Our apologies. No rudeness intended."

Benhu drew the wagon up, and jumped from his perch. "What, arguing with a venerable?" He pushed Quinn and Helice aside, bowing and making amends, as Quinn strove to bring his emotions under control.

Walking to the rear of the closed wagon, Quinn jerked open the double doors and gestured Helice inside. With the godwoman still close by, Helice couldn't protest, and allowed herself to be shut in.

Stepping back to look at the wagon and the hauling beast, Quinn's mood wasn't improved. The skinny beku hung his head as though defeated by the prospect of heading across the veldt. The wagon looked like a doghouse on wheels, painted a green so vivid it hurt the eyes. On the side, it sported an elaborate painting of the grinning mouth of the God of Misery.

Benhu approached, having at last shaken the old woman. Quinn circled around to the wagon's other side, with Benhu following. There, the design repeated, but the mouth frowned rather than grinned.

Quinn muttered, "God will be watching us across the whole cursed veldt."

Benhu beamed. "And I only paid fifty minors. Room enough for two to sleep, if curled a bit. Perhaps the girl will enjoy it." He leered at the wagon, where they could hear Helice swearing already, in Lucent.

"*You* might try lying with her, Benhu."

At Quinn's expression, Benhu sobered. "Causing trouble? If she displeases you, Ren Kai . . ."

"What? You'll send her away, the long way home?"

Benhu pulled on his wispy mustache, a sure sign that he was thinking and coming up empty.

Quinn stood by the wagon, imagining the Miserable God grinning at him. Did the cirque around his ankle threaten the land itself? Had he come here hobbled to some unthinkable destructive machine? Helice must be lying. But she had planted the doubt. He felt the weight of the chain resting uneasily against his skin. What now? He couldn't go back. But what lay forward? He needed time to think. Perhaps, in close confinement, he could wring a different story from Helice. He meant to try.

Overhead, an airship drifted by, barely higher than the tents and the beku, its motors faintly humming. Standing in the open hatchway, the rich godman they'd spoken to earlier peered at them, and Benhu bowed as the dirigible passed.

Rising, Benhu said, "Under way." The camp was on the move. "Our great mission begins," he said unctuously. He gestured to the door of the wagon. "Ride in comfort, Ren Kai."

"I'll take the reins, Benhu," Quinn said, climbing aboard. The beku turned as Quinn took a seat on the bench, fixing him with a baleful stare.

Benhu gave the beast an agile kick in the flank, provoking it to strain into the harness. Quinn handed Benhu aboard, and they joined a line of coaches and groaning beku. Since they had days ago decided to trade speed for camouflage, their journey would be long: a week to the place where a drove of Adda might be found. As Quinn had formerly conceived it, Helice would know her Chalin manners by then, the wagon serving for a private classroom. But now the world was tipping sideways. Unless she was lying. He held onto that notion. It was so like Helice to lie and twist facts to her purposes. Her purposes. Eventually, in the little green wagon, he'd discover what those were.

Benhu looked around him in satisfaction, drawing out his pipe and lighting it. "All according to plan," he sighed. "Proceed, Ren Kai." He waved in the direction of the Nigh.

CHAPTER TWELVE

Gond run no races,
Jouts release no memories,
Legates suffer no slights,
Inyx abide no roofs,
And Hirrin speak no lies.

—a saying of the Magisterium

"D

O YOU LOVE US, DEPTA?"

Lady Chiron sat in the garden by a small stone pool. Depta had not been long in Chiron's service; only one hundred days. Being new to her post attending the high lady, Depta had just lately become aware of how much time the bright lady spent in the former garden of Titus Quinn. In the center of the garden, a pool reflected the bright in a hot, silver circle. Chiron sat next to it, trailing a four-fingered hand in the water.

"I do love you, lady," Depta said in all truth. Hirrin couldn't lie without succumbing to panic, and it was for this reason that many Tarig, as well as other exalted personages, preferred Hirrin attendants.

Every day Chiron invoked the loyalty test with Depta: Do you love us? The day that Depta said no, she would be retired from service, one way or another. That day could not be imagined. Who could fail in devotion to such a lady—not only Tarig, but one of the ruling five? Depta had always dreamed of a lofty calling. Her parents, shopkeepers in Rim City, had instilled in her the love of service, pride in the meritocracy, and the hope of advancement. Growing up on the rim of the Sea of Arising, Depta had spent her childhood in full view of the Ascendancy, forever in the sky, forever beckoning. Rim City was a part of no sway. Existing to serve travelers on the sea and its rivers Nigh, it called for no allegiance from its varied inhabitants. For one such as Depta, allegiance was a necessity. In time the Magisterium fulfilled that need, and then the lady Chiron. Depta's appointment to the lady's service and her elevation to preconsul had been the culmination of her dreams; she could hope for no more. In the service of this exalted being, even minor tasks took on a nearly holy luster.

Today's work, however, was of the highest import, relating to matters of state: the capture of Titus Quinn.

Depta introduced the subject by reporting on Hu Zha's mission. "The legate Hu Zha has set out on his journey to Master Yulin's camp."

"The miscreant Yulin is no master."

"No, your pardon." Amending her statement, Depta said, "Hu Zha will soon arrive in the camp of your servant Yulin."

"Likely our quarry will bypass Yulin and so quickly go to Ahnenhoon."

"Yes, Bright Lady." Depta was sure that Chiron had spies everywhere near Ahnenhoon. All did not depend on one fat old former master of a sway, one of thin loyalties. But Chiron had offered him his life and restoration of his privileges, if he proved himself useful. Depta thought the chances good of Titus Quinn making his way to Yulin's camp. He would seek Ji Anzi there. He was a man of heart, not logic, and rumor had it that the two of them were lovers. She said as much to Lady Chiron.

"The girl Anzi. We should have brought her here to discover what she knows."

"My lady, I believe she told Yulin all that she knows. Their plans were simple: to meet at Ahnenhoon, so Yulin has affirmed. He claims she knows no more than that."

"In any case we do well not to alert Anzi that she is watched."

These secrets made Depta nervous. If she was questioned about any of this by others—by a lord, for example—she would have to disclose all, thus forcing her to betray the lady. May the Miserable God not look on me, Depta thought with desperate piety. For fear of this happenstance, Depta avoided meeting any other Tarig, and kept to her quarters when not on the lady's business.

The lords placed all their attention on the Inyx sway, thinking that Titus Quinn would come for his daughter, to finish the work he had begun last time. Depta's constant hope was that Chiron would quickly find the man of the Rose, and release Depta from her fear of inadvertent betrayal.

Chiron's voice became thoughtful. "Do you find it strange, Depta, that one who came to the All to save a child should have instead killed a child?"

As she sat next to the pond, Chiron must have been thinking of the Tarig child that Titus Quinn had drowned in another garden of the Ascendancy. He had pushed Small Girl's body under the water. Small Girl had time to shout his name, bringing Tarig rushing down into the garden. He had fled by then, an infamous defeat for the bright lords, and one that Chiron brooded upon.

"Strange indeed, lady. He was ever . . ." Depta fluttered her lips, thinking of just the right word.

"Malicious?"

"Well. I was going to say 'contradictory.'" Indeed, he had courted Lady Chiron, then abandoned her; accepted her protection, then rejected it. Such a rejection filled Depta with amazement. What manner of man was this? One could never quite know what he would do. And then killing Small Girl—no doubt because she raised the alarm, because she discerned his identity. Her last words were a scream of *Titus Quinn!* To stifle those words, he pushed her face under the waters of the pond. Depta shuddered, almost pitying him.

"You are too psychological," Chiron said. "He murdered the girl. A violent act. It must have quite thrashed the waters."

Now Depta too stared at the pond, much smaller than the one where Small Girl had died, but still. . . . "They found her floating almost peacefully, the rumor had it."

"Hnn. We will bring this matter up when we see Titus once more." As eager as Lady Chiron was to find him, she couldn't pursue Titus herself. But when warning came of the man's arrival, she would quickly pounce. Traveling by the bright, Ahnenhoon was as close as the other side of the garden wall. It would take as long to rush to her ship as it would to speed to the great fortress.

Once the lady had Titus Quinn, Depta didn't know how Chiron hoped to keep the other lords from their justice. Perhaps she merely desired to be the one who carried out that justice. Nor did Depta understand exactly how the lady was going to protect Yulin from the lords, when the time came. But her mistress had few doubts, and looking at the lady, clad in draped silver, her features so beautiful—no, Depta didn't doubt, either.

However, Depta worried about the lady's obsession with Titus Quinn. The fact that he had returned undetected to this very garden grated on Chiron. He had come to the bright city in perfect disguise and had even stood before Cixi and the doomed Lord Hadenth. At times, Chiron shook her head and laughed, as though a favorite enemy had won a game.

Chiron dipped her hand in the pond water once more. "Leave us, Preconsul. Send word the moment that Hu Zha reports from Yulin's camp. The very moment, ah?"

Depta dipped low, crossing her front legs in a complex movement reserved for important bows. Leaving the garden, Depta made her way along a narrow path toward her suite in the Magisterium.

In the canals of the Ascendancy, carp flashed under the bright, the closest thing to pets that the Tarig kept. As Depta watched them swim, she reviewed her report to Chiron. To her dismay, she realized what she had forgotten to say, that the agent in Yulin's camp must have access to the bright to send a timely message, and this secret means of messaging needed a lord or lady's permission. Once past his usefulness, the agent must be removed from life, to preserve secrecy, since it pleased the Tarig to limit knowledge of bright-speed communications.

When Depta returned to the arched doorway leading to the garden, she saw Chiron sitting in a chair, no longer looking at the pool, but rather gazing peacefully into the garden. She considered not imposing herself on this peaceful scene. Yet her report had been incomplete, and to rectify this, Depta walked softly toward the lady.

She was resting. As Depta drew near, the lady appeared to be in a profound sleep. But her eyes were open.

Depta fluttered her lips. Then softly, "Gracious Lady?"

Chiron took no notice. She gazed outward, unseeing, Depta thought with a pang of alarm.

"Bright Lady," she said. "May I have leave to interrupt?"

As she stared at the Tarig lady, Depta's resolve trailed away. Chiron's left hand rested on the arm of her chair, as though growing from it. Her face wasn't relaxed, but frozen in a terrible, calm beauty.

Depta looked around her, up to the high walls with their stony windows, but the manse looked empty, its windows sparkling with the light of the inner precincts.

Stepping close to the lady, Depta extended her long neck within a hoof's span of Chiron's face, trying and failing to make eye contact. She whispered, "Lady Chiron . . ."

Chiron jerked her head, focusing her eyes on the startled Depta. "Ah?" Chiron said with great vehemence. "Ah?" She rose, coming to her full height so quickly that Depta staggered backwards.

Chiron's face folded into a deep scowl such as Depta had never seen before. The lady bent over, staring into Depta's astonished face. In a voice too loud for such close quarters, she said, "Left, then came back?"

"Yes, Lady, Bright Lady, I forgot—"

Chiron's expression was awful. "Forgot, ah? Now coming here, sneaking . . ." She advanced as Depta inadvertently backed away, her whole body trembling. Surely the lady's pique would pass. Oh, let it be soon.

But Chiron's energy only mounted as her voice rasped, "Spying, Depta, does one spy?"

Spy. The word stunned Depta. She opened her mouth to deny it, but in a lightning move, Chiron went to one knee and grabbed Depta's neck, holding it so that she couldn't move her head. The fingers closed around her throat, constricting.

Depta's vision blurred in pain. "Lady," she whispered. "Gracious Lady. I do not lie."

The fingers opened a little, allowing Depta to breathe. The lady still knelt in front of Depta, locking gazes with her.

Lowering her voice, Chiron said, "Preconsul, do you love us?"

With a visceral shock, Depta realized that she did not at this moment. She tried to control her panic, regulate her breathing. Gathering her courage, she whispered, "No, my lady. I am afraid to die."

Chiron's gaze was steady and long. In a quiet voice she asked, "When you came back to the garden and passed through the arch, did you love us then?"

A tear forced its way out, falling down Depta's cheek. She whispered, "Yes, I did love you then."

Chiron released her grip, watching Depta with such intensity that Depta feared she had resumed her catatonic state. The garden trees rustled under a breeze, and the pond waters lapped against the stone sides.

Finally the lady rose, smoothing her soft metal skirt. "We will not speak of this again, Depta. We have the world to govern. You cannot know us, nor think that we see things as you do. Leave off curiosity, and only serve me, Preconsul. You understand?"

Depta crossed her legs in a shaky bow. "Yes . . . yes, Lady." She eyed the arched gateway, yearning to be beyond it.

Chiron followed Depta's gaze, and laughed. "Yes, go then. Compose yourself, Depta. Never worry until the day you wake and find you do not love us."

Depta stumbled away, dizzy with relief, her stomach roiling. Then, remembering her reason for returning to the garden, she turned back to the lady, saying, "Our agent in Yulin's camp needs the bright to—"

Chiron interrupted, waving a long-fingered hand. "Granted. Let him send word by the bright."

Depta nodded dumbly, and stumbled away. What was that posture of stone a moment before, and the terrible gaze in the lady's eyes? Truly, Lady Chiron was right in saying, *You cannot know us.* How, Depta thought, had she grown complacent so easily? Depta had assumed a level of worshipful comfort around her mistress. Oh, mistake, mistake. Depta would not again commit the error of thinking a Tarig was like a Hirrin—was like anything but a Tarig.

Yes, that was an important lesson. But more—Depta now wondered if it was possible to feel love and terror at the same time. Her heart held great love for the noble lady. And now for the first time, fear.

CHAPTER THIRTEEN

The Three Vows are these:

Withhold the knowledge of the Entire from the non-Entire.
Impose the peace of the Entire.
Extend the reach of the Entire.

—from *The Radiant Way*

ANZI CROUCHED BEFORE YULIN, her head on the floor in obeisance. Although her uncle held court in a ragged tent these days instead of his Chalin sway palace, he still ruled his few followers, and her. Now he intended to marry her to a man she didn't love—an officious, strutting legate whom she could barely tolerate. That man stood in the shadows of the tent, watching her.

"Uncle of My Deliverance," she murmured by way of greeting to Yulin.

Yulin waved a hand at her in impatience. "Yes, yes, all the titles and so forth. Get up, Ji Anzi."

Anzi stood, wishing, profoundly wishing, to be elsewhere. "Uncle. You are looking fit." He had lost weight in his trek across half the realm. His neck hung with folds of loose skin. He wore a dark green sash over his humble silks, the only strong color or ornamentation that distinguished him from the beku tenders outside.

"You will not flatter, Anzi. I have no time for your foolishness." From Yulin's haggard appearance, he hadn't slept in some time, yet she sensed a new vitality about him. Her uncle had lived for his palace gardens too long; now he concentrated on outwitting the Tarig. It made him more alive. This was, in

Anzi's view, the thing that one learned from the Rose: to strive, to burn intensely. Everyone who touched Titus Quinn came away changed—sometimes for the worse, it was true, if one longed for something one could not have.

Her uncle had visions of aligning with powerful human traders when the barriers between worlds softened. But today the barriers remained, and the Tarig were on alert. Worse, the lords had discovered his recent complicity in hiding Titus Quinn. Yulin had fled, abandoning the sway to his ambitious brother, Zai Gan. Also exiled and in hiding were Anzi and Yulin's oldest wife, Suzong. Fortunate to escape the slow death meted out for treason, they had taken on disguises and fled separately across the sway and beyond it, to meet up again near the plains of war. Yulin had become a beggar, and Suzong a half-mad scholar, wandering. Anzi had attached herself to a military enlistment squad and traveled on an army transport down the Nigh. All the while her thoughts were on a man of the Rose, praying that he had escaped God's notice and reached home safely. So that he could return.

Old Suzong sat at Yulin's side, warning Anzi with a pursed look to be amenable to instruction.

"How may I serve, Uncle?" Anzi whispered.

"You can serve by curbing your plots." Yulin pointed a finger at her. "Do not speak." When she shut her mouth, he went on, "You can serve by restraining your instincts to disobey, willfully cross me, and flout convention. That's how you can show me your loyalty, and your gratitude, which you can never repay if you live one hundred thousand days, which you will not because of errant adventurism."

Suzong coughed, keeping her eyes on the floor.

Yulin rounded on her. "You have something to say, wife?"

She pulled her high-necked jacket more closely around her, but didn't avert her eyes. He had been young and she, old, when he married her, but that hadn't affected their devotion—or the distribution of power.

"I would only say that marriage should be a happy topic, husband."

Yulin snorted. "And so it would have been, if my niece had been properly appreciative of Ling Xiao Sheng."

Stepping forward, the odious Ling bowed—a long drop for one so tall. He was the heir of a wealthy family with ties to high consuls in the Magisterium. Somehow, Yulin reasoned that such a match could help his precarious position. But surely there was only one way to survive now: to elude the Tarig completely. How could a minor marriage weigh in against treason? And besides, she had no intention of marrying anyone, much less Ling Xiao Sheng, who was too anxious for children and domination over a pregnant wife. Add to that, the man picked at his teeth with his nails, and stank. Even if it was true that they all stank in this hideaway, she couldn't bear him.

Ling Xiao Sheng rested his right hand on his sword pommel, watching Anzi with eyes the color of urine.

Yulin adjusted his sash and waved at Anzi's suitor. "Speak, and tell us what you have told me privately."

The man smiled at Anzi, receiving her cool gaze in return. "Ji Anzi, we have had our betrothal announced some forty days, and now comes time to set our marriage day, which is your privilege to do." When she didn't respond, he added, "Which you have not seen fit to do."

"No," she agreed. Cutting a glance at her uncle she added, "Yet."

"Yet," Ling repeated in some confusion.

As hard as it was, she managed a tepid smile at him. "Yet."

Yulin looked from one of them to the other, and exploded. "Yet, yet, yet! What game is this?" He stormed forward. "Farting Gonds, I'll have an answer."

Anzi held her place, but averted her eyes so as not to challenge her uncle. He did need her agreement. And she heartily wished she could comply, wished that she were the kind of woman who wanted a household to manage, and a high station in the meritocracy of the Entire. But Anzi had dedicated herself to the welfare of Titus Quinn. If he came back, she would be at his side, both because of how much she owed him, and because it was inconceivable to stay at home when adventures beckoned.

"Surely, One Who Shines," Anzi murmured, "you have higher concerns than Ling Xiao Sheng's marriage date? One dislikes to waste the time of the master of the sway."

Yulin darkened. "Am I so? The master of the sway?" He spread his arms to encompass the tent, the camp. "I am master of nothing. And we know why. We know why I have left my beloved halls, left my gardens. And who sits there now."

His half brother Zai Gan sat there. A bitter blow. Anzi whispered, "But you are always the master of the sway to me." Zai Gan was a fat imposter, by all accounts a lackey of the high prefect Cixi.

Suzong now stepped in. "The date, Anzi. We will have the date."

Thinking quickly, Anzi said, "Ten days to finish my purities. That will be the date of Ling Xiao Sheng's wedding."

"Purities," Suzong mused. "A young woman must purge herself of other lovers, before first entering her husband's chamber." Her voice dropped an octave. "We waive the purities. She is pure enough, eh Ling?"

Ling Xiao Sheng blinked. As to Anzi's other lovers, he might not have thought that she had had so many. Dozens. Hundreds, perhaps. He looked at her with a new appraisal.

Anzi murmured, "I would not want to bear my husband another man's child, mistress."

This utterance hung darkly in the room. Let them wonder about Titus Quinn and if we are lovers, Anzi thought. That must give them pause, to think that she was so favored by him. Yulin must still wonder what power Titus Quinn had, and if he spoke for the Rose, or whether he was just a man acting on his own, pursuing a lost daughter. This was Yulin's dilemma, whether to be for him or against him—for converse with the Rose or, according to the vows, against it.

But this wasn't a dilemma for Anzi. She was for the Rose. That realm of vast space, that place that held the Earth . . . She should have been born there, not here. Her longing for the place was the reason she had snared Titus Quinn's escape capsule so long ago and brought him here. Hers was the first act of treason, by the vows. That it had destroyed his family caused her deep shame. But now she would make it up to Titus. If he came back.

Yulin scowled at the possibility that she might be bearing the man's child. "Have you not . . . Since then, have you . . ." He gave up, glaring at Suzong.

Suzong beckoned Anzi forward and pulled her down so she could whisper in her ear. "Courses, girl. None?"

Anzi murmured back, "We may know in ten days, Aunt. Wait that long, I beg you."

Smiling sweetly, Suzong whispered. "I'll have your liver on a skewer if you're lying."

Anzi turned to Yulin and Ling. "Ten days' wait, for the sake of the purities." It would buy time. It would give Titus Quinn a few days to come back. To find her. Then, after ten days, she could claim she *was* pregnant. That would buy even more time. But of course there had been no intimacies, so that excuse would last only so long.

Anzi gave Ling Xiao Sheng a large smile, and his face brightened. I would rather lie with a Gond, she thought.

Yulin dismissed her, but despite her acquiescence, he felt no happier. Anzi had always been an inveterate liar and a sometime thief, when it suited her purposes. But he thought that she loved him, and for his sake perhaps she would conform this time. He wanted to tell her that if she didn't, he might soon lie at the feet of the Tarig. He wanted to tell her that the Lady Chiron had discovered their hiding place, and that he had been forced to change allegiance. However, for the sake of trapping Titus Quinn, that must remain secret.

Yulin knew that he might be as good as dead right now. It kept him awake at ebb-time, and pursued his thoughts during the day. On the one hand, the gracious lords did wish to look *gracious* in the eyes of their subjects. It would not be seemly for them to subject the master of a sway to the garrote. Yet no matter how skillfully the Lady Chiron might argue on his behalf, she was only one among the five ruling lords. For this reason, he must forge alliances such as this marriage, so that when the time came, others would speak for him.

Yes, let her marry Ling, he thought. Yulin was more determined than ever to arrange his personal affairs. Anzi must relinquish her unhealthy devotion to the man of the Rose. Let Anzi not seek him out, nor help him, should he ever return. Let her turn her attention to a husband and the large household that Ling Xiao Sheng could provide. And let her reconcile herself to Titus Quinn's capture. If the man came here—and Yulin almost hoped he would not—he was Chiron's.

His gut churning with anxiety, Yulin turned to Ling. Was it possible for this vain lordling to curb his exaggerated self-regard? "Be courteous to her, Ling Xiao Sheng."

The man drew himself up. "Of course, Master Yulin."

Yulin waved at him in irritation. "Your posture, your attitude. Soften it. Understand that Anzi is proud. Woo her, man!"

Ling took that for a direct command. Stooping, he ducked out the tent flap in search of Anzi.

He was alone again with Suzong. She murmured, "He can never replace the other one in Anzi's heart."

"Ling doesn't want her heart. Let her flutter over whom she will."

"And what about *your* heart, husband?"

His wife well understood that he was uncertain where his best interests lay. The Rose might be as powerful as the Ascendancy—someday. In that day, Yulin could be powerful too, more so than any master of a sway.

Yulin sighed. "I tire of speaking of hearts."

"But you must choose," she murmured, "between the man of the Rose and the lady of the Ascendancy. A matter of hearts."

"A matter of power," Yulin spat. "In the end, what does Titus Quinn promise us? Dreams of alliances with the Rose. Dreams, not power."

Suzong waved her hand toward the camp. "*They* think he has power. He destroyed the brightships. He felled Lord Hadenth. Every sentient in the Entire has heard by now and wonders what power the Rose may have." She sucked on her teeth. "Choose carefully, husband."

What he meant for a whisper came out as a snarl. "It appears you and Anzi have already chosen."

Suzong demurred. "What does it matter what women think? The choice is yours, husband."

Yes, his choice. But not yet forced upon him. When and if Titus Quinn came to this camp, *then* he would have to choose whether to alert Lady Chiron. And if Anzi was safely married, then Quinn would have no reason to come here. Damn the girl and her pitiful excuses. Let her marry.

Ten days, and he would officiate himself.

CHAPTER FOURTEEN

The bright is high and the Tarig far away.
—a saying

SYDNEY LAY CURLED UP ON RIOD'S BROAD BACK, dozing in deep ebb-time. Around them the herd milled quietly, munching at tufts of grass, tails flicking at gnats. But they were elsewhere; their herd-thought ranging far outward, past the encampment, the roamlands sway, the primacy—to Entirean distances.

Riod guided his fellow mounts, picking his way through the eddies of the mental realm, tracking down Tarig minds, then skirting them, hovering to send a focused tendril inside this mind and that one. The Tarig so far were insensible to these probes, so Riod judged. In this heart-realm, he picked his way with the delicacy of a cat, the grace of a dancer. Tarig consciousness might be strange ground, but Riod and his legions were born to the territory, making few mistakes. Riod became the surgeon of minds, setting the point of entry and knifing a way through the maze of Tarig cognition. All the while, he performed an even more difficult task: to screen Inyx personal thoughts from leaking through, betraying a foreign presence.

What he sought was the color of fear. *Find the weakness, then strike*, Mo Ti had advised. If the Tarig had a place where their powers stretched thin, where they feared attack, that was what Sydney wished to know and exploit. Superficially, in their hearts all Tarig looked the same. Slide the knife deeper, and sprays of color came to Riod, nameless colors in far ranges of the spectrum.

They were getting to know this most particular, this most peculiar mind territory: the very psyche of the lords. But nothing could have prepared them for what the herd-gathering had uncovered an arc of days ago.

147

Riod had led the mounts into the mind of a Tarig child. It was not a pleasant visit.

As all sentients knew, Tarig bore few children. Fewer still were publicly seen. But Riod and his fellow mounts discovered that Tarig offspring were not only small in number, they were rare. The combined intention of the herd had then begun searching for youngsters to investigate. To the astonishment of the Inyx, and despite long hours of looking, the heart probes could identify only two young Tarig. Across the vastness of the Entire, there existed only two.

Curious, Riod led the search into the mind of one of these youngsters, a boy. It was a dark and twisted place, this child's mind. Immature thoughts of overweening selfishness combined with spikes of paranoia and desire. Returning ebb after ebb to this individual, Riod and his herd-mates became convinced that the creature combined aspects of adult mentation and childish incompetence. Hearing of this, Sydney wondered if the lords had chosen not to correct for birth flaws. Was the youngster mentally damaged?

But in days to come, Riod had touched the mind of the other child, finding the same kind of cognitive patterns. Eventually, the herd came to a startling conclusion: Not even these two were children. Though to outsiders they seemed to be youngsters, they were merely small, imperfect versions of Tarig adults. With the memories of one of their designated parents, they had remnants of selfhood, but were profoundly mentally diminished. They were like half-formed, half-mad Tarig.

The same insight came to the herd all at once, in a moment of consternation and amazement. The Tarig had no children.

How they reproduced could not be determined. If they didn't die as most creatures did, then they might not need children. But strangely, they spent effort on maintaining the appearance of having them.

Drowsing on Riod's back, Sydney circled this mystery, letting her thoughts hover near Riod's, but not intruding. Riod had claimed that Lord Hadenth, whom her father had killed when he stole the brightships, was not truly dead. Were the mantis lords immortal then? Why would they hide this fact with such elaborate deceptions? The dream visits would continue, with increased intensity. The Tarig were hiding things. These were the things Sydney most wished to know.

She stirred, moving closer to Riod's horned neck to grasp the nearest horn. Riod was her sole comfort these days, her only friend. Even Akay-Wat seemed blameful. The Hirrin sided with Mo Ti, of course, arguing for him until Sydney begged for quiet. Sydney's heart had cooled toward Mo Ti. His lies stung, that he had been sent by Cixi. So then, no one could be trusted whose mind was not fully open to her. How did sentients form bonds of love, and never know heart-thoughts? Things that you said could be made up on the spot. Only heart-thoughts were the truth. Her hand curled around Riod's posterior horn.

Riod dimly felt Sydney's weight on his back. The herd was hunting far away, circling the Ascendancy, where the Tarig clustered most brightly. Lately the herd discerned that the glittering in the center of the world was not just a concentration of individuals compounding their light. Riod was the first to sense that the quality of light was no massing of individuals. Rather, there was one Tarig whose light burned incandescent. Difficult to see or even approach, this individual's thoughts did not form the maze so typical of Tarig minds. For all their confusion, mazes were supremely organized.

This heart-scape was chaos.

Most interesting of all, the lords hid this individual most carefully. Somewhere in the Ascendancy stirred a being on whom shadows of fear fell in fantastic stains. Here was the place around which Tarig defenses bulked. Therefore an enemy would do well to discover its secrets.

As Sydney stirred on Riod's back, her blindfold fell loose, bringing the glow of ebb-time to her sight. She noticed that Mo Ti stood in the distance with his mount, his hand resting along Distanir's flank. She wanted to go to him, to ask him if his devotion was firm. But whatever he answered, it would just be words.

She adjusted the blindfold, lest the fiends see Mo Ti and Distanir. Sydney had become the instrument of her own destruction, a danger to her sway. Blindfold in place, and darkness resuming, she felt a pang of remorse for what she was becoming. Her hate of the Tarig seemed to be driving out all other feelings. What would happen if someday, nothing but hate remained?

CHAPTER FIFTEEN

Snatch a whisker from the dragon, steal air from an Adda,
skimp the profits of a Gond, but never rob God of misery.
—from *The Hundred Harmonies*

IT WAS THE THIRD DAY OF THE JOURNEY. The wagon jounced over the rutted land, bearing Quinn and Helice in the overheated interior. Above them, on the driving platform, Benhu drove the beku forward, his pipe smoke occasionally drifting into the wagon's interior, adding stench to the suffocating heat and wretched company. Quinn looked at Helice, crouching in the corner like a gargoyle.

She was lying, damn her to hell. Lying, and people would die because of it. Don't use the weapon, she argued. But if he didn't use it, the Entire would feed on the Rose. The Tarig were in beta testing mode now, taking one star at a time, but eventually, it would all ignite. The ultimate catastrophe was beyond what he could envision, but it was all too easy to imagine the small deaths of people like his brother, like Emily and Mateo. Like Caitlin.

From the corner, came Helice's murmur: "Get rid of the chain, Quinn. Get rid of it now."

"Do you want me give it to you? Is that what you want?"

"I really don't care. Think I want to blow the place up all by myself? Don't be stupid."

"Did Lamar know about the cirque? Is he part of your extracurricular Minerva group?"

"Lamar doesn't know. Think I'd tell a friend of yours?"

Quinn's frustration mounted. She was hiding something. Lamar had, in fact, known—Quinn was sure of it. *I'm sorry*, he said. *Remember that I'm an old man.* He didn't contradict her about Lamar. Right now he wanted to accumulate a list of her lies, and see if he could trap her into more.

The slats of the wagon let in a spray of light from the sky. Quinn saw Helice sitting like a demon in the corner, dark and intense, hiding behind a façade of woman-trying-to-save-the-world. "You disgust me," he said.

She jerked to her feet. "I don't have to listen to this shit anymore." She went for the wagon door.

In an instant, Quinn was dragging her back, yanking her to the floor. She reached up to claw at his face, drawing up her knee and aiming for his groin. She missed, and he pinned her down, trembling with anger. "You stay here. You belong in the dark. If I have to tie you up, you're staying inside."

The door of the wagon flew open, revealing Benhu with his hands on his hips. "By the mucking bright, be quiet! What's amiss?"

Quinn hadn't noticed the wagon had stopped. Beyond the door he saw a herd of godmen spread out over the veldt, stirring up boiling clouds of dust. As Helice scrambled back to her perch in the corner, Quinn crawled out of the wagon and shut the doors behind him.

He joined Benhu on the driving platform, and soon they were under way again, with the beku emitting short bleats of protest.

"Excellency," Benhu said, cutting a worried glance at him. "You should tell me if we've got trouble. The lord won't like there being trouble."

"Mind your own business, Benhu."

"The woman is causing an uproar?"

To shut him up, Quinn said, "Yes."

"Trouble from the beginning." Benhu snorted. "Perhaps she'll die of some mishap. The camp is full of thieves and malcontents."

"These are godmen," Quinn muttered.

"Yes, so we do well to go armed." Benhu glanced at the bulge in Quinn's jacket, where he kept his knife.

Quinn's adrenaline faded, but in his mind he heard Helice's arguments, the ones she'd been hammering on for days: In using the nan technology, he would loose a plague of matter that would overwhelm the Entire. *Imagine,* Helice had said, *the ground, the plains, the expanse of the Entire pooling into slag.*

Imagine the profound subsidence as the middle collapses, pulling the edges of the world into a spreading gravitational sink. Even now, she had asked, how do the walls remain standing? How little might it take for them to calve off from their foundations? No walls, no Entire. Is that what you want?

Quinn watched the miles pass, coming closer to the Nigh and transport to Ahnenhoon. He couldn't bring himself to trust Helice. Or the cirque.

That ebb, they cooked a meal at their small campfire, having bought meat from the provisioning wagons.

Helice had taken on a more conciliatory demeanor, attempting conversation over the cook fire and even being gracious to Benhu. Afterward, they sat gazing at the fire. Sitting next to Quinn, Helice murmured in halting Lucent, "No pretty colored plants."

Quinn frowned, not understanding.

"Flowers," she said under her breath, falling back on the English word. "There aren't any." He had told her before; now she was seeing it for herself.

"Don't use dark languages," he whispered to Helice, and she frowned at his curt response.

The Entire, for all its beauty, had no flowering plants. Nothing even remotely similar to a rose, for example, which scholars had no doubt seen through the veils. It had often struck Quinn how odd it was that the Rose universe was named for one flower on one world. Was the Earth so unique in that regard, that no flower on any world could rival what they saw? Even so, after all the things that the Tarig had copied from the Rose, the rose was not among them.

Leaving the cleanup to Benhu, Quinn left, walking alone through the camp. The bright fell to shades of gray and lavender, casting a rosy glow onto the white godmen's robes and the dusty wagons. The sky bulbs swayed at their ropes, including the one at the center, the dirigible of the Most Venerable, the high godman who had arrived in midcourse of the procession. From here, Quinn could just see the tall flank of the great airship looming over the smaller vessels and carts.

The camp teemed with the varied species of the Entire, including the Chalin—in this primacy, the majority—as well as the agile and hairy Ysli, squat Jouts, and four-footed Hirrin. Gonds could be seen as well, borne on litters by their more mobile fellow godmen. Conspicuously absent from the throng were the Inyx. There were different styles of sentience here, ways of knowing that represented the pick of the Rose universe—or at least what the Tarig had chosen to copy. Some, like the Adda, knew direction and magnetism. To these floating gasbags, perhaps non-Adda sentients appeared inept. And to the Inyx, those who spoke audibly might also seem hobbled. Quinn wondered if the chief who had befriended Sydney read her thoughts. Benhu implied that Sydney had some measure of happiness, and Quinn hoped it was true. It would be some time until they were reunited. After Ahnenhoon. He would find a way.

His thoughts circled back to Helice. To his surprise, he found himself certain for the first time. She was fabricating a story about the cirque's flaws.

If what she claimed were true, Helice would certainly have told Stefan. No one, not Stefan, not Helice, wanted to ruin the Entire. Helice maintained that telling Stefan would expose her schemes at Minerva—her secret effort to penetrate the Entire on her own. She was planning to replace Stefan at the helm of Minerva, and she had her supporters, including, she said, Booth Waller and others. But would she jeopardize the Entire for the sake of that job? She didn't need Minerva. She could take what she knew about the Entire to any of the giant companies and name her terms.

So why hadn't she told Stefan about the cirque's defects?

Although he didn't know the answer, he was sure she was hiding something. Whatever her goal, he wasn't going to help her. The vise that had been gripping his heart since the day before began to loosen. He still didn't know the course he should take, but he was coming down on the side of the cirque.

He had walked farther than he'd planned, so that by the time he headed back to the wagon, most of the camp slept, some on the ground and some in tents or their wagons. From a distance, he saw his green wagon. With the fire gone out, Benhu stood by it, kicking the ashes. Helice must be asleep inside, perhaps helped by the godman's potions. Benhu stood before the wagon door, staring at it.

Then he removed something from his jacket. It was a knife. He reached for the wagon's rear doors.

Quinn's hand went to his side. The knife was gone. Benhu had it.

He broke into a run, racing to the wagon. By the time he got there, Benhu was inside. Quinn nearly tore off one of the doors as he launched himself inside. In the darkness, he heard a struggle. Helice cried out. He caught a glimpse of Benhu stabbing down at a mound of blankets. Quinn smashed Benhu's arm against the side of the wagon, drawing a cry from Benhu as he fell on Helice. She swore, struggling to free herself.

Quinn had Benhu's arms pinned, and the godman ceased struggling.

From the corner Helice said, "You son of a bitch."

"Shut up," Quinn hissed. He yanked Benhu's arms behind the man's back, telling Helice to find a length of cloth to bind him. She tore at something, and presently they had the attacker bound.

Helice muttered, "Asshole tried to rape me."

"No, he tried to kill you." Quinn turned to Benhu, who sat with his mouth hanging open, still gasping for breath. "What would your lord think of you now, Benhu?"

Spittle flew as Benhu rasped, "He'd thank me, that's what. For getting rid of this creature who'll get us our grave flags early. And I would have succeeded, if you hadn't broken my arm."

"It's not broken." Turning to Helice, Quinn said, "There's a knife around here somewhere. Look for it." She riffled through the covers until she found his knife, then handed it to him.

"Did you think, Benhu, that with her gone, my troubles would go away?"

"She's the cause of all this strife, isn't she?"

Helice blurted out, "What's he saying?"

"Be quiet," he warned her. "Talk Lucent or not at all. Half the camp may be awake listening." Quinn wiped the sweat from his face. "Benhu, I'm going to loosen your bonds. Will you behave?"

"Yes, if I must."

Quinn untied him. "Listen, now. I don't like Helice, but I don't want her murdered. I have a lot of problems; she's a minor one." He waited for that to sink in. "You know how the gracious lords punish murder."

By his expression, Benhu did. "I didn't want to do it. I had to work myself up to the task, but I'm no murderer."

Quinn forced himself to pat the man on the shoulder. "I know. You've been told not to fail, and you figured she's in the way. Well, she's not." It pained him to say it. Needing some fresh air, he made his way to the door. Pausing at the door he said, "From now on, Benhu, when you get an idea, tell me first."

"Yes, Excellency."

Turning to Helice, he murmured low, in English, "He won't hurt you now. He thought I wanted you dead, that's all."

As he left, he heard her mutter, "Not far from the truth, is it?"

In the morning a heavy fog greeted them, a brilliant scrim of air lit up by the bright, but obscuring the view of the march. Globular clouds floated by like mirror images of great dirigibles. Helice and Quinn sat on the driver's bench, with Benhu in the wagon, nursing his sprained arm. All three of them were quiet after the altercation during the ebb.

At last Helice whispered, "What will you do when we reach the Nigh?" When he ignored her, she went on, "I know what I did was wrong. Not telling everyone ahead of time."

He stifled a caustic remark, but his face must have been expressive.

"God, you hate me, don't you?" She pulled her jacket more tightly around her, unhappy not to be able to see the bright and the veldt one of the few times that Quinn allowed her out of the wagon.

"This isn't about you, Helice. None of it is. Chew on that a while; it'll do you good."

The beku stopped to pee, sending a sharp-scented gush of urine onto the ground. Helice liked the beku, and had even begun grooming it. But still, she had to smile at its timing. "I thought you said the Entire was a miracle of technology."

"If you want fancy, you need to make friends with the Tarig. That's more or less your plan, isn't it?" A wild guess. Whatever her ambitions, they wouldn't be small. "Helice, why didn't you warn Stefan about the nan, and then pack your bags and offer EoSap what you knew? Or TidalSphere. They'd have fallen all over themselves for you."

"You think they'd want me, after how I've behaved at Minerva?"

She had planned to develop her own going-over capabilities. She had a secret group. It was damning, but still, he didn't believe her. He was done giving her any credence whatsoever. He had once been a captain of starship crews, carrying colonists and visitors on long-haul transport voyages. He had learned to take the measure of all kinds of people. In Helice Maki he sensed a deep but empty well that she strove to fill at any cost. He was wary of her hunger, yet her arguments against the cirque still chafed at him.

Perhaps there was a way he could resolve this—Lord Oventroe. Although Quinn didn't relish relying on a Tarig, he had spent years in their presence, and thought them capable of loyalty as they saw it. He had seen divisions among the Tarig, though they disliked to admit them. Lady Chiron, for instance. She had once stood against the others to protect him. Similarly, Oventroe might stand against his kind, for the Rose. Why he might do so remained uncertain, with Benhu's answers less than enlightening. But there were factions among the Tarig, despite their tendency to be secretive. He thought of Chiron's secrets: among them, her strong attachment to him. She hid that as well as she could; but it was, at the end, an open secret. He wasn't proud of what had transpired between the two of them. He had been her prisoner. They had used each other. In any case, Chiron would never help him now. But Oventroe . . .

He made up his mind. If Oventroe was on his side, then here was the test: He should examine the cirque and pronounce it usable—or give Quinn a better device.

Benhu must find a way to contact the lord. And the cirque wasn't the only reason to do so. Quinn needed a way home. Sydney needed a way home. When he found her—after he was free to find her—he would need the correlates. Let Benhu arrange a meeting with the damn gracious lord, and soon.

Something caught his eye. A hulking form off to the side.

Through a tear in the gauze of fog, the great dirigible sailed into view, so close that it startled Quinn. It hovered near the ground, keeping pace with the wagon. On its huge flank, the face of the woeful god laughed, painted in orange and blue. From an aperture in the passenger cabin a pipe jutted. It moved slowly sideways, aimed at them. Quinn's pulse raced. Someone was watching them through the device.

Quinn turned to Helice and whispered, "Don't look around. Just do what I say."

He hugged her around the shoulders. Close to her ear he said, "They're spying on us."

"Who?"

"The godmen in the dirigible. Let's give them something to watch." He turned her face toward his and kissed her. She pulled back, but Quinn pulled her to him again. "Just act playful for a moment, can you?"

"God's beku," she murmured in Lucent, but threw her arms around him and kissed him with less enthusiasm than a cadaver, despite him muttering that she should make a good show of it. He'd been thinking of a story to explain the fight in the wagon if it came up: that he and Benhu were fighting over her. A good story, but now, to his disgust, he was kissing Helice Maki.

He looked up in time to see the rudder and horizontal stabilizer of the dirigible drive into an obscuring cloud bank.

Quinn's mind raced, thinking of reasons why the Most Venerable would watch them. Perhaps they were watching everyone, and his wagon happened to be in the path. He prayed that was true.

He flicked the reins at the beku to spur him on, an action that had no effect whatever. "I couldn't think what else to do, but give them an eyeful. Sorry."

Helice snarled, "Me too."

"If this is the worst the Entire does to you, count yourself lucky."

Ahead of them, now that he was listening for it, the whir of the great dirigible's motors came to them, near at times, and then far.

Helice sat in the cloud-soaked world, able to see nothing and having to endure the jolting of the wagon and the company of Titus Quinn. She'd rather have walked alongside the beku, getting some exercise and enjoying the quiet company. Beku were amazing. Big, loyal beasts, and patient with their caretakers, even with Benhu, who was bad with animals and smelled worse than they did. For some reason, Helice felt tenderness only toward animals. It proved, though, that she wasn't a cold-hearted person. She would rip the throat out of anyone who tried to hurt an animal.

She'd had a moment's panic when Quinn kissed her because he'd put his arms around her for a moment. He didn't snug up close enough to feel the items sewn into the generous seams and hems of her garments, or she might have had some explaining to do.

He'd let the matter of Lamar drop. Good thing, too. There was really no way Quinn could know anything about her plans, but she had to admit Lamar was a weak point in her group. He had ties to Quinn's father, and he'd been out of circulation for so long he'd forgotten his office politics. You lost the killing instinct once you were on retirement income. Like a lion at a zoo, trusting in a pail of meat to show up three times a day, you lost your edge.

That business with the dirigible worried her. Someone was spying on them. Godders were superstitious, inbred morons, but it wouldn't do to get crossways with them. Helice wasn't ready to hold her own with godman potentates. It was difficult to manage people when you couldn't speak their language, and when, in addition, they were likely to fear you because you were from a different universe. That was another good reason to go to Sydney Quinn first. She was an uneducated horse-woman—Inyx rider, whatever—but she was also a citizen of the Rose, like Helice. She was sure that she could manage the girl. It would be good practice for the Tarig. Everything was practice for the Tarig. Here were beings of prime intellect who had, apparently, purged their own kind of hangers-on and the feeble minded. Their technologies—the Nigh, for example—showed what could be accomplished when the average no longer dragged down the advanced.

One hole in her strategy: She didn't know the name of the defector. One lord was a bit of a loose cannon. He might be a key chess piece, but naturally, Quinn held back on the lord's name.

At her side, Quinn drank from a sack of water, holding the beku's reins in one hand.

"I'll drive," Helice said, gesturing to the reins. He passed them to her, and they plodded onward to the Nigh. Each step brought them closer to Ahnenhoon, because the Nigh brought it close, being a space-folding transport system, if Quinn's stories were to be believed. Once at the Nigh, Quinn would be in the homestretch. So she would have to get the cirque before then, if she had to take his foot off at the ankle to do it.

CHAPTER SIXTEEN

A clever general awaits the appearance of disorder among the enemy. Then he falls like a hammer.

—from Tun Mu's *Annals of War*

IN DEEP EBB, when decent folk, innocent ones, slept, Johanna made her way through the corridors of the centrum. It should have been dark for her purposes, but the walls, metal-smooth, sparkled with the ever-present light that the Tarig craved.

The basso thrum of the great machine grew louder as Johanna approached the engine chamber. SuMing wasn't following her this time. Pai would make sure of that, distracting the young fool in one way or another, serving Johanna in all things and never asking to know Johanna's business. Nevertheless, at every turn in the passageway, she looked for sentients who might be abroad: soldiers, servants, even legates come to Ahnenhoon to confer with Inweer. The centrum was a vast and empty place, however; the Tarig could conceive of no trespassers and desired few courtiers. They had grown complacent. Inweer had. He thought that his gifts bound Johanna to him.

She held in her hand something finer than any present of Inweer's, Gao's gift: the key to the maze, gleaned from Morhab's stone well computers in his den. Other keys and maps that Gao had copied had proven partial or false. Not this time. *The design emerges*, Gao had said. If she truly had a schematic showing the way through the chamber's maze, then she could lead Titus here when he came. Tonight, she would test Gao's work.

To provide a cover story for Johanna to be abroad this time of the ebb, Gao's wife Wei had come to Johanna's chamber with a tale of domestic trouble and Gao in a rage. Johanna had quickly dressed and hurried away to quell the family dispute. Wei and Johanna had parted company at a stairwell, with the woman unaware of Johanna's purpose. Perhaps she thought Johanna went to meet a lover. However, she might wonder why Johanna bothered with secrecy. Lord Inweer didn't demand exclusivity, nor did the Chalin culture, unless children were planned. No, no children planned.

The engine's churning vibrated in her shoes. *Kill the thing*, she thought. *Titus must kill the thing.* She rushed on. Though the corridors remained empty, she had the unnerving sense that Titus was at her side. She imagined the time—perhaps soon—when he would be, when she would guide him, to bring whatever force the Rose could devise against the engine. Perhaps the Rose would strike with nuclear force, eliminating Ahnenhoon in one stroke. If so, there was no need of a key to the maze. The Repel would be gone, and the Entire, so fragile in its configuration, would be gone as well. But they might choose a more limited weapon. Might. So much of her urgent mission was based on the hope that Titus had received her message. On the hope that he would believe her about the threat.

Oh, Titus, she thought. How have we come to this, so far from each other? Entangled in war instead of each other's arms? The thought caught her by surprise. Ten years without him. Now came this image of him gathering her in his arms. She pushed the thought away. She would be true to the Earth, but as to Titus, no, it was too late. Do you see, Titus? Tell me that you see. She couldn't imagine his answer.

Hurrying with all her senses alert, she descended a ramp that, curving, brought her to the ground level of the centrum. The stone on her finger guided her, glowing a soft gold instead of white in the illumination of the corridor.

The diamond stone of her wedding ring was no longer merely a gem; it was an optical computer—a very simple one. Gao had borrowed her diamond for a few days. When he returned it, the stone read the path, guiding her by changes in the spectrum of light. She had to squint to see the variation; but she was good with color. Gao, it turned out, was good with espionage.

Morhab tugged at his burden, unused to heavy lifting. It was difficult for Gond—particularly Gond of a certain heft—to lift things without the leverage of a wall or tree stump for support. With his short arms he finished hauling the sack onto the access platform of his sled. Then, in a convulsive motion, he humped his body forward, pulling himself onto the platform as well. Activating the lift mechanism, the platform came even with the sled's bench. He pushed the sack into place on the deck of his conveyance and eased his bulk onto the bench, panting.

Then he maneuvered the sled out of his den and into the halls of the remote wing of the centrum where his family nested.

Tonight would herald a new accommodation between himself and his heart's desire. At this thought, he pulled his wings tightly against his back, calming himself. For days he had lain in misery, rejecting his nest mates and reliving his mortification at the hands of the Rose woman. It was not that he especially blamed her for failing to appreciate his magnificence. Many sentients were prejudiced against beings of other sways, despite the Tarig braying about equality. Hirrin, for example, could not abide Ysli, as all knew. Rather, it was that the woman had drawn him toward her, affecting interest, arousing his matching interest. Otherwise he would never have presumed, she being a favorite of the lords, after all, and a human at that—sentients known for rigidity and intolerance. No, he would never have presumed. But now, he was helplessly snared by her. That would require snaring back.

As he rounded a corner, the sack lying at his feet almost rolled off. He slowed to a more cautious pace. His spy in Johanna's chamber had come just an interval ago with the intelligence that Johanna was abroad. Plenty of time. She was on foot, after all, and he had his sled.

Johanna was close now. The drumming sound hammered at her, rushing at her like harpies.

She passed empty stone chambers, some of them huge. She wondered if the centrum had once housed many Tarig. Had the Tarig once needed halls in which to confer, to plan against the Paion? Had there been an era when the Tarig were not so confident? The thought led her back to an idea she had had before: that the Rose might persuade the Paion to a joint cause. However, the Paion came from someplace that was not the Rose, and not the Entire. If they were the supreme sentients in their universe, they likely needed no such help as humans could offer.

She hurried past a colonnade of pillars through which she spied a dark garden with fruited, black vines. Sometimes Lady Enwepe sat in this one. Enwepe—so lonely a figure, and seldom with Inweer. They didn't love each other, she believed, but couldn't know. Much of Inweer's life was closed to her. She saw him only when summoned, at his sole pleasure. But he had a realm to govern, and a war to wage. More wars than he knew.

By the gold fire in her ring, Johanna found her way to the correct door. Gao had said one must select the right door to enter the engine containment chamber. Though Johanna knew some routes, this one was new to her. She opened one of the matching pairs of great doors and slipped through as the engine's drumming became a roar.

Her first impression was of the soaring vault of the ceiling. Far away and high on the wall was the catwalk from which soldiers might aim defensive weapons in case of attack. Looking around her, she saw stonewell computers held in rows by racks. Between the racks, apparent paths stretched away to shadows. Her map would have to be very good. Gao had said it was—because Morhab had taken the trouble to learn the maze. Although the Tarig allowed no outside help with the engine and its containment chamber, Morhab took pains to study these things. This went far beyond Morhab's duties in other areas of the Repel, where he provided for structural modifications to serve the servants of the Tarig: to modify their quarters, to create spaces that pleased Chalin, Hirrin, and Jout. All within strict parameters.

But Morhab was a creature obsessed with details; he collected vast files of arcane knowledge on things such as the history of Ahnenhoon's architecture, its record of growth and alterations. The great chamber's maze didn't escape his curiosity. She and Gao had gambled that this was so.

Johanna waved her hand in front of the paths formed by the instrument racks, watching her diamond. Finding a direction that deepened her ring to amber, she set out.

It was working. Oh, Gao, she thought, well done.

She had never told Gao the purpose of the engine, or why the Entire so desperately needed the engine, to fuel the life of the All. Why the children of his children's children would need the Rose to burn. He would never help her if he knew.

How ruthless she had become. As ruthless as Inweer. Perhaps, she thought, God chose a good partner for me, after all.

Her stone burned sodium-bright. She darted down a path to the left.

Peering into the chamber far below, Morhab caught a glimpse of movement. Why, the woman wore blue, a fine beacon to announce her whereabouts. Time then. Using all the strength in his delicate arms, Morhab pushed the sack onto the lift platform. He struggled to dislodge Gao's body from the bag, a harder task than he had supposed. Finally it came free.

The miscreant's body bore only a few wounds, but these had bled rather more than Morhab had planned for. The death must look like a suicide. The fall from the balcony should accomplish this, it being a drop guaranteed to produce breakage and blood.

He looked down on Gao's surprisingly peaceful face. Morhab regretted killing him. Gao had come under Johanna's spell; he had romanticized the woman, and taken gratitude to treasonous heights. Morhab could empathize. Still, Gao had known things he shouldn't. He'd known of Morhab's predilection for historical record, including records of things that were just as well to leave alone. So besides the theft of information, Gao could damage the chief engineer beyond repair. Thus he was dead, and thus he must fly from the balcony.

Producing a distinct whine from his sled's motors, Morhab tipped the lift into a ramp over the railing, letting the body slide.

Coming to a cross corridor, Johanna held up the stone. It shone pure white. Not the way. She turned around. Not the way. Faintly, a spike of noise came to her, as though a mosquito whined nearby.

Minutes passed, as sweat trickled down her sides. The stone glowed with an ordinary, diamond gleam. Worry mounting, she pressed on, hoping to pick up the way again—but white, white, the diamond showed. The center of the cavern eluded her. She remained on the edges. In a blur, she passed racks of computer wells, all the same, all wickedly conspiring to spit her out to the sides of the chamber. Under the great balcony.

The perimeter of the cavern formed a corridor of its own, with many paths leading inward, none of them gold. She followed this corridor, worry giving way to panic.

A smell came to her—an earthy, sour smell.

The path angled to the right and she turned to follow, soon brought up short. On the floor in front of her a body lay, the skull caved in. Someone had fallen from the high balcony. Whoever it was wore the green silks of a clerk or steward. She approached, dreading to confirm what she suspected, that it was Gao. That their sins had been discovered.

She had always known that if the worst happened, she couldn't protect Gao. She had told him as much.

His answer: *I have had a thousand days of happiness.*

Noble Gao. She kneeled by his body, now certain of him. Yes, the worst had happened.

Did Gao, at this moment, know the next kingdom? Did the Chalin merit the grace of God? It depended on whether the Entire was God's creation or Satan's. Strangely calm, she wondered which it was.

She hoped that he hadn't taken his own life. No, surely he was braver than that. She put a hand on his head and asked God to receive him. And to receive her, if that was what came next. She looked up to the catwalk. Something moved; a sled glided away.

The truth settled over her, bringing an icy calm. Morhab had taken matters into his own hands. Perhaps the engineer had planted false information in his computers to test Gao. Perhaps, indeed, he had seen through Johanna's meeting that day with him in the gathering yard, concluding that Gao was the point of it all. Yes, she could imagine that this all had been doomed from the beginning.

However, the implications worsened. If Morhab meant to tell Lord

Inweer, he would have brought the lord here as a witness when Johanna made her way into the chamber. Instead, Morhab had killed Gao, silencing him; warning her. So the creature had her at his mercy.

She thought for a long, slow moment about being at the Gond's mercy.

Tempting, that jump from the balcony. If she could be of no use to Titus, then why tarry here? She found herself at an exit door, and stumbled into the cold hallway. Finding a wash stall, she kneeled down and retched into the toilet aperture. At length she roused herself to wash her face in the basin.

Later, Johanna didn't remember her return journey through the centrum. Her mind was dull, and her thoughts mere fragments. Creeping back to her bed, she lay awake the rest of the ebb, until the waxing sky ignited a halo of light around the fringes of her drapes.

Morhab drove back to his nest slowly, his mood climbing. Now Johanna would seek him out. He would make sure that she did so, and frequently. Though she would hate him at first, he would persuade her otherwise. After all, no one could wish to force their attentions upon another sentient. It was beneath his dignity to bear her disdain. No, she must be properly wooed, in ways appropriate to human females.

And she must teach him how to do it.

CHAPTER SEVENTEEN

There are no strangers on the Radiant Path.
—from *The Twelve Wisdoms*

THE NEXT DAY WAXED CLEAR AND DRY, sandwiching the godder convoy between the golden tundra and silver sky. The dirigible of the Most Venerable floated far in front of the wagons, surrounded by smaller sky bulbs, including, Quinn supposed, the one he and Helice and Benhu had ridden down the minoral. If there had been suspicions after the argument in the wagon, perhaps they were forgotten now. Next to him on the driving platform, Benhu held the reins. Helice sat on the roof of the wagon, looking at the vast plain broken here and there by prairies of lavender grass. Sometimes she leaned back on her arms and closed her eyes, letting the rays of the bright fall on her face. She gloried in this place. It made Quinn uneasy.

Helice had destroyed his peace of mind. The chain cinched his ankle, dragging him down. Why had he agreed to bear this cirque into the new universe? The knowledge of the place, and the threat, should never have been Minerva's alone. Perhaps with more resources, with the checks and balances of other corporations and governments . . . His thoughts fell away on that note. He had little faith in any congress of firms or bureaucrats. As a result, the decisions fell to him.

He thought of the people whom he might have turned to for counsel: Anzi, most of all. Su Bei, the scholar who'd set him on the trail of the correlates. Even the steward Cho, who had befriended him at great risk. But even if they were here, they couldn't solve his dilemma of the chain. For that, Benhu had to summon Oventroe.

Reluctantly, Benhu had agreed, but had warned Quinn: *I'll have to find a navitar to take a message by ship. It could take a hundred days, a thousand days.*

Do it faster, Benhu.

If the two of them had tolerated each other before, now they barely spoke. That suited Quinn, as long as Benhu produced his end of things.

When the bright softened into Twilight Ebb, the caravan halted to pitch tents and bring the sky bulbs to ground. Quinn helped Benhu lay a fire with logs of condensed resins that Benhu had lashed to the wagon in bundles. As they cooked an evening meal and the bright edged toward evening, a Ysli approached their fire and bowed.

"Brothers and sister of the Woeful God," the Ysli said. "A word with Ren Kai, please, and if he will follow me."

Quinn and Benhu exchanged glances. Benhu took the cue, saying, "Born in a minoral? Ren Kai and I are having our meal. Come back later."

The Ysli smiled, revealing pointed teeth. "Zhiya was born in the Chendu wielding. No minoral."

Benhu rose, his beard stuck with bits of food. "Pardon. Of course. You should have said so at once." He turned to Quinn with a pointed look. "The Most Venerable requires your presence. Don't keep personages waiting."

Helice had by now taken alarm, but could do nothing except watch. Quinn followed the Ysli godman as he led the way through the milling camp.

So they hadn't escaped notice, after all. It was too much to have hoped for, with Helice as careless as she'd been, and talk of knives and murder that night in the wagon when anyone could have lurked nearby. He devoutly wished that he had left her at the reach. And why hadn't he? Because she would have fallen into Tarig hands? But perhaps she could have lasted at the reach with Benhu's stockpiles of food—and bound strongly enough not to break free for enough days to allow Quinn to get a head start.

Now the grinning god had noticed him.

He watched the Ysli for some clue as to the mood of the summons, but the creature did not respond to attempts at conversation. Too soon they approached the dirigible.

On the ground it looked enormous, a big-bellied fish at least sixty feet long. Extending from the gondola of the airship was a ramp. It was clear he must walk inside, and he did so, summoning his stories and lies. He could still brazen it out. He'd done so many times in the Entire, by reading his interrogator, by not losing his composure.

He stood in a large central cabin where several Chalin servants watched him with keen interest. The Ysli led him to a forward hatch, opening it and gesturing him inside. Behind Quinn the hatch closed.

Occupying one end of the cabin, a woman sat in a nest of colorful pillows. He thought it was a woman, though her face looked large for her body, and mannish, except for bright red lips and gloriously long white hair that curled to her waist. They were alone.

When the Most Venerable spoke, the voice was deep, adding to the gender puzzlement. "Sorry about your supper." The smile that accompanied this pronouncement held amusement more than regret.

The personage looked him up and down. "I suppose that by the time we're finished you won't much feel like eating. I'm Zhiya, by the way."

His heart began to cool. This person didn't look merely curious, or confused, or easy to beguile. "Venerable, have my companions given offense? Or have I?"

Zhiya chuckled. "Yes, you might say that." She gestured with her short arms at a pile of cushions opposite her. "Too tall. By the bright, sit down before you give me a crick in my neck."

Mind racing, he sat cross-legged, trying to guess what she wanted, what she knew. He took in the surroundings: on the deck, a litter of scrolls and boxes, plates with scraps of food, and stone well devices; on the bulkheads, faded draperies, pulled back from the viewports. A smell came to him, of some pungent herb or cosmetic, perhaps.

Uneasy under her scrutiny, Quinn said, "We had a falling-out that night. It's over now."

She smirked. "We heard. So difficult to keep secrets among such as we. If you hoped to keep secrets . . . well, you have a lot to learn about us."

"I am new," he admitted.

"Yes." She smiled an awful crimson smile. "For example, you're a handsome man to have chosen life as a godman."

"No sentient is without hope," he intoned.

Her amusement increased. "Look around you, Ren Kai. Do you see hand-some godmen?" She paused, grinning. "Or women?"

"Venerable . . . ," he said, with no idea how to finish his sentence. She didn't help him, but raised an eyebrow, still mirthful. "Venerable, I have long given up judging beauty."

Her face fell. "Oh. And I fussed with my hair."

He looked at her, his confusion mounting. "Very nice," he said.

Her smile became less playful. "Do you think so?" She ran one hand through her hair, caressing it. "It's my one indulgence."

The room was hot, and the smell of food or ointments or whatever it was had become nauseating.

She gestured at the cabin. "The sky bulb is a luxury, I suppose. But my brothers and sisters expect it, the ones who scurry after god and handouts. They expect a certain amount of *grandeur*, you know. They're content to be poor as beggars—well, they *are* beggars—as long as a few of us sit on pillows and travel in style. The way of things, isn't it?" She regarded him with an unsettling vigor. She put her hands on her knees. "So."

The way she said it signaled a change of topic, and he suspected he wasn't going to like the new one.

"Perhaps I should stop playing with you." She cocked her head. "Are you ready for business, Ren Kai?"

"If you please, Venerable."

"My name's Zhiya. You can drop the Venerable stuff."

"Zhiya, then," he murmured.

She rose, revealing her diminutive size, a height of perhaps four and a half feet. She walked across the small cabin, ambling slightly, and kneeled by a stone well computational device. Having second thoughts about activating it, she turned around and looked at him, her face losing its laughter. "I don't mean to be overly dramatic. But what you see may shock you." She thumbed a nodule on the stone well and dropped a redstone into the master cup.

The walls enlivened, filling the room with harsh light.

On every wall, his face appeared. Different views, different dress. But it was him.

He stood up, turning in a circle, looking at the images. They were from a time when his hair had been shorter. In one of the images, in the background, was a person he recognized from the back. It was Anzi. Otherwise, only him. All were images from his stay in the Tarig bright city last time. When he had been incognito.

She knew who he was. A hot stone lay in his gut. He looked at the pictures, some of them from the dock in the Sea of Arising, others of him walking along the canals of the bright city. One was an image of him walking with the steward Cho.

"Seen enough?"

He nodded, and the walls went dark.

"I know you carry a knife," Zhiya said. "My people could have disarmed you before you came in. So you won't run at me with the thing, will you? You'd never get out of the ship. And you'd be sorry, later." She swept a hand through her hair. "At least I hope you'd be sorry."

She found a cup and poured an amber liquid into it.

He didn't care what it was, he drank. It was fermented and strong.

Zhiya watched him drink. "People say you're unpredictable. Personally, I like that in a man. But I wouldn't want to die if I'm wrong."

He returned a bleak smile. Now that it was all out in the open, he felt oddly light-headed.

As though reading his mind she said, with some compassion, "Pretending is such hard work. I know. It makes you dark and a little mad. That's why I like to laugh."

"What gave me away?"

She poured herself a drink from a jar by her pillows. "Curious about that rather than your fate?"

"Sometimes it helps to fix blame."

"I know what you mean. Keeps regrets at bay." She settled herself comfortably in her nest, tucking her stubby legs under her. "You make a good Chalin, Titus." She blinked. "Can I call you that? You prefer Ren Kai? Dai Shen? Venerable?"

"I go by Quinn."

"Ah. Well, your Lucent is very good, Quinn—no distinction from a native, I assure you. But the female you're traveling with . . ." Zhiya shook her head. "The throat. Any Tarig who began a garroting would not stop halfway. We all discussed it."

He thought of how naïve he had been, and wished to holy hell he could begin over again. "All of you?"

"Yes, my fellow thieves and miscreants. You've been the subject of discussion for days. Anyway, I take no special credit for figuring it out. You knew your picture was spread around?" She shook her head wonderingly. "Oh yes, the lords sent it by navitar down the five primacies. So once we were watching—what do you call her?—Oh yes, Li. Once we began watching Li, we saw you, and eventually matched you with the visuals." She grinned, half evil, half sweet. "I must say your vanity got the best of you. You made your new face too handsome. You've changed your face before, the second time you came here. Why, coming back here this time, didn't you alter yourself again? That's one thing we couldn't figure out."

"There wasn't time."

Her eyes narrowed. "In a hurry then. You shouldn't have been."

"More true than you know."

She twisted her long hair around one finger, forcing it into a curl over her shoulder. "I feel so selfish. I promised you I'd get to business, and here I'm just enjoying our little chat." She watched him with an almost feral intensity. "You understand that you're famous? I never thought I'd be overimpressed with celebrity. I'm almost one myself. A dwarf, a Most Venerable. Draws attention. But you. Prince of the city, voyager from the dark, slayer of Tarig." Her face lit up. "My, that's good, isn't it?"

He had hoped that his exploits hadn't had time to travel. The Entire being so vast, and communications limited to light speed, there was a chance no one would have heard, outside of the Ascendancy. It was one reason that a quick return to the Entire had advantages. But the Tarig themselves had spread the word. And they, he knew, weren't limited to light speeds.

"Anyway," Zhiya went on, "most sentients are aware that you had a Tarig at your feet. Took away their toys. The big ships. How did you destroy all their ships? Dying to know."

He murmured. "They were conscious beings. I released them."

Zhiya sat in silence for a moment. "Released them."

"They were interdimensional beings. Framed tightly to take on a ship aspect. Prisoners."

"You empathized."

"Maybe. And I didn't want to be followed in the one ship I flew."

She smiled, but the humor was more sober. "Compassion tinged with practicality."

"I wanted to live." He had had reason to want to live. To bring home the discovery of the threat to the Rose. But by then, he had also wanted to live in general. He wanted his life—a far cry from the years when he hadn't.

"The lords have new ships," Zhiya said.

"Not made of flesh, I hope."

"One could hope." She stood. "Forgive me. I always love good company, especially someone new. But you're wondering what comes next, and I'm remiss in dragging this out."

As she stood in front of him, they came eye-to-eye. Her skin was pock-marked, but his attention went to her startling eyes, so deep an amber that they looked like melted gold.

He said, "The man Benhu. And Li. Can you let them go? I dragged them into this. They don't know anything. Let them escape. If I get one wish, that would be it." If Quinn's companions weren't put to torture, maybe Lord Oventroe's cover could be preserved.

After a pause, Zhiya said, "There's something I want to show you." She turned, beckoning him to follow.

She led him to a hatchway in the far bulkhead, which she opened to reveal a dimly lit cabin, narrowing into the nose of the airship. The smell as she opened the door revealed that the stench he'd been aware of had come from this room.

On a bunk in the center, a form lay. This was a sickroom, and one long occupied. The drapes covering the bulkheads reeked of medicinals and illness. They approached the bed, and Quinn looked down on a face that seemed to spread onto the pillow. Beginning at the line of the nose and forehead, the skin sagged away to either side, as though the bones of the face had given up. One arm lay outside the covers, and it too had a deflated look. Looking up at Quinn were two elongated eyes that no longer looked human—or Chalin. A miasma rose from the bed. The flesh wasn't rotting, but changing, flowing onto the pallet.

"My God," Quinn whispered.

The patient moaned, saying something like, *Gaaaaaa*. It was a pitiful sound, from a throat that could no longer enunciate.

"She's been like this for ten thousand days," Zhiya said. "It's one reason I keep this big ship. She likes to float in the sky."

Zhiya bent down and whispered in the woman's ear. "Mother, would you like the drapes open?"

The eyes looked frightened, tense.

Zhiya glanced at Quinn. "That means yes." She moved to the bulkhead and pulled aside a length of silk to reveal a viewport. A circle of molten silver appeared there as the bright shone in. The room filled with light, revealing more details of the woman's condition. Her mouth was elongated, but it had knitted together, forming a half moon on the lower part of her face. In the center a small hole allowed her to breathe, since she had no nose.

"Mother," Zhiya said, holding the woman's hand. "This is a new venerable, come to pay respects."

The hand was a cup of flesh, with fingers melted together. Zhiya held it tenderly.

The mother's eyes fixed on Quinn. "Gaaad," she said. Then, with great effort, "My God."

Quinn made a startled reaction.

"I should have warned you," Zhiya said. "When you spoke just now, was that in the dark language?"

He hadn't realized he had spoken in English.

Zhiya continued, "Her mind is very vivid."

He asked Zhiya's mother in English, "Do you speak my language?"

The woman struggled to push words out. They came in a warble, in his language: "God speaks." At this effort, the woman closed her eyes, her eyelids operating perfectly, even over such eyes as these.

Zhiya said, "I don't know how she knows your tongue. I never knew how she knew things." After a pause she added, "She is a navitar."

Quinn bowed. He didn't know why he did. But a sense of profound respect induced him to bow low. The navitar had traveled in the paths of knowing, where the worlds mixed, where dimensions blurred. Where futures were probabilities. Mere under-sentients slept on the River Nigh, their minds too exhausted to make sense of the exotic matrix. But navitars were transformed to bear it.

"Did you ever think," Zhiya said, "what happens to navitars when they burn out?"

Quinn hadn't wondered. And now he wished he didn't know.

Seated once more in Zhiya's cabin, they shared a meal brought in by a Chalin godman. Quinn began to hope that the Most Venerable wasn't his enemy.

As they partook of the meat-filled dumplings, Zhiya was silent. Only when a godman came in to pour steaming mugs of oba did Zhiya speak.

"Most of them kill themselves. It's not so bad. They do what they love for a long time, and then they can't imagine living as under-sentients. The traditional death is to weigh themselves down and sink into the River. My mother came home, instead."

"Is there nothing to be done for her? With all the medical knowledge of the Tarig?"

Zhiya's eyes snapped up at him. "But then we'd have to ask them, wouldn't we?" The bitterness in her voice wasn't hard to miss. "Mother and I would rather not. But I didn't introduce you to her for you to fret about her condition. Only to show you why the lords aren't . . . gracious, in my view."

She noted his inquiring look. "Yes, Mother chose her vocation. The lords are careful that way. It all looks so consensual. But it's how they've set things up, isn't it? One can't travel anywhere worth going without using the Nigh. But the Nigh needs special navigators. Sentients are drawn to the service, drawn to esoteric knowledge, but must submit to morphing in order to survive it. God's beku, why don't the lords just inscroll the knowledge, tell all the secrets? More to the point, why don't they just devise a better way to travel?" She waved away his arguments, although he wasn't going to make any. He'd had the same thought many times. The Tarig hoarded their knowledge. "They play with us, you see. I don't like to be played with." Glancing up at him, she said, "Neither do you, I think."

"No. Not by the lords of my universe, either."

"The same everywhere, eh?" She laughed soundlessly. "I should have guessed. Anyway, my mother went for a navitar, and I went for a godwoman, and begged and cheated my way to wealth, and now I travel about and spread misery. That is, I take on the miseries of the world, or whatever you want to believe about the Woeful God. It's been a good life, if a cynical one."

After a period of silence she murmured, "Not everyone is happy on the Radiant Path, Quinn. People would follow you. They think you are a *hsien*. One who has become immortal. It's a term of the Rose. Chinese, I believe. Anyway, you are dragging a big reputation around. And didn't know it, did you?"

"Immortal?"

"Well, we're a bit loose on theology, you know. The Tarig fill the awe-and-power slot. So god gets the leavings, bits and pieces of things. Some folks think you're a hero. Killing Hadenth, that ugly fiend. Killing one of the little lordlings."

Quinn must have visibly winced, because Zhiya said, "Don't ever waste time about that. It only added to your mythos." She smiled. "That and the brightships. You have no idea the terror of watching those ships skim down the bright, falling on the land, dispensing what they call justice."

He had never much considered what denizens of the Entire thought about him. *Hsien.* Immortal. Strange, from a people for whom life was as long as any could wish.

"People would follow you," Zhiya said again.

"I'm not going anywhere."

"What did you come back for? Your daughter, still?" He nodded. "That's not all of it, though, is it?"

He greeted this question with silence. He wasn't about to confide his mission. "Why don't *you* lead the opposition, Zhiya? If I lived here, I'd follow you."

She drew out a mirror and a cup of red paste, reapplying her lip color. Smacking her lips together to spread the gel, she said, "A dwarf? A godwoman? I think not."

Quinn murmured, "I'm no hero, no *hsien*. I want my daughter. I want peace between your world and mine. And I have no idea how to accomplish either one, much less making the Tarig behave. Don't think of me to save you."

Zhiya's smile became fixed. "A shame." She sighed, spreading her hands to encompass her quarters. "You're welcome to ride to the Nigh in comfort, Quinn. We could talk. Oh. I didn't make it clear, did I, that I'm on your side? My people won't tell. They practically worship you. Damn annoying, when I used to be the big deal."

He considered the advantages of getting Helice out of sight. When they reached the gathering place of the Adda, Helice could be crowded in among other sentients for that leg of the trip. She would never escape discovery, he knew now.

"Benhu and Li, as well?"

She considered this. "If I must."

"I may accept. If you're not worried about being seen with me."

"Not at the moment. These godmen are poor and without communications or stone wells. I'm known to take my pick of lovers. Let them think that's the case." She glanced at him coyly. "If it *were* the case, I would be delighted, by the way." She held up a hand. "Don't answer now. You'd hurt my feelings."

She pulled her hair away from her face and smiled mischievously. "Besides, we hardly know each other."

CHAPTER EIGHTEEN

The opportunity of defeating the enemy is provided by the enemy itself.

—from Tun Mu's *Annals of War*

O TI WAS GOOD AT HIDING HIS THOUGHTS. From the time when he had grown up in the wicked Magisterium, he had survived the tauntings of other children by hiding his hurts. The bunched muscles of his misshapen body formed a fine armor around his heart. But it concealed a passionate nature. His loyalty to Cixi was absolute, his love for Sydney unshakable. However, for the sake of his young mistress, whose sufferings were worse than his own, he would not reveal how it cut him to be fallen in her regard.

He walked alone into the steppe, seeking the peace of its scoured ground. To outward appearance, Mo Ti was the same Chalin fighter who had become Sydney's champion and closest advisor. But today he walked alone, and that was more the truth of things.

Some days he wanted to leave the sway, or die by his own hand. But that would only distress Sydney more, since she held—he presumed she did—some feelings for him. She didn't say that she blamed him for her poisoned sight; she even claimed to understand why he never told her that Cixi had sent him; but she stood apart from him even so. He saw it in her every gesture around him.

It was with great surprise, then, that he saw Sydney on her mount galloping toward him from the encampment. He knew it was her from a great distance, because no one rode a mount like she did. Here on the steppe, your riding style was known before your name.

Mo Ti did wonder why she would come out here, alone and in such a hurry. He kept his thoughts guarded from Riod, his emotions tucked into a small core of regret. But as Sydney drew near, he read her face: an expression of pure joy.

Sydney slid off of Riod without waiting for the mount to bow his front legs. Striding toward Mo Ti, she stopped short of the embrace that was clearly in her mood.

"My lady?"

"Mo Ti," she breathed, "they are false. False!"

Were there others besides Mo Ti who were considered false by Sydney? He waited.

"Mo Ti, the fiends aren't themselves. They aren't like us, nothing like!" She glanced back at Riod in triumph, and Riod's thoughts came tumbling toward Mo Ti. *Not born, not dying, not flesh as Inyx are flesh. Not separate as other beings are separate.*

It was Early Day, and Riod must just have come back from the herd and its heart-probing work. "Immortal?" Mo Ti asked. If so, that was not so great a surprise.

Sydney shook her head. "No, not that. Or maybe that." She grinned. He hadn't seen so broad a smile on her before. She took him by the arm. "Come." She led him to Riod and insisted that they ride double to find a spring that she knew was nearby.

Mo Ti mounted Riod and Sydney sat behind, her arms coming partway around his broad girth. It was a happiness that he used to take for granted; and though he didn't think that Sydney had forgiven him his failures, his heart lightened to ride with her again.

They found the spring, managing not to bring up the subject of the Tarig for a few intervals. By the time they sat next to the rare pool of water, Mo Ti had regained his composure and waited for good news. By the bright, he thought, let it be good news at last.

She sat cross-legged in front of him. "They are controlled beings," she began.

"The Tarig?"

"Yes, the mantis lords! Who else? Listen, Mo Ti: Riod says they come to us as consciousness fully formed, set into the Tarig form. But they aren't individuals. Not like we are." She looked up at Riod and grinned. "I can't get this straight."

Tell him in your way, Riod urged. He could have helped her convey the matter, but he held back, letting Sydney have her moment.

She took a calming breath. "Riod says that there is a being among them. Perhaps he is a Tarig lord—but he can't tell—who speaks continually with the old world where they come from."

"The Heart." The Tarig always said they came from another universe. The Heart.

"We always assumed it was a place. But it's a place without physical space. We can sense a chaos of thought. Riod calls it a swarm. A swarm of consciousnesses. When the fiends come here, they insert themselves into a created form. And when they pretend to die, they return to the swarm. They start out, Riod thinks, having one of just a few common personalities. Then, as each Tarig has different experiences, they become more individual." She shook her head. "They used to say that they were cousins. That they were of one mind. I thought it was their way of bragging about how unified they were. But what it really means is that they started out in a template form."

Mo Ti had a vision of robotic Tarig strutting the land. It caused him to smile. "They are not alive."

"Maybe they are alive. But it is a strange kind of being alive."

Riod sent, *The swarm is vast. Some strands in the swarm fear to come here. They despise physical form. Some choose to come. They are few in number.* Riod conveyed a brilliant universe of pure light and thought, and the revulsion that the swarm had toward fleshly being, the fear of being in a physical place. Only a few strands of thought wished to have that experience. They weren't necessarily the best strands of the bunch.

Sydney nodded. "The older they are, the more particular they are. And maybe some can't handle the stress at all, and go mad. Like Lord Hadenth. He wasn't like the rest. As bad as they all are, Hadenth was worst. . . ."

Her memory of the lord who had blinded her cast a shadow, and Mo Ti put a hand on her arm, touching her for the first time in many days.

Her excitement bubbled back, though, and she shook him off. "Mo Ti, that's why there are no Tarig children, except they want us to think they are normal, so they create beings who seem childlike. If you've ever seen a Tarig child—what they claim are children—you'd know there was something wrong with them."

"How do they create their own bodies?" Mo Ti asked.

"We don't know. Wouldn't it be simple, though? They created all forms in the Entire. No doubt their mantis form is copied from the Rose like they copied everything else. Everything except child-bearing, birth, and death."

Mo Ti sat, considering this revelation. He felt his heart thudding in his chest. He thought of Cixi, imagining her joy at learning the true nature of the Tarig. He would tell her at his next opportunity, though it was never an easy task. He dared not ask Distanir to send a heart-thought that any mount and his rider could pick up.

Setting aside his excitement, Mo Ti sifted through to the crux of the matter: "How do they cross to and from the Heart?" That would be the lords' great weakness.

"We don't know yet. They hide, oh Mo Ti, they hide so much, being cowardly. But we'll find out. We'll hunt down all their secrets. They've lied to their subjects. Lied in everything. Gracious lords." She shook her head. "They are simulacra. Afraid to live as we do."

"We have them, my lady. When we find how they convey to and from, we destroy their ability to do so. Yes?"

"Yes." She stood, brushing the dust off of her riding pants, and Mo Ti rose with her. She looked out onto the steppe, and beyond, toward the River Nigh, as though she were even now ready to board a navitar's ship. "I think it's time to let this secret out." She turned to him. "What do you think the sways would think of lords who aren't alive?"

Mo Ti whispered, "The Tarig will be lower than Gonds."

"Yes. The Entire will find them strange. Ugly. Cowardly. The mantis lords keep all this secret. They're ashamed of what they are." She smiled. "I have it in mind to send dreams to the sways, Mo Ti."

"Dreams, my lady?"

Sydney had already thought it through, without him. "We'll sneak in, in dreams. We'll share this vision of the Tarig simulacra with our fellow sentients. Riod will send them dreams."

Mo Ti was stunned by the audacity of her plan. But he shared his first thought: "It is no proof, to send visions."

Sydney smiled, but he saw that he had displeased her by offering doubts. "Sentients don't need proof. They just need suspicions. Of those, we have plenty."

After considering a moment, Mo Ti nodded. "It will sow distrust across the primacies. A good beginning, Mo Ti thinks."

"I wasn't asking for permission."

Nor had he meant it as such, but his heart fell. "No, my lady. Never."

In the distance, a galloping sound, and Distanir came into sight.

Mo Ti said, "You have made me glad that you came here yourself, mistress. Mo Ti thanks you."

Sydney nodded, her smile not unfriendly. She mounted Riod. "Now here is something for you to do, Mo Ti."

He paused, wondering if he had not already been doing all that he could in her service.

"Tell Cixi. However you communicate with her, do so as soon as you are able. Tell her what we have learned." She nudged Riod forward, then turned back for a moment. "And greet her for me."

They shared a brief eye contact, the warmth of their conversation gone.

As he watched Sydney depart, he felt a swelling of pride. He had taught her to think like a leader. To formulate strategies and tactics. Now she had outdone her teacher.

In his heart he saluted her as she sped away on her mount.

CHAPTER NINETEEN

The Ascendancy lies between bright and bright. Bright above: the gate of heaven. Bright below: the Sea of Arising. Between these shining places, the place of blinding power: the Ascendancy. Look up, see the city of the gracious lords, the source of all gifts, the fountainhead of the land wherein you dwell.

—from *The Book of the Thousand Gifts*

DEPTA PAUSED ON THE NARROW WALKWAY LEADING TO THE GARDEN— Titus Quinn's garden, that favorite haunt of Lady Chiron. The path followed a line of topiary trees, engineered for order and tidiness, qualities that Depta had once admired but which now seemed slightly ominous. Looming nearby, Lady Chiron's mansion formed one of the walls around the garden.

Although Depta had urgent reports to make, she feared making them—feared saying the wrong thing, or offending her mistress. She remained haunted by the vision of Lady Chiron sitting in her chair as though turned to stone . . . then, rising up to grip her throat, that terrible look in her eyes. Depta's hide rippled with uneasiness. Gone were the times when, anticipating meeting with the bright lady, Depta's thoughts had been gold-tinged. Now, all had gone gray.

But the lady's command remained: *Send word the moment he arrives.* Chiron's spy had arrived in Yulin's camp. Reports could not be delayed.

As Depta rounded the bend in the pathway, she found Lady Chiron waiting for her, a glittering figure under the bright, her skirt and vest like melted silver.

Depta approached, and bowed, trembling. She knew what Chiron would ask. With no other greeting, Chiron murmured, "Do you love us, Depta?"

"Yes, Lady." Depta remained standing, not falling into that fatal swoon. So here was her answer to that perplexing question: could fear and love dwell together? Yes, they could.

By the garden's wall, the steward Cho crouched, weighed down by a shackle that he wore over his shoulders. He couldn't run far with such a necklace. Catching Depta's eye, and taking that for permission to acknowledge her, Cho bowed nearly in half. Somehow, he managed to pull himself upright again.

Chiron regarded the steward without malice. "Cho does not love us."

Hearing his name, Cho bowed once more. His face was bruised where he'd been stoned by his associates in the Magisterium, but otherwise he had weathered his confinement well. Depta knew that his days would not be long, that he was alive only to preserve the option that Titus Quinn might confound all expectation and return *here*. Although Chiron was convinced he would go to Ahnenhoon, the man was unpredictable. He might wish to rescue this steward who had once helped him.

Depta regarded Cho with misgivings. How had such a timid sentient dared to break the vows? But of course at the time he hadn't known that he played a role in exalted matters. This was a new anxiety for the Hirrin, to know that one could fail in duty without intending evil. She saw Ascendancy life as more perilous than before. Stewards wearing prison collars, Chiron falling into a stupor for no reason, Depta—briefly—accused of spying. These shocking events trickled darkly through her mind, eroding the firm ground upon which Depta had always stood. This garden was the center of that darkness: Titus Quinn's old quarters. Lady Chiron came here day after day, obsessed. Perhaps mad. That didn't bear thinking of, that the lady might have become logically unbalanced. Especially, that she hid things from Nehoov, Inweer, Oventroe, and Ghinamid. The latter was excusable, since he slept. But the other three . . . unforgivable. Yes, the lady might well be mad.

"Bright Lady," Depta said, hoping to introduce a safe topic, "the legate Hu Zha has arrived at Yulin's camp. He reports that he has been received with courtesy, and finds Yulin ready to comply with all duties."

"Ah." Chiron looked as though she hardly remembered Yulin or her spy.

"As you commanded to know," Depta said, bowing again, trying to fill an uncomfortable silence.

Chiron finally said, "Hu Zha, the legate. Hnn. But Depta, even with Hu Zha watching, Yulin might secretly hear from Titus-een." This term, Depta had heard a few times before; a pet name for the man of the Rose.

"Lady, Hu Zha is a most resourceful legate. Not easily deceived if Yulin turns against us, heaven give us mercy."

She resisted the urge to bow. Standing so close to Chiron, Depta found herself staring at the lady's hands. Hands were a wonderful feature, and all creatures rose high in service who had them, such as Chalin, Jout, Ysli, and even Gonds. Chiron's hands weren't as lovely as her other features. Ridges on the top of her hands showed where the sheathed claws lay. Depta's prehensile lips were no match for hands and claws.

The thought of a physical fight with a Tarig alarmed her, and she forced her mind back to dwelling on Chiron's higher qualities. However, it was no use. Chiron noticed her discomfort.

"Do not bow like a courtier, Preconsul."

"No, Lady." She began to bow anyway, and stopped herself.

Near the garden wall, Cho, no longer able to stand the weight of the collar, went to his knees in exhaustion.

Chiron turned from this sight. "He is a tedious companion. Let him rest in the mud, and contemplate the breaking of vows." She walked toward the open veranda that joined the garden with the apartment, signaling for Depta to follow her.

Chiron led Depta into a small but elegant chamber. In all the times of waiting upon her lady in the garden, the preconsul had never before been in Titus Quinn's former quarters.

In the center of the room, a sleeping platform was dressed with brocaded blankets. Two scrolls lay there, as though just yesterday Titus Quinn had put them down, intending to read them again. An ornate rug covered most of the floor. On two of the walls hung large tapestries depicting people in strange garb as well as bizarre animals. Scenes from the Rose, Depta suspected.

The lady murmured, "You have seen such tapestries before, Depta?"

Her conversational tone put Depta more at ease. "Only pictures of such, Bright Lady."

"Hnn. He would have the custom brought here, to fashion figures in woven material. We gave him this tapestry especially." She went to the closest wall and drew her long fingers down the cloth. The weaving depicted a lithe-looking animal, like a Hirrin, yet unlike. The prancing animal was pure white in color, with a beard. Crowning the head was a single upright horn.

"What is the creature, Lady?"

"A strange one, ah? We have no term for this beast. He had a word for it, but we do not use dark languages." Chiron put her hand on Depta's back, causing an involuntary flinch at the unexpected caress. The lady pointed at the tapestry. "Here you see the white beast has a low fence around it. It prances as though it would leap free. Do you see, Depta?"

"Yes, Lady."

Chiron traced the fence with a finger, her claw slightly extruded. "But he does not leap free. Why, Depta?"

"Because he does not wish to leave." Depta noted a tear at the corner of the tapestry. That would be where Titus ripped the weaving from the wall, that day when, returning to his old prison, he had been followed by Lord Hadenth. Titus had escaped behind the tapestry, to that tunnel he had once created during captivity.

Almost inaudibly Chiron repeated, "Does not wish to leave. Yet does wish it." Then, turning to Depta, she said, "Do you wish to find him, Preconsul?"

Depta's heart jolted at the question. "Of course, Bright Lady. The Repel . . . he will likely assault it."

"Ah. But even if he came peacefully, you must wish for his capture, Depta. Do you know why the first vow commands that the knowledge of the Entire be kept from the Rose?"

"To protect us, Lady." All children knew that.

"Hnn. But understand, Depta, why protection is needed. Our land is sweet and bright, our lives long; the Rose is dark and fleeting. The ephemeral will hate us, and take what is ours."

A cold summary. After all, Titus Quinn was just one human man. . . . But Depta would never voice such a thought, especially not with Chiron staring at her with that dark, fixed look. The lady wished for Depta to hate what she hated. Depta tried, but all she saw was a white beast in a cage. A part of her wanted to see it spring free.

Chiron went on, "Scholars tell us that the Rose sentients breed without thought to sustain themselves. How many progeny did your parents have, Depta? One, ah? All in accordance with the long lives of the bright realm where we seldom step aside for new individuals. Consider now the Rose: their billions become many more, all rushing through the door that Titus Quinn would force open. The door, once open, channels a torrent of darklings."

Depta imagined hordes of breeding humans overrunning the Entire. They might breed more slowly here, but the doors would be open. . . .

Chiron went on, "Consider not only the inundation of our sways, but the nature of those invaders. Think, Depta. In their short lives, their ties are momentary. They do not feel loyalty as you do. Their worlds are shattered by war and strife because their paths are dark. This is why we have created a peaceful realm, where merit is rewarded and laws replace impulse. We have improved upon the Rose, and left the Rose in a jar to darken and die.

"Still, we are gracious, even when provoked. Finding the man of the Rose among us, we afforded him every courtesy. We could not allow him to go back, to invite more darklings through the veil, no. But we made him welcome. To prevent him breeding here as he might have, we removed his wife from proximity. For this, he murdered his host, the gracious Lord Hadenth. For this, he lay waste all our brightships." She turned to survey the bed-chamber. "We arrived home to find that he had fled."

The room seemed empty, despite Chiron's and Depta's presence. Titus Quinn wasn't here. But his memory was vivid for the lady.

Chiron's voice stretched thin. "We had given him the mansion to roam, the Ascendancy to enjoy. But he cast these things back in our face. He had no concern for ties of loyalty or graciousness. Nor will his cousins of the Rose, if they come." She turned back to Depta, and her eyes no longer seemed crazed, but sad. "Do you comprehend?"

Depta was shaken. Never before had the lady discussed such things with her. She spoke with conviction: "I do comprehend, Bright Lady. The Entire must remain separate. Always."

"Yes, just so."

The lady strolled to the bed platform. "All remains as Titus-een left it." She gestured at the scrolls. *"The Age of Simulacra. The Twelve Wisdoms.* We have kept all as it was. So that he will recognize his chambers when he is required to return."

Depta observed wryly, "He is fortunate to return to former rewards."

Chiron stroked one of the blankets. "Some things will change, though." She led Depta to the tapestry depicting the horned white beast and pulled it aside.

Behind the weaving was a gaping hole and, beyond, a smooth cylinder, a hollow tube through the stone. "Here," Chiron said, "is the tunnel through which he leapt the fence."

Depta strained her long neck to peer inside. "How could he have programmed the tunnel so exactly? It is perfect."

Chiron's voice grew wistful. "He did not. I have gilded the tunnel."

"Gilded?"

"Hardened it. The walls will suffer no adjustments; there will be no escape. We will seal both ends, leaving him in darkness. Thus will he die, eventually."

A sobering vision. A long death, giving him time to consider the proximity of his former luxuries. But the man had invaded this land, and might do so again. Behind him were waves of Rose invaders who would swarm through.

Depta gazed at the sculpted and elegant face of her lady, seeing there a great ruler who held the Radiant Path in her protection. Seeing there a generous being who had found it in herself to bestow favors on a strange, misguided intruder. Until he had betrayed her and fled, killing those in his path. Seen in this light, the lady was far from unbalanced. She was what she had always been: Tarig, unfailingly Tarig, with all the perfection that implied.

Depta took leave of Chiron, making her way through the garden where the despicable Cho cowered. The lady had dismissed her, but already Depta was looking forward to the next time she would be in her presence. Depta did have the high calling she longed for: It was to serve the Tarig lady, and her justice. To keep the Entire free of the dark.

Underneath that lofty viewpoint she felt a subtle and surprising emotion—something she could hardly have imagined just an interval before: empathy for the Lady Chiron.

CHAPTER TWENTY

There are many worlds. Worlds above, worlds below, worlds in between. If you doubt, ask where you go, in dreams.

—Hoptat the Seer

JANG, STEWARD OF TRAINS, tucked his blanket more firmly around himself, nearly waking from his remarkable dream. In it, a bright lord was sitting in his kitchen. The high honor of serving the lord sent Jang scurrying to present a beverage service. A problem was, there were now four lords sitting at his table, and he had difficulty bowing and paying respects to all four at once. A train was coming in, and passengers pressed forward on the platform, surging for the best seats. But Jang couldn't meter that flow because ten lords crowded into his small cooking room, jostling each other, helping yet more lords to step out of the oven, where, Jang could clearly see, dough rose on trays. Dough shaped like lords. One was even now stepping out of the bake-well, grinning most unpleasantly and smelling of yeast. Jang twisted on his bed, aghast even in sleep to be having such thoughts. The bright lords in an oven! Even worse, oh much worse, the lords were now inviting him into the searing interior of their birthing chamber.

Deep in the Magisterium, Consul Shi Zu woke, sweating in his silks. The dream was receding rapidly, hardly coherent anymore. What could have been so distressing? It was only a dream. He padded over to the drinking fount, filling a jeweled cup with water to wet his dry throat. Looking out of his window on the Sea of Arising, he bowed reflexively to the world the gracious lords had created. As he rose from his bow, he had an unwelcome vision: that of the lords hooked to strings from far overhead. Alien hands came down from the bright, pulling the lords this way and that. He shuddered. Magisterium-trained and therefore not a man of imagination, he wondered how such repellent notions could come to him. Knowing that they *had* come to him kept him awake for some time.

Dreams came snaking into the ebb-time rest of those in the Entire who slept most deeply. Among these, the Hirrin princess Dolwa-Pan, recovering from a bout of nervous palpitations, moaned in her long throat, protesting her dream. The lords were gracious and beautiful. In their great wisdom they had created the world. Yes! So lovely, their form and their law. She thrust out her hooves in her sleep, pushing the dream away, the dream that the lords were simulacra, not flesh, not gracious, not truly alive. Her prehensile lips unconsciously nipped at her chest, searching for the heart chime that used to bring her such comfort. She had lost it soon after she had traveled with a nice Chalin man she had met on a train. A man who journeyed with a young woman who was teaching him how to fight. She sometimes feared that the young woman had stolen the chime; if so, a shocking gesture of disrespect to the lords. She turned in her sleep, momentarily waking. Visit the girl with such poxy dreams, she thought. When she fell back to sleep the puppets were waiting.

Zai Gan, Master of the Chalin sway, roamed his brother's garden, shaking off unsettling night-visions. He thought of the animal park as his half-brother's, although Yulin had disappeared into the wastelands, abrogating his position and wealth. Around Zai Gan, growls and hoots came from the many cages. Despite the animal sounds, this ebb-time stroll calmed him and assured that he wouldn't entertain further dreams. He couldn't remember what they were, but once nightmares started, it had been his experience that they tended to play themselves out, especially after three helpings of dessert at table. Passing the tiger's cage, he recalled that this creature had recently given birth to three young. Sweet little fur balls, one of his wives had remarked. Tarig bear no children, the thought came. He had dreamed an awful dream, but he couldn't remember it. He was just as glad.

Though in a stuporous sleep, BeSheb the Gond muttered her prayers from deep habit: "O Miserable God look at me, O counter of sins, observer of sorrows, I am not afraid, I am not debased to attend thee. . . ." In the dream a Tarig lady stood before BeSheb, her eyes rolling backward like marbles. The high lady was a mechanism, unconscious, insensate, waiting the occupation of a higher sentient to sit in her body. "O Miserable God . . ." BeSheb's voice trailed off. The Tarig never gave the Woeful God his due. Nor did the Tarig give BeSheb proper respect, since she was a godder. BeSheb had never cared for the strutting lords. Too tall, disgustingly narrow, lacking in bodily joy and gusto. The Tarig lady rattled in front of her, horribly broken. BeSheb chuckled in her sleep.

In Ghinamid's Tower, the tallest point in the city of the Tarig, Cixi braced herself against the alcove walls. It was an alcove like many on the three-hundred-stair climb, but this one possessed a concealed stone well computational device with a small cup to receive a redstone. The wall before her had enlivened, showing Mo Ti's words.

Cixi slumped to her knees.

It was some time before she lifted herself up to read the message again. The words shimmered on the stone, and shimmered in her heart. Oh, my dear girl. The brave girl had done what no one else could do. Found the underbelly of the beasts.

The bright lords were nothing more than conveyances for incorporeal beings. They were not citizens or lords of the world, but interlopers, passing through, afraid to partake of life and death. Cixi had hated them before, as one hates and fears a predator; now the hate was sweetened by disgust. The

Tarig were monstrous in nature, nothing like a proper sentient. Not only that, they were controlled from outside the Entire, still tethered to the Heart. A thousand thousand days the Tarig had fostered distrust of the outside, the non-Entire, vilifying and despising the Rose. Today the Tarig were exposed as outsider themselves, continually passing to and from, a part of some uncanny swarm that all sentients would find abhorrent.

A better enemy could not be imagined.

Cixi's heart lifted, thinking of her dear girl's success. Sydney, my sweet and suffering girl. Soon to be Sen Ni, when she came to her proper Chalin name, when she would ask the Chalin sway to rise up with her against the river spiders. Sen Ni! Cixi was surprised to find a tear moving down the excellent thick paint of her face. She patted the wetness away. Her attendants must repair that before anyone saw that the high prefect went abroad in careless presentation.

She tapped the stone well to spit out her stone. Receiving it from the ejection cup, she strung it on the thong and placed it around her neck, tucking it in. She descended the stairs of the tower, emerging into the flat glare of the bright.

Her attendant on this outing was Subprefect Mei Ing. The woman bowed placidly, not understanding how the world had changed. Vacant as the Empty Lands, Cixi thought. Mei Ing's perfect features were framed by upswept hair spiked with decorative pins. As subprefect, she was supposedly in training for the office of high prefect of the Magisterium, the Great Within. That had always been a pretext, but now Mei Ing was surely as useless as legs on an Adda.

Sydney rises. The kingdom rises, Cixi thought. And you, Mei Ing, fall.

Mei Ing bowed once more.

Not even such groveling could tarnish Cixi's mood. Mei Ing smiled at the pleasant expression on Cixi's face. The subprefect was devoid of intrigue, ambition, manipulation, and cruelty. She would never have made a good leader.

Cixi managed a tic of a smile in return. Sen Ni would soon hold court in the bright city, and Mei Ing could watch from the gallery.

CHAPTER TWENTY-ONE

Hush and sleep, the Nigh flows in place,
Hush and sleep, the city floats in grace,
Rest and ebb, shadow time draws nigh,
Rest and ebb, violet cools the sky.

—Ebb song

IN THE DIRIGIBLE OF THE MOST VENERABLE GODWOMAN, Benhu and Helice took quarters with the rest of the crew—two Ysli, a Jout, and four Chalin.

Alarmed at first to be accepting a ride from a high-ranking godder, Benhu had listened with amazement as Quinn explained their good fortune. As agreed upon with Zhiya, Quinn claimed that the high godwoman was indulging in her pastime of raiding the pilgrimages to find lovers, and had chosen Quinn. Not as gullible as Benhu, Helice demanded the real story, but didn't seem surprised when Quinn didn't oblige her.

"What will happen to our beku?" she asked him.

He shrugged. "I suppose he'll keep pulling wagons across the veldt until he drops."

She looked unhappy. "I made the new owner promise to brush him. But the godman looked disreputable."

"You should have made him promise to shoot the beast. The beku might have thanked you."

Helice didn't smile, but waiting at the cabin hatchway, Zhiya broke into a broad grin. Quinn passed through to Zhiya's quarters, and the godwoman slammed the hatch shut.

"I don't trust her," Zhiya said. "She has slippery eyes."

It was true, Quinn thought. It matched the rest of her.

"Thank you for preserving our little story about my voracious sexual appetites. I don't think the Tarig would thank me for giving Titus Quinn a ride."

"Helice may suspect we're lying about that."

"Perhaps we should make it the truth." Zhiya put up her hands, stopping him from comment. "When you're ready, not yet. You can have this cabin. I'll sleep with my mother."

"We can share this cabin, Zhiya. It's large enough."

"Shall I take that as giving me hope?"

Quinn smiled in answer.

Zhiya needled, "You know that the longer we're together the less alluring we'll find each other. We'd better share a pillow now, before I start to look like a dwarf."

He looked at her, thinking how much he liked her. "You have no idea how long it's been, Zhiya."

"Oh," she murmured, "better and better." She nodded at her mother's door. "When you make up your mind you know where you can find me."

Zhiya's airship, although proceeding no faster than the rest of the caravan, kept Quinn and his party out of sight, a significant advantage. Quinn enjoyed the time apart from Benhu and Helice, but now, in the more leisurely company of the Most Venerable, Quinn found himself perversely aware of the chain around his ankle. It shifted when he moved. Waking in the ebb, he would feel for the cirque, thinking it had fallen off. When he touched it, it seemed colder than it had been. The sooner the dirigible brought them to the River Nigh, the sooner he might have confidence about the thing he bore—if Lord Oventroe could assess its potency. If not, let the damn gracious lord give him something reliable.

Meanwhile, Quinn and Zhiya spent hours by the side of her mother, where he witnessed a daughter's devotion, including humble tasks of changing the swaddling garments and daily recitations of the day's gossip and events, punctuated by the navitar's incoherent utterances. The woman was far gone, and by her nearly black hair, very old.

The days passed as the midlands of the Arm of Heaven Primacy passed below them. One day Zhiya said to Quinn, "You must grow a beard—muss up that nice face for when you get to the Nigh, where smarter sentients than godders will be on the watch."

Quinn agreed. Like his hair, his beard grew in white. Long ago Su Bei had altered his hair, thinking that one day Quinn would need camouflage. Bei hadn't realized how soon that would be.

Helice wondered what was up with the dwarf, and if Quinn was really going at her in the next cabin. Not that she wanted any details. She had barely fended him off the day before when he planted his lips on hers, and that had been quite as much of Titus Quinn's body as Helice cared to encounter.

Now she was relegated to a cramped cabin shared by seven other people—no, not people, sentients; she really had to get used to this. She even had to share the crew's wastery, no more than a hole in the deck that could enlarge to accommodate a Hirrin and smelled like it already had. It galled her that Quinn would travel in style when she was the one recovering from a painful burn. It was true that the burn was knitting smoothly, and she didn't really need medicinals to sleep. But still. It was a pattern; she always got the short stick around him. And never the truth.

For example, the business about Zhiya choosing him for a bedmate. It was laughable that he came up with that kind of story. What did he and Zhiya really have in common? Had they met on one of his previous jaunts in the Entire? So if Zhiya was a friend, did that mean she would risk the ire of the nasty Tarig? Helice filed that away for future consideration.

And why did people look at him like he was some kind of lord? Whenever he was in the central cabin, the Jout stared at him. The Ysli creatures, too. It was hard to believe *they* were intelligent. They watched him like a media star. Perhaps they suspected who he really was. And if so, why that mooning look? Because he had once been a prisoner in the Tarig city, and managed to escape? Was there some kind of big legend about that? Or was it about Quinn's second visit? He never said much about what he did last time. Looked for Sydney. Didn't find her. *Not* the whole story. This was her maddening disadvantage here. She didn't have the whole story. She was a fast learner—that was a fact—but she was in an alien realm and functioning at the equivalent level of a dred, for God's sake.

She settled into her nest of blankets, letting the hum of the dirigible's engine lull her. She would take some rest while she could, to improve her stamina so that in due time, and with Sydney Quinn's help, she could improve culturally. The Inyx nation—more likely, *pastures*—would provide a safe haven until she was ready to fry bigger fish than Titus Quinn.

But he was definitely going in the frying pan before anyone else.

Zhiya had a pot of wine by her side and poured liberally for herself and Quinn. Her mother had had a good night's sleep, and Zhiya was celebrating. She celebrated a lot, Quinn noticed.

The Most Venerable regarded him with friendly curiosity. "After all these days, you still haven't said why you're here. In the All."

"No." He smiled to soften his refusal.

"Actually, you don't need to say. I think I know." Zhiya plumped the pillows surrounding herself and murmured, "Ahnenhoon. You've given out that the battle plains are where you're headed. But that's not it, is it?" She went on without waiting for an answer. "Why would you want to go there, after all? Quite a distance. The farthest you *can* go. And full of danger, what with Paion wreaking havoc, and generals with weapons."

"It's better you don't know, Zhiya."

She sighed. "I know so many things that I wish I didn't. It's almost as though I can't help accumulating bothersome knowledge. Now you're here, and that's another thing I'm not supposed to know." She gave him a lopsided smile. "Still, it gives me some solace knowing why you take your celibacy so seriously. Very admirable. Given *how long* it's been." She took a sip of wine, then murmured, "It's because of the woman of the Rose. Your wife. Am I right?"

After a pause he said, "That was long ago."

"Yes," she allowed. "A sad story. I'm sorry."

"You've had your own sorrows."

"When we heard of her . . . preferences, it surprised us. Rumor had it that she hated them. Perhaps she succumbed to their charms."

"Succumbed?" Quinn wondered what she was getting at.

There was a long pause, during which Zhiya muttered, "Oh dear, you don't know." She put her hands on her knees, thinking. Then she rose, bringing the pot of wine over to him. She poured him a full cup. "Drink."

At the look on her face, he drank. Then, wiping his mouth, he said, "Stop pacing, Zhiya, and sit down. Just tell me, if there's something I have to hear."

She sat by his side, taking his hand in hers. "Did you think your wife was dead?"

The moment stretched out. "Yes."

"Quinn. She's not dead."

The whir of the dirigible engine came faintly to his ears, like a tiny drill into his mind. He pulled away from her, trying to hear her correctly.

Zhiya went on. "She lives at Ahnenhoon, still."

"Ahnenhoon," he repeated. Still at Ahnenhoon. His mind had slowed. "Everyone says she died."

"Of course that's what they say. That's all most sentients know. But I've known those who have seen her."

He closed his eyes, trying to absorb it. Johanna. Johanna. Her image came to him, and it overwhelmed him. "Alive," he whispered. "How can she be alive?"

Zhiya's voice was soft. "I know a thousand, thousand things that I'm not supposed to. I collect information, Quinn—haven't you figured that out yet? Someone has to know the truth in this *radiant place*."

He put his head in his hands. He saw Johanna, heard her voice. Dead, so long dead. He had thought.

"I thought you knew," Zhiya said. "I'm sorry to be the one to tell you."

"To tell me my wife is alive?"

"No." She took a gulp of wine. "To tell you that she has . . . a partner."

He nodded at this pronouncement, as though it were logical. Yes, she might find someone else after so many years. But on another level, he could not process what he was being told. His wife was alive.

Zhiya whispered. "Now, this will be hard."

"It gets harder?"

"You know how, sometimes, one becomes dependent . . . on one's jailor?"

He stood up. The room was so hot he could barely breathe. Dependent. On one's jailor. Is that what Zhiya said? He tried to concentrate. Johanna. Finding some peace in the only arms available. Yes, he remembered what that was like.

"With Lord Inweer?"

Zhiya murmured. "So the tale has come to me."

He went to the viewport and drew back the drapes, staring out. He stood there for a long time. He had made his peace with Johanna's death; at the time, a terrible peace. Hearing her name now, imagining her alive, loving someone else, brought his mind to a halt. He gazed out the window a long while, trying to absorb what he had heard. Zhiya didn't interrupt him.

If Johanna willingly stayed at Ahnenhoon, he could imagine why. The Tarig were, at times, fascinating. He knew it all too well. The psychological pressures of being a captive—gratitude for small mercies shown . . . it was easy, as Zhiya said, to become dependent. He pushed aside these thoughts for later. Because she was alive. Incredibly, he hadn't even suspected. He was so badly stunned that he could only gaze out the viewport, watching the relentless passage of the veldt.

Once, in the background, he heard Zhiya go to the hatchway and ask for a new pot of wine.

Eventually, the lights dimmed in the cabin. Turning back to face Zhiya, he saw that she had removed her clothes. The world presented one bizarre thing after another. Where was his solid base, his certainty?

"Lie down," she told him as she positioned herself on the pillows. "We can just lie here," she said. "I think we both need a bit of comfort."

He stood by the bulkhead, wondering what his life had become, wondering if he *could* find comfort with her.

"Come here, Quinn," she said. "In a world of misery, this is not wrong."

She beckoned him, and he walked toward her in a daze. He murmured, "I don't know what to do."

"Can I tell you?"

He nodded.

"Take off your clothes."

He did so, standing for a moment before her, feeling untethered, unreal.

"An ankle chain," Zhiya murmured. "Very attractive. The whole view, very attractive. I could die right now."

He kneeled beside her. Her face looked kind. Her body, sweet and mysterious. "You're bedding a crazy man, Zhiya."

"Oh, good."

She dimmed the lights with a wave at the walls. In the darkened cabin, he could just make out her ruby smile.

PART III

THE NIGH WILL KEEP

CHAPTER TWENTY-TWO

These are high stations: master of a sway, legate of the Magis-
terium, navitar of the river. And the highest is this: a happy
marriage.

— saying of Si Rong the Wise

SUZONG SAT BETWEEN ANZI AND LING XIAO SHENG in a small tent, deco-
rated for the ceremony of the marriage gift. The betrothal ribbons fluttered
on the inside, not the outside of the tent, to preserve their camouflage. Disastrous enough that the Tarig lady had an agent in the camp—but they must at
all cost avoid discovery by others. It was Chiron's command, for starters.

Seated on Suzong's right was Anzi, looking like a veldt mouse cornered
by a Gond. On Suzong's left sat Anzi's suitor Ling Xiao Sheng, handsome
with his freshly oiled hair pulled into a topknot. In front of him lay a small
parcel. Anzi would accept the marriage gift, and then Yulin would conduct
the ceremony at the first waxing of the bright. That was the plan. Lately
plans had tended to disorder, beginning with their flight from the sway, then
discovery by Chiron's spies, and now Anzi's stubbornness. Suzong sighed. No
wonder she suffered from fractious dreams.

The three of them sipped oba as small talk sputtered. Suzong let the
silence lengthen, her thoughts turning again to Yulin's heart, and what he
would choose. His insistence on this marriage was a clear signal he was
choosing the Ascendancy. Her husband forced this marriage on Anzi, to distance her—and by implication, Yulin—from the man of the Rose. It at least
gave Yulin time to play all sides, until the winner became clear. Though she

loved him, the old bear was cautious. Suzong, on the other hand, had urged defiance.

She could not love the gracious lords after watching them use the garrote on her mother. That day long ago, she had desperately hoped that her mother would tear the device from her throat and throw it in the Tarig's face. That was her first lesson in Tarig power. Suzong had waited sixty thousand days to commit an act of defiance. But she was not master of the sway, and she could not part ways with her husband. Therefore Anzi would pair with Ling Xiao Sheng, and that was the end of it.

The girl could no longer lie about being pregnant. Suzong had blood proof that Anzi carried no child. A simple matter of finding where Anzi had buried the rags, and then the not-so-simple confrontation with Anzi. The girl had cajoled and argued, sometimes brilliantly. *Save me for a marriage that can truly matter, when Yulin is restored to reputation. What good will Ling Xiao Sheng bring us?*

Poor child, Suzong thought. Anzi could not accept being a player in Yulin's larger schemes. Willful, spoiled. Suzong sucked her teeth.

Mistaking this sound for impatience, Ling put down the cup of oba and turned his attention to the packet lying before him. He unfolded the wrappings.

Anzi watched him, her face showing admirable control.

In the center of the wrappings lay a violet gemstone on a chain. Its gleaming facets and large size would have dispelled reluctance in most girls. Suzong hardened her heart. Let the girl accept it, and be grateful. Her uncle would have it so.

Ling waited for Anzi to voice her admiration. And waited. Suzong coughed softly to nudge Anzi, but still the girl remained silent. Ling, usually so confident, looked sickly at this fateful pause, his face greasy with perspiration.

Suzong had told Anzi last ebb, *You will not reject the gift, Anzi.*

No, Aunt.

Titus Quinn is not for the likes of you. Even if he succeeds in opening the door between worlds, he is not for you. If he takes a wife of the Entire, it must be a high lady.

Outside the tent, a beku brayed, mocking the solemn occasion of Ling Xiao Sheng's gift.

Anzi picked up the purple stone, turning it to catch the light. "Look, Aunt, how it shines."

Ling's smile was short-lived as Anzi said, "But too grand for such as I."

Suzong prompted him: "Surely the lovely Anzi is worthy of the stone."

"Truly," Ling hastened to agree. "The gemstone is beggared by the beauty of the breast where it will lie."

Suzong winced at the clumsy expression, but a man wasn't required to be good at conversation. She tried mightily to like Ling Xiao Sheng. A good family. He managed to dress well, even living in the wilderness. He did not belch at meals. . . . His qualities did not come readily to mind. Compared with Titus Quinn—well, there could be no comparison.

But why? Anzi had asked. *Why must he marry a high lady?*

To tie us together, the dark world and the bright.

But Aunt, I am of the bright.

The girl was stubborn to the point of blindness. Yulin had granted the girl's every whim from knee-high to the present day.

Understand, Anzi, that as the first envoy of the Rose, his station will be higher than yours. He will marry—if at all—a consul, or higher. They say that Subprefect Mei Ing at the Ascendancy seeks a husband.

But I am at least a niece of the master of the sway.

Nonsense. My husband took you in as a mercy. You are the child of a concubine of a distant cousin. You are no more a niece than I am a Jout. Marry Ling Xiao Sheng. You will learn to love him; and if not, you will love your children by him; and if not, you will have wealth enough not to care.

I will always care.

Suzong disliked to hurt the girl, but she had murmured, *My dear, does Titus love you?*

After a long pause, Anzi whispered, *He never said so.*

Suzong let that truth hang in the air between them. He never said so, no indeed. Anzi's resistance seemed to melt away after that. High time, Suzong had thought, not without sympathy for the girl's hopeless fantasies; but that, of course, was all they were.

In the murky tent, Anzi raised the pendant aloft, letting it turn on the chain, catching the available light. "You have surely paid too high a price for a marriage gift, Excellency."

Ling nodded. "It was dear." Glancing at Suzong he added, "But worth it, if it pleases you, Ji Anzi." The man was trying his best—on penalty of Yulin tying him to a beku and setting the animal's tail on fire.

Anzi looked up at him, and Suzong thought for a moment she would drive the bauble into one of the man's eyes. Instead, Anzi smiled.

"Put it on," he suggested.

Anzi complied, pulling the chain over her neck. Even against the dusty silk of her jacket, it looked handsome. Suzong thought the stone worth at least five thousand primals. It must have hurt Ling to lay down such a sum, especially given how little he, or any of them, had had time to salvage before the Tarig descended on the sway.

Anzi looked up. "Thank you, Ling Xiao Sheng. You can't know what this means to me. But I feel we have unfairly forced you to present such a fine gift." She lowered her eyes. "Because of my uncle's conviction that we must partner."

He was quick to demur. "My Anzi, never think that it is for his sake, or for the sake of formality. I would have given you this stone when we first met, you so moved my heart."

"Ling Xiao Sheng, thank you indeed. I pray you never hold against me that you lavished such expense on this unworthy person."

"Never," he said, with feeling.

Suzong expelled the breath she had been holding. She held out her hand for the stone, and Anzi deposited it there. Suzong would take custody of the gift until morning, when a plain and swift ceremony would finish the matter.

Sensing victory, Ling put his hand on Anzi's knee, and forced a smile.

Anzi's cheek twitched, and he removed his hand.

Noting the girl's cool reception of her betrothed, Suzong prayed that the Miserable God would not look on them in their long lives together.

It was the best she could hope for.

Anzi groomed the beku, shaking the mange nits from the brush. The beast craned its neck, grumbling in pleasure. Around her, the other beku were drowsy, swaying on their feet as they fell into a light slumber this late in the ebb.

Having traded places with a beku-tender, Anzi waited for Deep Ebb, when the camp wouldn't notice one lone rider on a beku slip away. No guards kept watch. They were too far from Ahnenhoon to suffer Paion attack, and they feared no other lawlessness. Still, she kept watch for spies, or Ling Xiao Sheng snooping about. She thought that she had succeeded in deceiving him today, since he had left the tent full of contentment. But since Ling was always satisfied with himself, it was hard to tell.

When the ebb darkened to its deepest phase, Anzi slowly walked the beku out of the corral, and into the folded hills.

She patted the belt around her waist where the gem resided. Finding it in Suzong's tent had been easy. Taking the stone but not the marriage was an unfortunate necessity. But hadn't Ling Xiao Sheng protested he would have given it to her the day he met her, regardless of the occasion? So the gem was hers by his own confirmation. In any case, it was hers in fact.

Selling it would finance her journey. She had no idea how far she'd have to go to find Titus. Would she be required to cross over to the Rose? The thought gripped her fiercely. With all her heart, she would like to see it.

Suzong lay awake as Yulin snored at her side. Anzi would be far away by now. Suzong had bribed her agents to smooth Anzi's escape. No one would follow the girl. By the bright, Suzong thought, if Anzi could help Titus Quinn, then she must.

She felt a twinge of guilt for intervening in her husband's plans. But they were small plans, both Anzi's part in them and—truthfully—overall. Yulin couldn't yet see that the Entire was on the verge of a great change, one way or the other. The Entire could become fearful, insular, and paranoid. Or it could open to the Rose. See what came of contact. And yes, dear husband, profit from it.

She turned over on her pallet, trying to find comfort for her old bones, but sleep would not come. *By my grave flag*, Suzong thought, *I have now chosen the man of the Rose over the Tarig. And my husband.*

The memory of her mother's terrible death came vividly to mind. Like mother, like daughter. Wasn't that a saying of the Rose?

CHAPTER TWENTY-THREE

Go not to the Midlands, far from the wall,
Nor to the Empty Lands, hearing that call.
Go not to the steppes, flat under the bright,
No ship plies there, no vessel in sight.
But come to the river, to the silver Nigh,
Five primacies claim it, but all of them lie.
Seek out the river, heartward to go,
All routes lead there, as the navitars know.
Fear not the river, trust the red pilot's throne,
Plunge into the deep, thence get you home.

　　　　　—"Home to the Nigh," a river song

THE DIRIGIBLE SHUDDERED IN THE WIND, skittering from side to side, making it hard to stand on the deck. Out the viewport, Quinn glimpsed the storm wall, a dark that sucked up the bright's outpouring light.

A jolt threw him against Zhiya for a moment as they stood in her cabin. "We're down," she said.

The passenger cabin of the airship jolted as the nose of the airship latched onto the mast. At this camp on the banks of the Nigh, permanent masts for airships eased the docking maneuvers. Quinn heard the ramp motors whine and then a thump as the ramp connected to the ground. Heavy footfalls announced that Zhiya's helpers had gone out to secure the landing.

She squinted up at him. "You look worse than before. Excellent." Free from the braid, his hair hung loose and unwashed. A growth of beard added to his unkempt appearance.

He knelt down and hugged her with tenderness. She hugged him back, then shoved him away, grinning. "Don't expect me to pine away for you. I serve the god, you know."

He laughed. "Yes, I know how much you do."

Smirking, she gestured to the next room. "A last visit with my mother?"

He followed her into the sickroom where the navitar lay, head turned toward the door as though she expected them, her long eyes fixing Quinn with a liquid stare.

Grasping the woman's hand, he said, "Journey well."

"Where bound?" she rasped, her eyes beseeching him.

They were among the few clear phrases he'd heard her speak in their nine days of travel.

The navitar gripped his hand with astonishing force. "Where bound? Where?"

"Ahnenhoon," he said.

The navitar looked at him in horror. He thought it was horror, but how could he tell? He glanced at Zhiya, who knelt by her mother's side, stroking her arm to calm her.

This caress drew the navitar's attention to her daughter. Her long, sloping eyes filled with tears. But she said no more. Zhiya wrapped her arms around her mother, quieting her. "It's all right," she whispered.

Quinn looked at the two of them, entwined in body and perhaps destiny. Zhiya to travel the primacy collecting her intelligences, and her mother to travel the inner paths.

He bowed to Zhiya. During the three-week passage, she had been his lover, and even better, his friend. She nodded, indicating she would stay by her mother's side. Gathering Helice and Benhu in the main cabin, Quinn led them down the gangway.

The sharp scent of ozone hit them as they gazed up at the storm wall, towering before them, at times appearing to fall, and then to advance, yet forever in place. The three of them stared like any newcomers would. At the foot of the storm wall, a silver ribbon glittered.

The Nigh.

Most inhabitants of the Entire never saw the River Nigh or traveled on

it. The passage was free, but filled with superstition, and mistrust of the navitars. Nevertheless, it was, as Zhiya had observed, the only way to travel far
and fast.

Quinn and his companions carried silk packs strapped to their shoulders,
bearing their possessions and gifts of food and money from Zhiya. Helice had
dispensed with her walking stick, traveling now with her throat carefully
draped in a scarf.

"I never met the navitar," Helice spat at Quinn in Lucent.

Startled, Quinn noted her vocabulary, her accent. Progressing fast. Soon
Helice would be more dangerous than she'd been so far.

"Old and sick," Quinn responded.

The pageant of godmen and godwomen had come to a halt near the river,
joining an enormous encampment of travelers, all hoping to embark on the
Nigh, but needing a ship of the river. The ships came on no discernible schedule.

He noted a bivouac of soldiers in the distance waiting transport to
Ahnenhoon. On the outskirts of this camp, ponderous forms milled.

Benhu noted his gaze. "Inyx," he said, exhaling a plume of brown pipe
smoke.

To keep their thoughts well hidden, the three of them would have to
shun the beasts. Proximity was a danger. Distance diluted Inyx communication with other sentients. But here they were close. *Don't think about the Rose,*
Benhu had advised. *Don't think about Johanna,* Quinn reminded himself,
veering away from his memories of her. So many thoughts to hide.

The Inyx were fresh arrivals, Benhu announced after a foray into the
throngs of soldiers. Here, they would train with the fighting units, and afterward depart in batches for the Long War. Quinn kept looking in their direction, curiosity plucking at him. Sydney was with such creatures. *Mustn't think
about Sydney.*

The turbulence from the storm walls spawned gusts of wind that yanked
on their silks and chilled them as they skirted the encampment to seek a place
to bed down. As Helice threw a barrage of questions at him about the Nigh,
Quinn finally tired of her. "Guard your thoughts. The Inyx are still close."

She raised an eyebrow. "Do you really think the Inyx would turn us in?
The way they despise the Tarig?"

Quinn noted that she had been gathering information on this subject, as well as other topics, no doubt. He preferred her ignorant, and didn't respond.

The three of them found a spot for a camp in an undesirable region of hillocks, a marsh where the river inundated in rivulets of exotic matter. With Quinn and Helice resting on a small rise, Benhu went in search of a tent where they could find some shelter from the wind. Helice chattered, and he humored her incessant questions, wishing mightily for better company but knowing that, from this point on, he wouldn't likely have any. In the distance, he caught a glimpse of Zhiya's airship, hovering like a mother bird over her flock. Despite the news she had brought him, which he must not think about, he was glad of meeting the godwoman.

Quinn broke out some food wafers and tubes of water, stored like loops of sausages in their packs, while Helice managed a fire with the last of their resin logs. She infused a pot of oba.

Quinn let her serve him. The bright ebbed as he drank from the steaming cup, his thoughts circling around Johanna, who was back in his life in a way he could not comprehend. A profound lethargy settled over him.

Benhu returned with a tent. Helice demanded that she and Quinn share the tent, but she would not, she said, consider sleeping in the same tent with Benhu, who after all, had tried to kill her. Quinn hardly cared. Sleep beckoned, though it was only Twilight Ebb. He helped Helice pitch the tent while Benhu set out in search of a second tent.

Climbing inside the shelter, Quinn listened to the wind punch at the fabric walls. Just before he lost consciousness he realized that he was ill. A dreadful sleep pulled him under. He tried to rise, to speak, but his muscles failed, and his tongue hung limp. He fell into the black.

Looking up, he saw the tidal wave of the storm wall wavering, ready to tip. Buckling high under the press of the shoreline, it had massed up to a dizzying height. Now, at last, it curled over at the top. It plunged down, engulfing everything.

The ocean surge tossed him, rolled him in a human ball. The chain on his ankle pulled him relentlessly downward. Must get the chain off. Must breathe.

"Me too!" Helice shouted. The chain, the chain. Helice was thrashing in the storm, sinking just like him, clamoring for the chain. But why did she want the thing that was dragging them to the bottom?

He fought back to a blurred and drugged consciousness. Helice was on top of him, facing backward, yanking at the cirque.

He growled at her, but his voice was a candle flame, flickering in the wind. *Four, five, one. Why was that important? Four, five, one.*

The chain fell off.

An alarm blazed through him as he fought for clarity. Helice was stealing the cirque. Her feet hit him in the face as she scrambled from the tent. She had the chain. The only hope of the Rose, he managed to remember.

Rousing himself with a supreme effort, he launched himself out the tent door, falling on her with such force that the breath left her lungs in a gasp. Swearing at her in two languages, he groped to find her hands, to find the chain. How many hands did she have? He found nothing except her nails digging at him. He struck her, his blow glancing off her temple, but she fled.

He followed her. The ebb was dappled gray and purple, reflected in the slicks around him. Helice's reflection ran through the iridescent pools, as if she took refuge in the exotic matter, rushing through a dimension he couldn't penetrate. Scrambling after her in a daze, he lost her in the hillocks. He staggered on, fighting the urge to lie down and close his eyes. But there she was again, just ahead, and he followed, jumping the pools, feeling like he might lose contact with the marsh and jump into flight. He saw her fall at the crest of the next hill, and putting on a burst of speed, he clambered up the slope, diving for her.

With the impact of his tackle, he saw the chain fly from Helice's grasp. Leaving her sprawled behind him, Quinn dove down the embankment, losing his balance but sliding within reach of the cirque. He grabbed it.

Helice stood at the top of the hill, bent over, gasping. Then she straightened. Walking down the embankment, she came to a stop, looking down at him. He lay sprawled on the hillside, gripping the cirque so hard his nails dug into his palm. Helice kneeled down and yanked at the chain, but Quinn had it in a death grip. She stood, kicking him viciously and trying again to loosen the chain from his grasp.

She looked up. "Benhu's coming," she rasped. She gazed up at the storm wall, her silks shuddering in the wind. Then she regarded him once more, her face flat and hard. "Kill them, then," she said. "Kill them, Titus."

He whispered, "Kill who?"

She looked at him with contempt. "Everyone." She pointed at the storm wall. "Everything. You can't use that kind of destruction in the Entire. Ever. You can't wage war here."

She crouched down, getting closer to his level. "The chain will mangle everything." She yanked at the cirque again, uselessly.

"My chain," he mumbled.

She snorted. "You arrogant bastard. Your chain. Your Entire. Your family. I'm sick to death of you." She stood, kicking her boot into his ribs. He barely felt it. She was moving off. Where was she going?

At some distance away, she turned back, saying, "Destroy the cirque unless you want to kill another child—your own this time. Maybe you don't give a damn about her. You left her—twice, didn't you?" Her voice lowered. "Family man. Big family man." She staggered away.

He closed his eyes. When he opened them, Benhu bent over him. "Excellency, Excellency." In the wind his beard and hair danced around his face, adding to his look of agitation.

"Helice ran away. Go get her," Quinn murmured.

"But you're hurt."

"No. She drugged me. Get me up." Benhu helped him to a sitting position. "Find her, Benhu. If she escapes, she's a danger to us."

At Quinn's urging, Benhu was finally persuaded to follow Helice, and he loped off, following her footprints in the marshy soil.

Benhu rushed through the quagmire, fearful of the tendrils of the Nigh, the little fingers of silver poison. He jumped carefully across the streams, finding dry footholds, rushing to intercept the woman before she ruined everything. What if a Tarig lord was here, as sometimes they were, watching crowds, mingling to confound simple folk? What if a lord should demand that she speak, demand who she traveled with? He rushed on.

A glimpse of her, ahead, winding through the campfires of decent godmen. She turned back and, seeing Benhu, ran away, drawing the notice of those still awake at this hour, sipping oba or wine and wondering at the fuss.

Benhu cursed himself that he hadn't killed her when he had the chance. It was what Lord Oventroe would have wanted. She's a danger to us, Quinn had said. Benhu's heart clutched at the thought of facing the lord and explaining why he hadn't taken care of the problem, why he had allowed Quinn to be captured . . . but surely it wouldn't come to that. Breaking into a run, he lifted his robes and pursued her with all his strength, but she was fast, and he lost sight of her amid the wagons and sky bulbs in the encampment of the godmen. Nearby, a ship had settled, a navitar's vessel, resting on its struts after skimming over the marsh. A huge crowd jostled to approach it, shouting destinations and pleading with the ship keeper who stood on the bow. He and Quinn ought to be on that vessel now, rushing to their task, not tending this miscreant Gondling who had poisoned Benhu's precious charge.

Catching sight of Helice again, Benhu followed her as she hurried past the camp and into a field that separated the decent folk from the herd of Inyx. To Benhu's horror, she made straight for the beasts. This was the worst she could do, to lay their plans bare before the devouring minds of the barbarians. He staggered to a halt, legs weak, lungs aching.

As he watched, Helice stood some distance inside the Inyx camp, looking around her. Perhaps, in their surprise, the beasts would tolerate Benhu rushing forward to claim her.

But before he could move, Inyx mounts and their riders began crowding around Helice, closing off his view. What could she have said to them? She knew few words. And what did she want from them? Sanctuary? But why should they . . . Benhu groaned.

She didn't need to speak. They spoke heart to heart. But what was in the woman's heart? He walked slowly forward, hoping for a glimpse of what was happening. Other mounts and riders had joined the throng around her, but most of the Inyx surrounding her were riderless.

Benhu knew what she intended. Had he figured it out, or did the Inyx speak to him in their cursed sendings?

Choose me, choose me.

Do you ride?

No, teach me to ride.

Whimpering, Benhu saw disaster coming. Helice was throwing herself at the Inyx, hoping to bond with a stinking mount. What would that mount discover, looking into her thoughts?

He took a few steps closer, trying to think of a way to prevent what was happening.

Then, to his dismay, he saw Helice perched on the back of a mount. It was too late. She had been chosen. Benhu groaned.

A broad-backed Inyx took a few steps in his direction. Benhu judged his chances of rushing in, pulling her off the mount she rode, and screaming for help from the army troops quartered nearby. He did not find the courage to pull this off.

Helice rode away, deeper into the Inyx camp.

The mount who had been watching him now took a few menacing steps in his direction, the horns on his back gleaming under the bright.

Benhu heard, *Leave quickly.*

Illogically plugging his ears against the beast's questing mind, he hurried away.

CHAPTER TWENTY-FOUR

An untold secret is a fire in the mouth.

—a saying

JOHANNA STOOD BEFORE THE OPEN ARCHWAY leading to the Gond den, a place few in Ahnenhoon had seen. At her side was the stalwart Pai, aghast that her mistress would come to this place. She dabbed a perfumed scarf at her noise to dilute the stench.

All the way from Johanna's apartments Pai had remonstrated against coming here. Johanna's determination only fueled Pai's suspicion that Morhab held her mistress hostage in some way. No doubt she suspected it had to do with Gao's death three days ago, but Pai could only guess. Johanna had often longed to confide in Pai, but in the end she trusted no one.

Pai pursed her lips. "It is not suitable, mistress. Have him come to you, if he desires company."

Company. If that is what Morhab wanted. It made Johanna ill to think it might be more.

Lurking a few steps behind them was the damnably quiet SuMing.

With the fortress in an uproar over Gao's apparent suicide, SuMing had yet to tattle that Johanna had left her chambers that ebb-time. Perhaps the girl felt some pang of loyalty toward the woman who had saved her from a fall similar to Gao's. Eventually SuMing might make demands in return for her silence. Damn the girl. Watching, ever watching.

"Ask the gracious lord for assistance, mistress," Pai whispered, plucking at Johanna's sleeve.

"I will go in." Johanna's tone brooked no argument, and she left her

221

women behind as she passed through the chamber opening. She breathed deeply to submerge her fear: He could hardly hurt her or leave bruises—Lord Inweer would notice. How trivial, that day on Morhab's sled, when all he wanted was for her to sit next to him.

We've gone well beyond that, now, she thought.

Johanna passed into Morhab's chamber, thick with the clotted air of decay. The glow from the corridor quickly fell away, and she found herself in a dim, vaulted room. She paused, letting her eyes adjust to the darkened premises. Here was one thing that she and Morhab had in common; they both liked the dark. Whatever she had to do, at least there would be an obscuring cloak. Oh Titus, she thought. I have failed you. I can't help you, my darling. You must come and wipe the Repel from the face of the Entire. Wipe us all clean. She wasn't afraid of that end. It had been quite a while since she had been afraid of dying.

Peering into the habitat of Morhab the Gond, she saw what looked like pillars holding up the ceiling. Coming closer to one of them, she found that it was a stunted tree, broad-trunked and leafless. Here was a sparse forest appearing to spring from the floor, a floor that couldn't nurture any real forest; it was a hard surface below a layer of debris and dust. Perhaps Lord Inweer had created a simulated native environment for his favorite engineer, just as he had for his favorite concubine.

That was well to remember: She was a whore. This next part shouldn't be difficult.

A light glowed in the inner recesses of the den. She made her way toward it, wending past the squat trees, worn smooth and shiny in places, as though from long handling. Off to one side she thought she glimpsed pale shapes among the trees. Morhab's family.

Although the floor was heavily littered with rubbish, the path toward the light had been worn clean by frequent travel. She followed it. In this inner region, the reek of offal vied with rot, smells that stuck in her throat.

In a clearing just ahead, she saw a Gond resting. He was surrounded by well stone computers. The light from the screens spilled into the stunted forest, illuminating one tree in particular, one splotched with dark red. The flickering light lent a surge to the red stains, as though they still held some essence of life, of Gao. May God have mercy on him, she thought.

Johanna entered the clearing. There Morhab lay prone along a limb of a particularly massive tree, a startling feat for one of his bulk. His face and wings glowed from the screens of his stone wells, fixed to the branches by wire cages. She had never known that Gonds climbed in trees.

Morhab, who had been resting his chin on the smooth bark, watching his screens, turned to watch her approach. "Johanna," he said, his voice throbbing low.

She gave him the briefest of nods. "Chief Engineer."

"Johanna. So pale. Not well? Perhaps not sleeping peacefully?"

It was true that her dreams were salted with nightmare images. Some of Gao's broken body. But some too, of the Tarig. Not that she would ever tell Morhab anything so personal as a dream.

"Do you dream, Morhab?"

"Of you."

Heaving his massive body into a curve, he slid the lower part of his body backward toward the trunk of the tree. With surprising agility, he coiled himself around the trunk, moving in a slow, controlled slide to the ground.

He lay propped up against the tree trunk, his head at the same height as her own, his limpid eyes focused on her.

His well screens filled with numerical runes, lending a purplish twilight to the clearing. He noted her gaze. "Yes, Morhab's collection of knowledge. All is here. All that you worked so hard and so uselessly to uncover."

"Since nothing of importance went missing, why did you slaughter Gao?"

Morhab tucked his wings closer, creating a soft, crinkling sound. "Killed himself. Perhaps you can say why he did, Johanna. Did he love you, beg you for respite, pine for you in secret? Did you pretend to find him interesting, only to humiliate him at the last?"

She knew they weren't talking about Gao. "No. I was drawn to him, and he to me. Being human, perhaps I mistook the protocols."

"You mistook nothing." He waved at the screens, and they darkened to black, flaring now and then with sporadic bursts of numerals. "Yes," he said, pleased with his numbers, "it is all here. My obsession. The proportions of Ahnenhoon. Did you think you could take what I have spent twenty thousand days assembling?" Without waiting for her to answer, he went on, "The

Repel has an ancient story, going back to the Age of Nascence, when the lords first created the sways and preserved them from the vile Paion. The fortress once was comprised of the centrum alone. Then came the watch, the sere. As the Paion strength waxed stronger over the archons, the lords created the outer terminus, which the grandfather of my grandfather helped to design. My predecessors recorded their work. Still, it was never a matter of maps. It is all mathematical, Johanna. A concern of ratios and proportions and the correlations between shape and time. The fortress is designed to change, to confound visitors, and this is the supreme puzzle and mystery of my life, even though I know more about Ahnenhoon than any other creature of the All who is not a lord."

He smiled, open-mouthed. "You knew that. You sent Gao to steal."

"Yes."

His smile elongated. "So, a small, pure truth. There will be more."

"Or you will bleed me on a tree?"

A sigh gusted from his great mouth. "You do make me sad. You think I am a monster." His voice went quiet, sending a chill through her. "Come closer to me."

Father in heaven. Hallowed be. She walked toward him, stopping an arm's length away. In his short beard lay pieces of his last meal. She noticed for the first time that his horns were covered with a delicate fuzz. He was not satanic, she told herself, he was not. Mary, Mother of grace. Deeper in the chamber, a plopping sound announced that they were not alone.

He stared at her and rustled his vestigial wings. "Your scent," he said. "Insulting."

"Then stop trying to frighten me." How, she wondered, could he possibly smell her sweat with the load of rot in the air?

"If I wished to frighten you, would we be talking now? I show restraint, Johanna. Restraint." He grimaced for a moment, and from the folds of his skin came an extrusion of liquid that spread over his hide, turning it glistening. "Formerly, I mistook your scent as signaling pleasure in my company. But now I know my human smells. The fear smell. You always feared me. Why?"

Johanna thought quickly. "Your large form intimidates."

"And?" He waited.

"The horns. They look . . . dangerous." Her mouth had gone dry. You are a beast of hell.

"Dangerous. Intimidating." He murmured, "Sometimes. I would have you know other sides of Morhab the Gond. Are you ready for your instruction?"

She nodded.

"First, as to your plot with Gao. Know that I am not a political being. I am scientific and mathematical. I have no interest in outside affairs. So I do not care why you seek to destroy the engine, woman. I do not ask you to tell me what you would not reveal to Gao. I am no traitor, but your plots do not alarm me. Being an ignorant woman, you can do little against the machine.

"Know, Johanna, that the future of your habitat is dire and certain. Your unfortunate land is condemned, and must give way to ours. That is the pattern of the future, and the bright lords only know why. Useless to thwart them. This being so, you must give up your meddling. Undertake no further attempts to intrude on my workmanship or my private knowledge. I do not fear what you may discover, for you, like Gao, are supremely uninformed. But I would not suffer your indignities to my stone well files or my private theories. Do you submit to this injunction?"

"Yes." She knew there was more, and waited.

His voice lowered to a rumble that passed for a whisper. "You have thought me dangerous, political, and vengeful. There you have been wrong. I am emotional. My kind" —here he glanced toward where rustling sounds still persisted in the dim chamber—"are practical and remote. But I have lived among many sentients, and I have learned their ways. I no longer crave the company of my nest mates. I have craved your company, Johanna."

His eyes darkened. "It could have been mutually pleasant." He folded one wing into a wedge and scratched the back of his head. "You could have come for conversation long ago, but you despised me, all the while leading me to believe that you found my company inspiring. That was deceit. Now I propose that we begin again." He fell toward her, rolling easily onto the floor to spread full length; then he humped along, pulling himself toward a broken limb that lay felled nearby. He heaved himself up, and spread along its length. "Sit here by me."

She watched with revulsion as he slithered across the floor. Finding a place on the limb, she sat as close to him as she could bear.

As he clung to his perch, his body sagged down the sides of the branch, his chin resting on the branch. "Now you will talk to me."

"What shall I say?"

"No, that is not how it will be, Johanna. When I say talk to me, I mean talk without constraint or limits. Tell me your heart."

"My heart?"

"Your feelings. What you think about when you lie in your nest at night. What you never share with others."

"I have no thoughts like that. I am a simple woman."

"Johanna." He paused, making sure he had her attention. "I will have this intimacy. It is the price you pay for my silence with the lord. Be assured that I could demand very much more." He drew himself up into a lecturing posture, gesturing with his little hands. "Begin with what you do in a day. Everything. From first waking. Leave nothing out. I wish to participate, to know what thoughts are in your mind with each undertaking."

But she didn't want him to know anything about her, much less such details. "Surely that is of little interest to one of such intellect."

"I have keen interest. Provided that you withhold nothing."

"I don't have feelings about mundane tasks."

"Now, that is untrue. You are an expressive, sensitive creature." He watched her for a moment, breathing heavily through his mouth, emitting a foul miasma. As she hesitated, his voice turned to a low growl: "Make it worth my while so that I do not take you to my nest."

While her mind searched for something intimate—but not too intimate—to tell him, he said, "To become bestial would destroy our emotional intimacy. But if you anger me, I will ask my nest mates to indoctrinate you. I would not approach you before you understood our ways."

A brief vision of herself in a Gond nest set Johanna talking.

She talked slowly, haltingly at first. What emotions did one have in getting dressed or eating a meal? Over the next two hours, Morhab led her to understand that emotions were never far from even the most ordinary tasks. She found a shadowy world of feelings that formed the background of her awareness. Morhab was patient, but relentless. Under his probing questions, she spun out the hours of her life, closing her eyes to remember the emotions that went with each thing. She hadn't realized the fine details of her inner life, nor that she in fact lived on two levels. Morhab taught her that she did.

The Gond listened with respectful attention, and at times, rapt excitement, when he would whisper encouragement and guesses of what she might reveal next. It was worse than disrobing. Morhab was indeed an emotional creature, and an observant one: He watched her for any sign of withholding.

By the end of their session she had revealed her love of Earth and her hatred of the machine. These were things that Morhab knew or could guess. But she carefully avoided the subject of Titus's expected return, or that she had summoned him with her message so long ago. Nevertheless, Morhab was very interested in what she felt for her former husband. It was then that she spun lies, because she didn't know what she felt, and hadn't known, for a long time.

The strain of lying and also telling the truth left her drained and sick. At last he released her with the instruction to come back tomorrow.

She wondered if the Gond's nest could be any worse.

That ebb she brought a blanket to her forest so that she could lie in darkness. Pai spread her own blanket nearby. There was no moon or stars. Lord Inweer hadn't gone that far with her forest cell, but she was content with the prospect of a clean, dark night. Tears came—for herself, for Gao.

Pai crept close, reaching out to pat her shoulder. "Find a peaceful ebb, mistress. It is over now. Do not go back to the engineer."

"I see him again tomorrow, Pai."

Pai voiced her astonishment. "Then he holds a threat over your head."

"Yes." Johanna looked into the dark forest to locate SuMing. She had made her camp farther off. Johanna was relieved to be free for a moment of that blameful look. If she could banish the girl, she would, but these were the servants it pleased the lord to assign her. She had always understood that they were her jailors as well as her servants. That Pai had grown to love her was only an accident, a cherished stroke of fortune.

"You bear more than your share of sorrow," Pai said.

"Thank you, Pai, but everyone has their burden, I am sure."

"But you have lost your daughter and husband both, though they still live. That is a heavy sorrow. Forgive me for speaking of them."

It was a relief to speak of them to someone who didn't take a prurient interest in confidences. "My daughter has never answered my missives."

"An ungrateful girl, to behave so."

"No, not ungrateful, Pai. The lords stole her away, blinded her. And I live with one of them. It cannot be forgiven. I leave it to God to forgive me."

Pai made a two-fingered sign by her right eye. "God does not forgive."

"Mine does." That was the only thing left to hold onto.

Pai lay down next to Johanna, looking up at the black sky. "I know you grieve for what the engine will produce. The engine will pull the life from your world, and draw it into ours."

Stunned, Johanna said, "Oh Pai, you know?" She looked around in the darkness to be sure SuMing wasn't lurking.

"There are rumors of the engine," Pai said. In a gesture of startling intimacy, she brought her hands to the sides of Johanna's face. "Why should we destroy your home? It's not right. I wouldn't blame you if you tried to prevent it."

Johanna let go of a pent-up breath. So, Pai knew. And didn't condemn her. That was a small but sweet consolation amid her troubles. "I am done with the engine."

"Morhab holds this knowledge over you," Pai whispered. "The stinking beast."

Around Johanna the forest hung blackly. "I am in hell," she said.

Pai put an arm around her. "No, mistress. This is not hell."

If it wasn't, then Johanna didn't want to know what was.

CHAPTER TWENTY-FIVE

Red for the navitar, gray for the Nigh,
Blue for the storm wall, fifty fathoms high.
Amber for the steppe lands, silver for the bright,
Copper for the gracious lords in their city heights.
New sways up the Nigh, strange lands down,
A ship keeper sees them all,
So traveler, where bound?

—"Strange Lands Down," a river song

QUINN WALKED ALONG THE BANKS OF THE NIGH, broad as the widest Earth river but deeper than any watercourse, so it was said. The curling waters lapped at the steep bank, a rocky outcropping where his hike had taken him after passing through the army camps.

He had been recuperating for fifteen days, and only in the last two days had he felt strong enough to walk. Benhu fretted about Quinn's health and pleaded with him to rest in the tent. But Quinn felt sluggish, and walked to get the poison out of his system, not to mention the foul medicinals that Benhu urged on him. With his legs suffering spasms at times, Quinn's gait was still shaky. Nerve damage. Helice might have killed him with her poison. He wondered what else she carried on her person, and why he hadn't thoroughly searched her.

Although Quinn had at first been alarmed at Helice's departure to the Inyx, he felt more secure now, concluding that the Inyx—whatever they knew—wouldn't turn him in or they would have done so by now. Meanwhile, he waited for Lord Oventroe to contact them. Benhu had managed to find a

229

navitar who would bear a scroll to him. Without betraying his secret affiliation, Benhu couldn't claim any special precedence with the ship keeper, and thus the message would have to wait until the navitar's trade took the ship to the Ascendancy.

The day before, Quinn had watched as Zhiya's dirigible droned away to ply the cross-primacy route, watching, listening, gathering truths on her way. She would minister to her brothers and sisters, and to the diverse sentients of the land, netting intelligence with good conversation, wine, and perhaps sex. If the Entire ever found its champion, Zhiya would be a good ally to have. He'd asked Zhiya how riddled with subversives was the service of the Miserable God.

More so than you might guess, she had answered. *Less than I might wish.*

Walking along the riverbank, Quinn watched the mercurial surface swirl into patchwork eddies, seething quietly and in a muted light, being near the storm wall. Close along the banks the winds died, nor did gusts disturb the heavy waters. Sometimes he sat on the edge, gazing at the river.

Helice's poison had left his thoughts slow and confused. Helice was gone. He felt relieved, despite the danger of her being loose in a world she hardly knew. It wouldn't keep her, he felt sure, from interfering in her inimitable way. But her midnight strike had deepened his distrust of the cirque. She had risked much in that attack, cutting herself off from his protection, ostensibly to make sure he never used the nan sequence. His thoughts eddied like river matter.

His eyes were drawn to the place where the storm wall and the river met, a distant fiery line like a fresh weld. The Entire, by rights, shouldn't cohere. By rights, there should be no sentient beings in this world. Why did the Tarig build this universe and lavish it as they did with civilization, technology, laws, and the comfortable strife of the Long War? Even when he had lived at the Ascendancy, he had seldom drawn them into such subjects. *You cannot know us*, was one stock answer, always unsatisfactory. Lately he had dreamed of them—odd, lucid dreams of Tarig as automatons. Strange that he would think of that now—years after he had lived with them and come to accept them as natural. Still, they remained puzzling. For instance, he wondered why the Tarig had gone to such length to keep this artificial cosmos, when they might have had worlds in the Rose with less effort. Was the Entire a simple matter to them? Or did they so despise the dark, that alternating of day and night required in the world of suns?

He became more aware of his surroundings. Standing a short distance away, where the bank cut down into a ravine at the river's level, stood an Inyx mount, pacing on the sand. The beast's great horned head came up, noting Quinn's presence and eyeing him nervously, but in a preoccupied way, as it stared at the river. Quinn had never been so close to an Inyx, and watched, fascinated, as the creature trotted back and forth along a short beach. Its black coat shone with sweat, and spittle hung from its great mouth. Although it was enormous and sported a double row of formidable curving horns, this animal wasn't well. Yet it wasn't an animal, he reminded himself.

You are no godman. The thought needled into his mind.

Too late, Quinn saw how effortlessly the mount knew his mind.

"No, I'm not," Quinn said. "But I mean no harm."

The Inyx looked at the shimmering river, seeming to forget him.

"You're sick," Quinn said. "Can I help you? I have water with me."

There is water enough.

Could the Inyx drink the exotic waters? Surely not, unless it was a powerful tonic for disease. The creature's flank shuddered with a convulsion. Sydney rode a being like this. He imagined a twelve-year-old girl on the mount's back. She was no longer twelve, of course. Too late, he remembered he shouldn't think of his daughter. But he thought of her constantly; it was a wonder that the whole Inyx sway hadn't heard him broadcast those refrains by now.

The Inyx slowly turned his head toward Quinn. *Rose. She is an Inyx rider, but of the Rose.*

Quinn's thoughts were wide open to this creature, as Benhu had warned him from the beginning. Now that it could not be undone, Quinn leapt to a decision. He approached the beast, but only near enough to present neither a threat nor a target. The Inyx turned to face him, swaying on its feet, staring at Quinn with rheumy, green eyes.

It was reckless to reveal himself. Quinn knew that. You can die of too much caution too, he thought. Quinn whispered, "Send her a message. I beg you. I will repay you in any way I can."

Rose. Man of the Rose.

It was all exposed now. Quinn didn't know how much the Inyx could take from his mind. The Inyx looked back toward the River Nigh, gazing at it with an unmistakable longing. This Inyx was going to walk into the river.

Speak, then, came the creature's thought.

Quinn felt adrenaline hit. "Tell her . . . tell her this: 'I will come for you. Watch for me. Wait for me.'" It sounded so flat. It fell like a stone in the river, sinking.

The Inyx walked into the river up to the hocks of his sturdy legs.

Quinn followed him to the edge, where the waters lapped against his boots.

The Inyx moved breast-deep into the glinting river. Around him, the heavy waters formed scudding waves in all directions.

In another moment, a word rang like a bell in Quinn's mind. *No.*

It came again: *No. You are dead to me, as I have been dead to you. Come near me and I will have my mount kill you.*

Quinn staggered into the shallow waters. Sydney had spoken to him. Her words hovered in his mind, the terrible words.

The mount swam away, conveying nothing back to him. Quinn splashed after him. The Inyx moved swiftly away from the bank, his back and the crest of his neck buoyed up, but sinking slowly.

Quinn stretched out his hand to stop the creature from sinking away. "Sydney. Stay . . ."

The Inyx fell beneath the coiling surface.

A funnel appeared where he sank, spiraling down.

Quinn backed out of the river. Greasy rivulets fell from his tunic pants and dribbled off his boots. He fell to his knees in a puddle of exotic matter. She had said, *Dead to me.* She had cut him away.

He watched as the silver grease burned into the sand.

The legate Hu Zha sipped a cup of thin oba in Yulin's tent as old Suzong poured from a blackened pot. To Hu Zha, the tent reeked, and the steaming oba did not much improve matters. As Lady Chiron's emissary, Hu Zha looked forward to returning soon to the Magisterium, where fine silks and exalted company would replace this tawdry posting.

Given a chance to redeem himself, the fat former master of the sway had failed. Yulin had let Anzi slip away. Both he and his decrepit wife would suffer the garrote for this lapse. Nor had Hu Zha, he had to admit, covered himself in glory. He had been snoring in his tent when Anzi fled, but who knew the girl would be so brash?

Suzong simpered, "More oba?" She blinked absently, as though she had not a thought in her head.

Hu Zha reached out his cup, and the hag poured. He waited for Yulin to broach the subject. What was there to say? Appeal for mercy? Hu Zha would convey no such request to the Lady Chiron. Rather he would say that Yulin had stupidly tried to force a marriage on Anzi, a match she could not abide, which sent her running from the camp, and now she was no decoy to lure Titus Quinn, and they would see nothing of the man of the Rose, and Yulin would see nothing of the clemency he desired. Hu Zha hoped to be there when Yulin went down at the Tarig lady's feet. It would be a glorious thing to recount to admiring throngs in the Magisterium, and to his children, how the master of the sway took his death, bravely or otherwise.

Hu Zha cut a glance at Yulin, wondering why the old bear had called him here.

Sitting on his cushions, Yulin felt the sweat pour off his neck and trickle into his jacket collar. The damnable tents at Heart of Day were fit to roast a slab of meat, and yet the meeting could not be postponed, as the miserable Hu Zha was eager to report to Chiron and hasten back to the rarefied comforts of the bright city. Nevertheless, Yulin forced a pleasant expression onto his face.

"Hu Zha, you are welcome to my tent. Now we must discuss matters of the highest import, so that you may tell your lady all that has transpired— despite my earnest efforts."

The man regarded him with insolent calm, his youthful face belying the high office he held—that of a full legate.

Yulin mustered patience. "Hu Zha, despite appearances, Anzi's departure does not suggest defeat. Quinn may yet come to our camp."

"Yes," Hu Zha replied, "and Gond may fly."

In the old days, Yulin would have split the man's tongue for such an insult. Today, he must ignore it. Suzong's lip quivered, and he hoped she would not drop the hot brew in Hu Zha's lap. He had seen her fury, and it was building now beneath her powdered face.

Yulin hastened to say, "Listen, Hu Zha, and hear my judgment of our enterprise." The minion dared to smile as though indulging a child. Yulin's voice lowered, forcing Hu Zha to lean forward to hear. "The reason that Quinn may come is this: He does not know that Anzi has fled. Of course, there is little chance she will find him. Therefore, he may still come, thinking her to be at her uncle's side." Anzi and Quinn had agreed to meet at Ahnenhoon. Yulin's camp being in the vicinity, Quinn could find it if he persevered.

Yulin sat back, having played his best card. But sweat beaded on his forehead. He slurped the oba, but it only made him hotter. They couldn't open a tent flap, because Hu Zha, disguised as a cook, could not be seen having oba with the master of the sway.

With silken nonchalance, Hu Zha said, "When do you expect him, then?"

"When?" Yulin drew himself up. "Am I a crazed navitar to predict the future?" The man had gone too far. *When, when.* He thought of strapping the man face up on a beku and letting him watch the bright for a few days.

As Suzong attempted to pour oba, she slopped on Yulin's hand. "Oh, so clumsy," she murmured, wiping her husband's hand with her sleeve. "A thousand pardons, husband." She turned to the legate. "As we've been saying, Quinn will certainly come, and you, Your Excellency, will have the honor of capturing him. So satisfying to all concerned. A fine atonement for those of us who have found ourselves in error, and a success for you, rewarding your patience. A lovely solution, and one the lady will certainly approve. More oba?"

Hu Zha considered her words. Simpering and cowed by Hu Zha's position, the crone had still stumbled upon a decent point. Suppose Titus Quinn *thought* Anzi was here? There was a chance the darkling could still be lured here. Hu Zha might indeed wait a few days before reporting the setback.

He put his cup forward to let Suzong pour. Certainly Yulin was not going anywhere, so that if the Lady Chiron chose to invoke Tarig justice, she would know where to find him.

He might not be remiss in waiting a few more days.

When Hu Zha left, promising restraint in his judgments, Yulin turned to his wife and took her hands in his own. "You charmed him, my sweet."

She snorted. "I dominated him, the young fool."

"For a time. But what will become of us if Quinn never appears in our tent?"

Suzong leaned in closer. "Then we seek refuge." She brought out a painted fan and whipped a welcome breeze onto his face. "There is one place the Tarig would never find us—the Rose."

His expression must have shown his astonishment. Whispering, she went on, "I have reason to believe that Titus Quinn was looking for safe passage to and fro."

"There is no passage to and fro. Not without great danger."

Suzong sucked her teeth and nodded. "But there is, husband. If one knows how to open the door."

Why, Yulin thought, would there be ways to open the door? Such things were forbidden. It was the first vow, after all. Did his wife flutter after rumors and superstitions?

Murmuring close to him, her breath was hot on his cheek. "They call them the correlates, so scholars say."

"Why would Quinn have such a thing, when the master of the sway does not?"

"Because, husband, he was *looking* for them. When he came to our sway, when he sojourned with us for a time, he was looking for them. You remember?"

"But, as to *finding* them . . . the vows forbid it."

"Some do not care what the vows forbid."

Yulin pulled at his beard, speculating. Might Quinn be so audacious?

Suzong said, "If Quinn did find them, we could cross over and take refuge with his people. Until they come in numbers. Until they return you to your rightful place."

Yulin looked at her fondly. She thought of things that most people did not. It made his younger wives seem vain and foolish. Back when he had had younger wives, and the leisure to criticize them. "Crossing over is a garroting offense."

She shrugged. "Nor is there any proof that he has acquired these secrets." After a time she said, "On the other hand, one can also lose oneself in Rim City. Even if it is under the nose of the lords."

"I would rather hie me to the end of the Radiant Arch, to the last sway of the last primacy, before I would live there, like a merchant."

"Merchants, husband, sleep in clean beds and do not suffer our deficiencies of table."

Yulin looked around his squalid quarters. He murmured, "The man of the Rose promised us more than squalor and the impudence of legates."

"Ah. But you have vowed to expose him."

"So I told the mincing legate."

Suzong let that statement lie. She seemed content at the moment to let him stew in indecision. But let Titus Quinn set foot in camp, and by the Miserable God, the moment of decision would be upon him.

CHAPTER TWENTY-SIX

Dread the gift of your enemy.

—a saying

IN THE PRIME OF DAY, as the bright raised wavering pools of heat from the steppe, Mo Ti and Akay-Wat rode out to meet the stranger.

Over the last few intervals, the stranger's mount had been sending guarded messages to Riod, that he bore a personage to camp, and one not blind. This was strange. Few outsiders found welcome in the Inyx sway, aside from the occasional itinerant healer or legate come to register deaths and births. And this rider was very much an outsider.

Drawing to a stop on her mount, Akay-Wat squinted in the direction of the Nigh. "There, Mo Ti. See the dark shape?"

Mo Ti shifted his weight on Distanir's broad back. "No one rides like that."

"Yet he comes."

"Sits his mount like a boil on a beku's arse."

Distanir pawed the ground, broadcasting a skittish anxiety.

As the mount and his rider drew closer, Mo Ti saw that the newcomer was a woman, dressed as a godder. Her thoughts, chaotic and rash, leapt between her mount and her welcoming committee. She was thinking of Titus Quinn.

Alarmed, Akay-Wat urged her mount forward.

Then Mo Ti thundered by on Distanir, rushing toward the stranger and raising a choking cloud of dust as he came to halt in front of the woman. "Shut your thoughts away," he ordered. It was one thing for Sydney to think of Titus Quinn; the herd was used to that. But if this stranger brought news of the man, it was best kept well hidden, lest the 'Tarig have reason to snoop here.

The stranger looked at him in confusion.

"Shut your thoughts away," Mo Ti repeated, "or I will knock you from your perch."

"Here bring news," the woman stuttered, "of man of Rose." She looked triumphant, until Mo Ti's blow felled her from her mount.

Akay-Wat rode up, her false leg sticking out farther than her other legs, though she still rode easily. "What creature is this?" she asked, looking at the godder lying sprawled.

Mo Ti dismounted and placed his hand on the new mount's neck to calm him. "A liar and a fool," he said, not knowing how true he would later find this summary.

The woman who called herself Helice sat on the other side of the tent wall, in a small enclosure that Mo Ti had erected for her. Sydney didn't want the Tarig to see this visitor, and therefore she couldn't look at the woman, either.

Mo Ti and Riod remained nearby, listening and absorbing the visitor's remarkable story. But since the two women spoke the dark language, Mo Ti was left with an imperfect understanding of what she said. From time to time Sydney would stop to translate for him, and he gleaned some remnants from Riod, who stood nearby where the tent flap had been pulled back. Mo Ti worried about the woman's presence here. Helice claimed to have crossed over from the Rose. Startling enough, and treasonous to boot. If the sway harbored her, they were implicated in vow-breaking. His mistress, however, had made it clear that she had no intention of reporting this stranger, who came with news, power, and promises. To ensure secrecy, Riod stood close by to hide the newcomer's thoughts from the nearby herd.

Mo Ti brooded on the new, disquieting revelations. Just when Sydney needed to concentrate on their enterprise of insurgency, now came plots from afar. If the stranger could be believed—and this Mo Ti doubted—her betters in the Rose had plans afoot to destroy the Entire.

Why would the Rose seek to destroy us? In answer, the stranger said that the lords had built an engine that helped them feed off the Rose universe.

But why, Mo Ti thought, would the lords need the Rose? Surely they did not need the frail Rose for their grand design. Surely the All could not be so bound to the darkling realm; he did not like to think so. The Entire was the proper and bright realm. What had we to do with the imperfect wasteland that was the Rose? Yet the woman named Helice talked of fuel, and energy, and words like *entropy*, to convince Sydney that even the high lords needed to sustain such artificial order that was the Entire.

And Sydney nodded, engrossed. Convinced.

In this woman's lengthy story, she warned that Titus Quinn had come back to prevent the destruction of his world. He possessed, she claimed, a catastrophic solution, one lethal to the Entire. The woman claimed she was in the radiant land to prevent this terrible outcome.

Why, though, would a woman of the Rose conspire to operate against the Rose's interests?

The woman had the temerity to admit that she wished to stay here for the sake of the long life the Entire bestowed. For this reason, she opposed Titus Quinn's mission, even if it eventually meant the destruction of her own world. If such a motive could be believed, it was a vile ambition. It was then that Mo Ti knew their visitor was without honor.

Riod sent, *Why come here to my roamlands?*

Helice answered that it was her only hope. She knew that Sydney dwelled here and that Sydney had been wronged by her father, and she hoped to find a receptive place to hide. She admitted that to save the Entire she had tried to kill Quinn.

This mention of her father both disturbed and gripped Sydney. She demanded to know more, and Helice obliged her. She told how Quinn had risen in the ranks of the leaders of the Rose, using his knowledge of the Entire as his leverage. He bragged of all that he had learned when he had been a prince of the Bright Realm. He alone, he said, knew the Entire's weaknesses and how it could be annihilated before it could endanger the Rose. Helice told how Titus Quinn had changed from former days, as his newfound power led him to large appetites, for both sexual exploits and control of the giant enterprise called Minerva.

Relating these things to Mo Ti, Sydney's frown lines deepened. But Mo

Ti saw something else: that Helice's stories gave Sydney the pleasure of having her opinions confirmed. Her father deserved the enmity she harbored in her mind, as well as in the book of pinpricks where, when she had been blind, she had recorded her troubles.

Mo Ti listened to them talk until his legs cramped and he could sit no longer.

"My lady," he interrupted. Sydney looked at him with some impatience. "My lady, I would speak with you in private." He rose heavily to his feet.

"About what?"

Mo Ti glanced at the thin wall separating them from the newcomer. "About our enterprise—our enterprise of dreams."

"It goes well, yes?"

"Yes, lady. Slowly, as we know we must be cautious. But . . ." Sydney waited for him to continue. "Not everything is for outsiders to hear," he murmured.

"She doesn't speak enough Lucent."

"Still." He rose to leave.

Sydney murmured, "Be patient, Mo Ti. I've waited four thousand days to hear of the Rose. I've waited four thousand days to know what my father intends, and how far his ambitions stretch. Now you can wait, Mo Ti." To soften the rebuke, she added. "Can you wait?"

He bowed. "Mo Ti will wait. Outside." He left her to whisper through the tent wall with the liar.

Outside, Akay-Wat paced up to him, her ears lifted. "She comes, oh yes?"

"No," Mo Ti spat. "Not with the guest having more words than a beku has fleas."

"The guest," the Hirrin sighed. "I do not trust this stranger. Her mount says that all the way here, she was unhappy to ride. And did not wish a good bond with him. That is unnatural."

"And why, Akay-Wat, does she not like her bonded mount, do you think?"

"Because she is a bad rider?"

He glanced back at Sydney's tent, murmuring, "I think it is because she does not like to share her heart."

"Oh dear," Akay-Wat said, straining her long neck around to peer at the closed tent flap.

Mo Ti stood inside Helice's tent. Distanir was just outside, ready to relay Mo Ti's thoughts to Helice.

The woman had commandeered a small table on which now resided many small metal parts. She sat on a stool, hunched over the metal pieces.

He began by bidding Distanir to send Helice this question: "What are these things?" He pointed to the objects on the table.

To his surprise, she spoke in Lucent. Halting, but clear enough. "My business. My tent, Mo Ti."

She looked up at him from her seat at the table. Most people were wary around Mo Ti at first because of his size, but this woman was not intimidated. He decided to go to the point. "My mistress has duties in the camp that require her attention. Do not discourage her from high tasks. A thousand mounts wait on her."

"Is that mount still lurking, waiting for me to ride him?"

"Vichna and you are bonded. It is the custom to ride."

Helice was assembling something, and she continued to work as they talked. "I usually like animals, but the mounts . . . I'm not sure I care for them."

"They aren't animals."

"Well, tell him to find another rider. I don't like my thoughts tampered with."

What was she hiding? He watched her with a new sense of antipathy. "Be aware that I suffer your interference only so far. You may not wish to test me."

She bent over the task of assembling two of the metal pieces together. "You're using long words, Mo Ti. Try to speak simply."

"Endanger Sydney's leadership, and I will kill you."

Helice put down the metal fixture with elaborate care. "I'm not happy with you, Mo Ti. You talk against me with Sydney. I hear you in the tent, saying she must be cautious with me."

So she spoke better Lucent than she admitted. "Yes, my mistress should be careful. Any advisor would say so."

She prodded her little pieces of metal, turning them, fitting them together. "Advise her better, Mo Ti, or you won't be an advisor long."

Distanir, who stood outside, was sending distress and anger. But Mo Ti remained calm. This small, scarred woman meant to challenge him for his standing with Sydney. She had been here only three days, and already she presumed to hold power. Luckily she didn't know that the herd had broken into the mind of the Tarig; she wasn't yet Sydney's confidante, in that, at least. He would pick his time to take this newcomer down.

Helice looked up at him. "Let me show you why you're not going to kill me."

She gestured at the pile of metal fixtures. "This will be an assembler. I'm sure you don't have a word for it in Lucent. Think of it as a very capable stone well computation device. That can make things."

Mo Ti peered down at the bewildering array of small mechanisms and apparatuses.

"Where did these come from?" He had seen nothing like them, nor had Helice brought anything with her when she first rode in on Vichna.

"Sewn into my undergarments."

She looked at the array of parts spread out before her, as though daunted by her task, but determined to finish. "Fitting this together will take a few days. I first create an assembler, and the assembler will fashion what I need. It takes a little while to build a machine that can perform delicate surgery. Sydney understands she must be patient."

Sydney? The two of them had discussed this apparatus without telling him?

Helice went on. "I came here to restore Sydney's sight. We knew from Quinn's first visit that she'd been blinded and sent to this sway. I meant to restore her vision when I found her. Now I've learned that the procedure will have to be a bit different than I expected—given the Tarig implant. But I can figure it out."

Mo Ti understood he had been outmaneuvered. She was going to repair Sydney's eyes. And Sydney would be grateful.

Helice had taken out the golden eye lenses that chafed her eyes. With the odd brown eyes gazing at him, he was conscious of the kinship between Helice and Sydney. These two were not Chalin. They were human. It unnerved him.

Still fixing him with her steady gaze, Helice said, "Do you see now why you shouldn't get in my way?"

Sydney rode out, Riod under her, surging in long strides across the steppe. At her side, Mo Ti rode on Distanir, his thoughts in as much turmoil as hers.

Never before had either Sydney or Mo Ti considered the Entire as a threatened world, a *temporary* world. Today, in one stroke, they had learned that the Entire was the target of a terrible weapon—and not only that, but the Entire had exhausted its energy sources and now required an outside source: the Rose. How could such things take root in the mind and seem normal? How could one look on the steppe, the sway, the primacy, the very bright of the sky, and think that they were soon to pass?

Of one thing Sydney was sure: If the Entire needed the Rose for energy, then the Entire must have it. She didn't hate the Rose, but her loyalties had long since faded for a land she had difficulty remembering. *One universe must die; let it not be ours.*

Titus Quinn was for the Rose, of course. At least he was loyal to *something*, she thought bitterly.

Sydney could let the mantis lords handle her father. She could send word to the Ascendancy, much as she hated the thought of collaborating with them. But Helice cautioned against this, saying that they would find and kill Quinn, which would be good, but then they would likely accelerate their plan to burn the Rose. Knowing that the Rose was alerted to the engine at Ahnenhoon, the Tarig would be forced to act before the Rose sent more instruments of destruction. Helice had a desire to let the Rose live for a few more years.

Why? Sydney had asked, suspicious that Helice's stories might not add up.

Let me bring my friends here first, Helice answered. I have a few key people that I want around me. People who work for me. Give me this one thing: a little time before the lords descend. A dozen people, no more, she promised. Quinn could be stopped by an assassin. No need to get the Tarig involved, no need for them to flock here to the sway, asking questions and taking Helice in custody, as it seemed likely they would.

These arguments gave Sydney pause. She must prevent her enterprise against the Tarig from coming under scrutiny. If the lords came here, could Riod hide the herd's thoughts from them? The lords weren't receptive to speaking heart to heart, but some of the attendants who traveled with them would be. No, the Tarig must not come here.

All these ruminations kept at bay the dark thought of whom she would have to kill.

Last ebb she had taken out her journal and written down all that Helice had told her about the man's ambitions. How he had set his heart on great things, and never on her. How, from the beginning, he had insisted that he alone return to the Entire so that he could forge the alliances that would bring him influence. He pursued something he called the correlates, so that, with this knowledge, he could be a captain of ships once more, finding ways through the Entire to access the stars. He had always loved his starships. Where was Sydney in all this talk of alliances and starships? How utterly forgotten she had been by the one man who could have helped her, back when she was a slave, and blind. When he sent a message to her at last, it was only to bid her wait longer. Why had he bothered to say such a thing?

He had come to destroy the All: the great Repel of Ahnenhoon, the primacy itself. And—the nan spreading—eventually all other primacies. Helice said the nan would race along the bright, jumping the Empty Lands, and bring down the world in but a short while. So coming for her was a pretense. Not that it mattered. These were a child's hurts. Her life now was with Riod. She would have been content never to hear of her father again. But back he came to the bright realm, again and again, ripping open the sealed drawer where she kept the broken things of her life.

She set down these truths in her book, writing in her pinprick code so that the Tarig could decipher nothing. Here was another misery to lay at Titus Quinn's feet: The Tarig had poisoned her sight in order to watch for her father.

"My lady," Mo Ti said. They had dismounted for a rest. Riod and Distanir fed on nearby tufts of goldweed while their riders drank from their canteens. Mo Ti had been trying to speak against Helice for days, but each time Sydney turned away. Mo Ti was jealous; that was clear.

"What is it, Mo Ti?"

"The woman Helice has told me of her machine."

Ah, the machine. The one good thing that Sydney could count on amid her troubles.

"I don't trust her," Mo Ti said.

"Don't trust her to tamper with my eyes? This caution comes rather late, Mo Ti." She regretted her remark, but something in Mo Ti's tone prevented her from withdrawing it.

"You trust her, I fear. But think: Why would she condone the destruction of the Rose? She is lying."

"Helice says that the Rose is corrupt. The Rose has become a place where the idle live off the gifted. Those with schooling must work like slaves because the lazy want riches and entertainments. So Helice says."

"You believe her."

"Neither yes nor no. I don't know her very well. But the Rose technology can make me whole again, Mo Ti. Unless she plans to kill me with her machine. I don't think she does."

"No. But there are other reasons for not doing it." She waited while he went on. "If the Tarig view through your eyes fails completely, they will be alerted. Who could have the knowledge to undo their handiwork? They may come here to determine causes." His crumpled face fell into a scowl. "They must not come here. How would we keep all thoughts secret, including all that the riders may suspect of our enterprise?"

First he had insisted that she have the Tarig surgery to restore her sight. Now he insisted that her eyes remain blighted. "I thought you would always be my protector, Mo Ti."

He winced inwardly. "I am, on my life."

"And keep me from my healing?"

"My lady, how can we trust the woman to have such a perfect machine?"

"Hasn't Distanir already probed Helice's mind and found her true?" She noted Mo Ti's consternation that she had found out about that. "You sent Distanir to spy on her. Did you think Riod wouldn't notice? Did you fear I wouldn't allow it, and so neglected to tell me?"

Mo Ti's voice went soft. "Yes."

Sydney's anger flared. "Helice felt your probe. She called it mind rape."

He went on doggedly. "She is hiding something."

"Don't we all." She turned from him, stalking over to Riod, and climbed on his back. *Ride with me, beloved*, she sent.

Mo Ti strode to her side, taking hold of one of Riod's horns to make him pause. "My lady?"

Looking down on him, Sydney rasped, "I can't bear having Tarig eyes. Not even to raise the kingdom."

She goaded Riod into a leaping start, and he set out at a furious gallop, one that brought the wind into her face and turned the water around her eyes icy cold.

Helice stared at her handiwork, the labor of four days: the assembler. On the outside it was a box, higher than it was wide, big enough to produce something the size of a boot; smart enough to produce anything she could program. On the front face was the screen that served as her input pad. The screen had actually been the hardest part to conceal in her clothing. It had been secured into the back of her tunic, which is why she had always slept on her side.

Mo Ti was worried about the device. He'd be even more worried if he understood anything about molecular manipulation and quantum processors. But it was enough for the brooding troll to realize that he was no longer in charge. He had lumbered off to convince Sydney not to submit to modifications. Busy man, Mo Ti. He had to pedal furiously just to understand that the power structure had changed.

In any case, here was the assembler. It would take her Oriental jacket and pajama pants—the ones that looked like ordinary green silk except weren't—and use them as raw materials from which to construct the mSap with its specialized arms.

The assembler had already given birth to a quite satisfactory ink pen. Delightful. Small beginnings in the service of profound ends. Someday she would show her children the ink pen and tell how she had come to the Inyx sway a poor sojourner—well, the story needed a few tweaks—and how her ascension to power had been just a logical journey from one advantage to the next. The Tarig? Why, they had to step aside. They were so used to lording it over the inadequate that when a true contender entered the fray, the lords had to bow the knee.

Even her subconscious agreed. Some nights she felt on the verge of knowing the chinks in the Tarig armor. Lucid dreams came to her, promising that the lords were weak and afraid. It would be helpful if they were, but even if not, she meant to banish or command them.

So far, she was pleased. Although round one, she had to admit, went to Quinn. He had managed to keep the cirque. And despite her attempts, she had never discovered the name of the lord who was the Tarig traitor. Useful intelligence. But she could never pry it out of Benhu.

Coming up, round two: assembling the mSap, so that Sydney would owe her a favor. Award that round to Helice.

Round three: getting rid of Mo Ti. A full-count knockout by Helice.

Round four: Quinn succumbing at last. And—this was the really excellent part—at the hands of his own daughter. It wasn't as though Helice had to force the girl to do it. You just worked with the material at hand.

Helice now wore the padded jacket and rough pants that the riders preferred. From a pile on the table, she slowly fed the assembler her old clothes, guiding them into the receiving gate.

CHAPTER TWENTY-SEVEN

Oh navitar, where are we bound?
My navitar, what paths are found?
Oh navitar, the binds deform,
But waking, we are then reborn.
My navitar, the river is deep,
What falls in, the Nigh will keep.
Where bound, Where bound, the keeper cries,
You hear the binds, not the replies.
But sways await, the travelers sleep,
Cast off, cast off, and into the deep.

—"Shanty of the Binds," a river song

QUINN WALKED ALONG THE BANKS OF THE NIGH. Across the river the storm wall bulked mightily into the sky, quaking with suppressed winds. Yet the air around him was tranquil. Far away, on the other side of the primacy, the matching storm wall spawned high winds, but here the Nigh imposed a slick calm, an unnatural quiet.

The poisons Helice had given Quinn still brought on regular bouts of nausea. Adding to this discomfort, his legs were swollen below the knees, the extent to which he had waded into the river. The cirque chafed against his ankle, its imprint now a circular greenish bruise, unless it was a stain from the metal links themselves.

He should rest. Instead, he had been walking for hours down primacy, away from the Inyx campsite. He must get far away in order to think freely. But how could distance make any difference to the Inyx capacities? Yesterday the mount had sent a message and received one back in a heartbeat.

249

His thoughts drifted to his daughter and to his wife. Sydney, Johanna. Round and round, spiraling down. He had never felt as bleak, not even after his starship broke up, with all hands lost. He used to think there was nothing worse than believing his family dead. Now he discovered there was: that they lived, and rejected him.

Anzi looked at the skewers of meat tended by a godman on an open fire. She could have devoured them all, burning hot. Having spent all her money on a tent, supplies, and bribes to ship keepers and travelers who might have seen a tall Chalen man with an Ascendancy accent, she had eaten nothing for two days except a few morsels. Six legs of river journeying, stopping in every travelers' camp along the Nigh, searching, searching. Ling Xiao Sheng's purple stone sold quickly in one of those camps, but reaped only a tenth of its value, and now those primals were gone. Her only item of value was the heart chime she wore around her neck on a thong. She pulled it out, watching the orb sparkle. Held to the ear, it emitted a range of tones indicating relative distance from the bright city. Titus had given it to her. "Stay far from the Ascendancy," he had said, as though she needed any inducement. The heart chime was a toy, or a devotional relic, depending on one's opinion of the Tarig. The loyal Hirrin who'd given it to Titus wore it to remind her of her connection to the lords and the centrality of their great city. It had become a token of Anzi and Titus's journey together, but she had resigned herself to its loss.

The godman noted the heart chime as she held it. He put on his bargaining face, turning the skewers over the coals.

"How many skewers for this costly keepsake?" she inquired.

He sized her up. "Three. No, I will go so far as four. Heart chime with thong."

"By the vows, I'll have all the skewers for this treasure."

He scowled. "Seven sticks of meat."

"Plus five minors in change."

She ended up with eight skewers and no change. It was worth it, but chewing hurt, with her face still tender where she had cut a long gash in it—her only disguise. As she ate, her cheek began to bleed, drawing the attention of a group of Jouts gambling in a line coin toss. Folding her skewers into their wrap, she walked away to find some privacy. Along the way she scanned the knots of Chalin men for one as tall as Titus, and with his walk, though he might have changed his appearance, she knew.

Finding a place somewhat removed from the throng of godly servants and the occasional soldier, she ate ravenously.

Meet me at Ahnenhoon, she had told him. If he wasn't in these river camps, then she would go to the plains of Ahnenhoon. But it seemed unlikely he would have been able to attach himself to a military unit this quickly. He would be coming into the Entire through a veil-of-worlds. He would cross the primacy, and travel the river to the Repel; he might be in any of these camps, or arriving soon. Arriving soon. The prospect of seeing him lightened her heart.

She couldn't remember when her feeling of obligation to him had changed to something more. Spending so many days with him she had learned what kindled him; the same things that caused the people of the Rose to burn with passion: family, honor, loyalty, ambition. Their short but intense lives made her own seem cold and shallow. She had always wanted a passionate life. And then, with Titus, she had found herself catching fire.

He is not for such as you. Suzong's words were caught in her skull.

There was a chance that Titus would become a personage of importance. Just as easily, he might remain an outsider. She wasn't sure which she hoped would be the case, but with his wife long dead, he might look at Anzi, mightn't he? On the other hand, she wasn't hoping for marriage, and not the role of first wife, necessarily. God's beku, who wanted marriage and its dreary routines?

In any case, and matters of the heart aside, he would need her when he returned. She knew he would return. *When I come back, Anzi*, he had said, *we'll be at war, your world and mine.* Ahnenhoon's terrible secret would draw him back.

She would do anything to help him. When it came to war, she had no doubt which side she was on.

Chang had a raging headache brought on by too much drink last ebb and a harangue from his captain this morning. Told to walk it off and be ready for

calisthenics by the first hour of Prime of Day, Chang trudged down the row
of tents and out of the camp, drawn by curiosity to the cluster of godders who
had arrived four days ago. Sky bulbs, wagons, broken-down coaches, and a
caravan of mite-plagued beku had descended on the banks of the Nigh like
an infestation of river spiders. His camp mates vowed that some godwomen
were eager for proper company, and Chang thought that might be the
quickest way to sobriety. The problem was, no decent woman could be found
among those who served the woeful god. They were all blackened with age,
sporting sores, or of the wrong sway for pillowing. However there was a Jout
once who looked ravishing after a jar of wine was pissed away. . . .

He stopped up short at the sight of a girl devouring her Early Day meal
like a Gond.

She was no godwoman, dressed in dark green silks, dusty from travel.
Though one side of her face bore a scabby wound, the other was as fresh as an
unplucked fruit. Even tucking her long hair into her padded jacket couldn't
hide her attractions.

Then lust gave way to curiosity. Her face looked familiar. His heart sped.
The girl watched everyone with a keen appraisal, even while eating. To cover
his interest in her, he mixed with a knot of soldiers, keeping watch.

God's beku, surely it was not the girl the lords searched for.

The girl turned her bright eyes to him, glanced past him, then turned to
wrap her meat sticks in a travel cloth. By the time she had done so, Chang
was sure.

When she rose and set out through the crowd, Chang followed. Keeping
the girl in sight, Chang also scanned the throngs for someone from his unit
so that he could alert Captain Dekisher what was afoot. Finally succeeding in
gesturing a fellow soldier to his side, he sent him off with the message that
he'd sighted an important fugitive. Above all, he mustn't let the girl slip
away, or Captain Dekisher, the ugly Jout, would have his balls on a skewer.

Benhu watched a ship approach over the marsh. On the crowded shore,
travelers pushed and shoved toward the river's edge. They needn't bother,

Benhu thought. This one is mine. Sentients shouted at the ship keeper for precedence, but the surge of travelers was largely futile. First priority on all ships went to soldiers, and with a massive contingent gathered here, there would be few slots left over. In this case, Benhu knew, not even soldiers would board. This was Lord Oventroe's ship, its small size and shabby exterior disguising the importance of the passenger it bore. This ship looked like no bright lord's transport, but it bore the markings the lord had told Benhu to expect. If Quinn hadn't gone walking, they could have boarded quickly and been gone before the crowd had time to protest it leaving with empty seats. The lord would ask why Benhu's charge was not at hand, and why he was in such a condition as he was, both in his mind and his body. Benhu pulled on his beard, trying to marshal a story that would convey the difficulty of controlling Titus Quinn. Worst of all would be explaining to the lord about the mount who threw himself in the river, jeopardizing the entire mission by speaking heart to heart with the girl of the Rose, who was, of course, Titus Quinn's daughter. Farting Gonds, how had he made such a shambles of his task?

By the time the ship sagged onto its struts nearby, Benhu's stomach felt like he'd swallowed a heft of river water.

As Anzi passed a group of Chalin she overheard the words *man of the Rose*. She paused, pretending to remove a stone from her boot. *Titus Quinn*, they said in hushed voices. The Chalin elders sat in a circle, playing a game of sticks and redstones. Stories of the man of the Rose had spread quickly, especially word of his involvement in the death of Lord Hadenth, who had bravely clung to the brightship as it sped away from the Ascendancy, bearing the traitor, the one who would bring the hordes from the dark Rose to swamp the Entire. So the Tarig version went.

However, these Chalin elders murmured of the cursed brightships and spoke Hadenth's name with a flat tone devoid of esteem. They had a another version of the story, one that Anzi had also heard, that Titus Quinn came home for his daughter, but seeing the Tarig domination of the All, sacrificed his intention in order to show how vulnerable the lords were. Their city could be compromised, their ships destroyed.

An elder reached out to scoop up the redstones he had won, and Anzi moved on, searching.

She chose a down-primacy direction to continue her search. Titus, if he were here, would camp as far from the Inyx assembly as possible. She walked along the river, into a region of hillocky mud. In the distance two tents rippled in the stiff breeze. Approaching, she found them empty except for three packs rich with provisions. Why would someone with such resources sleep in lowly tents like these, and so removed from likely docking sites?

Two sets of footprints dimpled the sand, one leading toward the camp, one away. She followed the latter. Putting her own foot into the imprint, she judged the size. It was a man's footprint. She turned around to assess the other footprints. Too small. Though she could see no one amid the marshy ridges, she set out with some hope.

This was a lonely wasteland, and her thoughts turned cold. By now her uncle Yulin would have foresworn her, and Suzong would be trying to scrape together payment to Ling Xiao Sheng for his wedding gift. On the other hand, Ling might claim that since Anzi had taken the gem, she had accepted him. Then he would force the marriage, even marrying her in her absence, making her the youngest of his wives, a slave, to punish her for as long as he liked. Provided, of course, that he could catch her. Anzi felt shame for disobeying Yulin, who had loved her like his own child and only asked that she marry a stable Chalin man for the sake of a potential reconciliation with the Tarig. If Anzi thought there was any chance under heaven of that reconciliation, she would have accepted Ling Xiao Sheng. But the lords would never forgive that her uncle had provided succor, alibi, and disguise to Titus Quinn.

Ahead she glimpsed a man walking along the strand, his gait uneven. Too far away to recognize, he looked up at the storm wall across the river as though trying to see past it to a more conducive view. Like a man imagining home. As though sensing her behind him, he turned and saw her.

Captain Dekisher set out with a contingent of thirty soldiers, rushing to join Chang, who was apparently tracking none other than the girl associated with Titus Quinn. Chang would have a promotion for this, the drunken sot, if he was right. Dekisher himself could expect a sublegacy, perhaps a full legacy, or mastership of the city in his Jout home sway. But if the girl slipped away, he'd likely get demotion to the ranks. She wouldn't escape.

Catching up with Chang, who was not far advanced from his original position, Dekisher saw the Chalin female that his subordinate was tracking. The captain was beginning to wish he had come with a larger force, but at the same time he was reluctant to alert the woman that a search was afoot. She might, after all, lead them to someone of even more interest. He took command of Chang and two other soldiers while directing the rest of the unit to split up and set out on different tangents to cut off escape. Keeping the fugitive in view, Dekisher's squad headed down to the marshes.

Once the captain and his squad reached the outskirts of the godder camp, they were exposed on the flats. Abandoning stealth, they quickened their pace.

Quinn watched the Chalin woman approach. She cut a path directly toward him. A doubt passed through him, whether his disguise held. He moved down the knoll, bracing for conversation with a stranger and trying to sharpen his wits for the encounter.

He squinted as the woman approached, and then found his steps quickening. By God, was it Anzi? He felt a broad smile cut into his face, and he stopped, drinking in the sight of a friend on this deserted marsh. She came within a few paces. "Anzi," he breathed.

Lord Oventroe's ship keeper was still fending off a crowd of travelers clamoring for passage as Benhu made his way down the deck to the central cabin to make his report. A commotion in camp diverted his attention and he turned to the rail. Benhu saw a mass of soldiers rushing through the camp, spreading out among the pack beasts and the godders, overturning pots of oba and ransacking tents.

Alarmed, he raced for the cabin, jamming through the door and blurting out to the surprised Lord Oventroe that the army was upon them.

The lord, still seated, looked up at him with eerie calm. "Compose yourself, Benhu. Now tell."

"Forgive me, Bright Lord. The army. Running through the camp, searching tents, and Titus still ashore!"

"Do not say his name, Benhu," the lord murmured.

"Forgive me, my life in your service, and no disrespect, Lord."

Lord Oventroe unfolded his long body from the chair, barely clearing the ceiling. "Where is our guest?"

Benhu pointed down the riverbank where, he fervently hoped, Quinn could be found. "Hurry," Benhu whispered. The lord climbed the steps to the upper deck to confer with the pilot. Ordered with a gesture to follow, Benhu obeyed. He heard the struts clunk against the sides as they folded. Through the portholes, he saw that the ship was moving off from the shore, steering toward the deeper river.

Once on the upper deck, Benhu found himself in the presence of the navitar—Lord Oventroe's navitar. Jesid, if he guessed right.

The navitar looked at Benhu with eyes so dark, the light in them seemed to have expired.

Benhu pointed down the shoreline. "Hurry."

Oventroe looked down at him as though he were a veldt mouse that had spoken.

The ship slowly lumbered over the marshland. Out the portholes, Benhu could see soldiers running along the shore, moving through the mud humps and jumping over pools of exotic water, but keeping pace with the ship.

"Faster," Benhu suggested to the navitar.

The lord nodded to his pilot. "This godman thinks we are slow."

The ship gathered speed.

Anzi's face bore a long and recent cut on one side, but her eyes were bright. In long white strands, her hair escaped the collar where she had tucked it. "Dai Shen," she whispered. "It is you."

"Ren Kai, now," he said. His voice had gone unnaturally deep. He was relieved to see her. "You're hurt," he said.

She seemed rooted to the marshy sand. "Not worth the cut, if you recognized me," she said.

"You did this to yourself?" Quinn stepped close, turning the cut side of her face toward him to look at the wound. It was angry-looking, but clean.

"I've been looking for you," she said. "I was afraid I wouldn't find you."

To his shame he realized that he hadn't been looking for *her*. He hadn't expected to see her here. Only at Ahnenhoon, and he'd held out little hope that he would find her there, or that he could take time to search for her, given what he came for.

In the distance, out on the marsh, he saw a ship. In its wake, reflecting the sky, the river bore a fiery crease.

Quinn looked over Anzi's shoulder where four runners could be seen— three Chalin and a Jout.

"Are you with anyone, Anzi?"

Turning to look, she drew in her breath. "No."

Captain Dekisher had watched with amazement as the girl joined someone standing where the marshes edged the river. A Chalin man—or was this the human man that the lords sought?

The couple had seen them. They began backing up, then turned and ran. Not the actions of the innocent. Dekisher instinctively suppressed his joy lest the Woeful God take notice. This was the woman Chang had identified as Ji Anzi. With any luck, her companion could well be Titus Quinn himself. "They are ours," he muttered to himself. Where could they go? There was nothing but desolate marsh and river country from here to the end of All.

Except now a river vessel cut a path toward his quarry.

Charged with excitement, Dekisher cried, "Take them," waving Chang and the others forward. He shouted after them, "Cut them off from the river!"

At Quinn's side, Anzi had her knife ready. Bad odds, Quinn thought: he and Anzi against three soldiers—or four, including a Jout lagging behind.

At that moment the distant river vessel again caught his attention. This time he saw that it was clearly bearing down on them, struts lying horizontal, ready to deploy. On the deck someone was waving wildly, beard flapping in the speed of the boat's passage and white garments plastered against a pot-bellied frame. It was Benhu.

"Friends," Quinn said, leading Anzi toward the river. He heard the shouts of their pursuers, whose faces he could just make out, fierce with determination.

He could hear Benhu shouting for them to run toward the ship, but if they did, they'd present their backs to the three coming at them with long strides down the flats. Instead, he and Anzi held their ground as the ship and the attackers converged. The ship bore down, drawing the attention of the three Chalin soldiers, who swerved to avoid collision. On the river side of the ship, Benhu threw down a rope rigging for them to climb the side. Too late. The soldiers rushed forward, forcing Quinn and Anzi to engage.

Leaving Anzi to the smallest soldier, two of them circled Quinn, knives drawn, lunging and swiping. Reflexes slow, poisons still weakening him, Quinn was no match for them, but kept them at bay, parrying thrusts, delivering a gash to a knife hand. His fighting instructor's advice surfaced amid the melee: When overmatched, cut at hands. Ci Dehai, though, had never fought half sick and out of practice, Quinn thought. Still, Quinn had already forced one man to fight using his clumsier hand. With better odds, Quinn came at them renewed, trying to maneuver toward Anzi. Blocked by his experienced opponents, he had a moment to see Benhu jump from the ship rail screaming like a madman, carrying the only weapon he could grab—a length of knotted rope. Landing between Anzi and her attacker, Benhu took a reeling blow to the head from his opponent's fist. He crumpled, but it gave

Anzi time to grab the bottom of the rigging and throw it over the head of the advancing soldier. Stuck in its mesh for a fatal moment, he took Anzi's knife in his belly.

Meanwhile, Quinn spun on a heel to keep the second, stronger fighter in view. An artless move, he opened himself up in back to a savage kick that sent him sprawling. His knife flew from his hand. Slow to rise, he expected a killing blow, but instead heard a whistling sound. And there was Anzi, standing among them, swinging Benhu's knotted rope in a vicious, fast circle, missing the kneeling Quinn but striking the biggest assailant in the face, drawing a bellow of pain. While that one staggered, Anzi rushed to the other, outfighting him, her good hand to his bad.

On his feet, Quinn advanced on the remaining man, just recovering from the blow to his face, when a voice came from nearby: "Hold." The soldier stared past Quinn with a look of astonishment.

A Tarig stood on the strand. "Hold," the lord repeated.

Anzi's opponent backed away from her, his knife lowering.

The Tarig strode forward, his slit metallic skirt clinging to muscular legs.

"Lord, Bright Lord," Anzi's opponent said.

Quinn's man still held his weapon, looking confused as to whether or not Quinn was a threat to the lord.

"No knives," the lord said.

All weapons were now on the sand, including Quinn's.

In the distance, shouts came from a growing number of pursuers. The ship lay between the lord and the converging men, preventing anyone in that group from seeing what befell on this side. The lord stalked toward the two soldiers.

"Side by side," the lord commanded the soldiers. They huddled together, kneeling.

Quinn went to Anzi's side. She was panting, spattered with blood and fearfully beautiful. Benhu lay huddled on the ground, but alive. Benhu, that excellent fellow, had brought Lord Oventroe.

"Look up," the lord told the kneeling soldiers. "At the bright."

As they did so, the lord extruded a long claw from his hand and drew it over two throats in one long swipe. Blood spurted onto the sand, onto the lord's vest and silver garment. The men fell, their blood darkening a tide pool.

Quinn and Anzi helped Benhu to his feet. Another figure appeared on the ship's deck: the ship keeper. He leaned far over the bow to extend a hand to Benhu. Then, with Quinn pushing from below, Benhu managed to sprawl over the rail and onto the deck. Anzi scrambled up the rigging after him.

Lord Oventroe stood beside Quinn, making a gesture for Quinn to precede him. Quinn nodded, hauling himself up the rope net, still heavy with its catch of a dead soldier. He saw the lord leap a twelve-foot height to grasp the rail. From there Oventroe swung himself over, landing lightly on the deck, then took a knife from Anzi and severed the rigging, letting it fall away.

In the next instant, sand flew up as the struts retracted, and the ship lurched forward with a powerful surge.

Behind the departing ship, a swarm of soldiers ran up to their fallen comrades.

A scowling Jout stepped from the group, watching the ship depart and following it a few paces into the tide pools.

CHAPTER TWENTY-EIGHT

There are three tests of a good life: a peaceful household, a contented heart, a fine enemy.

—a saying

CIXI PAUSED AT THE GREAT DOOR. Around her legates and consuls were bowing and smiling, offering to hold the door, trying to decipher her mood from clues in her expression, makeup, and hair. The boldest had scrolls under their arms, ready, should the chance occur, to present the high prefect with a petition.

It was the middle of ebb, and Cixi, as usual, was well awake, preferring as she did the twilight intervals to the glare of the bright. Now she wished nothing more than to take a walk along the canals of the Ascendancy—alone. No attendants, no legates, no sycophants. But of course the high prefect could hardly go abroad unaccompanied, so she chose Mei Ing with a flick of a long-nailed finger. Mei Ing bowed, accepting as her due the right to attend Cixi.

Legates bowed, smiling, holding the door. Fools and lackeys. "Go to bed," Cixi muttered at them.

She fled the Magisterium, down the stairs into the sunken gardens and up the further flight onto the plaza and thence to the great canal. Mei Ing hurried behind her, steps shuffling in her ridiculously tight gown. One pin in the woman's hair was askew in back, Cixi noted with satisfaction. The sub-prefect's servants must have wakened her in a hurry, in order that she might hasten to accompany the high prefect for an unannounced walk.

The plaza was deserted at this ebb-time. The sky simmered, the deep folds tinged with red, as though if you scratched the sky you could draw blood. Well, blood was never very far from the surface of things, particularly in this evil city.

She and Mei Ing walked along the canal in silence. The channel waters carried carp, and the occasional black vine strewn by the wind. In the quiet, the city seemed artificial—a stage set for the Tarig to act out their drama of happy sentients mixing in the city of princes. Somewhere here, Cixi had no doubt, the Tarig composed their bodies and entered them. But where? She knew the bright city as she knew her own face. Her glance went to Ghinamid's Tower, the monument to the Sleeping Lord, who having come here as the first lord, became homesick and lay down to rest, never waking again. A pretty tale, and a false one. The lord slept, it was true, but not from a broken heart. They had no hearts. Or rather, the Heart controlled each one, creating the same five individuals over and over again. Where did that occur? Cixi had been to the tower many times, carefully touching the stone walls, looking for secrets. But then there were the mansions of the five lords, and these too could hold secrets.

". . . nightmares, so vexing of course," Mei Ing was babbling.

Cixi slowed her walk, tossing a morsel to a carp that came to the surface, begging. "You are vexed, Mei Ing?" She had to look up at the subprefect—so annoying. But being unusually short, Cixi was accustomed to that.

"Some are vexed, it is said. By nightmares. That is the symptom of an undisciplined mind, of course."

What was she prattling about? Ah. Nightmares. Now here was a subject that commanded Cixi's attention. Sydney and her captain of mounts flooded the land with nightmare dreams of the lords. Mo Ti hadn't said so directly, warning only, *Sleep brings the truth to many.* It was obvious that Sydney was spreading rumors through dreams. The dear girl, so audacious! However, open discussion of such dreams would not do, not at all.

"Nightmares are for children, Subprefect."

Mei Ing's face tightened at the rebuke. "Of course." She simpered, "And it is better to be awake in the ebb, when Your Brilliance prefers to conduct affairs."

"Her Brilliance does not dally with nightmares even in Prime of Day, Subprefect."

Best to quash discussion of nightmares. It would not do to have the legates freely discussing dreams when one might conclude that they were unnaturally shared among so many. It had only been an arc of days since the dreams began—only ten small days since Mo Ti's great message—but rumors could travel faster than a navitar on the Nigh, at least here in the Magisterium. Once stories began, an attendant to a lord might well mention troubled sleep, and thus bring a lord's attention to the matter.

They crossed the canal at a small covered bridge. Vines formed a bower and afforded a sweet shade, welcome even in the ebb.

"Mei Ing," Cixi whispered. "You understand that dreams hold our hidden wishes. The ones we can never express."

Mei Ing breathed, "Surely not, High Prefect. Surely not all the dark things that come when one's mind loses connection to veracity . . ."

"Oh yes. That is precisely what I mean. The dark thoughts come then, Mei Ing. The lover one cannot have, the bloody deed that the vows forbid . . . the treason against the lords."

"Treason?" came the whisper. "Lord of Heaven forbid."

Cixi shrugged. "If one dreams what one cannot tell a lord, then that must be a high crime. For would the gracious lords punish a sweet dream?"

"Punish? Can dreams be punished?" Mei Ing held perfectly still, struck by the new thought.

"Would you tell a lord that he appeared in a dream"—here Cixi paused, not wishing to convey that she had such dreams, too—"in an unattractive guise?"

"Never, Your Brilliance. It cannot be imagined."

"And it must never be imagined. Not in the Great Within, not under my regency." Cixi let it sink in, that she had just given a command. "Should any legate suffer from such weakness of thought, let that legate know to remain silent and take medicinals to cool his mind."

The silence in the bower deepened as Mei Ing settled into what must be the unhappy conclusion that she was committing treason every night in her sleep. Or every night that the Inyx ghosts came knocking.

Cixi relaxed her voice to send Mei Ing to her duties, not as one terrified, but as one timely warned. "I depend upon you to school the legates, Subprefect. One must do so discreetly, as one would not wish to accuse high legates of treacherous dreams."

"Of course, Your Brilliance. Legates afflicted with such dreams will have my warning."

"Sweet sleep to you, then, Mei Ing."

It took a moment before Mei Ing figured out that she had been dismissed. She retreated in haste back across the bridge and toward the Magisterium.

As vacant as the Empty Lands, Cixi thought, watching the woman flee. Mei Ing would be a worried sentient from now on. Let them all worry. Let them indeed wonder why they hated the lords in their dreams when waking, they adored them. Let them begin to doubt their loyalty.

It was a good beginning.

When Cixi emerged from the covered bridge there stood before her a knot of Tarig lords gathered near the canal. *By my grave flag*, she thought. Why had her legates not told her of this gathering? She glanced down at her long index fingernail, seeing that it scrolled with messages—all unseen in the darkness of the covered bridge.

Lord Nehoov himself stood foremost among the Tarig. One of the ruling five, his presence augured some high matter. *By heaven, let it not be nightmares*, she prayed.

Nehoov regarded her as she bowed low. "Talking in darkness, ah?" His glance went to the roofed bridge.

"Bright Lord, my life in your service, and shall we share the rest of my walk?" She gathered herself up and glided toward the lords, keeping her composure, but barely. How much had they heard?

He didn't respond to the suggestion, but whispered to Lord Toth, who stood nearby—a lord whom Cixi knew well, and whom she knew not at all. All the lords were versions of each other. It utterly changed how she thought of them. But it didn't change their power, their absolute control over her and all others.

When Lord Nehoov turned back to her, he said, "Mei Ing is distressed, this lord believes. She dreams?"

Cixi's heart fluttered, but nothing reached her face. Through long practice, her face was placid. "She is afraid of dreams. Like a child. One despairs of training her for high office, Bright Lord."

"Do you dream, Prefect?"

"Yes," Cixi answered.

"Of what?"

"Of the murder of my enemies."

Lord Nehoov narrowed his eyes, but not dangerously. "Against the vows, ah?"

"The act, not the dream." She wasn't used to cowering before the fiends. The bolder her comments, the more natural she would seem.

His attention turned from her, and he looked up toward the palatine hill. The lords followed his gaze, talking among themselves. One of them pointed, and Cixi saw that a brightship streaked away from the city, having launched from the hangar just out of sight at the summit.

Lord Nehoov murmured to her, "Lady Chiron's ship. We have come to find you, High Prefect, to instruct the Magisterium on necessary new cautions. These are needed, since it seems that Titus Quinn has returned."

Ah, Cixi thought. So they knew.

She had already heard the report from Mo Ti, that a woman of the Rose claimed to have journeyed with the man. She put on an expression of surprise. "Titus, is it? May the lady's brightship find good speed."

"We do hope it is he. Events have transpired such that he may have been seen on the Nigh. The man—of Chalin form—has taken a navitar's ship."

"Mmm. Still stealing ships, then." But this time, if it was true he was on the Nigh, he couldn't be the pilot. He couldn't steal a ship—not to pilot it. For that, he would have had to subvert a navitar. Was it possible? Was it even thinkable?

Lord Nehoov's face was stony. "Lady Chiron will apprehend this individual on the river."

Cixi watched as the brightship—sleeker and more evil-looking than the old ones—climbed into the sky and, glinting against the bright, dove into its depths.

She hoped this time Chiron would draw a claw across the man's throat— although she had to admit that it was useful to have the lords looking for a villain of the Rose rather than focusing on their own kingdom. Quite useful indeed.

Cixi looked into Lord Nehoov's dark eyes, wondering what it was like to have been deposited in a form rather than to have grown up. She contained a shudder. "Lord, let us discuss all safety cautions that my small dominion can impose."

"No one believes, High Prefect, that your dominion is small."

Cixi allowed herself a smirk. "Compared to you, Bright Lord . . ."

In an offhand manner he responded, "One does not compare."

Except in dreams, she thought. She set out down the promenade with the cluster of lords walking in slow motion in consideration of her small stature and frailty of age.

CHAPTER TWENTY-NINE

When in power: inspire, reward, speak truth. When in weakness: divide, subvert, sow doubt. In the harmonious sway one force cancels the other.

—from The Hundred Harmonies

QUINN DRIFTED IN AND OUT OF A CRUSHING SLEEP as the navitar's vessel plunged and tossed. For the first time in his life Titus Quinn was seasick. He fought to contain his nausea.

Someone cried out, "Turn back!" It was Anzi's voice.

Opening his eyes, Quinn saw a smoky light bleeding through the portholes. Outside, figures moved—one a Tarig. Then, appearing at his side, a Ysli ship keeper peered down at him, frowning and muttering. The vision shoved Quinn under again.

When he opened his eyes again, the light had brightened, and his stomach had stopped lurching.

Anzi bent over him. "We came back." With her white face and hair, she seemed a creature of the exotic river—the undine of the Nigh.

"Where did we go?"

"We ran to the binds, but you can't bear the journey yet. You're sick." She wrung out a cloth in a bowl of water and dabbed at his forehead.

Outside the porthole, Quinn saw Benhu peering in. Still in his grimy godman's robes, the man bowed and smiled, showing where he had lost teeth in the fight on the beach.

Quinn struggled to put his thoughts in a row. "Why am I sick?"

"Benhu said that a woman of the Rose poisoned you. Yes?" When he nodded, she went on, "Going into the binds, you became violently ill, and the lord made the navitar withdraw."

The river, flashing silver under the bright, threw a shimmering reflection on the cabin ceiling. He wanted to ask where they were, but even in his muddled state he knew the answer made little difference. *Somewhere on the Nigh.* Theoretically, they were everywhere on the five Rivers Nigh. The time had come to decide at last, for or against the cirque. Lord Oventroe was here. Time to decide.

Bringing his knee closer so that he could touch his ankle, he found that the chain was still there. Cold, as always. And, as always when he touched the cirque, the activating sequence came to him: *Four, five, one, and then the reverse.* He looked at Anzi. The nasty gash on her face reminded him how many people he had risked or embroiled in his undertaking already. It was no time to back out. Nor would he, if he had to take the engine apart bolt by bolt.

He reached out his hand to her and she took it. "I'm glad you found me," he said.

She smiled. "You hid well, as always."

"Your hair grew long."

"It has been some time since you have been here."

"Yes. But not long in the Rose. Time passes differently there."

"Yes."

"I have a lot to tell you, Anzi." *My wife is not dead*, he wanted to say to her. *I thought she was.* He didn't know what he could say, or for that matter, what he could feel.

Instead, he whispered, "My daughter doesn't want to see me."

Anzi bent close to his ear. "Titus. Benhu has told me everything. You have cause to grieve, and cause for hope, too." She looked over her shoulder. A Tarig sat there. Oventroe. Anzi whispered, "Do you trust him?"

"No. But I asked to see him." He struggled, trying to rise. Anzi helped him to a sitting position.

The lord had come to the bedside and now stood over them.

Dressed in a dark great coat, Lord Oventroe looked less gaunt than many Tarig. He wore his blue-black hair clasped behind his neck, as he had the last time

Quinn had seen him, when Quinn had infiltrated the bright city. On his vest and skirt, remnants of bloodstains were disappearing like soap bubbles popping.

In a deep voice that Quinn well remembered, the lord said, "One cannot tell which poison your body hates most, the Rose poison or the Entire poison."

"Entire poison?" Quinn asked, his mind moving at half speed.

Oventroe took Anzi's place, crouching near. "Benhu's medicinals do not function in you. You are doubly poisoned." Noting that Quinn reached down to cover the chain with his hand, Oventroe said, "This lord might have taken the device already if we meant to control you." He glanced out the cabin portholes. "We have a pursuer. Speak quickly, if there is something we must know."

"The chain is flawed, my lord."

Hearing this, Oventroe cut a dark glance at the cirque. "Thus you called me here, at such great risk." The Tarig looked at Anzi with a feral black regard.

"She stays," Quinn said.

"She knows all your secrets. Is that wise?"

Quinn sharpened his tone. "I trust her."

"Perhaps. But she brought notice to you. She was recognized. Her presence might have ruined our purpose."

"She is on my side, Lord Oventroe. I need someone I can trust. You understand?"

Oventroe looked outside again. "We could ease your sickness if we had the means on board. But this is a simple vessel." He looked back at Quinn. "Nevertheless, be ready for my navitar to take us downward."

"I'm ready."

Oventroe gestured at the ship keeper to come forward. The Ysli obeyed, bowing deeply. A soft down covered him from head to foot, and he looked surprisingly steady for one in the presence of a Tarig.

"Tell Jesid to prepare," Oventroe said. The Ysli bowed again and disappeared up the companionway.

"Who pursues us, my lord?" Quinn asked.

"My cousins." That was ominous, but before Quinn could pursue the topic, Oventroe said, "Tell me of the flaw in the chain."

"It's a bad weapon, Lord Oventroe. Maybe a terrible one."

Oventroe looked contemptuous. "We need a terrible weapon, ah?"

Quinn shut his eyes momentarily against the nausea. Anzi brought Quinn a cup of water, and after sipping a moment, he felt steadier.

He fixed Oventroe with as steady a gaze as he could muster. "The damn thing doesn't work. Doesn't work right. You want to blow the kingdom to hell and gone?"

"You have lost your courage, perhaps."

"Listen to me." If Oventroe would just listen. Taking a deep breath, he began to tell what he knew. He related what Helice had discovered of the true nature of the cirque: its catastrophic flaw that would let loose a nan plague on the Entire, leaving behind chaos and slag. He explained that he had been pursued in the Rose, and left there quickly, perhaps poorly prepared. Helice, however, might have been more canny in her appraisal of the nan than Stefan Polich had been. He didn't necessarily believe her, but they couldn't afford to ignore her.

Oventroe's first utterance after he finished was that the woman lied. He examined motives she might have, or lapses in her methods. But Quinn had been there ahead of him, having had exactly those reactions. It couldn't be assumed that Helice was lying. Quinn wasn't willing to risk it, and he told Oventroe so.

The lord paced, a thing that Quinn had never known a Tarig to do. At last the lord muttered, "Does this woman Helice know who I am?"

"That you are a Tarig, yes. But not your name."

"So Benhu assured us as well." A claw extruded on the lord's left hand, stroking the metal of his skirt. "She has the protection of the Inyx." He continued pacing, lost in thought, ignoring Quinn and Anzi for now.

Quinn murmured to Anzi, "I told you that when I came back, I'd bring war. But I can't bring this kind of war."

Anzi crept closer to him, lowering her voice for privacy. "But you must," she whispered. "The Helice woman lied. How could she know what others did not?" When he didn't answer, she went on, "Take no chances for the Rose, Titus. Let the Entire stand or fall. The Tarig made it to be vulnerable. It is no fault of yours. The Tarig made the engine to destroy you, and that is no fault of yours, either." She put her hand on his ankle, near the chain. Involuntarily, he jerked, startled to have anyone touch the cirque. She removed her hand. "Use it, Titus. If one place must die, it must be us."

"I can come back with a better device." His stomach knotted for a moment and then relented. "Johanna said we have one hundred years. Let them burn stars. The great collapse will come in time, but not right away. I've got time to come back."

Still watching the Tarig lord pace in his long strides, Anzi hissed, "No. You have only this one chance. How long before the Tarig who are against us figure out that you know about the engine? Once they do, they will surround the fortress. You have only this chance. Tell Lord Oventroe that we will bring it to Ahnenhoon."

At the mention of his name, the lord stopped and looked down at them. Anzi gripped Quinn's arm, but whether it was to steady him or steady herself, he wasn't sure.

The lord announced, "We will open the cirque. Then we can know."

The thought of Oventroe opening the nan sent alarms down Quinn's nerves. "Why not give me something better to use? Give me a device I can trust."

"We cannot. Any Tarig methods would appear as such, exposing this lord, who is your only ally against my cousins. But you bear a sufficient device. Primitive though it is, it has destructive molecular power."

"Maybe you're not hearing me." Brushing aside Anzi's warning grip on his arm, he went on. "Helice thinks this will destroy your land. Nothing left, my lord— not the bright, not the Nigh, not the Ascendancy. Not you. Or your cousins."

"We always survive."

"All right, you survive. But everyone else dies. I won't do it."

Oventroe knelt down, regarding Quinn with disdain. "We require that you save the Rose."

"You don't require me." As Anzi's fingernails dug into him, he added, "My lord."

"Give us the cirque. We will open the chambers and determine potency. It is a delicate thing to undertake so far from devices that could assist. We have ability to compensate." He held out his long hand. "Give us the chain."

It could work. Oventroe would run his own tests with superior technology. If the chain's kill sequence was dependable, if the nan would limit its scope of destruction, then the mission went forward. It made sense.

He looked into Oventroe's stark face. He couldn't do it.

Anzi nudged him, eager to get on with it.

He put a hand on her forearm, warning her off. There was more to this than assessing firepower. Something more . . .

"Get me a chair, Anzi, please." Quinn struggled to his feet, swaying, whether from the ship's pitch and yaw or his own. He felt the chair in back of him and lowered himself into it. Oventroe sat on the bunk along the far bulkhead, waiting.

Finally, Quinn said, "Tell me one thing, first: Why do you *care*? That's the thing I've been struggling with. Why you care."

Oventroe said, "We do not have time for such a discussion. Do you know how fast a brightship travels? Even now, they come looking for this lord. And looking for you."

Anzi whispered, "Please, Titus." She looked out the porthole as though there were a chance of seeing a Tarig brightship approach.

"It's a matter of trust," Quinn said. He nodded at Anzi. "I trust *her*. She's the only one I trust."

Oventroe sat quiet as stone, murmuring, "We saved your life on the banks of the Nigh. Do I wish you harm?"

"I don't know. There are lots of ways to die. Maybe you're reserving me for something special." He ran his hands through his hair, trying to find a way to understand this Tarig and to find a way to put his fate in the Tarig's hands. "Lord Oventroe, I wonder what drives you to help me. Unlike everyone else, you favor the Rose. Why?"

Oventroe stood up and gazed out the porthole toward the storm wall, where its gloaming light fell on his face and bare arms. He said, barely audible, "This lord opposed the engine from the beginning. One believes the Rose is not for burning."

"Why do you care?"

Oventroe turned to face him. "Perhaps, Titus, it is for the same reason that you care for the Entire."

That the Tarig used his name startled him. He stared at Oventroe, trying to discern the creature's heart. He had just likened himself to Quinn. We have the same motives, he implied: to save a culture, a universe. But it was hard to trust a Tarig, particularly since their need for fuel was so great. If they *must* burn the Rose, how could Oventroe be against it?

He asked, "Will the Entire die without a new energy source?"

The lord paused. "One's cousins did not look deep enough for solutions. They found an easy answer: the Rose."

A spike of hope flashed. "Could you burn another place instead? A universe with no sentients?" If they looked past the Rose to another universe . . .

Oventroe put an end to that hope. "We have done so already. They are gone."

"Burned other universes?"

"Naturally. The Rose has some traditional value. We turned to it last." Oventroe glanced out the portal. He waved Quinn's brimming questions away. "No time. Know that the hundreds of realities are generally cold and empty. They lack matter, or if they had supplies, they were soon gone. The Rose is next. It is almost endlessly productive for our purposes. But this lord mislikes what his cousins will do. Those who dwell in the Rose are the template on which we based the sentients. The Rose is, in some ways, our root stock. We must find other ways to sustain the All. That is one's judgment, even if one must stand alone.

"Furthermore," the lord added, "we are curious about you."

"Curious," Quinn repeated.

"Yes. We long ago learned all that can be discovered of fundamental things. But of evolving sentients, we can never know enough. This is why we brought life to the Entire—out of our interest in all that our fellow creatures do. We do not slaughter sentients, as you have observed, but establish justice. Now the Entire prepares to slaughter sentients of the Rose. We do not concur. We will never concur."

They heard voices from the upper deck, the navitar's cabin. In another moment, the ship keeper came down to say that Jesid wished to be under way. The binds were disturbed, the overseer reported. It might be a brightship.

Lurching to his feet, Quinn waved the overseer away. "First, answer me this: Some time ago I came to you in the Ascendancy, and asked you for help. You turned me away. Why?"

"We suspected that you were a spy of Lord Hadenth, sent as a trap. Why should we have believed you? Then you fled, and we knew, too late, that you were not in Hadenth's service."

"I asked you for the correlates."

"So you did."

"I ask for them now."

Oventroe went silent. Quinn knew it was a gamble. But he saw a way to force Oventroe to commit to the Rose in an unambiguous way, and at the same time further an ultimate peace. Even if Quinn succeeded in destroying Ahnenhoon, that couldn't by itself ensure peace. Only a free exchange between the cultures could do that. They needed the correlates once and for all.

He said so. "You can't spy through the veils and expect to know who we are and how we live. Let humans pass freely to and from. Let your own people come to the Rose. If you share that vision with me, then give me the correlates. As a token of your intentions."

Oventroe looked from the companionway to Quinn and back again. He wanted to be gone. Were there brightships descending on them at this moment? Quinn didn't know, but he did know that this was the last chance he would have to force a concession from the lord.

Oventroe growled, "Is it not enough that we allow you to destroy the fortress at Ahnenhoon, against the wishes of the Five?"

Quinn didn't answer, holding his ground. Anzi came to his side to steady him as he stood.

The lord said, "You ask for much, but what do you give us in return?"

"My life. It should have been your job to stop the engine. Now it's mine. It's a job I may not survive."

"You will survive."

"Depends, doesn't it?"

Oventroe paced, while Anzi watched him with round eyes.

From the pilothouse above came Jesid's cry, "Poor under-sentients. Knowing nothing!" The ship keeper's voice followed, calming, cajoling.

The navitar's voice rose: "Dumb as piglets, blind as centipedes!"

Oventroe stalked to the foot of the companionway and thundered, "Quiet him! Feed him!" He turned back to Quinn. "At least he is quiet when he eats."

Quinn and Oventroe faced off until at last the Tarig said, "Are your people ready to have such a gift?"

It was an unexpected question. Quinn thought of Stefan Polich and Helice Maki, and he wasn't sure. Then, remembering Caitlin and Rob, he thought that decent people could make it work. In any case, humanity wouldn't be in charge. The Tarig would be. That wasn't particularly reassuring, but it did go some way toward the promise he had made, that humanity wouldn't overrun the Entire. "We're ready," Quinn said.

"It would have come to you in time, Titus."

"Time is the one thing I don't have."

The lord stood very still. Quinn remembered that flinty self-possession. The Tarig had few unconscious gestures; no pulling at garments, no bunching of hands. "We must first encode the correlates for use in your computational machines."

"Permit me, Lord Oventroe, to have the program in a redstone for use in a stone well—such as a scholar of the veil might use."

Oventroe looked at him as though incredulous that he could demand even one thing more.

Quinn went on, "There is a scholar of your acquaintance. The man who gave me your name so that I could find you at the Ascendancy."

"Su Bei."

"Yes. I want him to have the correlates. He has a lifetime work, a cosmography of the Rose universe. He has small bits of knowledge, a few data points. Give him the correlates and let him complete his cosmography."

A cold pause. "A rich gift for an old man puttering with maps." Quinn held his ground. "You test us," the lord said darkly.

Quinn let the accusation stand. It might give Oventroe pause, to know that Bei would verify the data.

"Send the correlates by the fastest way you have. Tell Su Bei that if I don't survive, he should send them to Caitlin Quinn. Into her hands, no other."

"As a redstone?"

"She'll figure it out."

Quinn knew he was pushing hard. He was desperate. He might never walk out of Ahnenhoon. Someone had to get the correlates to the Rose.

Oventroe was gazing out the porthole at the storm wall. "The correlates to Su Bei, then." Turning around, he held out his hand, waiting for the cirque.

Under the creature's skin, Quinn could see ridges under which his claws rested. Although this Tarig was no more alien than other sentients he had known here—the Hirrin, the Jout—those long hands were testimony to a species that killed with its hands. Quinn knew to be wary of this lord, ally or not.

From above, the navitar groaned in a mighty exhalation: "Oh pray, travelers, pray. . . ."

Quinn crouched down. Hands trembling, he touched the cirque. *Four, five, one. A total of ten.* He touched the depressions in the chain, in order, the right number of pinches at each node. The chain fell open. It lay heavy and cold in his hand. He delivered it to Lord Oventroe.

"It's military nan," Quinn said. "If it gets out . . ."

"Hnn. Molecular deconstruction."

It seemed a bland summation of the dangers. Quinn reminded him that if the sequence was pressed in reverse order, the nan would fly.

As a wave of nausea passed through Quinn, Anzi helped him to sit back down.

"You are not ready for the binds," Oventroe said. "But we must go in." He nodded to the ship keeper, who had once again come down the companionway. Receiving the silent order, the Ysli hurried back up the stairs to his master.

From the bottom of the companionway, Oventroe called to the navitar, "Go gently into the binds, Jesid. Our passenger is ill."

From above, Jesid's voice came in a mewling cry: "We will tiptoe in, my king."

But in the next instant, the bow of the vessel pitched steeply down, flinging Quinn onto the deck. The ship plunged headlong into the river.

Depta stood in the tent of Captain Dekisher, the Jout officer who believed the skirmish his soldiers fought in might have involved Titus Quinn. Already shaken by her ride in the brightship, both disorienting and nauseating, Depta summoned her courage to look on the injured soldier lying on a table before her and the Lady Chiron. His name, according to Dekisher, was Chang.

Two others who had fought were dead, their throats slit. This one was dying of a gut wound.

The frontal bone of the man's skull had been removed, and a delicate mesh laid over, touching the organ beneath. Depta felt her gorge rise to see the results of Chiron's dreadful, yet necessary, surgery. The patient was awake, but lay still, not in pain, so Depta hoped.

"Since he does not know what he saw, Depta," the lady said, "we must help him remember, and quickly." Even now, the man of the Rose—or whoever it was who had run from the soldiers—was no doubt fleeing as far and as fast as a navitar's vessel could bear him.

Earlier, under questioning, the badly wounded soldier had told them everything he could remember: *We ran into the marshlands. The ship came up fast, trying to cut us off. There were two fugitives: one woman, one man. From the ship's deck a man with a beard jumped on me. Above him, I saw a Tarig lord.* As to which man, which woman, which lord, the soldier couldn't say. Now, his memory would say. His visual memory.

Lady Chiron unfolded the scroll and lay it next to the comatose man. Between his forehead and the scroll she draped a long braid of sparkling filaments. The rolled-out scroll swam with colors, then formed into an image of Depta herself. The soldier, lying wounded, had seen her enter the room; he remembered her. She felt slightly ill to be called forth like this from the man's dying mind.

Chiron bent close to the man's ear. "Chang," she said, "think about the chase along the Nigh. You remember the chase. The girl. The man. Your captain bid you apprehend them."

The soldier remembered. As evidence that he did, an image appeared on the scroll, of a young Chalin woman thrusting her knife forward. A jolt of colors appeared as the weapon pierced flesh. Chang seemed to be caught in a web of rigging along the hull of the ship. In a moment the scroll showed a shocking image: a Tarig standing on the deck of the ship. But what lord would have been on that ship, and why?

"Hnn," Chiron murmured. Then bending close once more: "Remember the man you chased."

Memory flickered. The scroll showed a man and woman fleeing down the strand, jumping the tide pools. They pointed to something in the distance. One of them—the man—turned, exposing his face.

Chiron leaned closer. "Ah yes," she whispered. "His face is altered. But we have seen likenesses of his changed face. It is Titus-een."

The scroll went to swirls, then resolved into an image of Lady Chiron. The soldier remembered the moment when the lady tucked the painkillers between his lower teeth and gums.

Chiron stood up straight, bundling the scroll away, along with the braided tubes. "How strange," she murmured. "Titus Quinn has a friend among us."

Depta didn't recognize the Tarig she saw on the scroll. "It must be a minor lord whom I have not met," she said.

"In fact, Depta, this is no minor lord. Among the ruling five, Lord Oventroe now holds a place."

Depta's ears flattened in dismay. *Lord Oventroe?* "He who hates the Rose?"

"Who the lord hates is no longer clear," Chiron murmured. "How did my Titus come to have such a friend?"

Depta knew that the lady was no longer speaking to her. As she so frequently did, Chiron found her own company good enough.

Still, Depta offered, "Perhaps Lord Oventroe is not a friend of the fugitive, but has captured him."

"And withheld the triumph from general knowledge?"

Depta had never before considered that the lady's plans might not be the only secret designs under way. *We are all of one mind on these matters*, Chiron had once said. The Tarig were united in all purposes—so Depta had thought until the day that Chiron had bid Cixi not share with others that Titus Quinn knew the purpose of the great engine.

"If Titus has an exalted friend," Chiron murmured, "then Titus has a brightship." She cut a glance at Depta. "We must hurry, indeed."

Calmly, the lady placed her hand on the patient's open forehead. One of her claws snapped out.

Depta clamped her mouth shut. Must not vomit, must not. For a Hirrin to become sick in this manner was unthinkable—especially in front of the lady. Depta tucked her front legs down for a moment, resting her long neck along the tent's dirt floor.

After a moment, the lady came to Depta's side, saying, "This sentient would have died in any case, Depta. Now his death is worth something."

Numbly, Depta nodded. She rose to her feet, averting her eyes from the table.

At the flap of the tent door, Chiron stopped. She turned back to Depta, eyeing her steadily. "Do you love us, Depta?"

She breathed, "Yes, Bright Lady." For a moment her mind darkened, and she thought she might fall. Surely it was the nausea, from the brightship, from the soldier Chang's death. . . . But she held firm on her four legs.

The tent flap fell behind Chiron as she left.

Depta managed a ragged breath. Surely she *did* love the lady. The ungrateful fugitive running amok, the darklings of the Rose poised to infest the bright realm . . . the gracious lady, so serene and powerful . . . and the soldier, already dying, giving crucial intelligence. Yes, it was all proper and worthwhile. How could it be otherwise? If otherwise, Depta was preying upon the wounded; she was also hounding a man who merely wished to hold converse between universes.

On her uncertain legs, she managed to push the tent flap aside and follow Chiron outside. The lady spoke to Captain Dekisher, bending over the short Jout as though she were dipping down to peck at his eyes. As Depta approached, Chiron was saying that the deceased soldier must have a fine grave flag. A proper subject, even a noble one.

As the Hirrin approached, Chiron said, "Give us a grave saying, Depta."

Depta puffed air through her lips, thinking. "In death, served a Tarig lady."

"That will suit," Chiron said as the captain made note of the saying. Clustered nearby, soldiers bowed to the lady, their faces betraying their awe at seeing one of the Five. Chiron had already liberally distributed coins among them and promoted Captain Dekisher one rung, making clear her pleasure in their efforts, though their quarry had escaped.

As Chiron strode toward the brightship, she easily outpaced the Hirrin, forcing Depta to amble. The gangway was already retracting into the vessel as Depta made the leap onto the moving plate.

CHAPTER THIRTY

The pulse of the bright is thus: four of high phase, four of low. In the high phase of day are Early, Prime, Heart, and Last. In the low phase are Twilight, Shadow, Deep, and Between. In this manner the gracious lords keep back the dark, in grand progression from light to light.

—from *The Book of Ascendant Joys*

SYDNEY OPENED HER EYES. Her head throbbed with pain and the world was a blur.

Helice's voice came to her from close by: "Your sight will improve as you heal. The Tarig are gone, my friend. Of that I am sure."

Riod was nearby. She sensed that he had been with her every moment of the last hours.

Through the haze of pain-suppressing medicinals, Sydney received his heart words: *Best rider, we will ride again, free of the Tarig.*

The previous ebb, Helice had brought her small machine into the pavilion, making a tent over Sydney's face as she lay on the cot. Two cups had descended over her eyes. The chemicals Helice had brought dragged Sydney down to a sweet blackness. When the room lightened again, the thing was done. Helice pronounced that free sight had been achieved. Sydney couldn't verify Helice's judgment, but she felt the truth of it. The mantis lords were gone.

Sydney gripped Helice's arm. "Let me see you." She pulled Helice closer and gazed at her face for the first time. She was young, but already an engineer of nanotechnology and quantum things. She was educated, sophisticated, well traveled, and experienced—things that Sydney admired and envied. And Helice had defeated the Tarig, in this small thing at least.

Sydney clasped her hand. "Thank you," she said in English.

Helice made a nice smile. "You're welcome. You were very brave."

As Sydney fell into sleep again, Helice looked at her, searching for the likeness of the father. It helped that Sydney looked nothing like Titus Quinn. Brown eyed and sweet looking, Sydney must look like Johanna. Not much of a visage for a queen, but then maybe Sydney wouldn't be queen. The world was an uncertain place, and while one could wish the girl well, there might be other contenders. She smiled at Riod, who was no doubt trying to read her thoughts. Mostly she tried to think good, boring things so he wouldn't be interested. She could almost feel him pushing up against her resolve to remain blank to him. He might catch tendrils of things, but the creature couldn't possibly understand her purposes. If she couldn't outthink a *horse*. . . .

Riod sent, *Mo Ti wishes to enter to give respects.*

"Tell him Sydney can't have visitors."

She sleeps, Riod said, voicing the self-evident.

I am surrounded by simple creatures, Helice thought. To some extent, that was good. Folks hereabouts weren't prepared to play rough, and that would give Helice some leeway until they realized who they were dealing with.

While Sydney's little band of supporters gathered outside the tent to wait for her to wake up, Helice retired to her tent, ostensibly to rest. She carried the delicate medical sapient in both hands and placed it on the table next to the assembler. The mSap wouldn't need the little arms with tools anymore. With a little tinkering from the assembler, it would be strictly for quantum processing. For thinking. She sat back, surveying her two instruments. Assembler and mSap. Honestly, what more did one need in the world? In any world? She was almost content. But there was something else she wanted. A scarf. The little arms would go into the assembler to create a long scarf that she could wind around her head so she wouldn't be recognized when she went into the fields to see what those frequent herd gatherings were all about. Helice had gotten close enough to them to figure out that the beasts were in some kind of stupor. Something was afoot, and while Sydney's entourage was focused on the girl's recovery, Helice would take a little evening stroll.

It was Deep Ebb before the Inyx left their individual pastures and began gathering in one spot. Helice had taken a few stimulants to stay awake, and by the time the gathering started, she was edgy and sweating. This night's work was a tad risky, because she'd need to be open to the Inyx to figure out what they were doing. That raised the possibility that the beasts would mess with her mind, and she'd rather that didn't happen. They had come tampering with her before, and she had managed to resist them, or at least not think of secrets. She might have to be a bit more open tonight, though.

She pulled her scarf around her face and slipped among the tents toward the flats, where a massing of the herd was taking place in eerie silence.

The bright coiled above, a lavender-stained cloud that gave off a roseate light. She took a moment to absorb the grandeur of the sight. She was not insensible to beauty and tender feelings, despite what people said who didn't know her well. The Entire was a land both harsh and intoxicating, its wonders few but massive. She was going to like this place once she found her niche. However, that wouldn't be in a backward sway where the inhabitants' notion of high technology was a vole trap.

Lying on her stomach to watch the herd, Helice felt a nudge in her mind, an impression of thoughts on the verge of utterance. So, the beasts were thinking, perhaps in unison.

But of what?

She crept closer. Not even the closest of the mounts responded to her presence. The beasts stood without moving, eyes open but unseeing. Helice looked about for Vichna, the mount she was supposedly bonded to, but couldn't pick him out from all the others. Riod was no doubt in the thick of them, but there were thousands, and her view was restricted to those closest.

Here goes, she thought. Moving into their midst, she calmed her thoughts and listened. Wisps of impression came, like fleeting shadows. They were flying. Riod was flying. They were moving across the primacy. Opening to these sendings, Helice fell into them. She flew with the Inyx. There were colors of thoughts, a kaleidoscope; there was Riod's intention shaping them; there was a wave of stealth and hungry curiosity. . . .

She snapped out of the vision to see that she had her hand on the warm hide of an Inyx. Then she sank back into the vision of the pack hunting . . . finding the Tarig . . . swooping down and piercing a consciousness. Then another. She couldn't say what she was seeing, who she was seeing. Tarig thoughts bombarded her, shouting, screaming. She recoiled.

Helice fell from the sky where she had been swept. She hit the ground, hard.

Mo Ti stood over her. He raised his sword, and down it came in a great fall of metal. She rolled under the Inyx next to her, taking shelter between its four legs.

Mo Ti, more nimble than she had supposed, thrust the sword under the beast, following her. She spilled out the other side, seeing Mo Ti rush around with sword high once more. Instinctively, Helice held onto the mount's leg, hoping Mo Ti wouldn't risk the beast. She was right.

The giant bellowed, and reached for her where she cowered by the mount's hind feet. His big hands grappled around her ankle and yanked her out from under, brutally scraping her back against the rocky ground. Now the beast moved, throwing his head up and sending a spike of alarm so strong that Helice's head hurt.

Not deterred, Mo Ti lifted Helice from the ground in one ham fist and slammed her against the mount's flank.

Managing to remain standing, Helice sputtered at him, "Quite a temper, there."

Mo Ti, still holding the sword, yanked her down, bending her backward over his bent knee. The sword rested against her neck, which made her reluctant to thrash. She grew calm, even as the air around her was shot through with alarm and the screams of mounts.

"Stop, Mo Ti," came a voice. A creature with four legs and a long neck— they called them Hirrin—brushed against Mo Ti's arm, trying to dislodge the weapon. "Not the way, no."

Mo Ti growled. "She is a spider."

"Sydney will blame you. You risk all for just a spider, Akay-Wat thinks."

The sword took an edge of blood. Amid the cacophony of the milling beasts, Helice felt peaceful. She stared past Mo Ti's face into the bright. Its light fell on her face like the smile of God.

Bruised and thrashed, Helice allowed herself to be dragged from the field. She knew where Mo Ti was taking her. Perhaps clearer heads would prevail.

Inside Sydney's tent, Helice saw that Sydney was waiting for them along with Akay-Wat and Riod. How had they gotten there ahead of her? Oh. Mo Ti had paused to rough her up a little more. Then she had lost control of her bladder, and begged for new clothes, but Mo Ti had brought her straight to Sydney's tent, stinking and hurting.

Things hadn't gone well so far. Or had they? The worse Mo Ti acted, the better Helice looked.

"Spying, then?" was all the greeting Sydney offered.

Helice started to speak, but only a bark came out. She gathered her resolve and what strength she could muster. She coughed, testing her voice. "Neither one of us has exactly been honest," she rasped.

The group eyed her darkly.

Helice wished she could sit down. Actually, she was almost falling down. She grabbed onto the center tent pole. She needed her wits, and right now. The glimpse of the Inyx in flight over the primacy—only a vision, she knew—had told her a story, not only of the probing of the Tarig mind, but of Sydney's quest to raise a new kingdom. It was so close to Helice's own intentions that it staggered her. The girl had courage, but suffered from bad advisors.

Helice went on, "Honesty has been in short supply all around. You're hiding things; I'm hiding things. Not good for relationships."

Mo Ti stood with his sword drawn, but pointing at the floor. He looked at her like a hungry bear.

Her voice stronger now, Helice pressed on. "It's been disappointing to me that you haven't been truthful. I thought we were allies."

Sydney exchanged glances with Mo Ti. "Allies? You offered me some assistance, and I offered you a haven. We're not equals."

"I have a little more to offer than clearing up your eyesight."

"Why haven't you offered it, then?"

"A drink of water would be good. I've had a long walk from the pasture." She was sure she looked bad, beaten up and even bloody. Blood was on her tunic. It must be her own. But she needed water so badly she would have killed for it.

At Sydney's gesture, Akay-Wat lipped a canteen and dropped it at Helice's feet.

She took a long drink, and began again. "I was going to offer some benefits other than chasing the Tarig out of your sight. Although I thought at the time that that was a rather big favor." She paused, waiting for a reaction, getting none. "But then I noticed that you have weak links in your organization. That troubles me. Mo Ti, for example, isn't at your level. He isn't at home with complex situations. Good foot soldier though he may be, you really shouldn't take advice from your bodyguard."

"But I should take advice from you?"

"Yes. I've got an assembler that can make weapons and produce useful devices. You remember how to play chess? Well, that assembler is your bishop's piece. And then, I've got a way out of your larger difficulties. You might call this your best chess piece, your queen. Think of it as a renaissance. I do. It will involve a restructuring of fundamental issues here."

Sydney frowned. "Fundamental issues?"

"Yes. You think the issue is who rules the Entire. Fine. I like a woman who thinks big. But you have a much bigger problem than that." She paused for effect. "Do you want to rule an ash heap?"

So far they had been speaking in English. Now Sydney spoke to Mo Ti and Akay-Wat in Lucent, and Helice waited for her to finish translating. Mo Ti made his usual comments, but Helice couldn't spare any time to worry about him. Sydney was the one to persuade.

Helice continued. "The Entire is headed to be an ash heap. A few hundred years—you'll still be alive, right?—you'll be sitting on the throne of the Ascendancy, with me as your advisor. But we'll rule over an ash heap, because this place is running out of steam. The Entire is dying. No juice. That's where renaissance comes in."

Out of the corner of her eye she saw that Mo Ti was fingering his sword.

"To be completely honest," Helice went on, "it's your only hope of raising the kingdom." She cocked her head at Sydney. "Do you want to hear about it?"

"I want to hear."

Helice nodded. "Of course you do. But could your bodyguard just put the sword down while we're strategizing here?" She was strangely detached from any fear of Mo Ti, now that he had done his worst to her and she had survived, but he had to be put in his place.

Sydney glanced at Mo Ti, giving a nod.

Mo Ti didn't move. "I will not kill her yet."

Everyone's eyes were on him, as though at any moment they expected him to charge. His face was a weapon in itself, glowering and dark.

Sydney said, "Put the sword by the tent wall, Mo Ti."

After an interminably long moment, he did so.

The tension in the room subsided a notch. "Now," Helice said, "we can talk."

After Helice laid out her full plans, Sydney took new stock of the woman. Given this new information about a renaissance, as Helice called it, the woman should be seen as a considerably stronger ally than before. In light of this new information, Sydney decided she could forgive Helice's attempt to spy on the herd.

Mo Ti, however, could not forgive it. He instinctively hated the woman. Even the success of the eye surgery had made little difference to him. As though Sydney's vast relief counted for so little.

Clearly, Helice and Mo Ti couldn't both continue at her side, not with the enmity that now lay between them. One of them must leave.

It would be Mo Ti.

When she called him to her side, he was wary of her, surmising that Helice wasn't disgraced—far from it.

"Mo Ti," she said, her heart sinking that their friendship had eroded so far. She took stock of him. She had grown to love his bulging face, his stature, his chest as broad as a doorframe. Lately he had frowned at her every decision, drawing away from her. Did he tire of her so soon? They had once been so close, nearly lovers, except that he was incapable. Well, time cooled hearts, she had learned. If this was true now, perhaps it wasn't a bad thing that he had to leave.

A duty called to her—one she couldn't fulfill herself.

There were two lands; they couldn't both last. Sydney was saddened to hear this, because even though she had been cut off from the Rose, she didn't hate it. But: *They cannot both last.* And not only that, because of the competition between the universes, the Entire was under immediate attack. All this stood in front of the plans she had thought so grand: to raise the kingdom. To raise the kingdom she must first save the kingdom. From her father.

"Mo Ti," she said, "shall we stop Titus from hurting our land?"

His voice, though soft, always rang with authority. "We have many things to accomplish, my lady. Is this one of them?"

"Who else knows what he intends?"

"Send Helice to stop him."

She let that bitter statement sit for a moment. "Helice can't pass for Chalin, and is too small to overcome a grown man. I need a warrior."

Understanding dawned on Mo Ti. He looked away, his face grim.

"Will you go, Mo Ti? It will be dangerous to go. But who else can I trust?"

"Do you trust me? It seems that lately, you do not."

"Mo Ti you have my trust." She wanted to add, *And my love*, but didn't.

He seemed to sense that she might have said more, and his face crumpled. Finally, in the softest of voices, he murmured, "Will you hate me if I kill him?"

"No, never."

"Not hating is not the same as love." After a pause he said, "Command me."

From her throat came a whisper. "I beg you to do me this service." She couldn't meet his eyes. Her father's voice ghosted into her mind: *I will come for you. Watch for me. Wait for me.* He could still break her heart with just a few words. It's too late for that, she answered silently. You wouldn't have time to save me when the world ends. I will die under the bright. Or you will.

Mo Ti took her chin in his big hand and turned her toward him. "Say it."

"Kill him, Mo Ti. Kill my father."

He nodded, bowing.

CHAPTER THIRTY-ONE

My navitar, I see the shore
Where you will go, nevermore.

—from "Death of the Navitar," a river song

"**D**RINK," LADY CHIRON SAID, holding the cup and urging it on Depta. The brightship was aloft, traveling down the side of the storm wall, along the path of the Nigh, pursuing the renegade navitar vessel. Depta knew they would soon plunge into the binds, a maneuver that brought most sentients into a welcome stupor. Chiron, however, wanted Depta alert. Thus the vile potion, smelling like burned oil.

Why, though, should Depta remain alert? Sleep was the proper mode for those traveling the Nigh—surely the lady knew that. On the other hand, sleep had its own torments these days, as visions haunted Depta's sleep. Ghoulish images of Chiron staggering through the Magisterium, both dead and alive. The dream was too sensible to be normal. The dream *told* Depta that the lady was a false being, controlled by some unspeakable entities in the Heart, the Tarig ancestral land. Unthinkable. But dreamable.

Depta stared at the proffered cup, brimming with liquid. How could she gulp down the whole amount? Lady Chiron had thoughtfully equipped the cup with a feeding tube, but still . . .

Lady Chiron took some pity on the Hirrin's distress, saying "We will enter the binds, Depta. Have you ever wished to see a great thing?"

"Yes, Bright Lady. But . . ." She hesitated to admit her real fear. What if the potion was the same as navitars drank? Depta had no wish to travel the high-sentience path, no wish for sublime things at all; only a worthy calling such as a lowly Hirrin might hope for when schooled in the Magisterium.

Staring at the awful cup, Depta blurted out, "Will it make me a navitar?"

Chiron murmured, "We do not force a navitar." Her demeanor became very still, a mode that Depta had come to fear. Yet the lady also looked, if it were possible to believe, confused. "All sentients choose their path, Depta. Your doubts are troubling."

"Forgive me," Depta whispered. "Navitars choose what they are. Yet I fear them."

"They are feared?" Chiron moved her head to one side, as though preferring to look at Depta out of one eye rather than both.

"Yes, Lady. Sometimes the navitars grow so heavy their soft bones bend. Some cannot clean themselves when body functions require such. And the poor creatures are mad."

A curl appeared at the side of Chiron's lips. "Hnn. Mad, do you think? But they see more than you. They pity you. They love knowledge, whereas you, Depta, love only life. These are not the same things." Again, Chiron urged the cup toward her. "No more talk, Depta."

Her lady was in a most urgent hurry. That she took time to persuade Depta was high consideration. "I will drink, of course."

"Of course."

Depta addressed herself to the feeding tube and sucked. The liquid, despite its strong smell, had no taste. She emptied the cup quickly. The liquid ignited a buzz in her long muzzle, as though her teeth had been struck by a hammer.

"Do not fear, Depta," the lady said. "You will become more than you were. You will see what most under-sentients do not see."

Whether from stress or the effects of the potion, Depta felt her legs slowly folding under her.

Chiron's voice continued. "It is what Titus Quinn understood when we dwelled together. As strange as new things may be, they are also sweet and grand. It is always worth it to become greater than you are."

Depta didn't feel bound for greatness. From her position on the floor, she found herself staring at the lady's boots, noticing that the heels now bulged with little curving blades.

Depta was awake. The interior of the ship glowed with preternatural intensity, as though each thing, each piece of instrumentation, were outlined in fire. In Depta's eyes the Tarig lady bore an unsettling halo, making her hard to look at. Depta's stomach felt like it had sprouted a hot tumor.

They were deep in the River Nigh.

Chiron stared at the air in front of her, where a field of light occupied the space between her and the bulkhead. From Depta's angle of view, the display looked like curtains bulging and receding. From time to time, Chiron inserted a hand into the display, with a gesture like brushing aside a curtain.

"The binds," Chiron murmured. "He has gone deep. We will surprise this navitar." She turned from the display and sat in the chair she had caused to bud up from the floor. "If the ship bears our Titus, you will meet a person like few others. Stay alert around him, Depta. He will be desperate."

Her hand plunged into the wavering display. "Now, here is a hard maneuver. Hold fast."

With her prehensile mouth, Depta lipped a soft, tubular ring that protruded from the wall and held on, swaying and trying not to vomit.

Without windows, the brightship gave no views outward. The vaunted journey into the binds was a mystery so far, except for its effect of a hot, bilious stomach and forced alertness. Depta tried to imagine how she would maintain her equilibrium when they arrived wherever Chiron was driving them. She tried to imagine, as well, sharing this cabin with the man of the Rose, that tragic personage who had once risen high among the lords and in the lady's estimation, who had become a prince of the Ascendancy and thrown it all away. For this crime he would be buried alive in Chiron's manse.

The lady's words came to her with irony: *It is always worth it to become greater than you are.* Depta wondered if Titus Quinn would think so once sealed in the tunnel.

From her station across the cabin, Chiron cried out, "I have him." She rose from her chair, nodding at Depta. "Now let us see what we have caught."

Chiron gave a silent order to dilate the hatchway leading outside. In the cabin one of the walls dimpled, forming an aperture that quickly formed an open door. From this door a wave of pungent air shouldered in, bringing with it a flickering dark light.

Following Chiron to the hatch, Depta could see a gangway was moving out from the brightship to reach for a docking point.

It was a river ship.

Chiron rushed down the steeply pitched gangway, her face bluish in the light of the storm wall. Before her, the deck of the river vessel was deserted.

Moving onto the ramp, Depta looked around her. It appeared they were still on the river's surface, but she knew they were plunged deep inside it. It appeared that the storm wall loomed over them, and that the ship cut a white path down the molten surface of the Nigh. They were, however, in the binds. It was a sight that few had ever seen, and though she was grateful for the wonder, all that Depta could think of at present was that the contents of her stomach were trying to climb out.

She followed Chiron down the gangway, moving from the protection of the ship to a realm of noise and chaotic blue-gray. The wind, too slow to be real, pushed at her from various directions like the nudge of a ponderous beast. She set one foot in front of the other, eager to reach the deck of the navitar's vessel. It hadn't occurred to Depta that the wall continued into the depths of the river. But of course it would.

Once on deck, she was alone. Around her, the deck and air thrummed in a powerful, relentless rhythm. Nothing showed through the cabin windows but darkness. Chiron had gone inside. Depta struggled to remember her orders: *Remain on deck, allow no one outside.*

She looked above her. There hung a keel of a ship, an impossible rendition of the vessel she was on, suspended over her head. The bright was gone. The river moved from under her to over her. Where was up? Where was anything? The thought undid her, and she threw up over the railing, a terrible and prolonged experience.

By the time she got herself upright again, she saw someone standing on the deck at the prow of the ship.

A portly man with a venerable beard stood swaying. Depta called out to him, and he turned, looking alarmed to see her. "No!" he shouted.

"Go back inside," Depta said. She repeated this louder because the quasi-wind threw away her voice.

Ignoring Depta's command, the man climbed onto the lower rung of the railing, bracing his legs so as not to topple. Why would he climb the railing?

As Depta approached him, he looked half-crazed.

"Tarig," he said, pointing to the cabin.

Depta understood. Chiron had wakened him, alarmed him. "She is looking for someone. No harm comes to anyone, be assured."

His face flickered blue and silver in the fragmented light. "Looking for who? For me? Let it not be me."

"No, go back inside. You are not the one." As ill as Depta felt, she could only pity this man's terror. Awakened from a deep stupor, to look into the eyes of a Tarig. If he knew it was one of the Five, he would be undone.

His voice broke as he said, "I promised my father I would never suffer the garrote."

"Nor will you, Excellency. Be calm."

He nodded.

Depta was relieved that he seemed to be listening to reason. And perhaps he would have complied, were it not for the fact that Chiron just then emerged from the hatchway onto the deck.

Seeing her, the man drew back. Untangling his legs from the rail, he stood on the top, facing outward, balancing. Then he jumped.

Depta rushed to the spot where he had stood. Looking over the rail, she found the place where he had splashed into the Nigh: his plunge had created a sluggish silver whirlpool, but frozen to a standstill. She tried to process the thought: A man had just jumped to his death.

Chiron joined her at the rail. "This is not the ship we seek."

"He fell," Depta said numbly. "He jumped."

"Yes. He was not the godman who helped Titus Quinn. We assured him he was not. But he had not his wits about him."

Depta looked down at the frozen funnel. To her horror, she could still see the man's beard poking through. "We must save him, Bright Lady," she cried.

Chiron looked down. "No. He would not thank you for it." She strode off toward the waiting brightship.

Depta staggered after her mistress. Depta could have pulled the man from the river. But what would he be then? Would he curse her for it, or have the wits to curse? Taking a last look from the ramp, she saw that the funnel had disappeared from the river's surface.

Chiron was already gone, leaving behind too much death. Too little pity.

Her mind congealed in cold dismay. At this moment, Depta did not love the Tarig lady.

The steep pitch of the vessel's deck pinned Quinn and Anzi into the bulkhead. Far from tiptoeing into the binds, Jesid had them in a nosedive.

Heedless of the tilted deck, Lord Oventroe clambered up the stairs to the pilothouse, where, by the sound of it, he confronted the ship keeper and then Jesid.

At Quinn's side, Anzi said, "Did the pilot see a brightship?"

Had their Tarig pursuers found them, forcing the navitar to push the limits of the vessel?

Quinn looked around the cabin. They were alone, which meant Benhu had been stranded on the deck when the ship plunged. He staggered to his feet. "Anzi, Benhu is still out there." He picked his way across the lurching deck to the cabin hatchway.

Outside, Quinn shouted for Benhu, who rounded the stern and came wobbling forward, hands outstretched. As the ship shuddered and pitched, Benhu's feet slipped out from under him, and he crashed into the bulkhead. So fierce was the ship's speed that the fuel funnel on the prow dripped bullets of exotic matter, flinging them into the air and causing Benhu to cringe in place. Quinn staggered forward, from railing to bulkhead and back again, at last managing to latch onto Benhu with one hand. He yanked Benhu to a standing position and dragged him to the passenger cabin hatchway.

Anzi was there to take Benhu, and hauled him onto the floor where she had piled a few blankets. Quinn pressed his weight against the hatch and forced it closed against a heavy pressure of wind that now screamed over the deck.

"Down," Anzi cried.

Quinn went to hands and knees and made his way to the prostrate Benhu. "Are you hurt?"

Benhu grimaced. "I think I broke my head from that fall."

Relieved that it was no worse, Quinn said, "But Benhu, how will we know?"

The godman managed an indignant smirk just as the lights went out.

The ship had entered the binds. A purple light cascaded over them like a blanket of morphine. In response to the sedating effects, the three of them sprawled out, but Quinn fought it. "Stay awake," he urged Anzi, shaking her.

Anzi's hands groped for him, like some sea creature trying to pull him under. "Sleep is best, Dai Shen," she said, calling him by that former name.

No. Sleep wasn't best. Quinn looked down at the nest of blankets. Benhu was already out cold, and Anzi sinking fast. He backed up and leaned against the bulkhead, trying to stay upright.

The deck under him went from pitch to yaw with alarming abandon. Out the windows he saw a frozen landscape of storm clouds speared by hardened lightning. Like a series of snapshots, the picture changed. He stared out the portholes, watching for brightships.

No sound came from the companionway or the pilot's cabin. That, more than anything, gave Quinn concern. When he'd left to help Benhu, there had been shouting up there.

He glanced at the portholes. The blue-black wall surrounding them was rent here and there by incandescent cracks. These blinding glimpses mixed with the storm's purple glow to form a bruising light.

He woke with a start as his head bounced down at his sternum. Sleep had caught up with him after all. He had sunk to the floor against the bulkhead.

From above he heard the navitar moan: "Sleep, traveler, sleep. . . ."

The tone of the voice filled Quinn with dread. The fact that the navitar knew he was awake unnerved him. He remembered from his last trip on the Nigh that high emotion came with the territory. Even so, this time, something was wrong.

He went for the companionway. On the way, he knelt by Anzi. She lay on her back, her hair wild, static electricity sending white tendrils climbing up his legs. He backed away. The pilothouse. He had to get to Jesid.

Why?

Trying to kill us.

No, trying to save us from Lady Chiron. She is the one who is coming, of course. He was so tired. Perhaps he would just lie down with her once more. He loathed himself for the thought. With a massive will, he lunged for the stairs, dragging himself up the companionway.

At the head of the stairs he saw Jesid standing on his dais. He had dropped his red caftan on the deck, and was dressed only in a loincloth. His head and shoulders were thrust through the navitar's port in the ceiling, where Quinn could see him raising his hands to the sky, collecting the binds to himself. At his feet, his Ysli ship keeper slept in a hairy knot.

In the far corner, Lord Oventroe hunched over a shelf protruding from the wall, examining something.

Afterward, Quinn tried to remember the sequence of events. Had his coming up the stairs been the cause of the disaster, or would it have happened anyway? Did the binds show Jesid what would be, or what might be? Was there a difference?

Quinn thought he saw a spark come from Oventroe's hand. He moved closer to Oventroe's workstation.

Hearing someone behind him, Oventroe rose and turned in one movement, the claws of his hands extruding. Seeing Quinn, he relaxed a little. "Have you come for the great chain? We keep it in good hands, be assured." It dangled from his hand in a muted glow.

Quinn staggered forward a step. It was the cirque, the chain that had been given into Quinn's keeping. For the sake of Earth. Oventroe had opened the cirque. Yes, to analyze it . . .

A movement behind Quinn cause him to turn. Jesid had withdrawn from his post on the dais, and stood a few feet away, with an expression of agonized desire. He lunged for the chain, snatching it from the lord's hand.

Swiftly, the navitar backed up, holding the chain aloft in both hands. "Reverse the order: One, five, four. Reverse the order, release the fire."

Oventroe swept toward Jesid, stretching his hand out. "You will give it to us."

Jesid sneered. "Give it to piglets; give it to fools." As the ship yawed front to back, Jesid swayed, looking like an enraptured dancer. His face was alive with both ecstasy and suffering; the face of a man ready to die.

Then Quinn understood. In the binds, the navitar had seen a vision. One that told him they shouldn't risk the nan on his world. What had he seen? Quinn grabbed Oventroe by the upper arm. It was like clutching a steel railing. "My lord, is the nan safe to use?"

Oventroe's eyes were fixed on Jesid as he answered, "He does not think so. He sees the future he wishes to see. One where I have failed." Oventroe surged forward, saying, hand outstretched, "Jesid, give us the chain."

Jesid danced backward to the dais. Putting the Ysli's slumbering body between him and the Tarig, he groaned, "One." His forefinger and thumb depressed into the chain, pinching once.

Quinn dove for him.

The ship pitched, throwing him off his target so that all he hit was Jesid's right leg. Jesid lost his balance and crashed onto the deck.

Crashing to the deck, the navitar bellowed, "Five!"

As Jesid and Quinn wrestled on the floor, Oventroe raced past them and down the companionway. The navitar's body was slimy from leaning out into the binds, causing Quinn's hands to slip as he tried to pinion Jesid's arms, pinion the one holding the cirque.

Locked together for a moment, the two men faced each other a few inches apart. The navitar relaxed. His face looked indescribably weary and old. He was giving up.

"Four," Jesid whispered, pinching the chain four times.

Quinn knew enough to throw himself backward, away from the navitar.

Jesid stood up, holding a cirque streaming with nan. He smiled at Quinn. "I give it to the river. I give us all to the river." Calmly, he mounted the dais, stepping over the ship keeper, dripping nan on him in small, fizzing clots. Jesid assumed his position at the center of the dais, under the navitar's port. The Ysli didn't awaken. For the best, Quinn thought.

All for the best.

He was falling asleep on his feet. The world was coming apart. He was dying to go to sleep. Or going to sleep to die.

He staggered down the companionway, but stopped, transfixed, as he saw a shape outside the pilothouse. It was Oventroe, who fell upon Jesid as the top half of the navitar's body jutted out into the wilds of the binds. In the next moment, Jesid fell heavily to the dais, bleeding profusely from the stump where his hand used to be.

"Give it to the river," he groaned, managing to lock Quinn with a fevered gaze.

Quinn dashed down the companionway, coming into the main cabin just as Oventroe threw open the hatchway.

"Come quickly," Oventroe said.

Half awake, Anzi was huddling under one of the portholes, terrorized as she saw the ship deform around her. The bulkheads sagged inward. Quinn grabbed her by the arm and pushed her ahead of him onto the deck. But rather than the chaos of the binds, he found the long ribbon of the Nigh and the storm wall marching into the distance. They had surfaced. But the nan was loose and there was nowhere to go.

Quinn hugged Anzi to his side. Above him, the pilothouse was sagging, caramelizing, giving off a sheen of pinks and greens and oranges, like an oil slick in the sun. The roof sagged. Under its brown tent, a shape moved. The navitar, trapped in the embrace of whatever the ship was becoming. From amidships came a faint popping noise like something boiling.

"Quickly," the lord said.

Turning, Quinn saw that snugged up to the vessel and resting placidly on the river was a craft the size of a child's rowboat.

Glancing at Anzi, Oventroe said, "Leave her. There is only room for two."

"Then you take her," Quinn said. "You still owe me all you promised. Remember what you promised."

Oventroe went over the railing, landing in the small boat. From below, he said, "You have no more time, Titus."

"Anzi," Quinn said. "Don't argue. Please."

Her eyes pleaded. "You go, Titus. Leave me."

The air was filled with the sound of collapsing, heavy air pockets. A brown fizz surged outward from the pilot's cabin and sped for the rails.

Oventroe snarled, "Both of you, get in."

Quinn followed Anzi down the side of the vessel, where the small boat thrashed under the weight of the three of them. With a huge shove, the lord set the boat free of the navitar's ship, now listing toward the storm wall.

In that moment Quinn remembered the thing that had been nagging at him.

"Benhu," he said.

The stern and prow of the ship began to curve back on themselves, in effect rolling up the deck. Then, amidships, the deck and pilothouse began stretching away from each other, elongating the middle of the ship in a slick isthmus. Along this narrow bridge, Benhu appeared, lurching forward intently as though the other end of the ship might harbor safety. Looking up, he spied the smaller craft, and waved wildly.

There was no way to get to Benhu. "My lord," Quinn groaned.

"Do you speak to your God, or to me?" Oventroe muttered as he deployed a paddle, and used it.

Benhu's garments clung to his skin in an oily layer. He lifted his arms, puzzled by what appeared to be their extraordinary length. Dragged down by Benhu's weight, the isthmus of the ship began to sag.

At the last moment before the isthmus fell, Benhu locked a gaze on Quinn and bowed deeply from the waist. Then the isthmus collapsed into a seething pool amidships, where the pilothouse had fallen into the Nigh. The outer bulkheads went next, melting into the river's surface.

As the dinghy moved slowly to shore, the ship sank in unrecognizable pieces, leaving several pale scars on the river's surface.

"There is no God," Quinn said.

"Not that we have ever found," Oventroe responded. In the glowering shadow of the storm wall, his face wasn't the usual bronze, but iron.

It wasn't just Benhu's death, though. It was the cirque. Gone. The whole point of his journey.

Oventroe seemed to understand Quinn's distress. He pointed at a small round casing in the bottom of the boat. "The chain lives," he said.

"But the nan . . ."

"It is contained."

Quinn looked back at the now-empty river. "I don't think so."

Oventroe carefully transferred the paddle to the other side of the boat, where he continued his swift, sure strokes, making headway to the shore. "Jesid hit the chain in the wrong order. He knew the combination. But he did not know which indentations to press."

"What got out, then?"

"The analysis specimens. One fragment from each of the three repositories in the chain. The specimens clung to the chain. Jesid used your entrance to take us off guard."

Anzi was staring at the place on the river where the vessel had sunk. She shivered, and Quinn huddled close to her, putting his arms around her. "A fragment," he murmured. "That was just a fragment? It destroyed the whole ship."

"A small one, though," Oventroe said, as he brought the craft toward the shore.

Lady Chiron boarded four more ships of the Nigh. She required that Depta drink from the awful cup twice more, until Depta hardly cared what she drank, what she saw. In the end, it was all to no avail; they failed to find Lord Oventroe's ship, or any sign of Titus Quinn.

Depta lay on her side on the cabin deck, weak from the stresses of the journey. Chiron sat on the floor beside her, looking thoughtful. "Jesid is accomplished as a navitar," she said, her voice pitched so low Depta could hardly hear her.

"Jesid?" Depta repeated, wondering if she had missed something.

"We played among the curtains—he, slipping in and out, and we, following his wake. It was invigorating. For a time." She regarded Depta as though blaming her for Jesid's escape.

You created him, Depta thought. You created all the navitars. One part of her mind heard this comment with distress. Another part cheered her on.

"By now Titus-een has left the binds. Where next, hnn?"

Depta tested her voice, finding it raspy, but audible. "Ahnenhoon."

"Unless he surprises us, and turns toward the Inyx sway," Chiron murmured half to herself, "Strange. We have just now learned that the daughter no longer serves us with her eyes."

"No longer serves, Lady?"

"She is dark to us."

The startling thought came, and Depta put voice to it: "She put out her own eyes, do you think?"

"Perhaps. If so, we must wonder how she came to hate her sight. One could almost believe someone close to us warns her."

Depta didn't like that Chiron regarded her so closely. She fought back. "It is said that the high prefect doted on the girl."

The lady regarded her with a flat stare. "Cixi has served us for longer than you have had days."

"Of course. You are right, Bright Lady." But the more Depta thought of it, the more reason she could find that Cixi might be an informant. Depta had humiliated her. Chiron had forced her to withhold information from the ruling lords. The notion sent sparks through her body; the very idea that the old dragon would thwart the lords on her own! Was it possible?

"We will put questions to the high prefect. But not yet. First, our quarry closer to hand. We must wonder if Titus will go to the daughter. If he does, my cousins will have him first, and we must defer to them."

Chiron seemed lost in thought for many moments before adding, "That would be so like him. To choose the daughter instead of the world. What would you choose, Depta?"

Depta thought hard how to answer. "I do not know, Bright Lady. I have no progeny."

"Nor do we." Looking away, Chiron murmured, "One never could antic-ipate what he might do. We found it . . ." She paused.

"Stimulating," Depta offered.

Looking up in surprise as though she had forgotten about Depta, Chiron said, "Yes, a good word. He was stimulating. Most sentients do not require us to pay attention. Life passes in a succession of predictable moments." Chiron rose to her feet. "With you, Depta, it is different. You are learning to become great. You have taken your first steps."

But Depta didn't want greatness. Only a worthy calling. Watching the Tarig lady as she sat beside her, Depta found her oddly distasteful—this angular biped with bald skin and pretensions to greatness. Had Titus Quinn ever wanted greatness? Or had the lady forced him to conform as well, caging him in the gilded room and insisting he drink from her cup? Depta drew a long breath, trying to steady her careening mind. These thoughts were the spawn of too little sleep, bad drugs, and the death of strangers.

"No matter," Chiron went on. "We will hunt for him at Ahnenhoon. It is well that we have an excuse to go to the battle plains, Depta. The Paion are agitated, and they stream through in some number. This serves us well, making probable our appearance at Ahnenhoon."

Depta tried to absorb yet another new piece of information. "Paion? Paion come? The vows forbid, my lady."

"Hnn. The vows forbid, but do not prevent."

More blood then, Depta thought, her mood plummeting.

"Opening the door arouses them. Titus-een passed through recently. Here is another reason for you to abhor leaks, Depta: The Paion detect it, and draw inspiration."

Depta must have looked overwhelmed, because Chiron looked down at her with indulgence. "Sleep now. You have earned your rest."

Depta gave a relieved sigh, closing her eyes. They were finished with raids on the Nigh, and unnatural visitations. From nearby she heard Chiron whisper, "You look so content while you sleep, Depta. You dream, ah?"

"Nightmares, I fear."

Chiron was close to her ear, saying, "What is a nightmare?"

Depta murmured, "Do you not dream my lady?"

"No."

Halfway into a powdery sleep, Depta thought she heard the lady say, *That is a kingdom we would give much to rule.*

CHAPTER THIRTY-TWO

O God of Misery, look upon this one especially: my faithless friend.
—a prayer

T WAS SHADOW EBB AND TIME FOR BED. But Johanna put it off, having just come from Morhab's apartments and not wishing to trail thoughts of him into sleep. Her only friend in the Entire still alive, Pai, held her nightgown for her, waiting to help her mistress undress. Johanna was reluctant to disrobe, still feeling the beast's eyes on her.

Pai whispered, "Mistress, tell Lord Inweer that the engineer torments you. Why do you let Morhab command you?"

Because he holds my life in his hands, Johanna thought. My life, which isn't worth nearly so much as when I believed I might guide Titus to the engine. The engine in question thrummed, low and distant, yet ever-present.

Pai laid the nightgown on the bed. Her voice came gently: "Mistress, I grieve to see you so. Can you not find peace? Is it so terrible to talk to a Gond?"

Day after day Johanna went to Morhab's apartments, that ghostly den of dead trees. Day after day, he wanted to know her inmost thoughts. Oh, she lied, of course: made up events, softened others, all with the purpose of leading him away from her core self. But it made no difference. Morhab wanted the underbelly of everything, so that even the lies must have human emotion behind them, and she had to go to a deep well within herself to answer his inquiries. Sometimes, hearing her bland recitations, he chose his own topics, ones she couldn't evade: Tell me about the time of becoming a woman. Tell how it felt to be with child. She twisted and turned under his scrutiny, suffering his scowls if no intimacies were offered, then threats of the nest when one lie contradicted another. Evasions could lead to discipline. She began to think she would tell him some truths to avoid *that*. And then she told him some, keeping the nest at bay. Each day she returned to tell him her story, and each day he stripped away more and more of her privacy, her self-respect. At last, she had told him so much, a little more hardly mattered. These days she walked the halls of the centrum, dulled yet agitated.

Pai helped Johanna slip into her nightgown. At the door to her private rooms, she heard SuMing talking, turning a visitor away. Johanna had given instructions to admit no one. If SuMing was good for little else, at least she made a good gatekeeper.

"Mistress, talk to me," Pai pleaded.

Johanna was done with talking. Time was, when it would have been a relief to talk to another woman. But no one could be her confidante. She had too many secrets, and some of them could kill.

Why did Morhab probe so keenly? Did he suspect that there was more fertile ground than she had yet revealed? Was he suspicious that she had been in touch with Titus? As to that, she couldn't say whether she was or not. Had Titus ever received her message? Once, her faith had convinced her that God would have granted that, for the sake of all that would be lost. Now, she had grave doubts. God wasn't keeping a special watch over her. He might be well meaning and sad at ugly things occurring, but He was powerless.

"Tell the lord that Morhab plagues you," Pai whispered, pleading her cause. She couldn't imagine that Lord Inweer might fail to solve every problem. She couldn't imagine that Lord Inweer *was* the problem.

Johanna shook her head, letting Pai lead her to the bed, where, if she was supremely lucky, tonight she would sleep. She sat on her covers, murmuring. "Some subjects one can't raise with the gracious lord. Leave it at that."

As Pai dimmed the lights, Johanna said, "Bring me a sleeping powder, Pai."

After a pause, Pai said, "No. You've been saving them."

Johanna couldn't see her servant's face, and was glad for the darkness. "Don't tell anyone."

"No."

It felt like friendship, now that they shared a secret. Johanna hoarded her sleeping powders. In case she couldn't bear things any longer. In case the lord discovered her intentions and tried to question her.

Pai continued, "But promise me you'll give up your wish to take poisons."

"I promise."

There was a smile in Pai's voice, indulgent and temporary. "Too easily said."

"I won't take my life, Pai, be assured. I wait for Titus, you see."

The word *Titus, Titus, Titus* filled the room. Had she really mentioned his name?

At last Pai whispered, "You still hope for him to rescue you? But mistress, it has been many thousands of days. He will not come. Isn't it best to make your happiness here, with the lord who favors you?"

The darkness gave permission for so much. Things that could be said. Things that could be done. "He may come, Pai."

"That is high love indeed, mistress," Pai said, wonder in her voice.

"No, not coming here for me. But for the engine." She whispered, "I summoned him, Pai. Against the engine. He will come for that reason."

What must her servant think of this revelation? Simple Pai, more used to gossip than plots. The woman sighed, giving vent to her confusion. "Such high matters, mistress. Surely we cannot be certain what men of power will do."

"He knows why he must come." She had said too much, and let the conversation lapse. It was deep into the ebb.

She crawled into bed, hearing the bedroom door close behind Pai.

To her surprise, the sharing of secrets left her unguarded and relaxed; she fell into a welcome sleep.

Late in the ebb, Johanna awoke to a shuffling noise. She couldn't see in the pitch dark. "Pai?" she called out. Someone was in the room. A shadow.

Suddenly awake, she called out, "Pai?"

The voice came: "It is SuMing."

Johanna shoved the covers aside, instantly wary. "What do you want?"

Johanna swung her feet onto the floor. Did SuMing come to announce that Lord Inweer wished to see her? Had Morhab finally grown tired of her, and told the lord all?

But SuMing made no announcements. She crept closer to the bed, causing Johanna to wonder if her servant was armed. Come for revenge, at last. Johanna backed up, watching for the gleam of a weapon in SuMing's hand, but the room was too dark.

SuMing stood at the foot of the bed now. Her voice was even and low: "Remember the day, Johanna, when, for your sake, the lord hung me from the great height?"

Alarmed, and still not able to see SuMing, Johanna thought quickly about what she might use to protect herself. Slowly, she took a small blanket from the bed to fend off a knife. "I remember, SuMing. The lord would have dropped you. But didn't."

"Yes. I can't move my neck. It hurts."

Johanna remembered that moment that Inweer told SuMing to jump, and the flash of his hand as he snatched her long braid, breaking her fall, and her neck.

"But," SuMing continued, "I am alive. Because of you. Because you spoke for me, he let me go free." She moved closer. "I goaded you and spied on you, mistress. For that I am sorry. Now I will make it right." After a beat she said, "Pai is in Morhab's chamber."

Johanna thought with dismay, Does he torment my ladies, too?

"Pai has met with the Gond before. They are friends."

Johanna felt a pang in her chest. Friends?

"Yes, very good friends," SuMing replied. "Now I will lead you to them. You will observe."

Johanna followed SuMing from the room, her heart thudding, her mind frantic to forecast what would happen next. Johanna recalled her last conversation with Pai, how the woman had deftly drawn out her story, her most secret story. *Mother of God, what have I done?*

They made their way to Morhab's quarters, and peered into his den. All was quiet among the stunted trees. In her urgency to know the truth, Johanna left SuMing behind and crept toward the glow in Morhab's favorite clearing. There she saw Pai speaking urgently with the Gond. Johanna couldn't hear what they were saying. She didn't need to.

Pai knew that Titus was coming to Ahnenhoon, and that was subject enough.

It was the middle of the ebb, a poor time to rouse Lord Inweer, much less ask him for favors.

A cold gust of air met Johanna when she entered his chamber. Across the room she saw him waiting for her on the balcony, the storm wall frowning behind him. His long coat whipped about his legs in the wind. He didn't speak to her in welcome, and this made her watchful mood all the more cautious. Had Morhab come here already, whispering her crimes?

She crossed the room, forcing a lidded calm over her panic. She went past the sleeping platform—not disturbed, she noted—and through the wide arch onto the balcony.

"Good ebb to you, my lord," she said, casually bowing, affecting the confidence she had once felt around the Tarig lord.

"Johanna."

"A deep time of ebb, I know. I couldn't sleep." Despite the room's glaring light, the porch fell into shadow from the dark dance of the nearby storm wall. She couldn't see Inweer's face clearly. "And you, my lord, working so late?"

"We always work, Johanna. To keep the realm."

Against such enemies as she? Had Morhab come here to whisper Titus's name?

Inweer turned away from her and gazed down the profound length of the storm wall, toward the tip of the primacy, where the storm walls from each side converged in the greatest seam in the universe. He appeared surrounded by chaotic, silent storms. The lord's skin, shiny and bronze, made him look bloodless and unforgiving. How could she ever have loved him?

She moved closer to him, placing her hand on the railing overlooking the wasteland between the wall and the fortress. It was a blasted and muddy place, with no growing thing.

Inweer turned to her, gripping her chin in his long hand, and tilting her face to him. "Johanna. Do you love your husband of the Rose?"

She held herself steady. "No, my lord. Titus Quinn has faded from my heart."

She could barely breathe. Morhab had been here. Inweer was just waiting for her to compound her lies.

And, in the next moment, relief: "The Nigh, Johanna. We noted, forty days ago, a perturbation in the storm walls. Something tried to come through. Perhaps it was Titus. Come for his daughter again." Inweer moved his head imperceptibly forward, in that unnerving way he had of appearing ready to bite. "You are surprised?"

"Yes. He must know you would lie in wait for him there."

"This time, we will kill him. Are you ready for this?"

She knew better than to give him the obvious answer. "He is my husband. If I don't love him, at least I honor him. Would you ask me to condemn him?"

Not answering, Inweer strode away. He stood, back to her, looking in the other direction, along the storm wall.

Titus is back, she exulted. He has come back. She knew where he was bound. Not for Sydney. That was the past. For Ahnenhoon.

She heard Inweer say, "This lord wonders who the man loves more, his wife or his child."

Johanna saw the direction of his thoughts. Inweer wondered if Titus would come here, to rescue her. She hoped he wouldn't place the fortress on tighter security. "I doubt he much remembers me."

Inweer gazed at the storm wall as though expecting ships to appear, budding through from the Rose. He turned back to her. "But remembers a daughter?"

"Daughters do not fade."

"Ah."

She approached him, putting a hand on his arm. "He wouldn't come here for the sake of an old marriage. Nor would I want him to."

He was silent for a long time. Finally, he said, his deep voice nearly out of hearing, "You might have had your daughter, Johanna, had it been this lord's decision to make."

Don't say things like that, Johanna thought. Don't be kind. But it gave her the opening she needed to accomplish the night's purpose.

"Thank you, my lord. She hasn't faded from my mind."

"Despite the fact that she does not favor you."

"Yes. In fact, it would give me great pleasure to give Sydney a likeness of myself."

"Likeness?"

"A moving image of myself. So that she might remember me more favorably. It couldn't hurt, and it would put my mind at rest."

"You do not hope to bring it to the sway yourself." His tone made clear there was no chance of that.

"No, my lord. Send it to her as you deem best. But I would like this image created tonight. It is the day of her birthday," she lied, "making this an auspicious time to create the image." It was of the utmost importance that it be tonight. Everything must happen tonight.

"Johanna, we are beset with large matters. Yet you talk of presents."

"Is it a difficult undertaking?

"Not difficult."

She waited.

"Do you require the image at this instant?"

"Make it this ebb, if you will indulge me, my lord. All I need is time to change into a suitable gown. You could send someone to my apartments this ebb. I will be ready."

He waved a hand at her. "Yes, then."

"Also, I would like to have a device to view my image."

He nodded. "I will send someone."

"This ebb."

A sharpness came into his voice. "Yes, this ebb."

She glanced down, to deflect his irritation.

Then Inweer took her hands in his, and gazed at her as though trying to discern her thoughts. "Johanna. This lord may soon need your whole loyalty. Do we have it all? Do we have the devotion you once gave a husband, even if we can be no such thing to you?"

Standing near the soaring storm wall made it so much easier to lie to him. The storm could not stand up without devouring the Rose.

"Yes," she whispered. "I promise you."

It wasn't like him to embrace her, but he did. She clung to him for a moment, hardening her heart. All the while she watched the door to Inweer's chamber, and listened for Morhab's sled.

CHAPTER THIRTY-THREE

> *In the realm of existence, only the All.*
> *In the practice of war, only Ahnenhoon.*
> —a saying

LATE IN THE EBB, Mo Ti stood at the edge of the crowd of travelers, resting his hand on Distanir's forehorn. A cry went up as someone spotted a transport vessel on the Nigh, causing a general surge forward.

Now it begins, Mo Ti thought. My separation from her. Leaving her in the company of the she-Gond, the river spider. . . . He would never call her Helice. However, he would do Sydney's bidding. It was his mission, to obey her in small things and large. When he came back to the sway, he would bring Helice down, one way or another. Her reckless ambition endangered all that Sydney had worked for. The spider had her web, and Sydney was ensnared. The web was a grand scheme the spider called *renewal* or *renaissance*. *A bad plan*, he had told Sydney. *It will doom us*. No, Sydney had said, *it will save us*.

He hefted his travel bag and watched as the ship sped toward the bank.

Gathered at the forlorn river outpost were a few dozen travelers, mostly Jout and a knot of Hirrin godders. The Long Gaze of Fire claimed two sways, the Inyx and the Jout, bloth lightly populated, allowing an isolation the Inyx savored. Few navitars plied the Nigh hereabouts, and finding one after only one day's wait was luck indeed. The vessel neared the shore, pushing a mercurial wave ahead of it while at the same time taking the river matter into the funnel on the prow.

It was time to go.

At Mo Ti's side, Distanir looked anxiously at the ship. He distrusted the Nigh. It allowed strangers too near the roamlands. The Inyx considered the whole primacy as their territory. The Jout held a different opinion, but the vast primacy comfortably held both.

Mo Ti moved forward as sentients gave way before his bulk and that of his mount.

The Chalin ship keeper straddled the bow of the ship. "Where bound?" he shouted, looking over the prospective passengers.

"Ahnenhoon," Mo Ti called out. Around him, a clutch of Hirrin godmen flattened their ears. The Chalin man would have priority. He was bound for soldiering. These Hirrin had hopes of traveling together, but this monster and his Inyx companion would take up three berths, at least. Worse, an Ahnenhoon destination would divert the transport to the wrong primacy.

The ship keeper directed Mo Ti and Distanir aft of the passenger cabin to the baggage hold, a compartment large enough for an Inyx. Having the mount out of sight mollified the passengers, who resented having an Inyx nearby snatching thoughts. However, Mo Ti doubted that Distanir would care to browse in the hearts of Jouts and godmen, especially given Distanir's general agitation. Mo Ti steadied his mount as best he could by being steady himself. Mo Ti had no fear of the river or the binds, no more than he feared Paion onslaughts or the strutting Tarig. He had lived past fear. Now he lived for devotion. For Sydney. No one who knew him in former days would believe that Mo Ti the Horrible could have such tenderness in him. Since his twisted, muscular childhood, he had been dour and immovable. His mother foreswore her ugly child, taking her life by means of the four-minute ride from an outer balcony of the bright city. Ever after, his fellow clerks in the Magisterium had called him Son of the Falling Stone. But never to his face.

Soon he would come face-to-face with Titus Quinn. It remained to be seen how the man would handle death. Afterward, Mo Ti would strike off his foot and take the chain that held the plague. He would save the land. Equally important, he would earn back Sydney's trust.

Kill him, Mo Ti. Kill my father.

And so he would.

In the deserted marshlands at the edge of the Nigh, Anzi and Quinn sprawled in a fitful sleep. Anzi woke several times in the ebb, roused by Quinn's sweat-drenched moans. He was recovering from the poison that his fellow Rose personage had given him, but the navitar's headlong charge through the binds had also taken its toll. She wiped his forehead with her jacket sleeve. When Titus woke, they would set out on foot for Ahnenhoon, while Lord Oventroe would make his way up primacy to a place where he could find a vessel to command.

As Titus bent his knee in his sleep, his pant leg rode up enough to expose the chain around his ankle, drawing her eye. Why had the navitar tried to steal it? Did Jesid believe it spelled the ruin of the world? *Give it to the river*, the navitar had said, so Titus reported. Did the navitar know something about the river and the chain that others didn't? Of course, though navitars *thought* they knew more than normal sentients, they couldn't even dress themselves, or keep themselves clean.

Unable to sleep, Anzi sat up, wrapping her arms around her knees. She and Titus were alone. Earlier, the lord had hiked out of view, abstaining from sleep. She looked at the forever river, thinking ahead, thinking of what lay after the engine at Ahnenhoon. She imagined riding on the Nigh with Titus, traveling to strange sways far away. He might always be a fugitive, but if one wished to hide, the Nigh was very deep.

Earlier in the ebb, before she had lain down, she had seen a navitar's vessel far up the river. She had hunkered down behind the pillow of mud that masked their presence from anyone watching from the river. This section of the Nigh bore heavy traffic, as vessels disgorged heavy shipments of conscripts for the war. Levies from different sways took up camp in lodgment areas, awaiting orders, completion of their military divisions, and arrival of officers. Some of the camps were so old they had become permanent squatter settlements, military staging grounds dotting the banks of the Nigh for thousands of miles. No sense to bring green troops into range of the Paion zeppelins, nor was there a rush to battle, with the war always with them. A million days of war. And yet the lords claimed the All was peaceful. True, the sways didn't fight each other. But soldiers still died.

The plains behind the unstable marshes sometimes thundered with maneuvers and war games. Anzi could hear them now, far in the distance, and under the boom of the storm wall that hovered perpetually at their side. The sooner we are gone, the better, she thought.

She hadn't noticed that Lord Oventroe stood next to her. She rose, bowing.

The lord carried a dead steppe vole by the tail, its blood darkening the ground by his boots. So, he had been hunting. Oventroe gave her the carcass to skin and gut. She made short work of it, using Quinn's knife, the Going Over blade once given to him by General Ci Dehai. They could cook the vole on the trail.

"Now you will go to the engine, ah?" the lord said, or rather commanded.

"Yes, Bright Lord."

"Make certain he gets there. At any price to yourself."

She didn't trust him. But he was right in one thing: The Rose must not be fuel. Even if, to accomplish this, she and Titus did not survive.

"Wake him," Oventroe said.

She managed to rouse Titus. He sat up, coughing, and accepted a sip of water from the lord, who had found an aquifer last ebb, bringing back a pouch of it in a revised section of his great coat.

Crouching next to Titus and Anzi, the lord said, "We must leave here, each to our singular tasks."

"Not yet."

"The Rose is giving up its suns already," Oventroe said. "You do not wish to delay. Or have we misjudged you?"

Titus looked up at the storm wall, as though remembering for the first time where he was. His eyes traced the line of the dark barrier where it sloped into infinity. Setting his mouth in concentration, he said, "The ship and its crew went down. From a fragment of nan. Benhu went down, who helped me. That was a bad death, my lord." Oventroe didn't dispute this, remaining silent. "The nan looks wildly out of control. Is it?"

Titus should learn caution when speaking to a lord, Anzi thought. Oventroe watched him with hard, black eyes. Anzi knew how Titus wished to protect the Entire. To avoid bringing a bad war to a fragile land. He had promised Su Bei that he would protect the Entire. Su Bei, who had first brought Oventroe and Titus together. She didn't want the land to die. But surely the lords could devise a way to sustain the All without killing the Rose. If the Rose died, so much would be lost. The civilizations of Earth. Under the scholar Vingde, she had once studied these humans, following the lives of people for as long as the veil allowed, watching strings of days, observing the passions of the Rose.

The sentients of the Entire were copies of those beings. Pale copies, she had always thought. How could the Entire's one culture, the Radiant Path, compare with the evolved majesty of the Chinese dynasties? The Roman? The reign of the pharaohs? Even the American hegemony was a glory of striving, despite failures. She couldn't put into words the attraction she felt to Earth; she had been born with it, perhaps.

"We have told you," the lord was saying. "The assemblage will do harm, but not too much harm. When the human woman told you that it cannot be contained, she lied."

Titus glanced at the river, and Anzi knew he was thinking of the vessel, of Benhu's death. "How can you know?"

The lord murmured, "It would be difficult to explain all that we know, and how we know. You do not have time to assimilate this knowledge."

"Try me."

"You have not the vocabulary." As Titus remained silent, the lord went on, "We looked into the instructions imprinted on the molecular structures; they cannot feed on the bright. They have not the instructions to use exotic matter. The phage sentinels will disarm the activity within one hundred intervals. Redundancy designs, although crude, will ensure this." The lord stood up. "You fear what you saw on the Nigh. But we did not say the weapon was poor. Only that it could be contained. We have no proof to offer you. Decide whether we stand together or do not."

Anzi watched as Titus got to his feet. He looked haggard. "Yes, then." He looked at her as though asking whether he had done right. She grasped his hand in answer.

"Leave now," Oventroe said. "We cannot be seen together. Ahnenhoon is close—a few days away. When Jesid abandoned control of the ship, we made sure the river vessel arrived close to Ahnenhoon. Still, you must set out immediately."

They prepared to leave, with the lord providing a small pack that he devised from a section of his great coat. While Oventroe was thus occupied, Titus asked, "How much time is one hundred intervals?"

Oventroe glanced up. "Once you free the nan you will have a few minutes to flee. Be quick when you do."

"How much time, as I measure time?"

"Nineteen minutes."

"I thought I had an hour. My people told me—"

"They were wrong."

Anzi had seen the nan race over the ship. It would spread as fast as a plains fire.

"One thing more," the lord said. "Was there a happenstance in which you immersed the chain in river matter?"

Titus looked startled by the question. "I walked into the river once."

"That was not wise."

Then Anzi remembered Titus telling her of the Inyx mount who killed himself, who sent a message to Sydney.

"I walked in just a little way."

"It weakened the architecture. The structure is eroded."

A quiet fell on Quinn. "Eroded?"

"The tube is thinner than it was. The nan begins to assault from inside, feeding on the weakened reservoirs." The lord went on, "My judgment is that you have only a few days. Then, no matter what you do, the nan will come forth."

"How many days?"

"Five. Perhaps six. Enough time, if you travel swiftly and sleep little." Oventroe looked at the crumpled hills in the distance through which they would have to pass. "Best to leave now. You are recovered enough."

Quinn didn't need to be told.

Even though it was Deep Ebb, they took their leave of Oventroe. When they looked back, the lord was striding up the riverbank, toward the nearest military staging ground.

As they set out in the opposite direction, Quinn let Anzi shoulder their one pack and their makeshift canteen of water. He was unsteady, still, on his feet. They wound into the crumpled hill country. Sometimes they went over the crests of hills, and other times around them, frustrated that they couldn't shoot straight as an arrow to their destination.

As Quinn walked, he felt the cirque's weight against his ankle. It seemed to hug him more tightly than before.

They had been walking ever closer to the noises of a military exercise. From just over a rise came shouts and clanging metal mixed with the pounding of Inyx hooves.

Climbing to the crest, and lying flat to hide, Quinn and Anzi looked down into a basin milling with Inyx. Stomping feet, tossing heads, braying throats—the Inyx formed into battle groups and re-formed, then formed again. Their precision was their strongest talent. That and coordination at a distance. The riders seemed appendages to the great beasts, whose horns sported the colors of their divisions.

"Why do they practice in the ebb?" Quinn wondered out loud.

"It is cooler then," Anzi said. "And the Paion strike as often by ebb as by day."

Quinn delayed moving on, watching the maneuvers. "I want to say good-bye."

"Do not. These mounts may feel loyalty to the Tarig. A common enemy makes foes friends, Titus. These mounts could easily report you."

"They hate the Tarig."

She held his gaze. "Now you are an expert on the Entire?"

He barely heard her. This might be the last chance he had to contact his daughter. He might never leave Ahnenhoon. Nineteen minutes to escape. Perhaps Stefan Polich hadn't gauged the time precisely; or perhaps he had lied. In any case, Quinn was going to say the thing that he had meant to say to Sydney the first time he sent a message by Inyx: I love you. I have always loved you. He picked his way down the rocky slope. After some time of lying in wait for a stray mount, he found one who would send a message to Sydney.

He didn't ask for, or expect, an answer from her, but turned and rejoined Anzi to resume their trek.

Five or six days to Ahnenhoon. Once there, he would press the sequence into the chain. Then time would collapse into nineteen minutes.

How far could you get in nineteen minutes?

Remembering Benhu, Quinn hoped he could summon the godman's dignity when his turn came to face the nan.

CHAPTER THIRTY-FOUR

Deceive, deceive. This is the first principle of battle.
—from Tun Mu's *Annals of War*

SUMING TOOK A SHORTCUT OVER THE ROOF OF THE CENTRUM, hurrying to make a last visit to Morhab's den. At this hour of the ebb she had hope that few sentients would be afoot to delay her progress. Trying to curb an unseemly haste, SuMing moved toward a staircase and descended, entering a level that gave access to the storm wall side wing.

At a bend in the corridor she encountered a delegation of Hirrin who had come to the centrum to consult with the lord and were abroad early. She bowed, walking more slowly past them. Once out of sight, she rushed on. Johanna had her portrait only useful if used quickly. As SuMing hurried, she was aware of the pounding of the nearby engine. They said it generated a defensive shield around the fortress, but it was no such thing, no foil against the Paion. Instead, it drilled into the Rose, marshaling a great collapse that would occur, not today or tomorrow, but soon. Indeed, Johanna said, Lord Inweer had told her that the Entire was already burning some parts of the Rose for practice. SuMing loved her world, but what the lords were doing was wrong. Let them suffer a defeat for their arrogance. What had the Tarig lords ever done for her but bring her to this wasteland and then hang her from a railing? She lived not a single interval without jarring pain in her neck. And Lord Inweer had done all this with a casual gesture. When she had asked for healing, the lord responded, *Serve your mistress.* Now, she *would* serve her.

She entered a wing where the stench announced her proximity to the

319

Gond's apartments. Her footsteps slowed, and her skin cooled in the drafts from the arches up ahead.

At the mouth of the den she stood for a moment, looking into the tangle of ghostly trees. Morhab's lair contained no furniture or embellishments, but only the stunted trees, sprouting, so it appeared, from the litter and offal of the floor.

"Engineer," she called. She waded in deeper, calling Morhab's name. She prayed that Morhab hadn't already gone to Inweer to expose her mistress.

Then she heard him, his rumbling voice deadened by the mass of trees. "Who comes? By the vows, who?"

Following his voice, SuMing burst into the clearing to find the Gond sprawled on a fat tree limb. "My mistress," she blurted. "Engineer, hurry." She managed a sob.

He tucked his iridescent wings closer to his body in irritation. "Tell, and stop shrieking. Do not wake the nest."

SuMing drew closer to him, wringing her hands and giving vent to the panic she truly felt. "Mistress Johanna is distraught. She will do a terrible thing."

"Tell," he thundered.

Gesturing wildly toward the corridor, SuMing said, "She is going to kill herself, so she vows. Is there aught you can do? Tell her that you regret any insult, or whatever is between you, please, Engineer. She said you knew why she wanted to die."

In another moment she saw with relief that he had called his sled to him, not his Jout attendants. The sled was necessary.

Morhab half slithered, half fell down from the limb and began moving toward the sled, then lurched his heavy form onto the platform and swung his hindquarters in behind him. He coiled his upper body and thrashed once more, hoisting himself onto the driver's platform.

"Up," the Gond said, gesturing his small arms in SuMing's direction. She climbed into the seat opposite him, and the sled began winding through the Gond nest.

"Where is she?" he growled.

"Oh Excellency," SuMing wailed, "she is going to the sere."

His great round eyes looked at her in alarm. The fiery ground. One step into that killing yard . . .

She waved him onward. "Heaven give us mercy, she is on her way now."

Morhab expertly steered the sled into the corridor, rounding the corner from his den and accelerating down the hall. SuMing held on fast to keep from flying out of the sled on the turns. As they sped on, SuMing said, "Engineer, bring Pai, I beg you."

"No time," he shouted, coming to a lift and signaling the door to open.

It was the wrong way to reach Johanna's apartment. SuMing moaned, "She will never listen to you! Bring Pai, who is like a sister to her."

Morhab paused the sled, and the doors tried to close on the sides of the conveyance. "Why didn't you bring Pai yourself?"

SuMing didn't answer him. She let him assume she was witless enough to go running to and fro in an emergency.

Grumbling, he reversed direction, pushing the sled to speed again, heading for Johanna's quarters.

At Johanna's chamber they collected the groggy Pai and sped on again toward the outer defenses. With the effects of the powder Johanna had administered in her food, Pai did not question why she had not been wakened first, nor did Morhab take time to inquire. Profound creases cut across the Gond's face. SuMing wondered if he worried that his days of pleasant torment of Johanna would end if his victim killed herself, or if he worried that he might be blamed.

But in these conjectures, SuMing was mistaken.

Morhab drove in a frenzy of worry. *Johanna*, he thought with desperate longing. *Stop, Johanna, stop, and I will release you. Do not. Do not* . . . The two servants on the seat opposite him clung to each other with near hysteria, barely able to keep their seats. They would die for their dereliction, Morhab vowed. Glancing at his passengers, he saw perfect examples of the common Chalin woman—stupid and worthless, whereas Johanna was elegant and refined, the supreme jewel of his life. He had never meant to cause her misery, and that he had apparently done so filled him with remorse. He had only wished for her to share herself with him, and not in any base manner, but in a noble way. . . . She did not think it noble. Or even bearable. That she despised him, despite all that they had shared, saddened him beyond measure.

Coming to the parade grounds, he signaled the door open, and the sled shot over the yard at its maximum speed. To Morhab it could not be fast enough.

Had Johanna discovered that Pai was reporting to him? That was the only reason he could imagine for her suicide. She might rather immolate herself than face the lord's garrote. But Morhab had planned to beg the lord to put her under arrest in his own care. Lord Inweer would owe him some consideration for discovering the plot that was presently to bring Titus Quinn to Ahnenhoon. The poor, deluded woman, to think that she could bring the man of the Rose here, and no one the wiser! He would have spoken to the lord at first hour of Early Day. And of course, he still must speak to the lord whether Johanna died or not.

Across from him, he saw Pai's wild stare. She had never intended to doom her mistress. But Morhab had made clear that it was either spy for him or suckle his Gondlings in the nest.

Entering the great fortress of the watch, Morhab slowed, moving at a stately pace through a wide tunnel suitable for ten Hirrin to march abreast. He did not wish to raise alarms in the watch. If he succeeded in saving Johanna, no one need know. SuMing pointed the way into a remote corner of the watch, and he drove onward, chafing to speed ahead, racked with apprehension. Few soldiers billeted in this section of the watch, its silent corridors echoing with the whine of the sled.

As they approached the outer wall of the watch, SuMing half stood, waving her arms to direct him toward a heavy door. As the sled hovered in front of it, Morhab saw that the door was still partway open from Johanna's passage. He stared at it in dismay. "She has gone through already?" He eyed the hard-packed dirt. It looked quiescent. But it always did, while hiding its fire.

SuMing said, "Her lord has told her that today on the sere there will be a cycle of burning and not burning, so that soldiers can pass over. This is a quiet cycle, but hurry!" She jumped down from the sled and began pulling the door wider so that Morhab's conveyance might pass through. Pai rushed down to help, and the door came fully open.

Now they could see that someone stood far out on the sere.

From his perch on the sled, Morhab gaped at Johanna standing on ground that should ignite her. How could there be a cycle of inactivity that Johanna could predict? Looking to the other side of the sere, he scanned the fifth domain, the wall of that structure called the terminus. There were no soldiers waiting to cross. It made no sense that the lord had set a schedule of burning and not burning on the sere.

As Pai stood frozen by the door, looking out onto the dreaded black ground, SuMing grabbed her by the shoulders. "She will only listen to you, Pai. You must go."

Pai looked doubtful. "You come too."

SuMing's face hardened. "You know how she hates me. It is better for me not to show my face."

A sly look came into Pai's face. "You are afraid to step on the sere."

"Indeed not, if Johanna stands there safely." She turned to Morhab. "Shall I come along, Excellency, or just her friends?"

Morhab thundered, "Pai, step up to the sled. We go alone."

Having little choice, Pai relented. She climbed onto the sled.

SuMing watched as Morhab powered the sled onto the blackened ground.

"Now, Johanna," she murmured. And from the shadows, her mistress rushed to help her push the door shut behind the sled.

She and SuMing then crept to the window opening where she had set up her device to project her likeness. They watched as the sled moved forward. Under the platform of the vehicle, dust stirred, then purpled. As the sled churned forward, a seam of fire appeared underneath, spitting a plume to one side. Morhab looked down with a look of surprise tinged with sadness, as though the world had disappointed him. Beneath the sled smoldered an incandescent plate of fire.

The sled shook sideways, and a jet of flame ignited a pillow behind Morhab. Instantly the fire jumped to his person. Morhab bellowed. A curtain of fire swept onto his papery wings, incinerating them. The sled swerved around to make a turn and head back for the door as Johanna's image flickered out.

Standing on the sled's passenger seat, Pai wailed piteously. With the flames eating the pillows and drapes of Morhab's conveyance, Pai leaped to the ground and began racing for the door of the watch. Explosively, her feet burst into flames, shooting up her clothing, turning her into a torch.

Amid Morhab's terrible cries, the rear end of the sled exploded, crumpling it onto the ground, where a conflagration engulfed it, sending clouds of black smoke curling over the sere. The Gond couldn't move, but burned with his pillows and stone well computers, which popped and hissed like firecrackers.

Back at the window, Johanna tucked the imager into her tunic pocket. Pursued by the memory of Morhab's awful bellows, she and SuMing hurried back through the corridors of the watch. SuMing held out her arm for Johanna to lean on her, but found that she was scarcely more steady herself.

"We are safe now," SuMing whispered as they ran.

Johanna shuddered. "Did you see them burn? Oh, God, they burned like straw."

SuMing thought that image would stay locked in her eyes forever. But forever would not be long if they did not compose themselves and present a calmer façade. Gathering their dignity, she and Johanna took several steadying breaths and resumed their progress down the corridor.

At the next turn they saw soldiers racing toward them. Noting Johanna, one of them stopped to hear her story, that Morhab the engineer had threatened suicide unless she accepted him as a suitor. They heard how she had rejected Morhab, never thinking it would come to this. She only hoped the soldiers wouldn't be too late to prevent it.

They were far too late. From the thousand windows of the watch, astonished soldiers had seen Morhab's sled burning brightly. Some of those on duty claimed they had seen a woman standing there beforehand, but those who heard this story dismissed the notion.

No one could stand on the sere.

PART IV

A
PLAGUE
OF
MATTER

CHAPTER THIRTY-FIVE

To frighten one hundred, kill one.

—a saying

DEPTA STOOD ON A STEEP HILL overlooking the plains of Ahnenhoon. In the distance, skirmishes flashed as defensive units met Paion intrusions that appeared from nowhere. A light breeze soothed Depta's hide, and she reveled in four feet on solid ground. For the moment, at least, she and her lady were not racing after the man of the Rose, but stopping at a battlefield to inspect troops and carry out minor functions—or so Lady Chiron would have it appear.

At the foot of the rise lay Chiron's brightship, so small at this distance she could cover it with one hoof, outstretched. She saw the miniature form of Lady Chiron as she stood beside her ship receiving a delegation of officers. Once finished with formalities, Chiron would slip away to keep watch on the Repel. Chiron could not be far enough away for Depta's comfort.

She had grown to despise the lady.

The thought curled in Depta's gut like a tumor. Finally the truth. But what would happen when Chiron asked, "Do you love us?"

A minor general named Ci Dehai had been assigned to attend her, and now leaned in to say, "That is the high General Lehao who greets the lady."

"Impressive," Depta said, hardly registering the high personages below.

Depta could run into the hills. She could just imagine a court-bred Hirrin blundering about in the gullies, with no allies to run to. Perhaps the only recourse was to take her own life. Earlier, General Ci Dehai had given

327

her a most instructive tour of the armory, where a thousand different weapons might be used to good effect. She had paid strict attention, even to the point of testing a few of them, to the general's surprise and amusement.

"We have," Ci Dehai was saying, "thirty-two divisions of sentients, formed into eight regiments, each commanding a place on the grid where incursions are predicted by perturbations of the walls."

Divisions. Regiments. Depta tried to focus. But for what?

In the far distance, the walls of the world converged from both sides, pinching the world into a narrow strip of misery where the armies met, where Depta stood.

"On the instant, troops can reinforce each other across adjoining grids, then quickly re-form at stations," Ci Dehai droned on. "The Paion are methodical, allowing us to predict incursions as to grid placement, if not time."

Across the seven miles of battlefield between Depta and the storm walls, the armies mustered and engaged the Paion, creating snarls of troops and bursts of fire across the plains. So this is what war looked like, Depta thought. As isolated as she had been at the Ascendancy, it was easy to forget the war. It was also easy to miss the fact that she had given her life over to a fiend.

"See there?" Ci Dehai pointed. "The fortress of the Repel."

Crouching on the right side of the battleground was Lord Inweer's massive redoubt, at this distance a mere shelf of black stone. It was in that stronghold that the doomed Johanna Quinn lived her last hours. Lord Inweer didn't yet know it was she who had alerted Titus Quinn to the purpose of the engine, but Chiron would inform him soon. Since treasonous thoughts came so easily to Depta these days, she allowed herself to conclude that Johanna Quinn was a patriot of her own land, and shouldn't be held accountable to the vows of the Entire.

Once you decided to think for yourself, a great many ideas began to sprout.

At Depta's side, Ci Dehai kept up a running commentary for his important visitor. "See, Preconsul, the zeppelins cause consternation among the troops. Fear is the best weapon the Paion wield, not the killing rain."

Skimming over the war plain, Paion dirigibles swam, hailing down an ochre rain. The great airships, few in number, were fat targets, soon brought down by cannons shooting blue-white fire. The Paion used no great devices of war, nor did the Tarig grant such powers to their own armies. The Entire couldn't endure high disruption, and the Paion wished to claim the Entire intact, not in shreds. Thus, in the million days of the war, cannons shooting fire and zeppelins raining acid remained the most fearsome weapons of this contest.

The general pointed. "See there, Preconsul, an airship blooms." To watch this new zeppelin, he turned sharply to one side, exposing the mottled flesh of the ruined half of his face.

Depta watched as a smear of sky became an oblong ship, budding into existence before the walls of the Repel. She couldn't judge its size, and asked.

"The airship would not fit on this hill, Preconsul. It carries one thousand Paion." At her doubtful look, he shrugged. "They do not value life as we do, since they have so many soldiers to waste."

"Do they ever fight on the ground?"

"Certainly, Preconsul. Otherwise we would have merely an artillery war on our hands, whereas you see the infantries drawn up in divisions. But the enemy does come by ship. They bloom from nowhere, and wreak havoc until we have them in our sights. Then we obliterate them." They watched as a jet of blue fire snagged the zeppelin, sending a stream of fire along the top of the vessel.

Depta knew only one military quote, and she recited it now to maintain her end of the conversation. "'In all the dimensions of matter, only one enemy.'"

Ci Dehai responded with some irony, "Unless you count the Rose."

That was unexpected. "We are not at war with the Rose, General," she said. Not yet. Not unless Titus Quinn succeeded. "We withhold knowledge of the Entire, but that is not the same as war."

"Yes, Preconsul, that is more accurate, of course."

But surely they weren't at war in any sense. She cut a glance at this general, wondering if he would say more. He remained quiet—assigned to show her the sights, but not to trouble her preconceptions.

The Paion had been attacking for so long they had become a comfortable enemy, even while mysterious and feared. No one knew what manner of creature they were. They fought in short metallic simulacra—two-legged, two-armed torsos that lacked heads. Although only four feet tall, these Paion-driven machines were the images that children feared, the staggering robotic mechanisms armed with weapons that emerged from their armor in deadly sproutings. The Paion themselves rode in small humps on the backs of the simulacra, directing, controlling, or so it was presumed. No one had ever seen a Paion crawl out of that hump. When Entire soldiers felled a Paion simulacra and opened the housing, nothing remained but rotting biomass.

Depta wondered what would they do with the Entire should they ever conquer. If they came from another dimension, as legend had it, how could they hope to live in this one?

"Why do the Paion attack only here, General?"

He turned the good half of his face toward her, regarding her. "If they attacked elsewhere, Preconsul, do you think the Tarig would tolerate it? No. The Paion can dare just so much before the bright lords erase them from the universe." He noted the confusion on her face. "Does not the third vow say we must extend the reach of the Entire? Surely the lords show great forbearance in not conquering the Paion homeland. Wherever it may be."

What he was saying implied that the war was at the sufferance of the Tarig. All the conscriptions, all the deaths . . . She felt an intolerable weight bearing down on her. "I have seen enough death," she said, surprised in spite of herself to say anything of the sort to this general.

"Of course, Lady." He gestured her to precede him back to the camp. As a last impression, in the center of the plain a large clot of fire erupted, leaving behind a black pall that thinned out on the breeze. Ci Dehai led her away to a tent where she might take refreshment and rest. They walked away from the summit and down a short drop to a quartering area. A line of soldiers had formed to one side, snaking up from the other side of the hill and ending in a small clearing where a reviewing stand had been set up. Depta and Ci Dehai walked past this line. Soldiers must wait in line for food, for rest, for orders. The way of camp life. Depta wished that she could be so content with order, and doubted she ever could again.

"The lady has a grim duty here," Ci Dehai said, nodding at this line. "Perhaps she will consent to dispatch these individuals after dinner."

"Dispatch?"

"They have all committed treason."

"Surely not all," Depta blurted. She looked with dread at this line of ordinary soldiers: Chalin, Jout, Ysli, even Gond. Here and there a Hirrin.

"They deserve to die," the general said. He turned away from the line, murmuring, "For the peace of the Entire."

"How could all these soldiers have committed a capital crime?" she managed to ask the general, failing now to keep her voice neutral.

"Oh, they engaged in traitorous talk," he answered. "They spoke of Titus Quinn, and his escape from the bright city. Some claimed he killed a Tarig lord, and destroyed property. All preposterous, for how could a single human do so much? It doesn't do to make a hero out of a criminal. The dark can never become light. The Rose can never coexist with the Entire." He gazed at her directly as they walked side by side, and his voice fell low. "To think otherwise is treason. With the resulting penalty, as you will see."

Depta passed a Chalin boy who might have been conscripted yesterday. Her gaze fell on a Hirrin, staring at the ground, having given up already. The line went on and on. Each one would watch the ones in front die by the garrote. Depending on how tight Chiron strapped it, some would die sooner, some later.

"Certainly not all these," Depta protested. "There are a hundred of them."

"One hundred and eleven," Ci Dehai said. "It's too bad. Conscripts are fewer these days."

"Surely not all these," Depta repeated in a whisper.

The general turned to Depta, bowing. "A light meal is ready, if you will follow me."

"Please excuse me, General. I cannot eat."

His expression softened. "Do not trouble yourself, Preconsul, on behalf of these mere soldiers."

"Perhaps you should trouble *yourself*, General, on their behalf."

He turned his good eye on her, muttering softly, "Perhaps I already have."

Quinn and Anzi had been walking for two days, subsisting on catnaps. They wound their way through the hot, folded hills, traversing a gully, one of hundreds. With the Nigh far behind, golden hills surrounded them, an undulating geography so typical of the lands near the storm walls. Further into the primacy midlands, the veldt swept across ten thousand miles to the matching wall. But here at the tip of the primacy, the terrain buckled under the colossal forces of the Great Reach, where the storm walls met.

"Wrong direction," Anzi said again.

"Maybe." Quinn didn't want to argue about it. They had to keep going in order for him to have enough time to make a stop at Yulin's camp.

Anzi was dead set against it. "We have three days left."

"Four days," he said.

"No. Oventroe said five or six days of life left in the chain. If it was five, then we have three days left."

"I'm counting, Anzi, believe me. The camp is on the way." They had said all this before.

Still, she argued. "Imagine the chain falling apart here, or on the plains of Ahnenhoon. All the soldiers, gone—like Benhu. And the engine still standing."

He *had* imagined. The cirque clutched his ankle with a heavier grip—one that seemed to have grown brittle. Stepping in the Nigh to pursue the Inyx mount, Quinn had compromised the hollow loop. *Let's not chance getting it wet*, Stefan had said. The Nigh wasn't water, but something worse. He remembered Benhu standing on the sagging bridge between the vessel's bow and stern—his arms deforming, and his puzzled look as he sank into the river. It saddened him. Although their acquaintance had started badly, Benhu had won Quinn's begrudging respect. Quinn thought it was mutual. He knew others of his helpers had suffered for his sake as well: Yulin, certainly. And Cho, his guide at the Ascendancy. He could only hope that some had escaped notice: Ghoris, the navitar who'd set his search for Johanna's message in motion. Bei, who had restored his memories. When Quinn learned from Oventroe about Cho's imprisonment, he had asked the lord to intervene. But Oventroe had demurred, saying it risked revealing too much of his sympathies. At least he'd been honest about it, not that it helped poor Cho.

Quinn watched his steps. In this undulating landscape, the ground sprouted knife-sharp rocks. One slip could mean injury. Neither he nor Anzi could afford a further handicap.

He heard her scrambling to catch up. "Titus. You shouldn't interfere between my uncle and me."

Such brave words. As always, she was focused on one thing at a time, whereas he believed there was time and the need to do everything. He was aware that his life had become a stack of desires that clamored for settling. He had always believed it was because he loved things fiercely; any man would love his family; any man would love his world. In Anzi's case, she appeared to love the wrong world: his. Most of the time, he was grateful that she was on his side in that regard.

She continued. "My trouble with my uncle is not your business, pardon me."

But it was. Yulin had decreed a marriage for Anzi because of him. He could see the workings of the old bear's mind: Show the Tarig that Anzi was well occupied with a Chalin husband, and no longer embroiled in misdemeanors. Another proof of Yulin's change of heart for the gracious lords. Quinn wondered which side of the game Yulin was on these days. He hoped Suzong, at least, was on his side. She hated the lords for the terrible death of her own mother long ago. Her loyalties would never be with the Tarig. In any case, he wouldn't cut a destructive path through Anzi's life and leave her behind with hell to pay.

Quinn sat on a rock ledge and rested for a moment. Anzi pursued her topic relentlessly. "What if our estimates are wrong? What if it takes longer to reach the Repel?"

They had been through the calculations, drawing the route on the hard ground, planning the legs of the journey: three days to Yulin's camp. Another day to the battle plains, there to breach the Repel.

Anzi handed Quinn a strip of cooked meat, and he took it gratefully, counting on it to power another five hours of walking.

Anzi's voice broke into his thoughts. "Why go back where Ling Xiao Sheng is waiting? He can't marry me if he can't find me."

Quinn had a further logic to going to Yulin's camp, and perhaps now was the time to say it. "You'll stay in camp, Anzi."

She greeted this pronouncement with a stony silence. Tendrils of hair clung to her forehead as the day grew hot.

He knew she must want to be at his side. From the beginning, Anzi had felt responsible for everything: for his imprisonment in the Entire, for what happened to his family. She was determined about many things. So was he.

He softened his voice. "It'll be hard enough for one person to get through. Oventroe gave me what he knows of the Repel's defenses. It may not be enough." The fortification was enormous and sprawling, but not porous. Oventroe said the defenses were impregnable. There was the terminus, the sere, the watch and the gathering yard, the centrum, and the maze of the containment chamber. All these barriers could be crossed, but only by the Tarig. Last ebb, the lord had given Quinn the means to penetrate the place. Still, it would be like running a gauntlet.

"I can help you," Anzi said, looking at him with that amber gaze that seemed sun-struck, and a little fey.

"I don't want you with me." Harsh to say. Far harsher in the reality, when she attempted to enter the terminus and cross the sere.

She stared across the seemingly endless ravines and saddles. In the distance, the blue-black escarpment of the storm wall marched out of sight to the end of the primacy. Without speaking, Anzi stood, brushing off her tunic pants, and headed down the other side of the hill.

Mo Ti watched them from the peak of a nearby ridge. Neither of them was especially good in the wilds, whereas Mo Ti was a master of tracking and stealth. At his side, Distanir snatched the thoughts of the two fugitives, telling Mo Ti that Titus Quinn was ill, and that they were headed into Master Yulin's hidden camp.

They made one mistake after the next. How had Titus Quinn done the great things claimed for him? Here was the man himself, sick and stumbling. Best of all, he created a beacon on his position. His message to Sydney had been relayed to Distanir. Insisting that the ship keeper allow an unscheduled stop along the banks of the Nigh, Mo Ti had sped into the hills on Distanir's strong back, close behind them. Then the two fools had slept. While they had, Mo Ti and Distanir had crept within striking distance.

Still, there were two of them, and he wasn't sure of their weaponry. He didn't discount the woman, who was young and strong, with the muscular arms of a fighter. He would wait until the journey exhausted them; it couldn't be long now.

He watched as Titus Quinn picked his way up the next rise. Mo Ti couldn't see the chain around the man's ankle, but he knew from Quinn's thoughts that it was there: the machine filled with the seeds of ruin.

Mo Ti would take pleasure in severing the man from his string of days. Then, if Quinn's thoughts rang true as to the degraded state of the chain, Mo Ti would return to the Nigh and cast the infernal device into it. Three days.

Plenty of time.

Later that day Quinn found his strength returning. Perhaps the walking had finally purged his body, or perhaps it was just adrenaline. They set a better pace, traversing hill and gully without end. The bright was a boiling lid over the land, yet its rays were gentle in the ebb when they walked the fastest. Quinn had forgotten already what a blue sky looked like, and clouds. Despite his setbacks here, he didn't miss the blue; the silver seemed right.

Anzi was adept at catching the slithers that hid under rocks; and they developed a taste for the insectivores, even raw. He took a drink from their water bag that Anzi had replenished at wells she ferreted out. Accepting the water from her, he once called her Johanna. A slip of the tongue. His mind was on his wife. The closer they came to Ahnenhoon, the more his thoughts turned to her. If he did make it out of the fortress alive, Johanna might be with him.

He had asked Oventroe if the Tarig lord at Ahnenhoon treated Johanna well. "Yes," Oventroe had said. "He favors her." Quinn was glad of that, considering what the alternatives might be. Still, he wondered what was in her heart.

That day when Quinn and his family had been captured, when Johanna had first seen a Tarig, she was stunned by their towering stature, their predatory aspect. Sydney wasn't intimidated, perhaps because she was a child and didn't know how impossible they were. Within hours, the Tarig were speaking a halting English, and this encouraged Johanna. Yes, he remembered that she tried to talk to them.

Sydney had watched every move of the Tarig. She had said, "They smell burned." Johanna had said, "Be careful, Sydney. That's not polite." So even then Johanna had begun to make peace with them. So early.

That was unfair. No one had made greater peace with them than he had. It had begun, innocuously enough, with the Tarig lady. Once Quinn and his family arrived at the Ascendancy, the creature had come to him in the ebb, crouching by his bed. He had awakened with a start.

"They are gone," the Tarig being had said. This Tarig was smaller than others he had seen, wearing a jeweled net over cropped hair. He thought it might be a female.

They had told him nothing about his family, now separated from him. "Where are they?" Quinn had demanded.

"It would be difficult to explain," she said. "But far away. They are gone. Reconcile yourself."

She wouldn't say more, and soon departed. But now he had an ally of sorts. He knew something he wasn't supposed to know. He would learn to collect such pieces of intelligence, piecing it all together—eventually, and to his chagrin. Johanna and Sydney were a world away, a universe away.

Anzi set a brisk pace in the jagged terrain. He kept up, but barely.

"Anzi," he said. They were at the bottom of a slope leading to a rock saddle, some hundred meters above. They paused before the climb. Quinn said, "I'm going to take her home."

Scattering stone shards under her boots, Anzi went straight up the flank. At the top, Quinn joined her. Far in the distance the Nigh-ward storm wall met the anti-Nigh-ward storm wall at an acute angle, crushing the light from the basin between them.

"I'm going to ask her to come home," he said again.

"Yes. Of course."

"She may not come with me."

"Perhaps she won't."

The air was still and hot as the Heart of Day cast its fierce light on Anzi, making her seem struck from alabaster. She was quiet with her emotions, and always had been. So unlike Johanna.

Finally Anzi said, "I think she should go home. If she wishes to."

"She's the companion of Lord Inweer." He'd told Anzi this before. Why bring it up now?

"Then she may not choose to come with you, Titus."

"No. She may not."

Anzi plunged down the other side of the saddle. He followed. For months now he'd thought that Johanna was dead, until Zhiya had revealed the truth. So the past was not as over as he had thought. He had brought Johanna into danger in the Entire in the first place. And he would take her out.

He had recently loved her. How much of the old life was left? He found the answers skittering away into the ravines.

They ate the rest of their provisions and traveled a mile or two on the energy of the fatty meat.

During the trek, Anzi asked, "How will you persuade my uncle?"

"The same way I persuaded him to help me in the first place."

She murmured, "Humans will come. He must choose a side."

"Yes." He wondered if that argument would still hold. "We'll see if he agrees to give up the marriage. If he doesn't, you can come with me if you still want to."

He won a smile from her. But Yulin *would* agree. He didn't think he'd lose his way with the old bear on such a point.

Eventually they decided to allow themselves two hours' sleep. By Anzi's calculation, they wouldn't reach Yulin's camp until the third hour of Between Ebb. She knew, because she had come this way on her way out from Yulin's camp. Finding a rock ledge overhang they nestled in what shade the bright allowed, and dozed.

Mo Ti crept up the gully, having left Distanir behind to be sure his approach was soundless. Quinn and Anzi slept, so Distanir said. Now he could catch them unawares.

Mo Ti unsheathed the blade he carried at his side. As long as his forearm, it would cleave through such bone and muscle as these two possessed.

Behind him, Mo Ti felt Distanir's distress at being left out of the fight. Distanir's bulk and hooves were not made for stealth, and in a skirmish, surprise was a precious advantage. Distanir was sending his emotions rather too strongly. *Quiet, my Distanir*, he sent.

Once in the shallow basin, he spied someone lying in a small crevasse.

Sleep eluded Quinn, as his thoughts returned to Johanna and the decisions they would soon face. He rose after a few minutes, leaving Anzi in their snug retreat. But it wasn't Johanna who disturbed his thoughts. It was something else, a slipstream of distress, that edged into his consciousness. A familiar thing, but why?

It was very like an Inyx sending. Having experienced that strange sensation twice before, he now recognized it with certainty. If Inyx were nearby, why hadn't he heard their hooves and the cries of their riders? Hoping for a wider view, he climbed to the crest of the low hill, lying down at the top to be sure the ravines on either side were deserted.

They weren't. Down the next gully came a dark shape like a boulder moving. It was the largest Chalin man that Quinn had ever seen. His hair was gathered into a white topknot, in the military style, and sword drawn, the creature advanced on Anzi's sleeping form.

Quinn sprinted down the hill, making noise to distract the man from Anzi, who was sleeping and unarmed. Quinn carried their only weapon, a short knife, no match for the giant, who now turned his attention to the assault coming at him from above.

Quinn slid to a stop at the bottom, scattering loose rock. The giant turned to engage him, rushing forward to pin Quinn against the jagged slope. Guessing the man's strategy, Quinn moved to the center of the gully. Into his mind came the shriek of an Inyx mount, sending alarms.

The giant's shoulders loomed over a chest broad as a turbine, while his crumpled face sat athwart, looking itself like a dangerous weapon. The man charged, feinting left, and moving with a grace impossible to imagine in one so large. Drawing back his sword arm, he heaved the blade with a fierce slice into the air where Quinn had been standing.

Anzi emerged from the cranny, a rock in hand, ready to fight. She circled behind the man, creating two attack fronts.

The odds were against Quinn. His reach couldn't match the giant's arm. He shouted to Anzi in English: "Climb the slope; get above him."

Anzi continued to circle the giant, just out of reach. She removed her jacket, taunting the man, "Afraid to kill a woman, then?"

Quinn danced forward, then retreated, staying well away from the prodigious reach of the attacker, watching with half his mind for any fellow thieves to come down the ridges. Above him, he saw a massive shape on the crest of the hill. The Inyx mount came pounding down the hillside sending outrage in pulses of emotion.

At that moment, Anzi flung her jacket with expert aim, covering the giant's head to his shoulders. The man pawed it away, but not before Quinn charged.

Quinn aimed his knife into the giant's groin, the only vulnerable place he could reach as the man flung the jacket away. The blade slipped in, releasing a bellow as it drove home. Quinn yanked his knife back, determined to keep it. The giant went to his knees as the mount pounded into their midst, head bent down, horns to the fore.

Anzi raised her arm as though to finish the giant off. She bore no weapon, but her feint worked. The Inyx rounded, and came at her instead. This left time for Quinn to grab the giant's sword. He swooped down and took a firm grasp, but the monster held fast, looking into Quinn's face with the single-minded intensity of a starving bear. He hauled back on the blade, wrenching it free from Quinn's hold.

Lashing out with his booted foot, Quinn hammered the man in the chest, upsetting his balance just enough to send the sword blow awry.

But he wasn't hurt as much as Quinn hoped. He staggered to his feet and advanced. Behind him, Quinn saw the Inyx mount crash his forehorns into the rock overhang where Anzi had plunged.

To Quinn's astonishment, she was thrusting out a long knife blade that she could only have retrieved from the Inyx saddle sheath. The mount registered pain, sending out a wave of rage. She had sliced his fetlock.

Quinn circled around to Anzi's position, pulled her from the shallow crevasse, and hauled her up slope with him as the Chalin giant and his mount took stock of their wounds. Scrambling over rock scree, Quinn and Anzi climbed to the crest of the hill. They were breathless, dusty, and light-headed from the heat. But they were unscathed. To his surprise, their pursuer was kneeling to examine the mount's leg. Blood stained the ground where the massive Inyx stood, immobilized.

The Chalin man looked up at them, his face as impassive as it had been during the fight. He raised his sword and pointed it at Quinn.

"Soon," he said, in a chilling, soft voice.

CHAPTER THIRTY-SIX

Let your plans be dark and impenetrable as the storm wall, and when you move, fall like a Tarig's fist.

—from Tun Mu's *Annals of War*

THEY TOOK A MEAL TOGETHER, Johanna and Inweer. She wore her best blue gown, and forced herself to show an appetite.

"You are beautiful, Johanna," Inweer said.

"We have learned to see each other in kind terms, my lord." He might interpret that as an insult, but she was merely fending off his compliment, as she used to do, back when she parried words with him for his amusement.

It wasn't a Tarig custom to eat in company, and Inweer only did so now to honor her ways. Around them in the hall, the metal floor spread out like a skating rink to the distant walls. The drafty chamber didn't foster conversation, but Inweer still probed her about Morhab's death. After the soldiers had dragged the charred bodies from the sere, Johanna had wasted no time in suggesting to Inweer that Morhab had committed suicide for love of her. No point to deny a connection between her and the Gond; they had been seen together, no doubt. Perhaps it was settled. However, Inweer had his mind on other things, and might not give priority to the death of an engineer.

As a Chalin servant cleared their plates, Johanna poured skeel for him, wine for herself. Her hand was steady. She didn't think he would kill her tonight.

"You set store in kindness," he said, watching her rather too closely.

"It is my Savior's commandment, Bright Lord."

"Ah. The God who confers eternal life. After one loses one's body."

341

They had been over these things before. Though to the long-lived Tarig, the assurances of religion didn't compel, she and Inweer had an easy repartee about her faith. Once, such topics eased loneliness, in the days when she didn't have an impossible obligation on her shoulders. Oh Titus, come well armed, she prayed. Blow everything at once. There is no blame.

She adjusted the long pins in her hair, where they bound her hair into a simple twist. They would make good weapons, if driven into the eye. She smiled at Inweer. To kill him, it would be necessary to drive a pin into the edge of his eye. The orb itself was hard as glass.

Inweer's voice came to her, sliding to the topic she least wished to pursue: "We find it curious that Morhab had hope of you."

She managed a wry face. "Yes, strange, isn't it? I was determined to overcome my repugnance for his physical aspect, and I set myself a duty of talking to him from time to time. He made too much of that. He must have been troubled to be so mistaken."

"Talked of what?"

"Oh. My home world. He did seem interested. My family, little things I did as a child. It comforted me to speak of former things. Now I regret it." She sipped her wine. "Poor creature, to die so."

"And your serving lady, Pai. She was with Morhab. Why, hnn?"

Because she betrayed me, Johanna thought. She took no pleasure in that death. She didn't doubt for a moment that Morhab had held some terrible threat over Pai.

"I don't know, my lord. Perhaps, in death, he wanted to hurt me, after all. And knowing that I had no strong feelings for him, he took the one lady who I did love." She sipped her wine, hoping her flushed skin didn't mark her as an elegant liar.

Inweer hadn't touched his drink, but regarded her with icy stillness. "Have you told one all that pertains to the matter?"

"Yes, my lord. Morhab was deluded, and now I'm quite cross with him. I'll have to settle for SuMing as a companion." She put an edge to her voice, as though annoyed with the subject, but her heart was hammering.

They sat in silence for a time. Just get it over with, my lord, she thought. Whatever you're going to do.

"Johanna, we are dissatisfied with one thing: the image of yourself, that likeness you so earnestly requested."

Her tongue stuck in her dry throat. "My picture?"

"Did you wish the image sent to the small girl not for her sake, but for your husband's?"

"My husband's? Why would I care if he sees a likeness?"

"To prove that you are still alive."

"Well, a picture proves nothing."

"Unless it is a clue that you still live. That you wish to see him. Here, in my stronghold."

"He would hardly come here, to certain death."

"He is known to be bold."

What were they talking about? Titus coming for Johanna? Or coming for the engine? She pretended it was the former. "I don't want to see him here. If he tries to rescue my daughter, then I hope he succeeds, and never comes here. I'm a mother first of all, my lord."

"And second? A wife?"

She looked at the lord in some bafflement. If she didn't know better, she would have said that he cared whom she loved. It stopped her breath for an instant.

She said simply, "You think I still love him."

He rose, drawing himself up to his impressive height. "Perhaps."

"I will never go home, my lord. Not with my husband. And not without him."

He nodded. It was how everything had begun. That he, wishing her to give up longing for home, had told her that home would not last. But the conversation was over. Someone had arrived.

At the far edge of the hall, a Tarig waited under the gallery. It wasn't Lady Enwepe, because the lady hadn't been in residence for a week. Johanna hid her dismay. Too much was happening. She could barely control one Tarig. Two was not good news.

Inweer turned to the new arrival, nodding for him to come forward. "Leave us, Johanna," he said.

As the Tarig stranger strode toward them, his boots clanged on the tympanum of the great floor. His bearing suggested that he came as an equal.

Rising from her seat, Johanna murmured, "Who honors us with a visit, my lord?"

"One's cousin, Lord Oventroe."

"One of the Five." Her curiosity by now fully aroused, she had no choice but to give them the privacy Inweer demanded. "I leave you to important matters, then."

Inweer cut a sharp glance at her. "These *were* important matters, Johanna."

Chastened, she said, "Of course." Bowing low, she murmured, "My life in your service, Bright Lord." As she swept past Lord Oventroe he cut a glance at her that cooled her heart.

Johanna slept that ebb in her forest. SuMing made up the pallet amidst the trees, but not underneath, so that Johanna could view the stars.

Allowing SuMing the more comfortable rest of her own bed, Johanna dismissed her servant. She made her prayers. In the midst of them she remembered that when Lord Inweer asked about her portrait, she had failed to ask him whether he had yet sent it to Sydney. That would have been a logical question, had she really cared about sending a picture to Sydney. Eventually, to fulfill his promise, Inweer would send it. Suddenly, and with overwhelming longing, Johanna found herself wondering what reaction her daughter would have to receiving such a gift. She would throw it away, perhaps. But what if she was glad to have it? Johanna pushed the thought away. Her family was a thing of the past, and longing for it had long since dwindled to a slow, hard ache.

Hours later, she slept so deeply that when the shadow gripped her arm, she nearly cried out.

"Who?" she hissed.

"Your lord."

She sat up, dragging her fists over her eyes to clear them. She could see nothing, but she recognized the slender dark shadow of a Tarig. It wasn't Inweer.

"You aren't my lord."

"Perhaps you mistake him."

Lord Oventroe, she guessed, the one who had interrupted her dinner with Inweer. "Be welcome, Bright Lord," she whispered, knowing instinctively that he had come to her in the dark for secrecy.

"Gather your wits, and listen, now. These words come only once." Holding her arm, he pulled her closer, where she could smell his distinctive odor: a sweet, caramel smell that was both like and unlike Inweer. His grip was a torque around her upper arm, and he wasn't gentle.

"Do you wish the engine gone?"

She had never tried to hide that wish. "Yes," she answered.

"If that is so, then whatever you feel for Lord Inweer, set aside. Think of yourself now bound to Lord Oventroe, who holds your life, and the life of your world."

"Holds, my lord? How?"

"Say nothing. Your husband comes within two days. To be ready for him, we require you to memorize the sequence of the maze, so that you may lead him to the engine."

"Yes, the maze . . . ," she began.

Oventroe yanked her closer, his breath cold on her cheek. "Speak again, and we will cut you."

He went on, "Your husband will sow doubts. He will doubt that the All can withstand the onslaught of his destructive device. This you will not heed. Let no hesitation come to you, and by any means necessary—by love, or shame, or threats—bring him to the engine, there leaving the cirque that he carries on his ankle. It will annihilate the engine."

Annihilate. Yes. They were sweet words. But was this a trick to show her a traitor? Why would a Tarig lord do such a thing? She glanced about to be sure that she was actually awake and not dreaming.

He bent her arm so far she gasped. "Swear to your lord you will do so. You may speak."

She had prayed so long for help. Believing in miracles, she took this as one. "I do swear, my lord."

He released her arm. "I will tell you how it will be done."

Overwhelmed, Johanna whispered, "Thank God."

The starlight revealed the lord's bitter expression. "God does not look on such as us."

She wasn't so sure. Might not this be His hand coming through the wall of the world to change the heart of a lost creature?

In the shadows, her conversation with Lord Oventroe seemed charged with brilliance. She hung on the words of her new Tarig lord as he quickly and methodically explained the astonishing things that she must do.

General Ci Dehai watched as the Jout regiment dug at the hardened ground. Their coarse faces streamed with sweat, although Ci Dehai had given them leave to work under the cooler skies of evening. Grave digging was a chore proper to Shadow Ebb, he mused. If his arguments had triumphed, there would be no graves, but the Lady Chiron did not regard a minor general's protestations.

The lavender of the ebb eased his throbbing head. It had been a busy few days, with the bright lady's visit and the need to squire her entourage in the midst of a Paion incursion of some vigor. Now this chore, digging and filling, and having to endure the surly expressions from the work unit, who cast sideways glares at their general. Well, these sentients had reason to hope for glory in the Long War, not grave digging.

He turned to his aide, a capable lieutenant who had been standing well back from the summit of the hill, letting his general have a moment of contemplation.

"See them well buried, Han," Ci Dehai said, waving the lieutenant forward to command the unit. "Each with their flag."

Ci Dehai walked down the slope, away from the scene of carnage, where the last of the prisoners at last had died under the bright lady's ministrations. By the Miserable God, there would be no mass grave for these unlucky sentients, he vowed. Each would have their parcel of ground, even if it was in the blasted plains of Ahnenhoon.

Dotting the battlefield, points of campfires showed where the soldiers cooked their meal. A peaceful sight, those dots of light, each with its circle of weary sentients. There would be good rest this ebb, with the Paion retreated into their cursed land, wherever that might be, perhaps hunched over their own damnable food. For himself, Ci Dehai couldn't think about eating, after watching the lady do her work.

The Tarig dispensed capital justice. No other could lawfully do so, for the sways and armies were forbidden to kill, except in the case of Paion. It preserved the peace, prevented vendetta, and ensured justice. All good things. But it gave the Tarig lords and the Tarig ladies a dark aspect that no one forgot for long.

A rustle to one side drew his attention. Someone approached him, climbing up the side of the hill. A civilian, where none had leave to be.

"What's this?" he growled.

The civilian stopped climbing, and waved in friendly fashion. "A hard climb for one like me," the stranger said.

Ci Dehai would have ordered him away, but paused because of the self-assured, casual hail, and the man's strange physical appearance. When Ci Dehai drew closer, he saw that it was not a man at all, but a woman.

"Who the mucking bright are you?"

The woman clucked her tongue. "Such a greeting from an old friend."

"You're no old friend to me." Ci Dehai squinted. Or *was* she? Surely he would remember a dwarf with long hair, dressed as a godwoman.

The godwoman's face drooped in mock disappointment. "That's the trouble these days. Friendships don't last. Or carry over from mother to daughter." She looked boldly into Ci Dehai's face. "You don't remember Jin Yi?"

Ci Dehai paused. "But Jin Yi . . . she went for a navitar. That was long ago."

"Yes. She sends her greetings. She's retired now. Well deserved. I'm Zhiya, her only progeny." She gestured at her body. "A disappointment, to have only a dwarf for a daughter. But who can blame her for fearing to try again?"

Jin Yi. Once a charming, infectiously humorous, attractive girl. Long ago. But Ci Dehai himself wasn't much to look at these days.

"No longer a navitar? But I thought such . . . responsibilities . . . demanded one's all."

"Yes, it's rare to leave the Nigh. But she shares my sky bulb now." Zhiya sobered. "She's weak. Still, she remembers you."

"As the bright guides me," Ci Dehai murmured, taken aback, pierced by memory.

Zhiya gave him a respectful moment. Then she pointed to a sky bulb anchored on the plains below. "My conveyance. I have a godwoman's duties, and must waste no time, Excellency."

"Yes?" He now tried to imagine what this woman wished with him.

"I've come to suggest that we must help a mutual friend."

Ah. Now come the favors and demands, he thought. "If you're hoping for preference in a friend's advancement, I judge by merit alone."

"Merit." Zhiya smiled. "I used to believe in that, too."

"You're miserable indeed if you don't judge so yourself. What should we have otherwise? The vile and proud in positions of power?"

Zhiya murmured, "Perhaps we have such a situation already, General."

Did she insult him? He waited for her to explain herself.

"At the highest level, you understand." Zhiya turned away, looking up primacy, toward the Ascendancy.

Ci Dehai's awareness contracted into a very small circle. He remained silent, lest he be brought into treason.

"How go the burials?" Zhiya blinked innocently.

It could not be more explicit. His silence was now a disloyal act. Yet Ci Dehai held his tongue. Just over the rise of the hill, he could hear the clang of shovels on rock.

"Badly," he answered, letting the full impact of these needless deaths reach his heart at last. He thought he was inured to the slaughter of war, but not slaughter like this.

He spoke low. "What mutual friend needs help, daughter of Jin Yi?"

"The same friend who sojourned with you for a time." When he failed to pick up her meaning, she went on. "Who now carries the Going Over blade."

Ci Dehai knew quite well who now carried that knife.

He squinted at her. "How is it you possess information which any lord would pay handsomely to know?"

Zhiya smiled, enjoying herself a little too much. "I travel quite a bit. One can't help hearing things."

The godwoman now had his complete attention.

Ci Dehai asked, "Why do you care about him?" Let her commit the first treason, for it would not be he.

Her face lost its arch smile, and she glanced sideways to assure herself they were still alone. "To be frank? I'm a spy, General."

"Ah. But a spy for whom?"

"Sadly, I have no champion. Just enemies." She glanced up primacy again, making her meaning clear. "So as to why I care, let's call it affairs of state. We find ourselves suffering a great absence of statesmanship, General. I sometimes nudge people along to fill the gap. Can't nudge them if they're dead, of course."

Oh, it was treason and all. Ci Dehai was staggered. And intrigued.

Before the godwoman left, Ci Dehai had promised to help Titus Quinn. All quite rash, based on a long-ago connection to a woman gone for a navitar despite his offer of marriage. It was that connection, and as well, the fact that Titus Quinn was in the process of slapping the collective Tarig face. And Ci Dehai wanted in on the action.

CHAPTER THIRTY-SEVEN

When in difficult country, do not encamp. Do not linger in danger-ously isolated positions. The safest camp is on the plain, no walls but the storm walls small in the distance.

—from Tun Mu's *Annals of War*

THE TWO FUGITIVES had slipped quietly into camp an interval ago, using every precaution to avoid detection, and now knelt before Yulin. Suzong kneeled near the cave entrance, keeping a sharp eye out for spies.

Yulin glared at the suppliants before him, the two people who had caused the most consternation in his life: Titus Quinn and Ji Anzi. They were a con-tinuing source of aggravation, since now he must make the decisions that he had dreaded and delayed. A short walk from this cave where Yulin chose to receive the fugitives, the legate Hu Zha lay asleep in his tent. He could be wak-ened in a moment. Chiron could be here quickly. But Yulin must decide.

Instead of the momentous decision before him, Yulin found himself embroiled in a discussion of marriage. Is that why Titus Quinn had come there? To dispute Ji Anzi's betrothal? Truly, the man led with his heart, to risk so much for this girl.

Turning his regard to Titus Quinn, Yulin demanded, "What does it matter who she marries?"

Quinn said, "She doesn't love the man you chose." Quinn looked different than before, with the ministrations to his face and his long hair pulled back into a tie. In the flickering candlelight, he looked very Chalin. Very tired.

"It is a small matter, surely," Yulin said. "We waste time to speak of it, with spies everywhere." Anzi met his irritable gaze with the equanimity of a miscreant who couldn't comprehend her faults. "You," he snarled, "repay me with strange gifts, Niece."

She bowed her head to the dirt floor. Her muffled voice came: "So many pardons, Uncle. But everything was for Titus Quinn and our alliance with him."

"Alliance, is it? Now a faithless girl decides alliances?" She didn't know that Chiron had discovered Yulin's camp and held him hostage, so he couldn't blame her for the oversimplification. If Yulin had shared that piece with her, she would never have led Titus Quinn to the trap.

"I thought we *were* allied," Quinn said.

Yulin must tread carefully. Should he wake up Hu Zha, or not?

"Our alliance nearly killed me," Yulin growled. Now let him offer something to make it all worthwhile, or by a beku's balls, he would wake Chiron's spy and hand Quinn over.

"We warned you," Quinn said, as though that made up for losing his sway, his wives, and his palace. Yulin forbore to make a point of it. What was lost was lost. He cut a glance at Suzong, giving her leave to enter the tangle of the conversation.

Suzong hugged her jacket to her in the chill of the cave opening. "Why have you returned, Titus Quinn? We are sure it was not to inquire after our welfare." When Quinn didn't immediately respond, she prompted, "The Inyx was our guess. For your daughter, and all that you left unfinished."

Yulin pulled on his beard, listening with interest to hear why indeed Quinn had come back. What did the Rose universe intend, now that the doors were open between here and there? Or half-open. Or, at least, open enough to emit a draft.

Suzong sucked on her teeth, staring at Quinn. "Well?"

"Yes, to the Inyx," Quinn said.

Yulin thought the man an impossible mixture of the personal and the visionary. What good to save one child where dynasty, trade, and advancement were concerned? And now here he came meddling for Anzi's sake. Truly a difficult man to grasp. He shifted his seat on the hard ground, glancing now and then at the cave entrance, where the ebb's dour light began to wax toward morning.

Anzi looked sickly in the lavender light. He guessed that there was an issue between her and Quinn; she didn't look like a woman about to be rescued from a hated marriage, but rather like the niece he knew so well: the one who hated to be told what to do.

Yulin leaned forward, saying, "We must protect ourselves. Anzi's marriage offered stability, showed our loyalty. What do you offer us?"

"Nothing yet. But when my people come, then—"

Yulin waved this away. "Yes, yes. When they come. But again, you come alone, meddling with small matters. Is this the path of a prince?"

"Be glad I don't tell you everything, if you have spies in camp."

Quinn played his games, but Yulin didn't mean to be a piece in it, to be sacrificed at will. "So then, it would seem that you offer nothing new. Here is my judgment: Anzi—while of fond regard—owes help to our position, and will marry Ling Xiao Sheng. She has no other suitor, and high time she took a wife's place."

"She has another suitor," Quinn said.

Yulin growled, "Who?"

"Me."

At Quinn's side, Anzi looked carved in stone. Quinn turned to her. "Do you accept, Anzi?"

Staring at the floor, she uttered a barely audible yes.

Suzong and Yulin exchanged glances. This wasn't the response of a woman in love. Perhaps they had been wrong about that. In any case, Yulin was astonished that Quinn would make the offer when he would offer her so little.

Quinn snapped a glance back at Yulin. "Release her from Ling Xiao Sheng. I will repay the cost of the marriage stone."

Yulin grumbled. "You have coin?"

"Not at the moment. I lost everything in a sinking on the Nigh."

No time to hear *that* story. The time of choice was upon him. If he denied Quinn's suit, the man would know that their alliance was broken. Then Yulin must awaken the legate and align himself once and for all with Chiron.

Suzong's eyes beseeched him as though to say, *Choose rightly.*

Yulin let out a profound sigh. By the Miserable God, if Suzong wanted him to choose the Rose, he would. Anzi would marry Quinn; there would be no hiding of alliances after that. His despicable half brother would take his sway, and Yulin would be on the run again. By the mucking bright, how had he come to this? He well remembered the day that Quinn had arrived at his palace sealed in a jar and carrying the pictures of his wife and daughter. Yulin had known at the time that he should have sunk him to the bottom of the palace lake. Had he ordered it so, he would still be sitting on silk pillows and enjoying his gardens.

He nodded at Suzong. So be it, then. Turning to Quinn, he said, "Our camp is not a secret to some at the Ascendancy. There is nowhere to hide; if we form this marriage alliance with you, there will be no mercy for us."

"Hide for a while longer, Master Yulin. Then my people will come."

"I tire of waiting."

Suzong leaned forward, addressing Quinn. "The correlates. Did you find them?" When Quinn hesitated, she went on. "If you did, give them into our hands that we may flee to the world of your sun. The lords will never find us there."

Quinn hesitated. "Yes. I have them."

But Yulin wasn't as eager as his wife to fling himself into the darkness of the Rose. It might be no safer—and there, one could not rule a sway.

"A marriage like this," Yulin said, "binds your world and mine. You understand?"

"Yes."

Yulin drew himself up. "Then Anzi is yours. If you accept, Niece?"

She nodded, no more.

"Yes, then," Yulin said. "Anzi is yours."

Quinn bowed in thanks. "She'll stay here for a time. Protect her, no matter what you hear of me." He pinned Yulin and then Suzong with a stark gaze. "It will all be lies."

Mo Ti and Distanir followed the trail of Titus Quinn's thoughts to the outskirts of Yulin's camp. There they waited, picking up threads of conversation and trying to pinpoint Quinn's location.

Distanir could barely stand on his injured leg. The fetlock cut wasn't deep, but in walking so far, Distanir had gone lame. Dismayed at this turn of events, Mo Ti hardly noticed his own wound, nonlethal but burning.

Distanir turned his head, suddenly alert. *Yulin arrives*, the mount sent. *They have been outside the camp. With him, the one called Suzong.*

Titus Quinn also?

They are alone.

Where was Titus Quinn? The four of them had been together until a moment ago. Mo Ti's best chance was to turn Yulin against Quinn, and he thought he knew how this might be done.

Leaving Distanir in a small gully, Mo Ti crept toward Yulin's tent. Drawing close, he saw two soldiers standing guard. He walked forward, hands outstretched. "Peace," he said.

Weapons were at his throat in an instant.

"Tell your master that one named Sydney has a message for him."

In a moment the guard had returned, leading him into a spacious but humble tent where a heavy Chalin personage and an old woman sat on stools as though giving an audience. Mo Ti knew who this man was, and who he used to be. He also knew that the man's loyalties had been with Titus Quinn and might still be. But Mo Ti thought that after hearing what Quinn carried around his ankle, no sane being of the Entire could fail to sever ties with the outlaw.

For all the Rose spider's faults, she had painted an expressive picture of the fate of the world once the plague was unloosed. When the woman said that she wished to prevent that calamity, Mo Ti believed her. Because she had admitted her base motive: that she might live for one hundred thousand days. To achieve this goal, she must live in the embrace of the Entire, the embrace that Titus Quinn intended to shatter.

Mo Ti bowed low to Master Yulin and his wife. When they gave him leave to give his message, he told them the story of the chain, and the one who carried it into their land.

Yulin's alarm at hearing his story was all that Mo Ti could have hoped for. The former master of the Chalin sway loved his land—how could he not? Any mewling godman, any mincing legate would feel the same.

The lady Suzong cast out objections, clearly skeptical. But Yulin, glowering and muttering, was convinced.

He murmured to his lady, "Now we know why he came to Ahnenhoon, eh?"

Mo Ti was sure that Yulin had not been any more aware of the engine and its purpose than Mo Ti had been. But once past that, it made sense to him that the Rose would strike.

"He must suffer final justice," Mo Ti said. When they hesitated, he went on, "If you have no stomach for the act, Mo Ti does."

"Be it so, then," Yulin murmured. "But spare the girl."

Suzong, the old crone, slumped down off her stool, putting her head in Yulin's lap. Why she should weep, he could not imagine.

Yulin patted her old head. "We kept what faith we could," he said. "It is over now."

Quinn and Anzi had said their good-byes. With recent rest, Quinn needed no sleep this ebb, and would set out immediately for Ahnenhoon.

"May God not look on you," Anzi said with fervor.

There were things Quinn wanted to say. If circumstances had been different, he would have loved her. No, that wasn't it. If he scraped aside all the things he *should* do and feel, he found that in fact he *did* love her. It wasn't fair to say. He couldn't act on it.

Prior to the audience with Yulin, at his suggestion, they had agreed to say they would marry. Yulin didn't know Johanna was alive, and more than one wife would seem natural to him, in any case. The pretense of a betrothal would give Anzi room to negotiate. In the days to come, they might never be able to prove that Titus was dead at Ahnenhoon. Or, if he escaped with Johanna, they could never say with certainty that he would not be back for Anzi. So she could use that excuse as long as she wished. Unless they found his body. But he didn't think that likely after what he had seen on Jesid's doomed vessel.

She held out her hand to him. He took it. "I could still come with you," she said.

It would all be so easy if she just went with him. Somewhere. But Ahnenhoon couldn't be put aside. It governed everything.

"I'm sorry, Anzi." More sorry than she knew.

She nodded. She would stay. It was perhaps the first time in their acquaintance that she had given in on something she had her heart set on. He was grateful.

Behind them, they heard a smattering of small rocks.

To Quinn's surprise, old Suzong came scurrying up the gully, waving her arms at them. Rushing up to them breathlessly, she rasped, "Run, run." Then, having spent her energy on the race from the camp, she sat down on a rock. "Go," she urged. "The big man comes."

"What is it, Lady Suzong?" Quinn asked.

She waved her hands at him. "The giant comes from your own daughter, bearing word of the chain as a disaster for our world. With a command to kill you. He is lying. It cannot be. So go, go, both of you."

"But Yulin   ," Quinn protested.

Wildly, she interrupted. "Has chosen against you. Run."

He looked down the gully in the direction she had come. Still empty. But she need say no more.

Quinn and Anzi ran.

The camp crackled to life, with shouts and sounds of running and beku bleating in protest at the commotion. Hu Zha stumbled from his cot and grabbed his boots. He had been sleeping soundly after exhausting himself several ebbs trying to play the proper spy, listening at Yulin's tent. Now he scrambled to reach the tent flap to find out what had happened.

A great bulk blocked the way as a figure threw open the tent flap and closed it again.

"What . . . ?" Hu Zha growled. The stranger was enormous, with a misshapen head and beefy arms ending in fists like beku's hooves.

"You are Chiron's," the giant said.

Hu Zha sputtered into silence at the mention of the lady's name. How did this ugly stranger know of his duties to Lady Chiron? "I am a cook, no more."

"My mount says otherwise."

"Your mount?" Hu Zha wondered if the man were a lunatic, thinking his beku could talk.

The giant strode forward and grabbed him by the neck, squeezing. "Do you serve Chiron? Answer me. Does she wish to have Titus Quinn?" The stranglehold tightened.

"Yes," rasped Hu Zha, sinking to his knees as strength left his legs.

"I do not kill easily," he heard the monster say, not loosening his grip. "But Chiron may not have him."

As the man's hand tightened around his neck, Hu Zha had a split second to understand that he was going to die. The last thing he felt was a profound surprise that his end could be at the hands of such a beast. A jerk on his head, and Hu Zha's thoughts settled like dust.

Mo Ti snapped his neck. He looked down unhappily on the courtier, having little stomach for killing, even this Hu Zha, a miserable courtier from the Tarig queen. But it was necessary. Chiron might kill Quinn, but on the other hand, she might not. The Tarig lady, as all sentients knew, had taken the man of the Rose as a favored plaything. She might wish to do so again, and then the man would survive to torment Sydney without end. That would not be.

Mo Ti checked the vicinity of the tent for observers, and finding none, slipped from Hu Zha's tent.

Making a stop at Distanir's billeting, he quickly checked the leg wound. It was clean, but the tendons were badly damaged, and Distanir now lay on the ground, attended by a groomer of beku, who had supplied fresh water, but kept well away from Distanir's horns.

"Leave us," Mo Ti snapped at him.

When they were alone, Mo Ti knelt by Distanir's side. "I must leave you for a few days, my friend."

You must leave me, Distanir agreed in tones so final that Mo Ti lowered his head.

"You can heal. Stay here and heal."

Yes, heal, but never run again.

Mo Ti caught the picture of Distanir isolated in camp while others rode the steppe, a vision that came to him with a heavy mood of despair. Distanir did not wish a life without good, strong legs. In the next pulse of thought, Distanir showed him how Mo Ti, in loyalty to Distanir, would take no new mount, making both their lives darker.

Distanir's large eyes seemed as deep as a water well. *Release me, my rider. I have a tundra to roam in lands far from here. I will wait for you there.*

Mo Ti looked up at the bright, gone gray-blue in this Deep Ebb, with purple stitching in the folds of light. "Best mount. My heart," Mo Ti whispered. His vision blurred. He pushed this duty away, but it came back. Pushed it away once more.

Distanir's shadow voice came to him again: *My rider forever. I am ready.*

Mo Ti prepared himself, closing his heart into a tight corral. *Now a quick stroke, and I will run with my forebears.*

Mo Ti's blade was swift, severing the main artery in Distanir's neck. The blood pulsed onto the ground, and Distanir's eyes went glazed, then dark. By his mount's side, Mo Ti felt his own eyes darken. He knelt there beside Distanir until he could bear to move once more.

Rising, Mo Ti left, tossing a full sack of coin to the camp servant. "Dig a deep grave, and pay for help to lay out my mount properly. I will hear of your diligence and return to thank you."

Then, gathering his mission to himself once more, Mo Ti ran in the direction of the distant shouts.

Yulin stood in the gully by the cave, watching Mo Ti lead a small force into the hills.

Mo Ti had asked for and received fifteen servants to help him pursue Quinn, but the retainers had begun badly, trampling the area where they hoped to pick up Quinn's tracks and causing Mo Ti a prolonged delay.

Anzi had fled with Quinn, of course. But Yulin couldn't spare a thought for her. His thoughts were on what he would say to Hu Zha, and how to explain that Quinn had come, but escaped. He would think of something.

He motioned to a servant. "Rush to the cook's tent and bring him to me."

Then Yulin turned to Suzong, who stood waiting for his judgment, not trying to hide that she had been the one to warn them. With great dignity, she sat on a rock, gathering her knees into her arms. Her mouth twitched with things she would like to say.

"Say nothing," he warned her. They faced off, as Yulin's followers watched them askance. "Go back to camp," he told them, waving them all away. "Go back, I say."

When they had left, he slumped into a cross-legged position on the ground, facing Suzong.

"You chose against me," Yulin murmured.

"Yes, this one time."

He sighed. The sky held a glow of silver that presaged Early Day. The days would come and go, astonishing in their normalcy, but Suzong would not be at his side.

"How will you die?" he asked finally.

"Poison. Before Hu Zha denounces me to the strutting queen."

Yulin would never let her die like her mother had died. If she wished poison, so be it.

The day had begun so ordinary, and then Titus Quinn was among them, and the news that the world would not last, and lastly, most terribly, that his wife must die.

Yulin felt strangely empty. All his schemes and fears had wound down to this simple moment, sitting on the hard ground, looking into his wife's face.

"We had a glorious run," he said.

She clapped. "The saying for my grave flag. May I?"

Yulin nodded. "And I shall have the same."

"No, husband—"

He put up his hand. "I will decide, wife, whether to go on without you. Keep silent on that, but allow me your last minutes free of disorder."

Suzong put her hands on her bony knees, and looked around in satisfaction. "Remember the day we met? The day I arrived and I was twenty thousand days older than you'd been told?"

He felt a half smile slide into his cheek. "You wore a red gown. It swept the tally of days from your face. And then you spoke, and I came under your spell. After you, I could never stand my young wives."

"Nice girls. You should have given them babies."

"I did."

"But babies you could have cared for."

He looked into her face, familiar and dear. "I cared for you."

"Yes, my love, you did. To my everlasting delight." She slid down to her knees in front of him, holding out her hands.

He took them.

A messenger appeared in the gully, stopping respectfully, seeing the master and his lady sitting on the dirt. Noting him, Yulin beckoned.

Approaching, the messenger blurted, "Master, the cook Hu Zha is dead."

Startled, Yulin stared at him. "Dead?"

"Yes, master. We found him in his tent."

Yulin swung his glance over to Suzong. She had closed her eyes as though she would collapse.

"How killed and by whom?"

"We do not yet know, Master."

Yulin dismissed him. If Hu Zha was dead, then Chiron would not descend, not immediately. And Chiron would not know of Suzong's betrayal. There was time to escape, once again.

A surge of energy propelled Yulin to his feet. He looked down sternly at Suzong. "An apology, wife."

"I humbly beg your pardon, a thousand times. But you must admit that Titus Quinn is still our best chance—"

He held up his hand. "Just the apology."

She made obeisance on the ground, head on the dirt.

He took in a great breath of Twilight Ebb air and then reached down to take her elbow and help her stand. "Now, instead of poison . . . a glass of wine?"

"So early . . . ," Suzong tittered. "But perhaps a small glass."

They hobbled up the gully together, dazed and renewed. They would be on the run once more. But first, they would have wine.

CHAPTER THIRTY-EIGHT

To achieve my blessing, do not deprive me of a glorious death.
—Hoptat, seer of the Miserable God

QUINN AND ANZI SET A BRUTAL PACE, knowing that Yulin's guards couldn't be far behind them. Included in this pack was the man whom Sydney had sent to kill him. Sent to kill him. And he knew why: because Helice had found his daughter and told her about the weapon. Helice had gone to the Inyx military camp and then to their sway. That she was poisoning Sydney against him, he had no doubt. He'd give a lot to know what her larger plans were. Being Helice, she would have large plans.

Anzi crested a hill, swiftly taking her bearings. She knew this particular area only from reports of Yulin's scouts. She hoped to follow a minor canyon down primacy, but so far the canyon was hidden by the endless pattern of basin and ridge, basin and ridge.

The Repel was still a full day away, as Yulin had estimated, back when the man had found it convenient to help Quinn. Just an hour ago, but all had changed now. They crested a saddle and slid recklessly down the other side, with Quinn keeping the pack, and the Going Over blade in its sheath at his waist. Anzi, too, was armed, since Suzong had urged her own knife on her niece as a parting gift. Their only advantage would be to meet Yulin's men at the top of a ridge, keeping their attackers below them.

The cirque chafed on Quinn's ankle with each step. He resisted the urge to bend down and touch it, to see if, as it seemed, the metal sleeve was losing its frigid coldness. Two days of stability remained in the thing, three at the outside. Quinn tried not to think how the first leaks would feel. With any luck, by then he'd be at the foot of the great engine. Then let all hell break loose. It was what he had come for. It was what the Rose counted on, what Caitlin Quinn counted on—if she could have known his task—and what Emily and Mateo must have to live their lives in peace. To live their lives at all. By God, Yulin's soldiers weren't going to stop him now.

Anzi pointed down a ravine. "This way."

His instinct was to head straight to Ahnenhoon, a direction he thought he might gauge by the storm wall in the distance, but Anzi seemed certain of herself. He began to wonder if they should stand and fight. If he could get the giant near the edge of the canyon that Anzi had described, he might have a chance to maneuver him over the edge. Quinn was still weak from the poisoning. He needed an advantage.

"How far is the canyon, Anzi?"

"Not far." But he saw her lips moving in what he took for a prayer.

Mo Ti looked down in disgust as another of Yulin's servants pulled off a boot and dumped out a rock.

"Soft," Mo Ti muttered.

"You try running up hillsides in such shoes as this," the youngster snarled.

Out of shape, clumsy in his gait, and already hungry, the fellow wasn't much worse than the fourteen others Yulin had sent as a fighting force. They weren't soldiers, but courtiers, more accustomed to long parties than long treks. And this trek had just begun. Mo Ti knew this terrain around Ahnenhoon: gullies giving way to canyons gouged from the plains by the quaking storm walls. He feared that if he got much ahead of these idlers, they would never press on. On the other hand, despite his groin injury, Mo Ti had the stamina to double his pace.

He summoned the most able-bodied man and pinned him with his best glare. "Mo Ti will go ahead. See that you bring these men along in good order and without slacking. If not, our prey will report your camp and your master. You know the penalty for treason?"

The man did. He kicked the seated youth, and soon the group was slogging up and down the hillocks in better order.

Mo Ti swiftly left them behind. The bright waxed into Prime of Day, a dazzling blanket across the vault of the sky, like the plowed ground of heaven. By its harsh light, Mo Ti saw that the tracks of his quarry pointed directly to Ahnenhoon. He trod in their groove. By Heart of Day, however, he knew that Yulin's men, if they caught up at all, would never arrive in time for the coming confrontation. He would have to kill Titus Quinn without assistance. His wound still bled, though cinched close with a band of cloth. Even so, Mo Ti could overcome the two he pursued. They hadn't slept for days, whereas he had caught fistfuls of sleep riding Distanir on their way into Yulin's camp.

Distanir. The loss scared him. But it didn't slow his steps.

Quinn squinted into the distance, seeing a man the size of a bear lumber over a ridge. Their perch afforded them a wider view than before, one that showed them the giant was still hunting them. Although the big man was alone and limping badly, he was close: six hillocks away, and giving no signs of needing rest.

From your own daughter, Suzong had said. *Sent to kill you.* Over the last few days he had allowed himself to think that Sydney would soften toward him after his messages. But instead, she now thought of her father as someone who would commit genocide.

Leaving these thoughts to smolder, he concentrated on their predicament. The Inyx mount wasn't with Sydney's assassin; perhaps the mount's wound prevented him from undertaking the chase. However, even without the mount, and despite his wound, the man lumbered relentlessly after them.

At Quinn's side, Anzi said, "If he comes, leave me behind. He's wounded. I can delay him. Let me do this, Titus."

He looked at her, tracing her features, seeing her anew. Could he let her? What was one person's life worth now? But *this* person's life . . . *No, don't ask me, Miserable God.* He didn't answer her, and Anzi let it lie for now.

They crept back into the next gully and rushed on.

Anzi had been looking for landmarks, and now she found one. "This way," she said, pointing upslope. They clambered to a saddle of rock between two outcroppings.

"There. The fissures begin." Below them, a broad valley extended, cleft by a dark line. "We should go around, or we'll be trapped against the canyon edge."

She led the way. But by now they were both stumbling, and gave up the effort to move quietly.

Quinn wasn't thinking clearly. He should turn and wait for the assassin. Fight him now, before he grew weaker.

"Anzi," he said. "The sequence on the chain. You should know it. How to take it off me. How to activate it."

"Yes, teach me."

He did, as they loped along. They were talking about dying.

Nearby the fissure came into view. Beginning as a narrow crack, it widened to their right into the canyon proper. Seven or eight hundred feet to the bottom, Quinn guessed. A rock bridge crossed it. They could cross and defend the bridge easily against all comers. He pointed to it, but Anzi shook her head.

"Too fragile. No, we must go the long way." She pulled him onward.

He drilled her on the sequence of four, five, one to remove the chain and one, five, four to activate, but it was useless. She would never get into Ahnenhoon without him.

Anzi stumbled, going down to her knees. She clutched her ankle.

He knelt beside her, but she pushed him furiously away.

"Let me look at it," he said.

She shook her head, wincing.

"How bad is it?"

She groaned. "Bad enough. It'll slow me down." She looked back in the direction of their pursuer. "Go, get out of here, Titus." Seeing his expression, she said, "I'll get back to Suzong. She'll help me. Just go."

He couldn't carry her. Ahnenhoon waited. The giant pursued.

Still, he lifted her up and carried her a few steps to a place behind a cloven boulder the size of a beku. "Anzi . . . ," he said.

She shook her head. "Go. Don't say anything. Don't say farewell. For luck." She smiled and pushed him away.

He backed up. "My heart is broken," he said.

"It always was." She made pushing gestures and finally drove him into a desperate run. He ran along the canyon edge, keeping to the most open area, hoping to draw attention. He told himself that Anzi would make it back to camp. He took comfort in the thought even while knowing it was wildly improbable.

Mo Ti heard voices. He stopped to listen. Ahead of him, a woman's voice, proof that he had at last caught up to his quarry. They were nearby, but where? Closing his eyes, he turned slowly, listening. There.

He hurried down the cleft between the ridges and came out on a flattened shelf of land that abutted the storm canyon. There, on the rock arch spanning the end of the great fissure, he spied them trying to cross. He loped forward. No, it was the woman, alone. He drew his knife, watching for Quinn.

Anzi stood in the center of the rock arch, waiting. Every thought left her like a flock of startled birds. There was nothing but fright, sickening fright, of the drop beneath her feet. Her ankle didn't hurt a bit. Even if she had broken it instead of pretending an injury, she would have felt nothing but terror.

The giant strode onto the slab, walking toward her, sheathing his knife. He would just push her.

The arch was cracked in the middle. She stood on the crack.

The moment the giant left the buttressed sides of the rock bridge and entered the middle, the bridge gave way. It collapsed a section at a time, beginning under the man's huge weight, and falling toward Anzi, who just had time to scramble to a portion that held to the far side of the crevasse.

Anzi stood on solid ground, watching as he crashed onto a slope below, bringing down a cascade of rubble in a cloud of dust. The man lay dead, a boulder among the stones. She slumped to the ground, kneeling. When she finally looked up, Titus was standing on the other side of the crevasse. She was glad she couldn't read his expression.

She motioned that he should follow his side of the canyon and meet her at its head. She thought she could make it that far. But all the strength was seeping out of her body. She walked for only a few increments when she went to her knees in exhaustion. Not another step. Head on knees, she kept seeing the rock bridge sink and fall.

After an indeterminate amount of time, she saw Titus approach.

He dropped the pack at her feet. Crouching beside her, he offered her the flask of water, and she drank.

"I suppose I can't trust you anymore."

"No. It would be foolish."

"You planned this from the moment we left Yulin."

"For the Rose."

He sat down next to her and put his arm around her. "We'll sleep for an hour."

"*You* sleep," she said.

He pulled her head onto his shoulder, and against her will, Anzi lost consciousness.

CHAPTER THIRTY-NINE

The knowledge of Heaven is obtained by offerings to the Miserable God; the laws of the universe can be verified by mathematical calculation; but the dispositions of the enemy are ascertainable through spies, and spies alone.

—from Tun Mu's *Annals of War*

T HE SUN ROSE ON SCHEDULE, piercing the deeps of Johanna's forest with excellent lateral light shafts. It was all lovely, convincing, and false. She rose from her pallet, knowing that Early Day had come to the Entire and she could be properly abroad, appearing to engage in the petty concerns of her life, such as painting on canvases, maintaining the forest illusion, and tending to silk spiders. In reality, though she hadn't slept, she was renewed. The new lord had come to her side last night whispering in her ear, breathing life into her again. Breathing life into the Earth. The secret of access to the engine was now revealed. It could be brought down. Soon this forest, poor copy of Earth that it was, would buckle and fold. Let it all buckle and fold, she told herself.

She could bring the chain to the engine herself. She had said so to Lord Oventroe. But no, his answer came. In the aftermath—and presumably at least for the Tarig there *would* be an aftermath—her possession of such technology would throw suspicion on Lord Oventroe. His cousins would ask, Where could such destructive capability have originated? No, it must appear to come from the Rose; from Titus. Very well. So long as it accomplished the deed.

After accepting a light meal from SuMing, who joined her on the grass hillside, Johanna washed in a stream and set out for the battlements of the centrum. SuMing caught her mistress's somber mood, and didn't converse.

Once on the high ramparts, Johanna scanned the cascade of roofs of the great watch, and beyond, the fifth domain, the terminus. Hazy in the distance, the skies over Ahnenhoon were dotted with black ovoids, the war bulbs of the Paion. She couldn't care about their mystery: where they came from, or why they came. One thing was clear, and that was that the Paion were at war with the Tarig. And *she* was at war with the Tarig. Since Lord Oventroe's visit, she could be sure she was in this dark realm for a reason. It conferred immeasurable peace to think so.

"Shall I bring oba, mistress?" SuMing was nervous, wondering at Johanna's mood.

"Yes, thank you." They would linger here, drinking oba, chatting. Yes, it would look habitual, nothing out of the ordinary.

When SuMing bore the tray with an oba service, they drew chairs together and sat quietly for a time.

"Is it today?" SuMing asked. "Will he come today?"

The question startled Johanna. Had she betrayed her excitement so easily?

"I will wait to see, SuMing. Perhaps."

After an interval of silence, SuMing ventured, "If he does, and if we find ourselves under suspicion, the lords will never take me. Do not fear that I will betray you."

Johanna narrowed her gaze, surmising what SuMing intended. "Do not, SuMing. Death comes at its own time." She was a hypocrite; not long before she had been considering her own suicide. But she hoped that the more innocent SuMing wouldn't make such a choice.

"I will not die by the garrote, mistress. I have decided."

Johanna kept her gaze on the place that Lord Oventroe had told her would signal Titus Quinn's entrance into the terminus. "Don't be afraid, SuMing. It may not come to that. And if it does, God will take you to join Him."

SuMing made a warding gesture, not liking reference to the Woeful God.

Poor girl, Johanna thought, to live in such a place, where God bore only misery. "I have told you there is another god, SuMing."

"Yes, mistress. But how else explain where misery comes from if not from the dark god?"

It comes from the Tarig, Johanna thought. "Humans would say Satan."

"Two gods, then?"

"No, one."

"Then why does the god not get rid of such a being who hates him?"

"Satan does not hate God, SuMing. He hates people."

"Ah." SuMing mulled this thought.

They left these matters of philosophy unanswered, sitting in companionable silence. Early Day brightened into Prime of Day as Johanna waited for Titus, and SuMing waited for Johanna to tell her what came next.

Quinn and Anzi lay on their stomachs, surveying a dark-shouldered plain.

Ahnenhoon. Even the name struck a note of dread. Before them, in the far distance, the antlike formations of the armies who contended here. On the far right, the Repel, massive even miles away.

He had arrived. Quinn had come across two universes to defy these armies and this fortress.

It seemed odd at that moment to rummage in their pack for food, but that is what he and Anzi did. The few hours' sleep had restored them and their appetites, even for a few bricks of dried meat.

They had emerged at last from canyon country, breaching the last hillock before going to their bellies to observe the Great Reach. Now, in the vaulting shadow of the Nigh ward storm wall and the anti-Nigh-ward storm wall conjoined, the two of them took what meal they could, lying flat, eyes drawn to the immense vista before them.

On the far right of the vista, on the anti-Nigh-ward side, massed the great bulk of the Repel. Before the fortress, the battle plains stretched far away to the converging storm walls, its grasses lending it a lavender hue, and the enemies contending there giving it an even broader aspect than an empty one might have had.

They watched as the collective armies of the sways brought fire to bear on the dirigibles, and in the far distance, advanced on a ground incursion of what looked like black beetles.

The thought came to Quinn that this region should be more rumpled than any other in the Entire. Quinn had asked about this flatness before, in hearing the battleground described as plains. He wondered how such a basin could remain, subject as it was to the forces of the storm walls on two sides. He had been told that the shock waves of each side cancelled themselves out, leaving the plain in a state of perpetual calm. How, then, could the vast structure of the Repel endure so close to the wall? But that, of course, was Tarig doing. Quinn was starting to think like an inhabitant of the Entire. What the lords wished, they would do. Someday humans would learn their technologies. But he doubted that the Tarig would share willingly.

The noise of battle didn't come this far. They watched the contesting forces mill in eerie silence. Quinn pulled his attention to the enormous black complex squatting massively on the land, its central keep a dark smear far away. That was the end point of his journey. Now that he was so close, he longed to enter the place and deliver his chain; the drive was almost as strong just to have the thing removed from his body.

He stood, and Anzi hefted her pack.

This was the ebb of the fourth day. Oventroe couldn't predict exactly how long the cirque could contain its load. One day left, or two. He wouldn't assume he had two days. If one day, he hoped it would be enough time to get into the Repel.

It was time to go.

Cixi slowly lowered herself onto the cold steps of the tower. At the moment she didn't trust her legs to support her. Placing her hands on her knees to keep from shaking, she closed her eyes against the glare shedding from the tower walls. The fiends could bear no darkness, so even near the top of Ghinamid's stone tower, one could find no shadows, no calm.

She stared at the alcove where the message had been waiting for her these several days.

Faithful Mo Ti had sent a short message, each phrase bearing an awful weight.

A woman of the Rose now in the sway. Warns of a plague of matter that will dissolve the Entire. Mistress orders me to Ahnenhoon to kill her father, take the chain he wears that bears the weapon.

Cixi stared ahead, unseeing. So many questions. What woman of the Rose? How could she arrive? Why does she warn us?

But these questions paled before the awful warning: *A plague of matter that will dissolve the Entire.* These phrases looped through her mind as she sat on the stairs, clutching her knees. With such an inconceivable threat, what could be done? How could Mo Ti, after all only a single man, find and destroy Titus Quinn? Think, you old dragon, think. As she collected her scattered concentration, she reminded herself that Mo Ti wasn't alone. Lady Chiron also searched for Titus Quinn.

But the chain, the chain. The man carried a dreadful chain. Rivulets of acid trickled into Cixi's stomach. If Chiron captured Quinn, he might still have time to set the plague free. The Rose had quickly moved to the offensive, yes. Cixi was impressed. Although the Rose capabilities were backward, the people of the dark compensated with remarkable ruthlessness. No, Mo Ti wasn't the way to handle this. Nor was the Lady Chiron.

She rose from her position. How long had she been sitting here while her functionaries waited outside the tower, expecting her to arrive at the summit and look at the view, always her excuse for coming to Ghinamid's Tower? No time for pretenses. Down the stairs Cixi rushed, her short legs wobbling with the strain, her mind framing and reframing her plans. *By my grave flag*, she thought, *Chiron must not be the only one to know where Titus Quinn has gone.*

A hundred steps and still Cixi descended. A stark resolve gripped her heart. She would sever ties with the Lady Chiron. She should have done so days ago, when Chiron first left the Ascendancy, leaving Cixi alone with Lord Nehoov. He was the only one of the Five still in residence, not counting the Sleeping Lord. Nehoov must use every resource to find Titus Quinn. She had little doubt that he would.

She cursed herself for allowing Chiron to command her. Was it already too late? Was Quinn, even at this moment, loosing his pestilence on the world?

Her mind jumped from one question to the next: How can a small chain contain a plague? Why would a woman of the Rose work against the Rose? Answers would come, in time. For one hundred thousand days at the dragon court, Cixi had juggled fragments of information. She had learned long ago that waiting for complete intelligence brought paralysis.

She could only admit a certain portion of the truth to Nehoov, of course. She must say only why Chiron knew Titus was likely to attack Ahnenhoon if and when he came. She must at all costs hide the fact that she knew about the weapon he brought—for that brought the question of why she was in touch with Sydney, and how she was in touch, using the means at Ghinamid's Tower. No one beside the Tarig could communicate at bright speeds. Or so they thought. Thus, her plan must be to tell some but not all of the story, and summon her wits to keep all her lies in mind.

Even so, Lord Nehoov might kill her. Why had she allowed herself to be persuaded by Chiron to withhold the information that Quinn had discovered the great engine's purpose? I am an old fool, she chided herself.

Cixi arrived at the bottom of the tower stairs and threw open the door on her surprised attendants. Composing her face, she muttered at them, "The stairs are too steep today. I go to the palatine hill to confer with Lord Nehoov. Beg of him an immediate audience."

A Hirrin legate rushed off in the direction of the hill. Cixi turned to her remaining retinue—a Jout consul and two Chalin stewards. She brought them along as she hurried to Lord Nehoov's mansion. She might need them to relay orders. Or to witness her death. If the latter, then let the Magisterium sing of her glorious role in saving the All.

Arriving at the outer vestibule of Nehoov's audience chamber, Cixi conferred with the gatekeeper, who consulted an activated scroll and found that the lord permitted the entry. Opening the door, the legate gestured her through. Fear shed from her as she entered the chamber, her mind uncluttered by doubt. She did indulge a fleeting hope that, should Nehoov take offense, he wouldn't employ the garrote. Fling me from the city's edge, she prayed. Put *that* spectacle in the legend.

Shards of glass and ceramics lay around the lord as he paused in his rampage. It had been a most disgraceful display of temper. Unprecedented. Cixi found herself kneeling in front of him, although being half the fiend's height, she could hardly be more inferior.

Then Lord Nehoov began roaming his chamber again, looking for something else to break, but he had quite finished the matter in the first interval after hearing of Chiron's schemes.

At last Nehoov took a seat, his visage composed. His profoundly bass voice came to her in a whisper: "Cixi of Chendu wielding." He wasn't looking at her, but rather up at the ceiling, as though imploring the Miserable God for help. He would be even more alarmed if he realized the powers that Titus Quinn's weapon possessed.

He turned to face her. "Why would the bright lady confide in you, but not in us, hnn?"

"I know not, Lord. I simply obeyed."

"Is it obedient to withhold from us?"

"Obedient to the lady, but not to the lord. Until the bright burns out, I will feel that shame."

He remained silent for a time, not giving permission for Cixi to rise, or to speak. At last he said, "We will make a display of our displeasure."

Her chest cinched tighter around her heart. "Radiant Lord, I have served you for one hundred thousand days—"

"You have served yourself well indeed," he conceded, fixing her with that baleful stare.

Her mind had gone numb. In her vision she saw Sydney, so young and fierce, the girl she hadn't seen for so long. Oh, to say good-bye, to set eyes on her one more time. She had hoped to preside over her investiture; had hoped to be present when Sydney took on a new name: Sen Ni, her Chalin name. Go on without me, dear one, she thought.

Without being given permission, she stood.

Nehoov rose too, and in a few strides came to her side. He looked down on her. "You shall live in honor, High Prefect, for your actions this day."

She stared at him. *Live in honor*, did he say?

"Lady Chiron will unsheathe a claw or two, when she learns you abandoned her." He looked as though he enjoyed the prospect of Chiron's anger. "So you have shown courage, if belated."

"Bright Lord," she whispered.

As she took in a breath of cool air to steady herself, she heard the lord murmur, "But the steward Cho shall pay." He gestured her away. "Bring him to the lip of the city."

A small bulge in the platform formed a stage. It jutted out into the sky. Where Cho stood with the lord and the high prefect, the floor had been made transparent, so that the others could view him from the lower levels of the Magisterium. The thousands assembled there would all want to see the four-minute ride of Cho the steward.

No one had told him why today was the day of his execution, nor why they had delayed so long. He tried to compose his mind, but his thoughts skittered around like water drops in a hot pan. One of them was his grave flag saying: *Learned to live at the very last.*

He had served the lords, the land, and the Magisterium for six thousand days. Then he had met Titus Quinn in disguise at the Ascendancy, and everything had changed. He never knew why the man of the Rose had come here, but Cho believed the man was a personage of great import, that he had no venality in him. Cho believed that Titus Quinn had come to open the door between worlds, and he considered this a worthy goal.

Cho's crime had been to help Titus Quinn to find a redstone message from his wife of long ago. That message had changed everything. What could the wife have known that would cause the All to quake? Cho prayed that it was the secret of Tarig vulnerability. But even if it wasn't, he was prepared to die. I learned to live at the very last, he mused. Better than never learning at all. He had been born in the Magisterium and had occupied humble posts all his life. The Great Within held all his days, all his concerns. He had counted the chores of a steward worthy and interesting—even fine. Then he had stumbled upon personages like Titus Quinn and Ji Anzi who came from the Great Without and were driven to accomplish high things. Cho had been touched by greatness. He didn't regret this.

A gust of wind slammed into him as Lord Nehoov caused the field of the wall to evaporate. Cho faced the endless sky, seeing the glint, far below, of the Sea of Arising, its exotic matter sustaining the Ascendancy and the five rivers in one. His chest crimped at the glory of what he was now seeing for the last time. It was only justice that they kill him. He had well understood that to break any of the Three Vows was a capital crime, so he didn't feel bitter toward the lord. In fact, he rather pitied the lord for trying to keep the door of knowledge closed. Useless, now that many people knew that the man from the dark universe wasn't himself dark. He was a light, dispelling shadows. People talked of Titus Quinn that way.

Behind him Cho heard the high prefect murmuring something to Lord Nehoov, and the lord responding. He paid them no mind, instead looking down through the platform floor, seeing the assembled clerks, factors, stewards, legates, and consuls. Craning their necks to watch, they gathered— including some he recognized: GolMard the Gond, the Chalin consul Shi Zu, the clerks Fajan and Qing, and fellow stewards Haitao and Mi—each with upturned faces, each with glittering eyes and excited, pinched faces, waiting for the spectacle that came once in ten thousand days.

Lord Nehoov rested his cold hand in the small of Cho's back, making ready to push.

In the high winds, Cho could just make out the lord's rumbling voice. "It may be as you say, High Prefect."

Cixi replied, "In addition, it will cause quite a surprise among those assembled. Let them never guess at the lord's high purposes."

"Yet they may think us weak."

"Never, Bright Lord. Not when you fling Titus Quinn from this same platform. Now *that* will be a spectacle."

"Let us be content with that."

"As you will, my lord."

Nehoov's hand left Cho's back and took a grip on his shoulder, turning him around in a painful twist.

Oh, to fall *backward*. Cho tried to calm his dismay. He had mustered his courage about falling forward. . . .

Nehoov looked down at him, his black eyes gone almost white with reflection from the sea. "Bring Titus Quinn to us, Steward. Can you perform a last service?"

"Pardon, Lord?"

"Does Titus Quinn regard you as a friend?"

Cho's throat was so dry his words were glued inside it. Finally he stammered, "Friend? Oh. A short acquaintance. Only a steward, of course. No personage. Unworthy." He looked at Cixi in perplexity.

She sneered. "His wits are gone, Bright Lord. Leave him to me." She leaned in, whispering, "You will be under order of execution. That may bring the man of the Rose to us, eventually. That long, you shall live."

By the time Cho looked back at the lord, Nehoov was already striding away. Behind Cho, the field wall was knitted up, causing the wind to subside. He felt light-headed.

At his side, the high prefect made a grand gesture toward the assembled legates, commanding them back to their duties.

Cho started to shake.

Cixi cut a glance of pity at him. "You are delighted, of course. You might have had a glorious death, Steward. There is much to be said for a fine exit." She gestured him into the custody of guards. "Well, you may still have your chance."

CHAPTER FORTY

How can the Nigh be a river?
How can a city be in the sky?
How can a redstone be wise?
How can a storm be a wall?

—a child's bedtime questions

QUINN AND ANZI TOOK REFUGE behind an undulation in the plain, con-
templating the fortress bulking up before them. It didn't look possible
to enter it, but Quinn knew that the outer wall was riddled with openings.
He meant to pass through one of those holes.

Behind the fortress, the storm wall teetered like a tsunami of impossible
height. On the other side of the plains of Ahnenhoon, the Nigh-ward side
storm wall rose in a matching palisade. Between the two walls, the bright
squinted down from its narrow slice of sky, leaking a dull glow.

At a word, Anzi would go with him. But he wanted maximum flexi-
bility, with no one to hamper his movements. When he came out of the
Repel, Johanna would be with him—might be with him. She would be difficult enough to guide through the outer defenses.

"It's time, Anzi."

"Yes."

"Do I have to tie you down to make you stay?"

"I could be at your back in a fight."

He sighed. "I won't take you with me, Anzi. I'll be making sure Johanna
gets out. Three is too many." He didn't like bringing up Johanna. He saw her

close down, turn away. "Anzi," he said, taking her hands in his, "the nan . . . the fire in the chain . . . it will rush outward. Don't be here when it arrives. Please."

She pulled her hands away. "Where can I go?"

Oventroe said that forces in the storm wall would repel the tide of nan away, directing it onto the plains. If it weren't for this factor, Quinn's job would be somewhat easier. He might drop the chain anywhere close to the engine. Perhaps even outside the wall of the Repel. But it wasn't going to be so easy.

"Go to Su Bei," he urged her. "He has the correlates." If Johanna was with him, Quinn would also go to Su Bei. He couldn't think past that.

It was Last of Day when Quinn left the rumpled hills and walked out onto the plain. The bright simmered low, sinking into folds of amethyst. He didn't look back toward the ridge that hid Anzi. They would meet, if they could, at Su Bei's reach. Even to Quinn it sounded hollow.

The words he might have said to her felt like a bone stuck in his throat.

Chiron's formerly faithful servant Depta made her way through the pitted fields of the war zone. Her mind was strangely calm. She was a Hirrin with a purpose, a lofty one.

She stepped carefully, bearing the heavy instrument on her back. The tube shifted as she walked, falling first to one side and then the other. When she'd left the armory, Depta had been in a hurry. Chiron was only an interval ahead of her, and she couldn't afford to lose the trail. Normally Depta would have been a poor tracker, but Chiron's footprints were unmistakable: She wore boots with a distinctive bud on the heel, allowing deployment of a knife.

Since leaving the Ascendancy, Depta's journey had taken her from the center of the All to the ends of the primacy. She had traveled down the bright, and into the Nigh. She had toured the plains of Ahnenhoon with a general. Depta had seen a wonder or two. But her journey of the heart was more remarkable.

She knew a worthy undertaking from a false one and dared to disobey.

And more: She had become kindled by the notion that her beloved Entire wasn't in peril from a flood of Rose darklings. No, far otherwise. The Entire stood in great need of humans and other sentients of the Rose. They must come and hold converse with Chalin, Hirrin, and Jout. They must challenge and balance the power of the Tarig. Why, after all, should the Tarig reign unquestioned? They had created the Entire, and for that they earned honor. But when had honor turned to corruption? Perhaps long ago.

So, Depta reasoned, there must be converse between one world and the other. In fact, it had already begun.

Now there was only one more place to go. Depta prayed it wouldn't be too late.

Over the wide roofs of the watch and the terminus, Johanna watched the sky for the signal Lord Oventroe had devised, that of an illusion of a burning airship. When the dirigible appeared, when it was aflame, Johanna would know that her countdown had begun—that Titus had arrived in the Repel. She hadn't asked Lord Oventroe how this signal could be given. Nor would she be the only one to see it. What the generals would make of a burning ship that their soldiers hadn't attacked, Johanna couldn't guess.

Before her on a small table, SuMing had laid out a simple meal. Johanna turned to it gratefully. "My eyes hurt, SuMing. Watch the sky for me. Watch for a burning ship."

"Yes, mistress." SuMing didn't ask why. The young woman had committed to Johanna, and did her bidding. All because Johanna had once saved her life. That she was likely to die now was surely too generous a return gift. But on behalf of Earth, Johanna accepted it.

Not long ago Johanna had stood on this same spot watching for Morhab to cross the mustering grounds so that she could intercept him and give Gao the time he needed. Now both of them were dead. She had murdered one of them, but she didn't regret it. War had made her ruthless. War also had driven out all thoughts of Titus as a man she had loved. In truth, her life with Inweer had driven out thoughts of Titus long ago. She had believed she would never see her husband again, and gradually she had let him go, praying for his welfare, as she prayed for Sydney's. When at last it seemed he *would* come, she had nothing left of personal hopes. Had she forgotten how to love, or had it been stolen from her, day after bright-laden day? There had been a time in the Rose when she couldn't have imagined being as she was now, doing what she was doing. Doing any of the things she had done.

From time to time Johanna glanced at the entrances to their rooftop viewpoint, to ease her mind that Lord Inweer wasn't standing there. He had grown colder with her of late, perhaps suspicious. Now, of all times, he mustn't seek her company.

In front of the yawning structure of the terminus, a field of grasses lay over in a stiff wind. Three hundred feet of waist-high grass lay between Quinn's position and the great wall. It wouldn't matter which opening he passed through, Oventroe had said, so he decided on one closest to the line of hills through which he'd passed.

Quinn looked up at the sky, uttering in a small exhalation, *By the bright*. In the Entire, those not inclined to religion often swore by the bright, and he did so now. In the next hour, or perhaps two, he would find his way through the Repel's defenses. It might seem a nearly impossible task except for the aids that Lord Oventroe had given him, and the guides that waited for him. Odd as it seemed, in the end he had need of a Tarig to defeat the Tarig. It unsettled him.

Oventroe had no reason to lie. The chain would destroy this fortress. Repelled from the storm wall's superior power, the nan's molecular chaos would spread onto the plains in an arc. Then, overcome by phage sentinels, it would congeal, cool, and die. Let the Tarig learn that the Rose wouldn't be fuel. True, they might build another engine. On the other hand, they might wonder how strong a nan-force the Rose might bring *next time*. That was the thing to remember about the über-beings of the Entire: They lived in a glass house.

Crouching in the tall grasses, Quinn made for his chosen entry—a dark hole, rounded and gaping. There was no door; the Tarig seemed to welcome entry. In his pocket he clutched the bud that Oventroe had given him, the one that allowed infrequent movements of servants into the fortress, the one that would show the path. As he moved toward the wall, the cirque crimped against his ankle, feeling somehow heavier. The chain, so steadfastly cold to the touch, had in the last few hours been growing warm.

Left behind, Anzi had only a brief interval to make up her mind. Titus had said that he didn't want her along. But there were times when he was wrong, and this was one of them. He couldn't achieve his purpose alone, no matter how much help Lord Oventroe had given him. The lord was gone. Anzi was here. No question, then, who was most able to help.

Her feet started walking before she knew that she had come to a decision. She hurried over the ridgeline. In the distance she saw Titus, nearing the terminus wall.

Then, off to the side she saw another figure moving toward Titus. Someone very tall.

Alarmed, Anzi rushed forward, drawing her knife. She could barely make out a commotion ahead, but too distant to hear sounds of fighting. It was a Tarig. She was sure of it. Stuffing panic back into her chest, she crept forward, wishing for speed but needing stealth.

Titus, she thought. *Titus.*

Quinn saw a movement in his peripheral vision. He went to ground, but it was too late. Through the mesh of grass, Quinn saw a dark figure loping toward him.

A Tarig. Giving up his hiding place, Quinn bolted for the opening in the wall. He felt for his knife—still there. He had once killed a Tarig, but the creature had been half dead. Tearing through the field, he heard the grass crunch behind him as a part of his mind calculated his chances against the stride of a Tarig.

Soon answered. The blow came from behind, a sharp, glancing hit that sent him sprawling. He blacked out.

When he opened his eyes, a Tarig was bending over him. The net in her hair held small chunks of light. A steely hand clutched the front of his jacket, at the same time pinning him to the ground.

He knew who this was. It gave him a moment of hope, until she spoke: "We have been hunting you. Having caught you, shall we split open your chest?"

He tried to rise, but she held him flat.

Her deep voice sounded masculine. Once he'd been used to it. "We do not prefer game meats, but in this excitement, the meal might suit."

Staring into Chiron's eyes, he looked for a chance, a flicker of old affection. She was not in an affectionate mood. She jerked him into a sitting position, the strength in her arms impressive.

"I won't beg."

"You will beg, Titus-een." Her claws were fully extended.

He took note of his position. Still fifty feet from the wall. But the wall offered no advantage: She could follow him in—supposing he could make a break from her.

She noted his glance toward the wall. "There you would die. The rooms form, and you die slowly, of thirst, of terror, of the dark."

"Remember, my lady, I'm not afraid of the dark."

"Afraid of so few things. But then unable to live without that small girl you brought here. She was only a pitiful, immature being. We could have been persuaded to give her to you."

"No, Chiron. For that, I *did* beg."

She didn't argue the point. The pause lengthened. What did she want?

"We know why you came here," she said finally. "Not for the Rose wife. She lies, you must know, in the lord's bed and takes her pleasure. Therefore you come for the engine, ah?" Chiron looked up at the huge wall. "The great Lord Inweer will not be pleased to learn that the Rose wife summoned you. It will go poorly for her. We may take you to observe this."

"She only did what you would do, Chiron, if in prison in the Rose. That should count for something."

"We are not in prison in the Rose."

Winner take all. She wouldn't soften. He still had his knife. If he was quick . . . but his knife lay tucked in his jacket, and she was paying strict attention.

Chiron brought her hand up as though to caress his face. Instead, he felt an indentation down his neck, and a warm trickle into his collar. Methodical and shallow, the cut was just for play.

"Titus-een," she said, using a name she had once called him, "why did you rush from our chambers? We gave you our trust. One's standing diminished. One has been alone."

Her words took him by surprise. Chiron had always kept to herself. Aloof from the others, she had wanted his company. Eventually, he had wanted hers, as well. He hadn't thought of those times much. Initially he couldn't remember them. Later, he didn't want to remember them.

"I went a little mad," he said, to answer her, and to keep her talking. "I tried to kill Hadenth, because of what he did to my daughter. Her eyes, you remember?"

"We remember. We remember, too, the tunnel you escaped from."

No point in denying any of it. "I worked it for thousands of days. To find Sydney again, and Johanna. You stole them from me. You also offered me kindness. I thought I could forgive you. I was wrong."

Chiron watched him with rapt attention. Almost as an unconscious gesture, she cut him again, on the other side of the neck. With her claw slightly extended, she controlled the incision with delicacy.

"You will come home again," Chiron said. "The tunnel will be your home until you grow lonely." She cut a line along his hairline. Blood spilled down his cheek. She rose, gripping his jacket and pulling him up. "To Lord Inweer, then."

Something flickered in his peripheral vision. A Hirrin stood some hundred yards away.

Frowning, Chiron saw the creature too. Still keeping a grip on Quinn, she turned to face the Hirrin. "Depta, ah?"

The Hirrin didn't respond.

Chiron's voice took on a note of alarm. "Depta, do you love us?"

Beside the Hirrin was a cylindrical instrument. The creature sat on her back haunches, bringing the tubular device to the front.

Chiron leapt forward.

Out of the tube came a stream of black fire. It hit the grass to one side of Quinn, turning it to brittle ice. Chiron's great strides began closing the gap between her and the Hirrin.

Using her prehensile lip, the Hirrin fired again. Missed. And again. Smells of deformed grasses hung in a low cloud.

As Chiron approached the assailant, she jumped into the air and extended a wicked boot that struck the creature in the neck with a powerful, felling blow. But as the Hirrin sprawled, the tube coughed a point-blank volley into Chiron's face.

Chiron staggered backward, twirling in the grass, wiping at her face and chest. Whatever the black fire was, it didn't burn, but froze. It slowed her to a standstill. She stood amid the grasses as her vest and skirt disintegrated, taking hanks of skin, falling off in frozen slabs. She tottered for a moment, then collapsed.

Rushing toward her and pulling out his knife, Quinn found Chiron lying dead among the grasses, her body ravaged. Left behind were strips of muscle clinging to bone. Shards of frozen blood sparkled in the grass. He stared at the mangled body, still unsure if, even in this condition, she might rise to fight again. Quinn paused, trying to comprehend that he was still alive, and Chiron wasn't.

Turning away from Chiron's body, he walked over to the Hirrin, finding her collapsed in the grass. The Hirrin's neck was pumping out her blood in a wound that would kill her within moments.

He knelt down beside the creature. "Go in peace," he said.

The creature whispered, "Titus Quinn?"

"Yes."

She sighed raggedly. "Today I look upon a *hsien*."

"No. I'm nothing like that."

Blood trickled from the Hirrin's mouth. "Oh yes, a *hsien*," she whispered. "An immortal hero."

"No. Just a man, but I thank you."

Her eyelids fluttered, then closed. He put a hand on her long neck to let her know that someone was still with her.

She whispered something. He bent closer. Her voice was barely audible. "I didn't love her," she said. "The Tarig lady. I didn't. Love her."

It was the last thing she said. Kneeling by the Hirrin in the grass, Quinn wondered who she had been, and what had transpired between this Hirrin and the Tarig lady.

I didn't love her, either, he thought.

Then he rose and, quickly scanning for other pursuers, took what cover the grasses could provide and made for the wall of the Repel.

A burning airship appeared in the sky just beyond the fortress. SuMing saw it too, pointing.

It was a reasonable approximation of a dirigible igniting. Instead of falling from the sky, the burning craft hovered in place, its image wavering. Johanna staggered to her feet. The appearance of Lord Oventroe's signal stunned her for a moment as she watched it gradually fade from view.

The waiting was over. Johanna clasped SuMing's hands. "Take no more chances for my sake, SuMing. We come to the end, now. Thank you forever."

SuMing nodded, and Johanna hurried from the roof, starting the descent down the stairs to the next level. Halfway down, she stopped her headlong rush. Calming herself, she resumed a more deliberate pace. She thought of those who had already died for this cause. Today would give Gao's death meaning. May God have mercy on you, she prayed for him. And for Pai and Morhab, too. She thought of Titus as well, and what she might say to him. She couldn't imagine what either of them would say. It doesn't matter, she told herself. Nothing matters now, but the Rose.

Gathering her poise, she continued down the steps, emerging into a corridor at the bottom. She smoothed her blue gown around her, wiping the perspiration off her palms. Then she headed in the direction of Inweer's apartment.

Quinn's eyes hadn't yet adjusted to the murky light of the terminus. In the shadows, he squinted down at the palm of his hand, where the small device lay that Oventroe had given him. He closed his fingers around it to activate the bud as Oventroe had directed. He felt something move within the casing.

When he opened his hand, he found that a wasp had broken out of the case. It looked like a wasp. Winged and golden it sprang from his hand. If anyone saw it they would think it an insect. He followed it down a narrow corridor made of rough adobe. The empty budding case was now tucked away in Quinn's pocket, for later use. As the wasp flew, the corridor ahead of it brightened to a nearly blinding white light.

Side corridors emerged into view. Some of these the wasp chose, little wings a blur of industry. Behind Quinn, the corridor darkened. The guiding sprite carried its daylight with it, or enlivened the walls, but when it passed, the shadows returned.

The wasp set a stately pace, as though it needed time to figure out the route. Some corridors broke off at angles, and some were ramps, up or down. Quinn felt a moment of apprehension as the wasp chose one of the downward sloping ramps. No, forward, forward, Quinn urged. But he followed the wasp. *Do not follow your intuition or sense of direction*, Oventroe had said. *We have created the maze to ensnare.* Quinn was now in the midst of it, the place he had been heading since he came to the Entire. It would all play out now, but he found himself strangely free of worry. So few choices were left, and they were all simple ones. Follow the path in. Destroy the furnace that burned such precious fuel. Get out if you can.

He heard a sound behind him. Stopping, he listened for a moment while keeping his eyes on the wasp. He thought of Chiron following him. But he'd seen her dead, very dead. Silence pressed in around him, and he went on. The corridor ended in a small well from which stairs rose in three directions. The wasp chose one staircase, and Quinn followed.

As he climbed the steps, Quinn couldn't help but notice that his ankle chain pulsed at times with a fiery warmth. It was day four of the life of the chain. Was it already dissolving? He bent down to check the cirque. The carbon nitride links were fused to his skin.

Johanna stopped before Inweer's chamber door. He wouldn't be here at this phase of the bright. He *must* not be here. She put her hand on the door, and it opened to her command, as Inweer had long ago arranged. Sometimes he liked her to be here first, waiting for him. . . .

She entered the chamber, closing the door behind her. No occupant. There, just past the sleeping platform in a wall alcove, was a small metal vase that Inweer favored. At this location she could enliven the needles she brought. She hurried past the platform.

Someone was sitting in the corner.

A Tarig.

Her heart shouted, and she whipped around to stare.

Lord Inweer sat in a chair, watching her. Oh God. She went to her knees, weak with terror. When she dared look into his face, she saw that he wasn't looking directly at her, but rather over her shoulder. Johanna looked behind her, but no one was there. Turning to confront that black, quiet gaze, she saw that Inweer hadn't moved.

"My lord?" she whispered.

He didn't respond.

She stayed kneeling, looking at this specter. Was this some form of ultimate fury? Did he know why she came? "My lord," she managed to say again.

The longer she remained kneeling and watching, the more convinced she became that he couldn't move. She rose and backed up toward the alcove, keeping her eyes on Inweer. He remained immobile. The thought struck that perhaps Inweer was dead. Was this how Tarig died, stiff and vigilant?

No matter, she had work to do. Hands shaking, she removed the vase—heavy enough to contain something. Setting it on the floor, she removed the five needles from her pocket, sliding them out of their sleeves, each one as long as her ring finger. She carefully stuck them into the ledge of the alcove.

An instant later she had removed the needles and replaced the urn.

Tucking the needles into a pocket of her gown, she walked swiftly across the chamber. Lord Inweer hadn't moved, but she felt that at any moment he would spring up. She fled from the room.

Anzi followed the light. She crept carefully, her footfalls light as silk.

When she'd first entered the fortress, she had a moment's panic that she had arrived too late to follow Titus. But a brilliant radiance burned ahead of her, and once she saw Titus in the middle of it. She didn't know how he created the light, but she knew that light guided him through this tangle of halls. She held back as much as she dared. But not too far back.

Everyone had heard the stories of how Paion died who entered here. Riding on their four-limbed simulacra, sometimes they would venture in, or so the stories said, armed with an algorithm as a key to the endlessly repeating maze. Steering their simulacra down the byways, they would soon lose confidence in their calculations. Far into the path, disappointment decayed into alarm, and then to terror. There would be one, innocuous room.

When they turned to leave, there would be no door.

At times she thought she heard footsteps behind her. But those were likely the echoes of Titus, in front.

On the roof of the centrum, SuMing sat in a chair watching the domains of the fortress, expecting to see something terrible, but all was quiet. She had nothing to do but wait. Her mistress had gone to accomplish some ultimate task. SuMing expected that whatever it was, her servant would share the blame.

She looked out over the roofs of the Repel to the battle plains and the great storm wall. All these sights held mysteries: how the storm walls held; why the Paion attacked; what the Engine of Ahnenhoon was for. SuMing had never deeply pondered these mysteries, and now there wouldn't likely be time. Her hand strayed into a slit in her gown from time to time to reassure herself that the small poison stone was still there.

She remembered her decision, a thousand days ago, to take up service at Ahnenhoon. Her mother had grieved that she wouldn't see her again, but SuMing thought it a fair trade: her family for the grandeur of Ahnenhoon, with the great lord, one of the Five. Perhaps she would even see a battle with the Paion. She smiled at that long-ago innocence. Some of her service had indeed been grand. Mistress Johanna had been grand, of that she was sure. . . .

She spotted a shape against the bright. Standing up, she watched a speck approach from far up primacy, racing along the bright.

In a short while, it became clear: a brightship was coming.

SuMing would have been surprised to learn that in that moment she repeated a gesture she had seen Johanna use: She crossed herself.

Johanna made her way across the gathering yard adjacent to the centrum. Hindering her stride were the extra garments pinned under her gown. Once across the sere, Titus would need a disguise. In their favor was the fact that the fortress, even the watch, was sparsely garrisoned. The Tarig didn't think it would come to a battle within the fortress, and they might be right about a clash of forces. But a lone human could wage battle. They'd find that out soon enough.

Once inside the watch, she moved down the halls, wide enough to permit troop movement, devoid of cloaking shadows. Everything the Tarig built sparkled with light, a quality she had grown to despise. She strode purposefully toward her destination: the door where she had sent Morhab to his death. Encountering two small groups of soldiers, she nodded at them as she passed, walking as regally as she knew how. The lord didn't forbid her to come to the watch. It would be remarked upon that Johanna had come here, but by then it would be too late.

Titus, wait for me. She clutched the needles in her hand: one for the sere, three for the engine. Lord Oventroe had drilled her well. The lord was gone now, departed in a brightship, so that he could be far from the scene when Ahnenhoon fell.

Whatever the outcome, Johanna dreaded having to face Inweer. In her imagination, she heard him saying, *We gave you your forest and days and nights. Was it not enough?* Her swift answer: *No, my love, it wasn't. I wanted the real thing.*

She came to the door in the wall of the great watch. In a nearby room she took up her post at the window, the same one through which she had projected her image onto the sere the day that Morhab and Pai died. Here she watched for Titus.

From down the corridor came voices. She heard the four-footed clangor of Hirrin moving by, chattering. Their voices moved off.

Johanna hoisted her gown and unpinned the extra garments, laying the clothes out on the floor. Then, hurrying to the window, she identified the door where Lord Oventroe predicted Titus would emerge from the terminus on the other side of the sere.

An hour passed. She worried that soldiers might spy the signal of the burning dirigible and determine it to be false. It might be enough to put the fortress on alert. Then too, Johanna had been seen entering the watch alone; when she left in company with someone, note might be taken, and an officer informed. Worst of all, Inweer might wake up, and remember that she had been in his room. Leaning into the window, she watched for Titus with feral intensity.

Quinn stood before the door to the sere, the bud case in his open hand, an act that brought the wasp to him. It crawled inside the chrysalis. When the case formed around the wasp once more, he squeezed it, activating a diffraction of light that would confuse his image to any watchers. A blurring light curled around him, conferring, he hoped, a measure of invisibility. With that, he stepped outside the door.

Something caught Johanna's attention on the other side of the sere. It was a blur, like light viewed through a smeared lens. This blur stood in a doorway across the sere, pausing. At this particular door, it must be Titus. He knew to wait for her signal.

Johanna had been holding one needle in her sweating hand, and now, when she pricked the stone with it, it dropped from her slippery fingers. She fell to her knees searching frantically. She patted the floor as she bent close to find the thin spine of metal. With another sweep of her gaze she found it. Standing once more and clutching the needle, she inserted it in the window ledge. Twisting the pin to achieve the proper angle, she let the needle guide her by its warmth. She found that angle. The needle contained instructions to suppress certain defenses, among them, the response of the sere to pressure of any kind. Once satisfied that the needle was placed correctly, she rushed from the room, moving to the great door leading outside.

She opened it enough to show herself to the figure who stood on the other side of the sere. Then, she touched one foot onto the blackened soil in front her. Then both feet, doubting, with sudden misgivings, the strength of one needle against the burning ground. But it lay quiet and cold. The sere was disarmed.

Across the yard, Quinn saw her. She raised an arm, signaling him. Johanna. It hit him hard to see her, even at this distance, a small figure in blue, his wife. She beckoned him.

Quinn stepped onto the expanse of the sere. He walked slowly toward the watch, a curving wall of seemingly limitless span. The garrison billeted behind this wall, keeping watch for a larger enemy. Deep-set cavities in the wall gave defenders a clear view of the sere; in some of these embrasures, he saw faces of soldiers.

Oventroe had told him that Johanna would disable the sere, and so she had. But she couldn't disable the garrison. Behind him, he left faint footprints in the carbonized ground. With no wind today to blur them, his path was an arrow pointing straight at him. He passed a great burned area of the yard. Quinn wondered what unlucky traveler had been caught unawares. He neared the other side, where Johanna waited.

She opened the door a little wider as he approached. He slipped through, joining her in the cool of the watch. Once inside, he released his grip on the bud in his pocket, clearing the blur that had surrounded him.

She stood in front of him, dressed in a blue gown, looking no older, despite the time that had passed for her. "Johanna," he whispered.

She backed up. "You aren't Titus," she spat. "Who are you?"

"It's me, Johanna."

"No!" She glanced down the hall, ready to bolt.

"My features," he said. "Altered, Johanna. Listen to my voice. It's me."

She calmed somewhat, then. Still eyeing him, she nodded to one side. "Over here." She led him to a small room nearby, then turned to him. Her face, lit from the bright that fell through the window, retained its dark beauty. She was still nervous. "Prove that you're Titus."

"I don't know how."

"Figure it out." She spun away. "God, how could you come to me with the wrong face! I need to trust you, and now I can't."

"Won't."

They faced off. Her eyes slashed a look at him, familiar and fierce. "That sounds like you. You'll take no blame. Not the fine Titus I knew."

Her words wounded. This wasn't how he ever would have met her—with recriminations.

She jerked her head to listen to something, and moved swiftly to the chamber door. Looking out into the corridor, she satisfied herself there was nothing amiss. Then she turned back.

He was about to speak when she said, "Sydney . . . you've seen her? Found her?"

She was accepting him. But the moment when he could have embraced her had passed. He shook his head. "No. The Inyx have her. Still." There was so much to say, but they had little time, and every moment increased their danger. He felt the chain firing a welt into his ankle.

Still, there were things he had to say. "I tried to find you, Johanna. All these years. God knows I tried. And Sydney." He fell silent, hearing how pathetic that sounded.

She came closer. "Don't blame yourself. We were in hell. Hell is a strong place."

He reached out for her, and she came to him. He held her for a while, overcome. He would take her out of hell. She still wore her wedding ring, he had noticed. Did she think them still married? If she did, then they would be.

At last she pushed away, taking his hands in hers. She looked down, turning his hands over and examining them, as though trying to find the old Titus. "Have you remarried, Titus?"

"No."

"I've moved on," she said with perfect equanimity. "Past our old life. I had to."

Each word stung, though he had expected them. "Come home with me, Johanna." She deserved to be asked. He had promised himself he would say it. "Remember what we had?" For these last few minutes he had been remembering.

She shook her head. "No, Titus. I don't remember. I'm sorry." She turned away, looking out the window, checking for pursuers, then turned back to him, her voice steady. "The bright does that. It bleaches your mind of things. I'm sorry. I couldn't wait for you. Too long, my sweet." She gestured toward some garments that lay on the floor. "Now put these things on; we have work to do."

He didn't budge. "You could come home," he said. "Away from hell, if that's what this is. I won't hold you to anything. But I'll bring you home."

Her smile was tender. "Do you expect to survive what we're going to do?" When he didn't answer, she said, "Always optimistic, my Titus." She helped him undress, to don the clothes of a man she referred to as her overseer of forest grounds.

In the midst of changing clothes, Quinn inspected the chain, pushing at it. Without doubt, it had grown into his skin.

"Is that what you brought?" Johanna asked, kneeling down to take a closer look.

"I'll have to rip it off. It's stuck." The leakage itself was invisible. How many reservoirs were leaking? How much nan would it take to kill him? It was a good sign that he still had an ankle. This was no nano storm, not yet.

He stood, now dressed in the overseer's tunic and pants. They should set out, but he still had one more question. "Johanna," he said, "do you love this Tarig lord?"

There wasn't much of a pause. "Yes." She snapped a look at him, searching for blame. "Don't judge me. Don't you dare."

She hadn't heard about his own betrayals, then. He whispered. "I don't, Johanna, believe me." He turned to the window, gathering his thoughts.

She grabbed his arm. "The windowsill. Stay away from it. I'm controlling the sere. You can cross over it again when you leave, if you are able to leave. But don't touch the window."

In his peripheral vision, Quinn saw a figure out in the yard. Turning, he saw with astonishment that it was Anzi. She stood in the doorway where he had been a moment before.

"What?" Johanna cried, noting his gaze. She joined him at the window.

"It's Anzi," he said. "She followed me."

"A friend?" When he nodded, she said, "Send her back. She'll expose us."

Anzi had never intended to let him come here alone. He should have suspected. She stood there, looking up at the wall of the watch, no doubt seeing that it was patrolled.

"Wait here," he told Johanna. Despite her protests, he left the room and made his way to the door leading onto the sere. Once more, he activated his chrysalis, generating a smear of light to obscure his passing. He walked across the sere toward Anzi, hoping she would stay in the relative obscurity of the terminus doorway for a few moments longer.

When he reached the other side of the sere, he took her arm. "It's me, Anzi." He wasted no time on rebukes. "Stay by my side. We can pass unnoticed, but stay close to me." He pulled her onto the sere, none too gently, and they quickly crossed. No alarms—not that he could hear.

Johanna was waiting for them in the side room. She narrowed her eyes at the newcomer. "Who is this, Titus?"

"Someone who shouldn't be here. Her name is Anzi." He sighed, looking at Anzi, kicking himself for not anticipating this.

"Well, then, Anzi," Johanna said. "What do you want?"

"The same as you. To help him."

"This isn't helping," Johanna muttered. "Now what, Titus?"

He answered, "She must have followed me through the terminus. I can't send her back."

"Leave her here," Johanna whispered to him. "No one will find her in one of these many rooms."

"I'm coming with you," Anzi said. "Don't waste time arguing."

There was no persuading her to stay behind, of that he was sure. "All right," he said, "you're coming with us."

Johanna eyed Anzi critically. "The hair will give you away. Not SuMing's style." She whipped off her belt and handed it to Anzi. "Bind your hair back."

Anzi cinched back her hair, and Johanna led the way down the corridor, deeper into the watch.

At Titus Quinn's side, Anzi was where she wanted to be. Even if she was in the Tarig fortress as an intruder, she was still where she wanted to be. Ahead, she looked at the brilliant blue of Johanna's dress, and her long hair cascading down her back. She was shorter than Anzi, and this surprised her. She had pictured Johanna as tall and regal, and was relieved that she was only beautiful.

Anzi didn't begrudge Johanna's station as wife. She might have wished the station unfilled, but wishing for facts to be otherwise was useless. She'd tried it often enough, so she knew. Despite Johanna's presence, Anzi felt a rush of joy. She was with Titus, and the sere—the defense she had most feared—was now behind her.

She followed Titus and Johanna, watching their backs, ready to fight if need be.

SuMing hurried to the wing of the centrum housing the brightship bays. Near the main stairs she found a hiding place behind an abandoned Gond carriage. From her vantage point she saw servants rushing about readying a reception of whatever lord came on the brightship. Heart sinking, she guessed that this arrival came at a very bad time for her mistress.

A delegation finally was descending the stairs. She noted with astonishment the presence of seven Tarig—as daunting a line of individuals as she had ever seen. Tarig did not often travel together. They looked grim, and in a hurry. Their long strides soon took them from view.

Flustered servants ran down the hall after the lords, murmuring a name she had heard before: Lord Nehoov. One of the Five, come from the Ascendancy. But why? As she mulled over this development, she felt a hand on her shoulder.

Whipping around, she came face-to-face with a deeply frowning Jout.

"Hiding? What is this?"

"Many pardons, Excellency. I was nervous, seeing the lords, and hid in fright."

He hauled her to her feet. "But what business brings you here to be frightened by lords?" When she didn't answer, he gripped her harder and set out down the hall in the direction the lords had taken.

SuMing's stomach had cramped into a small wad. He would take her to be questioned. She had no answers she was willing to give. Any that she was forced to give might doom her mistress. By the bright, she would not be the cause of Johanna's downfall. Fear turned to conviction. Her hands were still free to seek the stone she kept in her pocket. Slipping her right hand into her jacket pouch, she found what she was looking for.

The Jout came to a halt just before the door of the captain's chamber, pausing to knock.

Pretending to cough, SuMing brought the stone to her mouth and swallowed it.

Entering the door of the watch, Mo Ti stopped, uncertain what to do next. He had kept the girl in sight all through the terminus and across the sere, but now he had lost her. He loped down the corridor, wincing at the jolts to his ruined knee, lately a casualty of a fall off a rock bridge. He wasn't sure how long he'd lain stunned, but when he came to his senses only a few bones were broken. None of them were in his sword arm.

Reaching a junction of corridors, he looked in both directions, but there was no sight of Anzi. Weak from the sprint, he leaned against the wall. With one of his lungs already collapsed, his strength was ebbing fast. He had managed to pop his dislocated shoulder back into its socket, a maneuver that had left his arm swollen, almost useless. His face was still a ragged wound of rock abrasions. By rights he should be unconscious. But not yet.

Sounds of footsteps drove him around the corner and into a chamber crowded with military stores. He waited by the door, knife drawn, as soldiers passed outside: two Jouts talking in their gravelly voices. When the corridor was quiet again, Mo Ti looked around him. Dun-colored blankets were stacked on shelves, along with bales of goldweed, a Hirrin's preferred bed stuffing. No weapons, no uniforms, or other things he could have used.

Mo Ti was still pawing through the storeroom when the Jouts returned.

They hesitated only for a moment, but it was enough for Mo Ti. He exploded into action, slicing his hand against the throat of one while head-butting the other one and sending him sprawling. Still on his feet, Mo Ti drew his knife, making swift work of one Jout as the other sidled back, drawing a blade too long for the close quarters. Mo Ti evaded the first thrust and smashed his good hand down on the Jout's hand. The weapon fell, and Mo Ti had him in a hard grip across the neck. The Jout, despite his considerable size and good health, was no match for his adversary.

Mo Ti sang softly in his ear, "Do you wish to live?"

Johanna kept Anzi at her side, the proper place for an attendant, and Quinn walked behind. Johanna had warned Quinn that they would encounter sentients in the precincts of the centrum, and they did—not many, for a place of such size, but each of them—whether Chalin, Jout, or Hirrin—bowed as Johanna passed. Some of these denizens glanced at Quinn and Anzi, assessing them, perhaps registering that they were strangers. It wouldn't matter in a short while, and for now, no one thought to detain them with questions. Oventroe had said the Repel was complacent. Perhaps too, no one could imagine that Johanna was not loyal.

The deference shown to his wife suggested to Quinn, more than anything, that she had a history here, not all of it as a hostage. If Johanna was in hell, then she had standing. Quinn knew that he had no right to judge her. Walking behind Johanna through the centrum, his thoughts spun away from him, but always fell back to the engine. Close now, by the reverberations.

The halls of this deep fortress went on too long and too far for Quinn's comfort, eating up the time they had, judging solely by the cirque's tightening grip. In an unhurried pace they went up broad stairs and through enormous galleries and chambers. Johanna knew the way.

Though their advance through the centrum seemed endless, it had been no more than a half hour, Quinn guessed, by the time they arrived at their destination. He felt a rumbling through his boots.

Johanna nodded at the massive doors before them. The containment chamber. The drumming sound they had been hearing all through the centrum clearly issued from this place.

"The engine," Johanna whispered. Pushing against the massive doors, she opened one of them, and urged him and Anzi to pass through. As the door swung open, the booming of the engine fell over them like a pall.

Captain Erd listened to the soldier's breathless report. He considered carefully whether his dignity as a captain of the guard required him to dismiss the report with impatience or take decisive action. It wasn't common in the Repel garrison for a Ysli like himself to rise as high as Erd had done, and the troops watched him constantly for signs of incompetence.

"A giant with a tuber for a face?" Captain Erd repeated the soldier's words so that the man might hear how foolish he sounded. "Crossing the sere like a maiden strolling to market?" He rose from his seat behind his desk, so as to muster a bit of height, but he was still far shorter than his subordinate.

"Well, he were no maiden, Captain. A monster, more like."

Erd regarded the Chalin man, still flushed from his vision and the strain of reporting high in the chain of command. Just a few days ago had come another fanciful report, with a few sentries claiming that Mistress Johanna had been on the sere, decked out in a fine gown and never a wisp of smoke to announce that her feet trod solid ground. Now come giants, and tomorrow, who knew?

It was time to put a stop to this breakout of hallucinations. "You see this?" Erd nodded at a quiescent scroll on his desk.

"Sir, it be a scroll, for certain."

"Well noted," Erd said. "Toss it out the window."

The soldier hesitated, snaking a glance at the window looking onto the sere.

"That's an order." Erd watched the slow-witted man with growing contempt. "So you claim the sere is cold? Let us see."

The soldier shrugged, then pitched the scroll out the opening. He peered down to see the effect.

"Satisfied?" Captain Erd remarked.

"Yes, sir. It's off, all right. Colder than a Gond's kiss."

It took a beat for Erd to register this remark. "Off, did you say?" He strode to the window. There lay a small object on the dirt, intact. The sere looked the same as always, but there the scroll lay with no hint of fire or even smoke. Off, impossibly off.

As the captain rushed from his office, he heard pounding feet. In another moment, around the corner came two soldiers, breathless.

They had seen a man crossing the sere, one so large he looked hewn from a boulder.

"A monster," one of them said.

Erd pulled out the orb he wore around his neck on a thong. He activated it with the heat of his hand, signaling a general alarm.

Once inside the containment chamber, Quinn found himself in the largest room he had ever seen. The ceiling vaulted far overhead, shedding a harsh illumination on a plain of machines that hid his further view, but left him a clear line of sight to a mezzanine that wrapped around the room some hundred or more feet high. A metallic churning came from the center of the place, setting up a vibration in the floor and in his chest.

Johanna crouched down, bringing something from her pocket. Needles. Slender but substantial pins. One at a time, she proceeded to prick them into the floor and twirl them. "To find our path," she said as she worked. "Every day Lord Inweer changes the maze. These needles will forge a way."

Satisfied at last, she rose from her task, her face gleaming with sweat. "Now we run."

Around them, the machines were moving. Some of them were sinking, melting down and disappearing into the floor or whatever was under it. A swath four yards wide was opening in front of them, and it led straight into the heart of the great room. At that distant point, Quinn could see a monolith, smooth and shining.

Johanna waved them onward. The three of them ran down the aisle formed by the vanished machines, their footfalls barely audible amid the engine's droning. As they ran, Johanna took Quinn's arm to command his attention. "The engine has two lobes. I'm the right size to fit between them. That's where Lord Oventroe said to place the chain. I'll take the chain."

"It doesn't need to be close."

"No, it does. What if the Tarig come in time to stop the nan? For the sake of the Rose, Titus, give it every chance."

He could barely hear her through the roaring throb of the engine. When they had gone halfway to the center, Quinn stopped and took Anzi by the arm. "Stay here, Anzi. If anyone follows us, prevent them. And shout for all you're worth."

She nodded, drawing her knife. He put a hand on the side of her face. "I love you," he said.

She held his gaze. "And I you, forever."

Quinn ran to catch up with Johanna. She was running, looking back to be sure he followed.

They came to the center of the sprawling complex. On every side, racks of instruments and the housing of unknown machines shouldered up. Clear passageways lay between them. Behind Quinn, a clear path stretched straight to the doors through which they'd come. It was deserted, though Anzi hid somewhere back there.

Before him the great engine towered some sixty feet above. Its lower half was embedded in a deep well. With smooth sides, it looked almost egglike. Innocuous on the outside, but it allowed the Entire to feed where it shouldn't, where it wouldn't in another few minutes. Its two lobes thundered in a split-second difference of timing. Quinn glanced at the mezzanine above: long and thin, empty of defenders. He wished more than anything that he could hear beyond the pounding of the engine, which cloaked any sounds of pursuers.

Johanna pointed to a railing around the engine where a ladder went over the side to the lower level. "Give me the chain."

Joining her at the rail, he looked down. Here, the drop was some thirty feet. At the bottom, he saw that the crack between the lobes was narrow, hardly a foot wide.

He sat on the floor, pulling up his pant leg. Blood welled from the crease where the chain cut into his ankle. He bent closer, repeating in his mind the combination to release the clasp holding the chain in a circle: Four, five, one.

At his side, Johanna gasped. "It's sunk into your leg."

"I have to yank it off. Give me some cloth."

Taking the knife Quinn offered, Johanna tore a strip of cloth from her dress.

While she did so, Quinn took the cirque between his forefinger and thumb. Placing his fingers carefully into the indentations in the chain, he pressed in the sequence to break the circle. Four, five, one. A total of ten, Stefan had said. And then, responding to the code, the chain opened at the clasp. It remained embedded in his skin.

Taking the cloth from Johanna and shoving it into his mouth to muffle his cry, Quinn yanked, letting loose a searing pain. But the chain still clutched the back of his ankle. Gritting his teeth, he yanked again. The chain came free, trailing blood. He didn't know if he'd cried out. By the way Johanna was looking up to the mezzanine, he figured he had. Grasping the cirque, he hobbled to the ladder.

Johanna rushed to join him. "Titus. Give it to me. You can't get close enough."

The gap between the two lobes was merely a crack. He could almost toss it there, but then he'd have to set the timing sequence before he threw. How fast would the nan rush out? Would he have time to throw it well?

Johanna saw him hesitate. "Titus, the storm wall will repel the nan, sending it Nigh-ward, not letting it spread back to the engine. It must go between the lobes." She looked back down the cleared path, becoming frantic. "Give it to me." She knew how to do it, she said. Lord Oventroe had explained it.

She was small enough to slide between the lobes. He had only a moment to decide. "Do it, then." He handed her the chain. As she listened intently, he showed her how to press the reverse code sequence into the links.

Drumming its two-part rhythm, the engine seemed a robust heart, but it was a doomed one. For Johanna, the awful booming could not be gone soon enough.

She took the chain, clenching her fist around it. Although she must hurry, she paused, looking into her husband's face. At this moment she desperately wanted to let him know that he wouldn't survive. He had a right to know this, to make his peace. Let him rush back through the fortress, and back onto the plains—but neither he nor anyone else would survive for long.

"Ask God for his mercy," she whispered.

"I leave the prayers to you."

"No, you must ask." She reached out to grip his arm. "It's over, Titus. We'll die of this. Make your peace with God so I can be at peace."

"We won't die. We'll have nineteen minutes. It's enough."

Johanna hated the deception. Titus still thought it was local destruction. When Lord Oventroe had come to her last night in her forest cell, he had told her the Entire's days were over. He said that in the natural sequence of things, the Entire couldn't be sustained, and it must give way to the Rose. The lords had had their Entire for a time, but it was artificial, doomed. With Johanna's help it would die early, cleanly. All at once. Oventroe couldn't save her, nor did she ask it.

Oventroe didn't trust Titus to remain firm. But facing the imminent release of the plague nan, Johanna couldn't bear to let her husband go unrepentant into that long night.

She told him what he had to know: "Eventually, the nan will take us all. Me, you, Sydney. Everyone."

His eyes locked on her. "What do you mean, Sydney?"

"No one is saved. Except the Rose." The basso thrumming of the machine was shredding her mind. She would put the nan in place just to be rid of that pounding forever.

"Good-bye, Titus." She swung herself over the railing. "Make your peace."

She began descending, but heard a commotion above her. Titus had jumped on the railing and was clambering down. From the rung above he reached down and seized her by the arm. "Why will Sydney die? Is it the nan? Is it out of control?"

What did it matter if the nan was out of control? The Rose was at stake. The Rose would die. She yanked furiously. "Let me go."

"Tell me, by God, or I'll take your arm off."

She spat out, "Yes, the nan will spread. Hell is about to fall. This hell. And we're all going with it."

"But Sydney might live. The sways far away might live."

Still denying it. Poor Titus and his optimism. "No one lives," she spat. "There's no stopping it."

Mo Ti crept through the massive door to the hall where the engine lay. True to his promise, he had let the Jout live. The soldier had brought him to this spot, hoping for his life to be spared. Mo Ti had told him, "I swear by my mother's grave flag, if you give warning to others, you are the first one I will kill. But if you guide me aright, you shall live." Just outside the door the Jout was firmly bound, and stunned by a blow to the back of his head.

Mo Ti knew where Titus Quinn was ultimately headed. The man's thoughts had been clear and obsessive, and Distanir had dutifully relayed them. Still, the destination was a murky concept: the engine room. Fortunately, every soldier in Ahnenhoon knew what the engine room was.

The soldier had said there was a maze, but he was wrong. Before Mo Ti was a clear path heading straight to the center. Anzi and Quinn were nowhere in sight. Fearing he might already be too late, Mo Ti ran, for Sydney, for the Entire.

A woman stood in his path, knife drawn. It was Anzi, whom he had fought before. She was small, and couldn't hope to stop him. He approached her swiftly, sensing she would feint to the right. She went left instead, ducking under his sword. Pivoting, he swung out his fist and knocked her senseless onto the floor. Barely breaking his stride, he rushed onward to the center of the cavern.

Looking into Johanna's contorted face, Quinn kept a tight grip on her arm. They were still at the top of the ladder, their goal close, but receding as his mind reeled with Johanna's pronouncements.

There was no stopping the nan, just as he had feared, just as Helice had said. He recognized what his intuition had been telling him for days, building as it did on small hints and evasions from the Tarig lord. There were things he knew about the Tarig from long experience, things that lay just out of his conscious reach. Such as when they were lying.

Still holding onto Johanna, he whispered, "Oventroe lied to me."

"Yes! Because he knew you wouldn't do it! The chain is all we have. For the Rose, for the Earth." She tried to yank away, nearly falling from the ladder as one of her feet lost its grip. But Quinn held on.

Had Jesid seen the outcome of all this? Had he seen the world collapse? But why did Oventroe insist upon placing the chain at the foot of the engine? Surely it could have been done anywhere . . . except the collapse would take time; even a nan plague would take time to spread. Oventroe was for the Rose, and he meant to destroy the engine first to be sure there would be no time to activate the engine's full powers. Quinn looked at his former wife. "The Entire," he hissed. "Everything that's here. Millions of souls, Johanna. Billions of sentients." How could one person be asked to destroy so much?

"In God's hands," she rasped at him, her face without mercy—an avenging angel, intent upon apocalypse.

It would be for the sake of Earth, its teeming cities and glorious lands. And for the universe embracing it. A land and a cosmos that would otherwise be fuel for these extravagant skies and storm walls. He had to choose now, and he was frozen. By the bright, he prayed.

By the bright, I can't do this.

When he thought of all that he had seen in the Entire—the vast, enclosed universe of so many miracles—he knew that he couldn't destroy it. He loved it. Now it was plain: He had always loved it.

"For the Rose!" she pleaded.

The Rose. Yes, the Earth must be freed from the Tarig, from the engine. But not like this.

Johanna's voice needled at him. "Don't be afraid of death. It's not the worst."

He looked down at her stricken face. She cared so passionately, but that didn't make her right.

"Let the Entire live, Johanna. It's not hell. It's heaven to some people. I can't kill it. And neither can you."

"I can!"

Snaking his leg around the ladder rung, he reached down and with his free hand caught the chain dangling from her hand. "Let go, Johanna." When she refused, he yanked it away.

Johanna moaned, "No . . ." She lunged for his feet, grabbing him around the ankles. The pain of his lacerations shot up his leg, causing him to jerk free of her. As he did so, she lost her footing and fell from the ladder with a sickening crash.

She lay at the bottom of the ladder, unmoving. He began to scramble down after her.

Before he went far, however, he felt a steel grip on his shoulder. Someone had grabbed him from above. An impossibly strong arm hauled him up. In another moment he saw who it was. On the other side of the railing stood his adversary from the hills—the Chalin man, face bloody and bruised, clutching him in a ham-fisted grip.

The giant lifted him bodily over the railing, dumping him on the floor. Quinn scrambled to his feet.

The man looked at the chain in Quinn's hand. In his oddly quiet voice he said, "The chain is still intact."

"Yes," Quinn said. This bear of a man had been after the chain all this time.

"You came to kill us," the giant said.

"To fight the Entire. Not to kill it." He saw the man's hesitation. "If that's what you're worried about, it's over." He raised the chain, offering it. "I can't use this." He was a man of the Entire now. It made him dizzy to think so. Who was he, then? A man seduced by a new land? Johanna lay at the base of the ladder. He had changed allegiance.

"Why?" the big man asked.

It was too much to say why. To say that he had lived in both places and loved them both. He said simply, "For Sydney." It was the one thing he felt at peace about. Sydney would live.

A bang from across the room jolted their attention. There, down the pathway to the edge of the chamber, they saw that the doors had burst open. Soldiers ran through.

As the Chalin man turned to note this, Quinn bolted down the corridor, calling for Anzi. Drawing his knife as he ran, he came into a knot of four soldiers, and lunged at the first one.

The fortress was awake.

As the soldiers advanced on Quinn, he heard a commotion behind him, and there was the giant, slicing with terrible accuracy at the soldiers. The big man was fighting at his side. Quinn didn't have time to wonder why, but parried the thrusts of the Chalin soldier in front of him. In his peripheral vision, he saw Anzi just stirring from the floor where she had fallen.

With a well-aimed strike to the soldier's temple, Quinn knocked his adversary down, then fell on him with his knife. That done, he turned to the rest, but found that the giant had herded the three remaining soldiers into a side aisle of machinery where the narrow confines split their attack. The giant fought like a madman, crushing the skull of one soldier and fending off the other two. At twice their size, he might prevail. Quinn heard him shout, "Run now. Mo Ti has them."

Quinn rushed to Anzi, helping her to her feet. She was wobbly, but not bleeding. He hesitated. The man called Mo Ti was beating back the two remaining assailants, but not finishing them. Meanwhile, Anzi swayed against him, struggling to stay upright.

"Leave now," Mo Ti shouted, "or the Tarig will have you."

This giant was offering him his freedom. With the alarm raised, it wouldn't be long before the Tarig would have them both. Mo Ti was offering him a gift, and he would accept it for the sake of all that remained to be done. He bowed to Mo Ti, and the big man grinned, fighting on.

Quinn backed away with Anzi, down the cleared path among the machines. Then, gripping Anzi firmly, he broke into a run. The sounds of clashing blades resounded behind.

Once outside the engine chamber, Quinn ran with Anzi down the path he had taken with Johanna, trusting his memory to follow the path in reverse. The way was charted in his mind, but even as he ran forward, he thought of Johanna lying at the foot of the engine, needing help. It seemed impossible that he was leaving her there, lying in her own blood. Leaving her again. But beyond every other consideration, he had to dispose of the chain. It was disintegrating. The metal tube housing the nan was in the last hours of its useful life. The plague of matter would run free. All Quinn knew to do was to let the river Nigh take it. As Jesid had said: *Give it to the river.* So yes, he was leaving Johanna behind. Mo Ti had given him his chance, and for the sake of the Entire, he took it.

They swept on through the corridors, rushing as fast as Anzi's weakened state could handle. He walked with his knife in hand, ready to fight. As they hurried, the sounds of shouting came from several directions at once. And grew louder.

Retrieving the wasp case from his pocket, he clenched his hand gently around it while bringing Anzi close to his side. Around his hand, the familiar disruptive spray of light appeared, crawling up his arm and jumping to Anzi.

She flinched. "The nan?"

"No, it's our protection." Hearing guards approach, Quinn pulled Anzi against a wall, and they flattened themselves as a unit of soldiers rushed by them, unheeding.

Then, under the shelter of the cloaking light, Quinn broke into a run, supporting Anzi at his side. The chain lay heavy in his pocket, a burden he would gladly have thrown off, but couldn't. He hoped for enough time to bring the chain to the Nigh; he hoped that Oventroe had been wrong about how long the chain would hold. This was likely to be the last day, and the day was ebbing.

At last he and Anzi came to the outer door of the centrum leading to the gathering yard. He pulled the door open. As he did so, he heard a bellowing far in the distance. Someone was shouting Johanna's name. They raced across the yard toward the watch.

Soldiers carried Johanna up the ladder, supporting her, not knowing why she was here, but careful for her injuries. Her arm was bursting with pain, a bad break already swelling. The blow to her head had made her dizzy, and she struggled not to faint against the soldiers. They urged her to lie down, but she demurred. It was important to stand upright.

Lord Inweer was striding down the corridor. Behind him came a second Tarig lord.

Around the containment chamber on the high mezzanine, soldiers began massing, flocking to protect the engine. This was unnecessary. The engine endured. Damn it to hell forever. In time she might damn Titus as well, but she hurt too badly.

Inweer approached her, his face unreadable. Ignoring the soldiers who held her upright, his eyes fell on her, terrible and dark, as she had known they would. His voice was calm and low. "Where is your husband?"

Her own voice was also calm. "I don't know," she said. "Somewhere here. You can look."

The second lord came forward, saying, "The traitor Johanna, ah?"

"Yes," Lord Inweer said. His hand swept back.

The blow sent an astonishing pain through Johanna's body. The first blow was to her chest, the second, to her head. She blacked out. The next thing she knew, she was being hauled up, and another blow came, electrifying her body with a hideous pain. Oh stop, make it stop. Thrown into the railing, she crumpled, gasping through clots of blood in her throat, fighting for breath.

After a second or an hour she opened her eyes a crack. She saw a lord's boot close to her face. A knife had extruded from the heel. He would kick her now, slicing off her face. She hoped the blow would kill her.

"Leave her," a deep voice said, and then there was the sound of booted feet.

The sound faded. The world faded. All so cold. Death is so cold. When does God come? she wondered. Does He wait until all is cold, or swoop down now?

Now.

CHAPTER FORTY-ONE

Hush and sleep, the bright turns blue,
Hush and sleep, the Nigh bears you.
Rest and ebb, the Entire is wide,
Rest and ebb, the lords provide.
                              —a child's bedtime song

THEY PASSED UNNOTICED ACROSS THE SERE. Later, Quinn surmised that the garrison had rushed to the center of the fortress, weakening the guard in the outer domains. Entering the terminus with Anzi, Quinn freed the wasp to guide them through the tangle of corridors with their silent, bony chambers. As they ran, Anzi leaned heavily on Quinn. He bunched his fist around the chain in his pocket, wondering how fast he'd be aware of nan release.

In fits and starts as they ran, Anzi learned that the engine still stood. Her mood seemed to darken then. It wasn't the choice that Anzi would have made, but he'd made his own. Meanwhile they had far to go, to reach the Nigh where he would drown the chain.

The race through the terminus brought them out of its coils faster than they had traversed it before. They emerged onto the plains of Ahnenhoon. It was Twilight Ebb. The Paion were active, and armies moved in the distance, accompanied by pulses of light where dirigibles met a fiery end. In the nearby hills, units of soldiers swarmed, so he and Anzi couldn't head that way. With the wasp scrambling the light around them, they struck out across the middle of the plain, but knowing their camouflage wouldn't last long.

For some time the light around them had been dimming. Anzi wanted to travel more furtively, hunched down to take full advantage of the cover of the grass. But that would slow their progress, and besides, the grass was thinning, offering less camouflage than before.

At last Quinn saw Anzi clearly, and knew that the wasp had lost its function. He had been clutching the chrysalis so tightly that his hand had almost frozen into a claw. Opening his fingers, he found nothing in his palm but dust.

The fighting was closer now, and the cries of soldiers could be heard less than a mile off. In spots across the plain the airships of the Paion welled out of nowhere, drawing a wave of troops to set up fire-launching defenses. Quinn and Anzi would need to circle around the skirmishes—a longer, more time-consuming route. They took stock of their situation. Exhausted and hungry, they needed rest. Most critically, they needed water.

"Into the hills, then," Anzi said. She held Quinn's hand, sounding lost but at peace.

"The long way . . . ," Quinn mused.

They looked Nigh-ward to the storm wall in the distance. They could never walk so far, not without rest. They had no time for rest, if Oventroe's prediction of the chain's life was correct. The lord might have been lying about that as about so much else, Quinn knew. The thought kept his hopes alive, of reaching the Nigh in time. Whether to trust the lord at all was a constant thought. Why had Lord Oventroe risked so much to save the Rose? Was he just a ruthless ally, determined to keep Quinn on task, and in the end, the best hope the Rose had for succor? Or was he something worse? In time, Quinn meant to find out.

The memory of Johanna slipping from the ladder sickened him. The fall might have killed her; certainly it would have been a terrible injury. If the latter, she would face Tarig justice by herself, and the thought weighed heavily. He knew now that Johanna had never planned to survive the experience, but her willingness to die made her fate at Tarig hands all the more unjust.

Anzi pointed across the plain. There, an airship approached them at a stately pace.

They crouched down in the sparse grass. Perhaps the craft was heading for some point beyond them, Quinn thought. But soon they heard the airship's humming motor, and the dirigible dropped ropes for landing. They had been seen.

He turned to Anzi. "I'm sorry," he whispered.

A small smile came to her lips. "I'm not. It has been the life I hoped for, Titus."

"Too short," he said, embracing her. He looked at her brave face, and loved her painfully more than a moment before.

They stood as soldiers shinnied down the ropes from the cabin. One of them approached as the others pulled the guy ropes, securing the craft.

The soldier bowed to them. "General Ci Dehai will have you come aboard, Ren Kai."

Anzi looked up at Quinn in astonishment, instantly recognizing the pseudonym that he had used. They still had cover.

Ci Dehai. Yulin's man, once.

Quinn and Anzi followed the soldier to the craft, where a hatchway opened to receive them.

Johanna floated free of her body, the pain in one place, her mind in another. She heard distant voices, speaking too weakly to be heard. A cold wind swept across her mind. She was in motion, moving toward some last destination. She thought it might be an angel who carried her, but then, against her cheek, she felt the metal weave of a Tarig vest, and knew the angel must wait a little longer.

The movement stopped. Something warm fell on her face. It felt like the sun. She opened her eyes but could see nothing. She was blind.

"Johanna."

She knew that voice. Was it her father? Was it Titus? Those memories were falling away, now. Best to receive the Kingdom with nothing in your arms.

"Johanna," came the voice again.

A strong hand came under her head, creating a pillow. "This is your forest."

The sunlight fell on her face, her open eyes. She tried to speak, failed.

After a time she heard, "Who told you how to approach the engine?" The voice was gentle, yet insistent.

She thought it would be polite to answer. She tried, but nothing came out. Finally she managed to whisper, "Morhab." It was the lie that Lord Oventroe had suggested. It was such a good lie.

"Ah. Morhab," the Tarig lord said. "So we have guessed." A long time passed as the lord held her. His deep voice came to her through a fog: "And now Titus Quinn comes to the engine to destroy it. So the Rose knows our purpose."

She tried to shake her head. *No, no.*

"Do not lie again, Johanna. They do know."

With great effort she whispered, "But they have. Nan plague."

"Nan? Molecular breakdown?"

She mouthed the word yes. The lord held her with such tenderness. She knew that if he had wanted to kill her, he would have. He had beaten her so that Nehoov wouldn't garrote her.

The sun was sweet on her eyelids; she fell into unconsciousness. But it wasn't over yet. She blinked her eyes open. Mustering herself, she pushed out the words, "You don't. Dare."

"What do we dare not do, Johanna?"

"Kill the Earth."

"Because of Titus Quinn?"

"He has the nan." She wanted to say that although the secret of the engine was out, the lords dare not strike against the Earth. Oventroe had told her what to say. Had she said it all? She hoped so. There was no more breath left.

She lay in Inweer's arms, her breaths farther and farther apart.

He spoke again. But by then she was far away.

Ci Dehai pointed out the viewport of the dirigible. "See that distant vessel?"

Looking in the direction that Ci Dehai pointed, Quinn saw a godman's airship in the distance, the face of the Miserable God an angry red blur.

The general smiled on the half of his face that wasn't too scarred to move. "I never knew you for a religious man, Ren Kai. But that godwoman is fond of you."

For now it was understood between them that Quinn was Ren Kai, a simple godman who had once been in the company of Benhu, and had come to minister to the troops at Ahnenhoon.

"The Venerable Zhiya," Quinn acknowledged. "I am as religious as she is, as it turns out."

The general threw him an ironic look. "No doubt true." He looked around his private cabin, to be sure that an aide had not entered. "She thought you would need help, and I agreed that once again, you did."

There had been a time when Quinn first came into the presence of Master Yulin that Ci Dehai had helped a great deal. He had taught Quinn to fight like a Chalin warrior, and hold himself as one. Now the general was doing more than help. He was taking sides. Quinn knew that Zhiya could be persuasive. He owed much to her, and hoped to repay her someday.

As Quinn watched out the viewport, the airship shrank in the sky. Quinn silently thanked her. Perhaps she thought he had come to Ahnenhoon to spirit Johanna away. She would be surprised to learn what he had really come for, and perhaps not so surprised at what he ended up doing.

Anzi came to his side, bowing to Ci Dehai. The general scowled at her. "In the center of trouble again, Anzi."

"Yes, thankfully."

Ci Dehai squinted his one eye, wondering if she was being impudent. His response was cut short as Quinn removed the cirque from his pocket and examined it. The general regarded it with loathing, having heard from Quinn about its contents.

The chain coiled there, warmed by its raging metabolism. "A plague," Quinn said.

The general's voice came out in a rumble. "Take it to the middle of the Nigh. Do not risk the shallows."

"I'll need a vessel," Quinn said.

"Would the navitar Ghoris suit you?" Ci Dehai smiled at Quinn's surprised reaction. "She is waiting for you."

"How—," Quinn began.

Ci Dehai's glance slid to the viewport. "Zhiya has connections to the navitars—personal ones. She said Ghoris would help you, but how she can be sure of such things, I prefer not to know."

Ci Dehai likely knew a good deal more than he claimed. Quinn had asked the general why he was helping them, but all he would say was, "A favor to an old friend." Ci Dehai had made a choice, and it was against the bright lords. Against Yulin, even. In the march of events, it was a time for choosing, whether you were high or low. The steward Cho, Suzong, Mo Ti, the Hirrin servant of Chiron—all had been forced to decide.

Thinking of his own choice, he gazed at the chain in his hand.

Hold on, he urged.

Once on board the navitar's vessel, Quinn and Anzi stood on the deck, the sole occupants of the ship. Greeted by the Ysli ship keeper, their only glimpse of Ghoris was a red swath of cloth in the pilot's cabin, a deck above. She brought the vessel far out onto the silver stream. There, the ship hovered, one side of the vessel in deep shadow from the storm wall.

Whether Ghoris understood the thing Quinn was about to do, he wasn't sure. The ship keeper hadn't allowed him to speak with her, but had conveyed Quinn's request for transport to the river's middle.

Anzi stood next to Quinn as he brought the chain from his pocket.

"Did I do the right thing, Anzi?" he asked.

"I don't know," she answered. "But throw it, Titus, since you must. Throw it."

He balled his hand into a fist around the cirque.

She whispered to herself, to the river: "We each love the wrong universe."

Quinn answered her: "No. We love them both, that's all." With a powerful cast, he hurled the cirque into the Nigh. It fell without a splash, like a rock into a cloud.

Then, in the spot where the chain had fallen, a funnel appeared. A yellow-and-green froth spat up from it and sucked down again. For an instant the river itself became an iridescent gold. Then it lay silver and flat once more.

The ship keeper watched all this from the door to the passenger cabin.

"Where bound?" he asked, the immemorial question of the ship keeper.

Anzi turned to answer him. "As far as we can go," she said.

CHAPTER FORTY-TWO

Three things attract the attention of the Miserable God: an earnest godman, a vain beku, and a hopeful sentient. But only one makes Him laugh.

—Hoptat the Seer

SYDNEY RODE HARD, with Riod's hooves thundering beneath her. At her side rode Akay-Wat, Takko, Adikar, and a multitude of others, some of them new to her.

They were fifteen thousand strong and growing larger every day. The camp was on the move, but the strongest mounts ran a race, kicking up the steppe into a storm of dust. Perhaps they would let their leader win this race, though she urged them on, sending through Riod her challenge to the best riders of ten encampments: "Ride, ride!" Under her, Riod took up the cry subvocally, urging the mounts to do their best, to surpass him if they could.

At last Ochrid, a mottled brown-and-white mount, dashed ahead, taking the lead, his rider whooping with joy.

It could be no proper race with so many running, but each group of mounts and riders formed their own competitions, and in the end, there were a hundred winners, including Ochrid. Sydney and Riod were pleased to be second in their group, as out of practice as they had grown during the time when Sydney stayed close to her tent, hiding her co-opted sight.

By Heart of Day, the massive herd turned back, heading to a camp that had begun setting up in the rear.

The only shadow on the day was the lingering sadness over Distanir's death, an event that had come to Riod's mind the moment it happened. Mo Ti was still alive. This was the last thing Sydney and Riod had heard from them.

Riod felt Sydney's changed mood when she thought of this. *Best rider*, he sent. *Mo Ti will return.*

She prayed that he would. When he did, he would have news of the thing she had asked him to do.

"I'm sorry," she whispered. It startled her that she had spoken. It surprised her even more that she was thinking of Titus Quinn. No one should have their father's death on their hands. But she wouldn't permit him to ruin her world, her sway, and all the mounts and riders she held under her protection. Not even having heard his last message to her: *I love you.* After so long, those simple words struck hard. If he had said more, or justified himself, she might have closed her heart. But simply, *I love you.* It both lifted her spirits and darkened them. What was done was done.

Helice wasn't riding today. She never rode, being uneasy around the Inyx and unable to bond with her mount. In time she would find more comfort here, as Sydney had. There were times when Sydney wondered if Helice had lied about the cirque and what it would do. But Riod claimed she spoke the truth. Over the days since her arrival, Helice had tried hard to be a friend. But she wouldn't ride, and this was a barrier between them.

As the day burned to its hottest phase, Sydney and Riod at last returned to camp. When they approached their pavilion, a stranger waited.

Akay-Wat dismounted and went forward to determine who it was. Returning to confer with Sydney, Akay-Wat announced it was a Chalin woman come by caravan with a gift.

A gift? But from whom? Sydney was on the verge of asking, but Helice approached, eager to know, curious as everyone was. A small knot of riders watched Sydney approach the stranger.

"From Ahnenhoon," is all the stranger would say in front of so many.

As Sydney motioned the newcomer into the tent, Helice made as though to follow, but Sydney stopped her. "I will call you in. Let me discover what gift this is, first." She had an inkling that the gift was personal; that she might have to fight to keep her composure. What if it was news from Mo Ti? A heavy dread fell over her. She invited the traveler into the tent.

Helice stepped back, her cheeks red with the rebuke. She would see it that way. Sydney was learning that Helice was only happy when she knew as much or more than others. But Akay-Wat remained outside as well. For now, she wanted no company.

Once inside the tent, Sydney let the woman unwrap the package from Ahnenhoon. It was a mechanical device. For viewing a likeness, the messenger said. This wasn't from Mo Ti; it was from her mother. Expecting to hear of her father's death, she had instead received a recording from Johanna. A stab of relief hit her, making her almost glad to have news of her mother. Receiving instructions on how to activate the portrait, Sydney sent the messenger from the tent.

She and Riod were the only ones to see Johanna's image that day. Johanna wore a gray gown with a belted blue coat. Her hair fell down her back, still long and dark as Sydney remembered it. She had not aged. It seemed wrong that after so many years, there would be no testimony in the face. Sydney stepped closer, looking into Johanna's face.

Her mother's gaze at close range was certain and strong, as though she had vowed to do something of supreme difficulty, as though she urged Sydney to do the same. Sydney could not have said why Johanna looked so brave in that image. She had never thought that her mother might have need of bravery. She fought tears. So much was lost.

It was best that Johanna had chosen not to say anything. There was nothing Johanna could know about Sydney now, or about what her daughter had chosen for her life. But as her mother looked at her with such conviction, Sydney knew that she had been given a gift, just as the messenger said. It wasn't merely a portrait, but in a way, a promise—a reassurance that the striving was worth it. She took that meaning from Johanna's strong gaze. It would all be well, eventually. All well.

Johanna had survived the Tarig, and in some way overcome them, of that Sydney was convinced. They could be overcome. Even the Rose in its dark purpose could be pacified. It would all be well.

She thought of Mo Ti, and she silently urged him, Come home again, Mo Ti. We have much to do. Come home.

Leaning against Riod, and taking comfort from his steady heart, Sydney let herself hope.

EPILOGUE

OR A REASON SHE COULDN'T QUITE SAY, Australia's New South Wales looked like home to Janna Weer. But she had never lived on plains like these.

According to her official story, she was a city girl, born and bred. Janna doubted this, although she couldn't be sure. For the benefit of other people she had a background story, but for herself, the past was a blank. Sometimes her imagination conjured up false memories. One was a recurring fancy that across these grasslands armies passed back and forth like scythes harvesting souls in a never-ending war. She didn't talk about this for obvious reasons, nor did she talk about her past. That was good enough for her neighbors, who knew that wealthy people could do or say as little as they pleased.

On the western edge of Janna's property grew an ancient stand of eucalyptus trees clinging to the boundaries of a submerged watercourse. Today she lingered there, intending to write in her journal, but instead transfixed by the enormity of the grass-clad desert. No wraithlike armies appeared today—the plains were empty all the way to the horizon. She leaned against a eucalyptus tree, catching her bright blue shirt on its crackled bark. It was her habit to wear blue, and only a certain shade of it. Du Peng bought her clothes, and knew what she liked, though he advised her to add an extra color. Perhaps white? No. She held onto the things that seemed linked to her previous life, even though that life must have been a bad one, dangerous even to remember.

The ranch lay between the inland desert and the Murrumbidgee River, a property that Du Peng had found, and researched, and prepared for her, as he

421

prepared everything. With no interest in ranching, Janna had converted the place into a nature preserve. Where does the money come from? she asked Du Peng. From before, he said, his eyes snaking to the side, avoiding more questions. She learned to be content with what was here now. The porch of her ranch house looked out on the grassland with its patches of desert peas, prickly weed, trefoil clover, saltbush, and, in places, waxy succulents bearing extravagant, short-lived flowers.

She had been here six months, and still had a dry and pitiless summer to endure, but she looked forward to it. She would record the days of summer as she did all her days, creating a record of who she was now. Opening her journal, she began her day's entry.

Thursday, October 4.

I flew the flyer to the eucalyptus grove, and landed it well away from the trees as I promised Du Peng, who worries too much. He means well, and what, after all, would I do without him? The cumulus clouds are crowding eastward, turning the golden grasses pale and the drifts of red dust to purple. I shouldn't stare at the sky. It's peculiar behavior, as Du Peng has warned me.

Every day I reread my journal to remind myself that I exist. That I have had a life, though I don't remember it. Here in this journal is my only record. It appears to be in my own hand, from a time when I had all my faculties. It is an account of who I was, but it says little, as though describing a phantom. Du Peng will say nothing: not who sent him to protect and serve me; not where his family is or where he came from. Much is lost, my former self tells me in the journal. Don't seek to know, but be grateful for the Earth.

That's a strange thing to say. Be grateful for the Earth. Still, I am grateful. It's one reason I sit under this eucalyptus—the big one with the gnarled, split trunk—and stare at the sky. Clouds bulk up into the heights, carrying rain sometimes and lightning. I never tire of looking.

There are times when I think I can remember things. Sometimes I believe that I had an accident. There was such a flash of light. I seemed to lift above my body and watch myself catapult like the fleshy discharge of a cannon. Du Peng will say nothing, so I read my journal for clues. Don't seek to know, my former self writes.

Despite such warnings, I do remember one thing: a creature tall and beautiful but unearthly. He spoke to me, something very kind, I think. He warned me to be brave. That must be a dream, but such a persistent one. Du Peng won't talk about the creature, but from his expression when I told him, I feel he knows something. It will be our secret, even if I'm the only one who thinks so.

Neighbors come by bearing gifts, invitations, and small talk. There are some people they want me to meet. I know enough to be wary of matchmaking, and turn down offers of company. Still, I wonder what kind of man would choose to live in this harsh and beautiful land? I will meet some of them, eventually. Du Peng encourages me. He wants me to be happy with someone, as well as just happy. So there are layers of happiness. More to come? I'll wait and see.

The morning was well along before she finished writing. Janna stood and brushed the dust from her clothes. Slipping her journal into the pack, she headed for the small flyer. Du Peng would have lunch waiting, and she would join him for it, she decided, although she could also follow the watercourse gully to the hills or fly southeast into the tablelands, or simply watch the sky, high and blue and bright. Across all the prairie she could choose where to go. It felt like extravagant freedom, and earned.

ABOUT THE AUTHOR

KAY KENYON grew up in northern Minnesota, where winters are long and books, particularly science fiction books, could take you away—the farther the better. She was in thrall to the alien worlds of authors like Silverberg, LeGuin, and Herbert. She never lost that early love of alternate worlds, but creating her own would have to wait through several careers in the real world. After professions in TV and radio copywriting, acting in commercials and promoting urban transportation alternatives, she turned to fiction writing. Since then she has published numerous short stories and seven science fiction novels, including *Tropic of Creation*, *The Seeds of Time*, *Maximum Ice* (Philip K. Dick Award finalist), *The Braided World* (John W. Campbell short list), and *Bright of the Sky*, the first book of her present series, The Entire and the Rose. Kenyon's work has been anthologized, podcast, and translated into Russian and French. She chairs a writing conference, Write on the River, in eastern Washington State, where she lives with her husband. You can visit her blog and her Web site at www.kaykenyon.com.